Swing Shift

By William D. Arand

Copyright © 2019 William D. Arand
All rights reserved.

Dedicated:

To my wife, Kristin, who encouraged me in all things.

To my son, Harrison, who likes to just play on the ground with his toys in my office now.

To my niece, Kaylee, welcome to the clan. Going to buy you so many drum-sets just to antagonize your mother.

To my family, who always told me I could write a book if I sat down and tried.

Special Thanks to:
Niusha Gutierrez
Bill Brush
Gavin Lawrenson
Michael Haglund
Steven Lobue
Kyle Smith
Matt Gough
Robert Hammack
Zach Johnson
Roland Jackson
Caleb Morris
Chris Bastion
Troy S. Cash
Brian Walker

Books by William D. Arand-

The Selfless Hero Trilogy:
Otherlife Dreams
Otherlife Nightmares
Otherlife Awakenings
Omnibus Edition(All Three)

Super Sales on Super Heroes Trilogy:
Super Sales on Super Heroes 1
Super Sales on Super Heroes 2
Super Sales on Super Heroes 3
Omnibus Edition(All Three)

Dungeon Deposed Trilogy:
Dungeon Deposed
Dungeon Deposed 2
Dungeon Deposed 3 (To be released 2019)

Books by Randi Darren-

Wild Wastes Trilogy:
Wild Wastes
Wild Wastes: Eastern Expansion
Wild Wastes: Southern Storm
Omnibus Edition(All Three)

Fostering Faust Trilogy:
Fostering Faust
Fostering Faust 2
Fostering Faust 3 (To be Released 2019)

Books in the VeilVerse-

Cultivating Chaos: By William D. Arand
Asgard Awakening: By Blaise Corvin

Chapter 1 - Cold Coffee

Groaning, Gus rubbed at his eyes. No matter how much he ground his fingers in, though, it wouldn't change the view.

He sighed, then leaned his head back and stared up at the ceiling above him.

The view there wasn't much better, honestly. Unless you liked the stucco perfect squares you found in office buildings.

Getting to his feet, Gus went over to the coffee machine and rapped it with a knuckle. The glass was cold through and through.

Which means that damn coffee is like ice.

Muttering under his breath, Gus fished his mug out of the sink next to him, filled it with some of that black nastiness, and put it in the microwave.

He flicked the popcorn button, then sighed and stared blankly into the appliance.

As it rotated slowly, the "Pancakes!" porcelain cup was his whole world.

When the timer ended, he found his own face staring back at him in the darkened glass.

His reddish-brown hair reflected oddly in the poor excuse for a mirror. Reaching up with one hand, he fingered the two inches of length before letting go to run a hand over his face and stare into his dark-brown eyes.

Looking pretty tired there, bud.

Opening the microwave, Gus grabbed his cup and went back to his desk. When he sat down, he was treated to the decidedly chipper login screen that loved to immediately pop up after a single minute of inattention.

Setting the cup down to one side, Gus immediately typed in his credentials.

With a chime, the display flashed back to the home-screen for the Paranormal Investigations Department.

Gus smirked as he opened the file he was filling in with information from the hard-copy report.

Not quite like it is in the stories.

Kinda hard to keep all this shit under wraps with cameras on every corner and in every person's hand.

Then again, I suppose that makes it more surprising that the majority of everyone out there doesn't know.

Filling in the box for "number of citizens aware" with a single digit, Gus shook his head.

Or is it that people don't want to know? They see something and write it off, or explain it away themselves.

Finalizing the report with a tap of the enter key, Gus leaned back in his chair and looked around.

He was alone, of course. There was never anyone around during his shift. Technically it was the swing shift for the department. What was normally called graveyard in other places.

Except it was the middle of the day.

Glancing at the clock, Gus saw it was about noon.

"Fuck it, lunch it is," he grumbled, getting to his feet. He opened the drawer to his desk and pulled out his sig with the magazine for it.

It wasn't a personal favorite of his, but it was department issue. Department issued, modified, and made to handle the various types of ammunition they used.

With a fluid motion, Gus loaded the weapon and chambered a round. Then he flipped the safety on, slid it into his shoulder holster, and went to get his coat.

***

Sitting on a bench outside the Rit Memorial Hospital, Gus tried to enjoy his lunch break.

Thankfully, the entry to the emergency room and ambulance bay was nearby but not directly in front of him.

It made eating easy, and it kept him well away from prying eyes.

Feeding off the fear of others was awkward when they were watching. Quite doable, but uncomfortable.

Gus took in a deep inhalation, and the fear of the emergency room pulsed brightly as someone was wheeled through the doors. It filled him, gave him strength, and made him feel infinitely better.

Being a Boogieman wasn't all it was cracked up to be. Even just the name was something most children would laugh at. Though it was the most accepted term by the general Para community.

Possibly because it downplayed how frightening they were.

One of the better things of being a Boogieman, though, was that the meal requirements were significantly easier to come by than many others.

I mean, really. All things considered, it could be worse.

I don't even have to bother anyone to eat.

Hospitals, dentist offices, and normal police departments were great places to feed at.

The greater the fear, the more intense, the quicker Gus fed. The better he ate.

When he got to his feet, he felt quite a bit better.

Full and satiated.

If things went well, he wouldn't have to feed again for several days. Even though it was easy and he didn't actually cause anyone distress in his feeding, it still felt weird.

Hi, I'm Gus, the Boogieman. I sup on your fear and worst thoughts. Don't worry, it's harmless, just… really fucking ooky-spooky, yeah?

Shaking his head, Gus strolled toward the front of the hospital without much of a care or worry. Being part of an almost extinct species wasn't particularly fun.

Though it did make hiding easy. Especially with how easy it was for a Boogieman to live as a human would. Gus's life was a fairly easy life in the world of paranormals.

When he stepped out onto the sidewalk, he collided with a woman in a blazer and slacks. She had dark-brown hair, light-brown eyes, and a slightly brown skin tone.

She was also half a foot shorter than he was at five-foot six, but she looked feisty. Feisty and angry.

There was also an undercurrent of fear in her.

Then again, Gus had just practically run her over.

Grabbing her by a shoulder rather than send her tumbling, Gus began to trip forward, his coat flapping outward.

"What the hell are you doing?" she asked as he moved toward her with his stumble. Her left hand lashed out and grabbed Gus's right wrist, locking it to his side. "And why do you have a gun?"

Gus's first response was to floor her. Floor her and stomp her head flat against the curb.

Thankfully, he'd learned to curb those instincts since returning to civilian life. He wasn't running around in the desert with a rifle anymore.

Instead, he grabbed her wrist with his free hand, holding her in the same way she was him.

"Because I'm a cop," Gus said in a low voice. He couldn't blame her for reacting poorly. If the roles were reversed, he wasn't sure he wouldn't just punch the other person. "Look, I'm sorry, didn't see ya, wasn't minding my surroundings."

The woman glared up at him, looking annoyed and angry at being stopped in her tracks with his clumsy grab.

"I'm a detective. Out of precinct forty-two," she said, trying to jerk her hand out of his grasp. "So how about we let each other go?"

Snorting, Gus let go of her, then gave his right hand a wriggle.

"Bit young to be a detective, eh?" Gus asked. He wasn't in the mood to be polite. His question wasn't purely a jab, though. She looked just barely old enough to have graduated the academy.

Which meant she was either a rising star in her precinct, or something much worse.

Glaring up at him, the woman seemed to be considering her options.

"Is it so threatening that I'm young? Are you already writing me off as some sort of charity case?" she growled. "Don't you dare think I didn't work my ass off to get my badge. I earned mine through the normal channels, thank you."

Releasing his hand, she gave him a once-over.

"And what exa—"

There was a soft crackle on Gus's portable radio. As part of the PID, he always carried one with him.

"Code eight," said a calm voice without Gus's prompting. The hair on his neck rose up, and he felt his skin go cold. "Cat-one disturbance and E-break in public. Officer needs assistance. Rawlin High School."

Turning away from the detective, Gus set off at a fast run for his car. He pulled the radio off his belt and held it up to his mouth.

"Received code eight. This is Hellström, en route," Gus said.

Code eight was an ironclad rule in the PID. If you heard it and didn't have a collar, you went.

After getting into the driver's seat, Gus turned to the computer display from his PID laptop and tapped in Rawlin High School as he pulled his seat belt over his shoulder.

Beeping, the display populated the fastest route assuming no traffic.

I'm only two minutes out. That'll make me practically the first backup unit.

Category one means I need my rifle.

The passenger door opened and the detective got in. Gus briefly considered arguing with her, but he realized there was no point.

He needed to go. Now.

Someone from the federal office would wipe her mind of the incident by tomorrow anyways.

Toggling the emergency lights and siren on, Gus pulled out of the parking lot at full speed.

"So… what's a cat-one E-break?" asked the detective.

Gus glanced over at her, then looked back to the road ahead as he slipped past a stop sign.

"If you stop here and now, you won't get your memories wiped. At least much more than hearing it. You won't get a red rubber stamp next to your name in the personnel files," Gus said. "Going any further will get you a whole laundry list of things that'll fuck up your life."

"My memories wiped?" asked the detective, sounding confused and unfortunately interested.

"Yeah," Gus said, sliding through an intersection after making sure everyone was respecting the emergency lights. "Wiped. They usually do a good job of only taking what they need to. But that isn't a guarantee. They also tend to peek around to see if you've been up to anything you shouldn't."

There was a brief silence in his car.

"Cat-one and E-break?" she prompted.

"Right, whatever. Category-one disturbance, enchantment break," Gus said, pulling the wheel sharply to the left through another intersection.

Should be up ahead on the left.

Killing the siren and lights, Gus weaved his way through traffic, now looking more like a crazy person than a cop.

"The list of things that could mean is kinda short. Troll, Ogre, Warlock with a broken Soul Contract, something like that," Gus said, looking to his left.

Then he saw it. Or what he assumed it was. There was a mass of teenagers all standing outside of a large set of buildings.

"Question time's over," he said.

He pulled into a side street that ran parallel to the school and drove down it as quickly as he dared. The wall turned into a chain link fence. He could see up ahead where it opened, but it was locked shut with a padlock.

Wedging the corner of his car against the point where it opened, Gus gassed the engine once.

There was a strange pinging noise, and then the locking mechanism sheared off from the gate. After pulling the car back several feet, Gus popped the trunk, turned off the car, and got out.

He grabbed his SCAR-H and pocketed several magazines as well.

"What the hell is that?" the detective asked.

"Department-issued cat-one rifle. I'm personally not a fan of it, but they won the contract so… here we are," Gus muttered, loading the weapon with a mag. With a negligent pull of his fingers, he racked the slide. "Grab the shotgun, fill your pockets with shells. Need to go."

"This is insane," said the detective.

"Not really. And you chose to be here, you'll remember, without even knowing what it is. Only crazy thing here is you.

"Though truth be told, it's definitely a bit abnormal, I guess, but it's not the first cat-one this month." Gus pulled off his jacket and flicked it into the trunk, then glanced at the detective who was stuffing her jacket pockets with shells. "Close the trunk when you're done."

"This is Hellström, moving to scene. Last known position of cat-one?" he asked into his radio.

"Code eight is main building agent. Proceed with caution. Reported as Troll," came back the dispatcher.

Gus pulled the rifle up into his shoulder and held the weapon.

It felt right.

He felt right. Holding a rifle, adrenaline pumping in his veins, heading into danger.

Not in the sandbox anymore, idiot.

Moving at a jog Gus headed toward the main building of the school. It was a large three-story building that looked like a giant rectangle made of bricks and windows.

"Your name is Hellström?" asked the detective, moving along beside him.

"Yeah. I go by Gus. You?" he asked.

"Vanessa," said the detective.

"Fine, Vanessa," Gus said as he reached the door. Flinging it open, he was momentarily stuck when Vanessa rushed in first, the shotgun fetched up to her shoulder.

"It's a Troll," Gus said, following her in. "You can expect it to be big, green, and very—"

A roar came from down the hall. It was followed by a wall literally being knocked down. Stepping over the rubble was a massive monstrosity of a creature. Its head bumped the ceiling and it was partially hunched over. Its shoulders practically went from wall to wall.

It looked like a moving green wall.

"Loud," Gus finished. Lifting his rifle, he pointed it at the Troll and slipped his finger up against the trigger.

"Sir," Gus called out, getting the Troll's attention. Trolls always responded best to respect. "Please put your hands up, and don't move. A—"

Roaring at the top of its lungs, the Troll started moving forward toward the two police officers.

There was no fear in the Troll. None at all.

After tapping into his other inherited ability, telepathy, Gus knew where this was going. There wasn't a single rational thought in the Troll's head, in any way, shape or form. Just rage.

Unrestrained, animalistic rage.

Gus waited as long as he could, hoping the man would snap out of his berserker rush. Except it didn't happen.

Gus realized the Troll wasn't stopping. There was no going back from this point.

Then he pulled the trigger, leveling the muzzle at the charging Troll's center.

It wouldn't be hard to aim. Trolls were big. But center-mass was center-mass.

Set to full auto, the assault rifle emptied its magazine in the blink of an eye. The rapid-fire booms of the shotgun followed the retort of the rifle.

It was all absolutely deafening.

Explosions of green blood and flesh went in every direction as the Troll was hit repeatedly. As if it'd been hit with actual explosives, giant craters in its flesh appeared.

Tapping the mag release, Gus reloaded his rifle as quickly as he could, chambered a round, and brought it back up.

The Troll staggered to one side and slumped against the wall. Black blood pumped out of its gaping wounds.

Dropping to its face, it lay there unmoving.

Gus pulled out his radio.

"Suspect is down, in need of immediate emergency medical attention," Gus said. "Gonna need Enchanters on site."

"Received," replied the radio.

Setting his rifle down to one side, he immediately went over to the downed Troll and started doing what he could for him.

"What the hell did I just fire? My hands are aching and my shoulder feels like it's broken," Vanessa said.

"Uh… basically it shoots small rockets filled with blessed materials, and silver," Gus said, trying to find a pulse in the Troll. "Works for most things."

It was weak. Almost not there at all. Holding his fingers on it, Gus literally felt it stop and cease to beat.

Shit.

Gus grabbed his radio again.

"I need an emergency doc who can work on Trolls on location. No pulse here and I don't have the tools for a Troll," Gus said.

"Affirmative. Magical medical en route for a Troll," the dispatcher reported back.

"I don't… I don't even know…" Vanessa's voice trailed off.

"Yeah, well, you won't real soon. Those Enchanters are gonna pop your memory. Don't fret it much," Gus said.

He tried to turn the Troll over but had no luck with it.

Damn it!

There wasn't anything he could do about this one. Not a damn thing. Trolls were almost impossible to help without being in the right place at the right time.

Sighing, Gus went to press a hand to his head and stopped. It was covered in black blood.

Staying put, as that was the doctrine for the situation, Gus waited. Feeling helpless.

Going to have to do a walk-through by the watch commander, get interviewed, and probably… probably have more counseling sessions later.

Great.

***

Four hours later, and with another report to file and fill out, Gus was staring at his computer screen again.

He needed to get this bit of work done because he already knew he'd be put on administrative leave for the next few days.

It was standard practice and procedure, even for the PID.

Most of the report would be standard. Especially since he wasn't the first responding officer. That'd been someone from another precinct. Someone who'd had their head pulled off by a very angry Troll.

Shaking his head at the thought, Gus focused on his screen.

He filled it out as best as he could, right up to the point where he got to the list of impacted citizens. Those who would now be classified as in the "know" and get flagged accordingly.

He typed in the detective's first name, then realized he didn't know her last name.

Not that it matters. She'll get her day wiped and that'll be the end of that. With any luck she'll get a bonus for her assistance and it'll just be some strange attendance award or something.

After finalizing the report, Gus leaned back in his chair as the file was submitted.

The cleaning lady emptied a trash can across the way. She was always here at the end of his shift.

Since this was the swing shift, the best time for cleaning was now, right before the "day shift" came on duty.

Adjusting her cap, the woman dumped another small trash bin into her much larger one. Her uniform looked rather worn, and it definitely fit the "not a real person, please ignore me as I work" shapeless lump that such services tended to aim for.

Reaching under his desk, Gus fished out his own trash can and held it out to her.

"Here," he said. It was something they did almost every day. He saw no reason to make her work around him while he was here.

"Thank you," she said, emptying the trash bin and then setting it down next to his desk rather than hand it back. Without another word, she moved on to the next desk.

As was the normal case, she gave off a flash of unassociated fear whenever she got close to him.

He figured it was just the aura he put out. Quite a few people seemed to inherently have a negative reaction to him.

Same way the detective had earlier.

Picking up his coffee cup, Gus took a sip and immediately spat it back out into the cup.

It was cold.

Again.

Except the day was over now. It was the end of his watch.

Setting the mug back down, he tried not to think about his day. Except he kept coming back to the fact that he'd killed an unarmed Troll. A Troll in a rage unlike any he'd seen before.

Something out of history books that simply didn't happen anymore.

Then his computer blanked out and the screen locked.

Rolling his eyes, Gus got up and ended his day.

"Have a good night," Gus said to the cleaning lady as he headed for the door.

Chapter 2 - Partner Up

A loud and lively chime dragged Gus from a deep sleep.

Prying his eyes open, he managed to glare at the offending device. His cell phone, sitting on the wireless charger across from him on the dresser.

Buzzing, chiming, and happily throwing flashing lights around, it was an annoying monster Gus wanted to destroy.

With a groan, he rolled out of bed and stumbled over. Snatching it up, he tried to thumb the alarm off.

Only to realize it was an incoming call instead that he'd just accepted.

"Uh, hello?" Gus asked, pressing the phone to his ear.

"Good morning, dear," said his mom in a cheery voice.

"Mom," Gus said, closing his eyes. "Why are you calling me at whatever it is in the morning?"

"Because you're supposed to come over for dinner this weekend. And if I don't remind you and get you on the phone, you'll forget," she said, still just as cheerful. One would never suspect her of being a Boogieman. "Your sister will be there along with her boyfriend."

"Uh huh," Gus grumbled, yawning. "If that's your way of asking if I'm seeing anyone, I'm not. Still pretending to be human and just… not interested. Remember?"

"That doesn't matter at all, dear. Human, Boogieman, Troll, or otherwise. I was pretending to be human when I met your father, after all," his mom said.

"Dad read your mind," Gus said, standing up straight and scratching at his head. "After that you weren't pretending anymore."

"Mm. True, I suppose. It was rather nice to find someone who wasn't afraid of what I was," she said, her voice turning predatory. He imagined she was now looking at his father.

There was a certain feral desire that apparently all individuals of their race had. To hunt, invoke fear, and devour it. In the past, they had even gone as far as eating humans' still-beating, fear-filled hearts.

Or more.

"Mom, don't look at Dad like that," Gus grumbled. He knew exactly what look she was giving his dad.

"Hmm? Oh, yes, sorry. Anyways. Dinner, Saturday, see you then," his mom said, then disconnected the line.

She's going to jump him.

Gus shuddered away from the mental thought. His mom was a true apex predator in the paranormal world. She had no problem dipping into what she was. From what he knew, the only reason she wasn't a terror in the city—and hunted by someone in his department, the Para National guard, or the Fed—was his dad.

Or more precisely, the taming effect he had on her.

Shuffling his feet one in front of the other, Gus made it into his bathroom. Staring back at him was his own reflection.

Except it wasn't at the same time. Gus knew he was the same as his mother. He could see it. See it in the eyes of the reflection. The chained and desperate hunter that wanted to break free. Break free and feed.

Except it couldn't. Where his mother had his dad, Gus had a previous life spent dodging bullets. Running from building to building with a rifle.

Checking every bump, hole, or crossing for IEDs.

He'd had his fill of fear and killing.

He glanced at the clock; it was six in the morning.

Might as well get the day going.

***

It was a determined pounding on the door that got Gus out of the shower quicker than normal. It wasn't really something he could ignore. He knew that knock.

Anyone who had ever served a beat knew that form of wall-shaking greeting that one put to a door.

A policeman's knock. Three deep slams of the fist that were more likely to wake the dead than ever be considered knocks.

Wrapping a towel around his waist, he shambled over to the door and peeked out the peephole.

And found only blackness. Whoever it was had decided they didn't want to be seen.

Frowning, Gus reached down to the coffee table near the front door. He pressed his thumb to the electric reader underneath the lip, and the false drawer opened up below the table.

Reaching inside, Gus planned on drawing his off-duty weapon, a duplicate firearm of his issued pistol. He'd bought it on his own from the same company that supplied his department.

"Gus! Open up the door already—it's Vanessa!" called a feminine voice from the other side of the door.

Huh?

Confused, and not really sure what to make of the situation, Gus unlocked the door and pulled it open.

Sure enough, the detective from the previous day was standing there, staring back at him.

"Sorry, do I know you?" Gus tried, wondering what the hell she was doing here. And how she seemed to know his name.

"Yeah, nice try," Vanessa said. Then her eyes tracked down from his head to his feet and back up. Her mouth turned into a dark frown, and she raised her eyebrows at him. "Do you always open the door like that?"

"No. But I don't normally have people who shouldn't remember me showing up in the morning either," Gus said. Stepping beyond the doorway, he looked up one side of the street, then the other. Everything was as it should be, though there was a car he didn't recognize parked in front of his house. He assumed it was the detective's.

"You can invite me in, or I can stand here and make a scene," Vanessa said. "I grew up in a big family; I can really project my voice if I want to.

"Would you prefer angry ex-wife or insane girlfriend?"

"Damnit. What the hell is wrong with you?" Gus grumbled and stepped to one side, gesturing to the interior. "Well then, by all means, come on in."

Walking into his home, the detective did an immediate scan of the area. Something Gus had done many a time.

Is there anything visible I should be aware of?

"Off-duty sidearm is in a bio-reader drawer in the coffee table. Everything else in the bedroom in the gun cabinet," Gus said, walking back toward the bathroom. "So, care to tell me why you know who I am? And where I live?"

Being called out as she was, Vanessa immediately shifted her body posture to something more casual. "Sorry, force of habit."

"Yeah, got that. Do it myself. Now, how do you know?" Gus called, walking into his bedroom.

Pulling open the top drawer, he fished out a white undershirt and some boxers. He threw both on top of his bed, then went to his sock drawer and pulled out a pair of black socks.

It was all he owned now. When you had to wear black socks for work, there wasn't much of a point in owning anything else. You just ended up having to do more laundry to keep up on your black-sock inventory.

"That… Enchanter… showed up after you left. She took one look at the scene and said she was going to be too busy to 'blank' me," Vanessa said, an edge to her voice. "Your watch commander told me to take a few days off, then called my boss and made that happen. Apparently I'm supposed to not do anything I wouldn't want to forget."

Part of Gus wanted to make a comment about how seeing him the morning after was indeed a forgettable experience, but the wisecrack died on his lips before he even started.

The strange dull ache came back instead, making his chest hurt.

"Yeah, standard procedure in that case," Gus said, moving into his walk-in closet. "They've got you listed and registered for a wipe. No time to do it right now. I imagine that Troll was seen by a number of people who aren't police, and those take priority."

"I figured… if they're going to take the memories from me anyways, I might as well find out more," Vanessa said, her voice muffled by the interior of the house. "So I tracked you down in the police database and… here I am. You didn't mention you were a detective yourself, Agent Hellström."

"Doesn't really matter, does it?" Gus asked, pulling down a polo shirt from the rack.

"I suppose not, if you thought I'd forget about you. Oh, your watch commander said he was going to call your boss. That you were probably going to go in to work today. Apparently he wants you to track down who did his 'mask' and then where he'd been the last few days, and everyone else has cases," Vanessa said. "He either didn't care that I was listening or forgot what the Enchanter said."

Sighing, Gus put the polo back onto the rack and pulled down a white button-up shirt and a navy suit.

"He probably forgot. Most people get wiped same day," Gus said, marching back out of his walk-in. "Wait. Then why are you here?"

"Because I want to know more. I don't like… not knowing. Even if I forget, I'd rather know. So I figured I'd take you to breakfast."

"Huh… fine. Mark probably won't call me in till noon anyways; he's my boss. Trying to get anything done at the DME before two is pointless, and that's where this would start. Not enough employees," Gus grumbled.

"DME?" Vanessa asked, her words followed by a soft clatter.

Frowning, Gus whipped off his towel and pulled on his boxers quickly. Peering out from his bedroom, he saw Vanessa.

She was poking through the pictures on his mantel.

"Department of Magical Enchantments. It's where Paras get their masks assigned by Fairies, Spell users, or Fae," Gus said after moving back to get dressed. His assumption was that something had gone very wrong with the Troll's mask. Especially since he hadn't actually been wearing it. Which wasn't technically possible without breaking it outright. "So, breakfast?"

"Yeah, my treat. But we need to go somewhere cheap. I'm still paying off student loans. Apparently your department's version of a detective makes a lot more than mine."

"Yeah," Gus said, that cold ache coming back. "Hazard pay."

"After yesterday… I'm not sure they can pay you enough," Vanessa muttered.

After getting into his clothes quickly, Gus finished up by loading his duty weapon and holstering it. Then he walked back into the main part of his house.

Vanessa was sitting on the couch, flipping through something on her phone.

"Ready?" he asked.

"Oh, yes. Sorry. Was reading a book," Vanessa said, pressing the lock button on her phone and getting up.

"Anything fun?" he asked, then moved to the door and opened it.

"I'm not sure it'd be your cup of tea," Vanessa said as she passed by him.

"And how do you know that? Maybe I like all sorts of tea," Gus said, closing his front door and locking it.

"It's a romance novel, and I'm driving," Vanessa said, and she moved toward her car.

"Hey, I like romance. Especially the kind that ends with a lot of grunting and moaning," Gus said, catching up with her.

"Of course you do," replied the detective. "Then again, maybe I do too, for all you know."

Thirty minutes later, she pulled them into a greasy spoon. Gus had never been inside this particular one.

In fact, the last time he'd gone somewhere like this was before he'd joined the military. He tended to stay away from places like this because Paras liked to frequent them.

And Gus might as well have a neon sign above his head that said Para-cop. There really wasn't much else he could be, since he had a mask but was entirely human behind it. Any other human who would appear as such could almost always make their own mask. Usually one that was infinitely better, too.

No such thing as an undercover human Para-cop.

Sure enough, the hostess looked like some type of Fairy behind her glittering spell mask. Her eyes were a full blue color without any whites. She stared at him, the recognition instant.

"Booth preferably, two people," Gus said, trying to get the girl moving. The longer she sat there staring at him, the harder it'd be to get her rolling.

Giving her head a quick shake, she smiled at him in the same way all waitresses did. Though she did have a set of overly large canines that visibly slipped free from her lips. "Of course, right this way."

Vanessa pulled off her jacket when they got to the booth and tossed it lightly into the corner of her seat. The gun in its shoulder holster was very visible.

Reaching into her blouse, she fished out her detective medallion and set it beside her clothes so it was visible as well.

Also visible was the fact that Vanessa was stacked. And she had a narrow waist that spoke to a lot of walking. There was no denying that she'd be worth approaching by any number of men.

Now that he was looking, she was actually rather pretty, too.

Deciding he might as well follow suit since she was openly professing she was a cop, Gus pulled off his coat and ditched it in the same way. He didn't pull out his medallion, though. His was also his mask, and he didn't want to put himself more on display if he didn't have to.

With eyes on the hostess, Vanessa waited till she was out of earshot.

"Let me guess—she's not normal, and she knew you were a cop," Vanessa said.

"Fairy or somethin'," Gus said with a shrug of his shoulders, opening the menu. "All mask holders can see through other mask holders.

"Keeps everyone playing fair and in the open. It also makes it a lot easier to pick out Paras without a mask."

"She gave you the same look I get when I go home," Vanessa muttered, pushing her menu to one side. "Order the waffles, trust me."

"What? Eh… whatever," Gus said, closing the menu. "No matter what I order, I'll probably get something special added."

"You won't. I come here often enough that they know better," Vanessa said. "So… tell me what I need to know?"

"Need to know?" Gus asked, getting a sinking feeling.

"Yeah. Need to know. If I'm only going to keep these memories for a few days, I might as well help you work this case. Your watch commander already got me several days off, and I'm not going to just sit around in my apartment."

"No. Just, no. You're not going to do this," Gus said, shaking his head. "You'll just—"

"You can clue me in and bring me along, or I'll just follow you. What are you gonna do, call the cops on me?" Vanessa asked.

"Are you serious—"

A waitress who was very clearly not human to Gus walked up with a pad in hand. She had short black horns coming out from her brows and long, downturned ears.

"Uhm… I," she said, staring at Gus.

"Hi Judy," Vanessa said.

"Oh, hey… Ness, who's your friend?" Judy said, somehow breaking her eyes from Gus.

"I'm not working, and she didn't know till yesterday, and she'll forget the next time you see her probably," Gus said with a sigh. "I'll take the waffles and whatever dark soda you have."

Judy the waitress looked back to Vanessa.

"The same but coffee," she said.

Judy went off toward the back to put in their order.

"Her too?" Vanessa asked.

"Yeah, looks like a Demon of some sort," Gus said. "Fine, ok. Fine. You can come with me. If—and I mean *if*—my boss actually calls me and puts me on the case. Otherwise, you're going home, and I'm going to go run some errands."

"I can agree to that. So… what do I need to know?" she prompted.

Gus pressed a hand to his face; he didn't know where to start. "Right, uh. All the things that go bump in the night are real.

"Humans outnumber Para something like three to one in general. They're moving into the cities faster and faster as the government makes it easier. So you'll find much greater concentrations of them in cities. Outside of some dos and don'ts, that's most of what you need to know."

"Dos and don'ts?" Vanessa parroted back.

"Yeah. Don't make a deal with a Warlock, Fae, or Fairy. Vampires and Werewolves can turn you if you get bitten. It's not a guarantee you'll contract the disease, but chances are one in five you'll catch it.

"After that it's like fifty-fifty you survive it. Vampires get rolled into a coven through the blood bond of the disease. Werewolves can go rogue."

"What… what if you were bit?" Vanessa asked.

"I've been bit before. Werewolf. Not a fun experience," Gus muttered. "CDC kicks over a regimen to take if you're bit. It decreases the chances of developing the disease. If it's vampirism, you end up having to leave the force, but with a pension and usually a bit more power in your life than if you were a civilian. Werewolves get reassigned if they turn and survive."

"Can Vampires and Werewolves just bite whoever they want?" Vanessa asked.

"No. There's a bunch of paperwork people have to submit to get converted. Mostly because it's a coin-flip whether it ends up being suicide.

"Illegal bites get run as attempted murder or murder," Gus said. "Kinda easy to track that back with DNA on the bite."

"There's a prison for Paras?"

"Yep. The medium-security and max prisons are mostly run up north across the border. Stick 'em in the middle of nowhere and deep in the wilderness. Then just make it a giant armed and armored fortress. No visitations or anything.

"Non-violent Para offenders end up in normal jails with humans," Gus said. "Anything else you wanna know?"

"I mean… there's lots I want to know, but I don't know what to ask. I don't know what I don't know," Vanessa said, looking frustrated.

"Yeah, I get that. Honestly, the Para world is just a giant gray space. You fill it in bit by bit, do research, and try your best to keep both sides of the equation safe," Gus said, leaning back in his seat. "Paras can end up having it almost worse than humans at times. Especially in the smaller places."

"I'm not sure how I can see that. That Troll the other day was, ah… frightening," Vanessa said.

"One on one, sure, they're terrifying. Except all you have to do is drown them in humanity," Gus said. "If you want a good example of that, just rewind history a few hundred years and start going through witch trials, crusades, and inquisitions.

"Sure, a strong and prepared group of Paras can really cause a problem. But it's their numbers and inability to band together that endangers them. A Vamp would rather drink from a hobo on a ten-day bender of black tar and booze than compliment a Wolf."

"How does one get into your department?" Vanessa finally asked. Gus had been expecting it for a while.

"Recruited by watch commanders usually, since they have the most overlap with normal police officers. They usually do a yearly review of all the other forces they can pull from and go from there if there are open slots. Those recommendations get kicked up to captains."

"And how'd you get in?" Vanessa asked.

Gus blew out a breath and finally met her eyes. He gave her a cold smile and let out just a hint of what he kept bolted down inside his soul.

"I spent a month holed up in a tiny village in the shit-hole end of nowhere with nothing but my squad, sand, and an entire clan of Elves out for our blood.

"Not all Elves, either. Pretty sure there were a few sub-species in there as well, but that's how it goes," Gus said. "Me and two other guys walked out. One ate his gun the week after that. The other works in my department, but he works day shift and I work the overnight."

"You work overnight? But... you said you worked during the day," Vanessa asked. At the same time, Judy came back with their food and set it down on the table.

"Yeah, I guess that wouldn't make sense at first," Gus said, paying Judy no mind. "Because the Para community is more active at night. That's the day shift. I'm the swing shift agent."

Judy finished up, looking from Vanessa to Gus.

"Thank you, Judy," Gus said, giving her a genuine smile. "Your horns are quite lovely, by the way. It's like they're polished. I bet they shine beautifully in the sunlight."

Judy gave him a sudden and bright smile, surprised and flattered, and nodded her head.

"Thank you. I gave them a good buffing last week," she said.

"Last week? I'm surprised. You look more like you just walked out of a salon," Gus said, maybe laying it on a bit thick. If he could get the waitress on his side, though, he might be able to come back here another time.

Judy wrinkled her nose with a grin, shaking her head at him. Flattered and clearly liking it. Her large ears were also very bright red.

"Ah, let me know if you need anything and I'll take care of it," she said, giving him a hand wave.

Vanessa was giving him a strange look, unfolding her silverware from the napkin.

"Demons take pride in their horns. Hers were actually rather pretty," Gus said, looking at his food. "No reason not to compliment her on them. That and it'd be nice to come back here sometime."

That sentiment was mostly because the food smelled really good.

And it didn't hurt that there was an undercurrent of fear in the place coming from the patrons, all directed at him.

His inner demon chuckled smugly.

Meal with a meal. Should have thought of this before.

Chapter 3 - Breadcrumbs

Gus was steadily working through his waffle when he felt his phone start vibrating in his pocket. Reaching down with his left hand, he pulled it free and glanced at it.

Of course it's Mark.

Gus swiped the accept button and pressed it to his ear.

"What's up, boss?" Gus said, looking at Vanessa.

She gave him a pretty smile that was equal parts "I told you so" and saccharine sweet.

"Hey Gussy," Mark said, using the same nickname he'd been given back in their unit. "I need you to pull a shift today. Somethin' like twelve to nine. Can ya hack it?"

"Yeah. I'm on it. Got a hitchhiker though," Gus said, still staring down Vanessa. "The detective from yesterday tracked me down."

"What, the Norm? I saw her when I came to see the mess you'd left me. Watch-Com wasn't too happy with you.

"Eh... she's going to get blanked anyways. She was hot," Mark said. "I'd say why not give her a roll or two?"

"No, Durh," Gus said, hitting Mark's nickname a little hard. "Listen. She wants to work the case with me."

He wasn't about to walk her into this without Mark knowing and maybe saving him from it.

"Huh? Really? Hm. Really," Mark said, his voice fading out near the end. It sounded like he was typing something into a computer.

"Durh, what are you doing?" Gus asked, getting a little nervous now.

"Nothin'. She there with you?" Mark asked.

"Yeah... why?"

"She wearing something fun? When she pulled her coat off the other day, she had some great cleavage."

"What the hell is wrong with you? And why are we having this conversation?" Gus asked, getting more than a little nervous. Vanessa was actively watching him.

"Cause she was hot," Mark said. "I mean, if you're not willing to make a play, maybe I will. She's got that feisty thing going on and you know I go in for that.

"Remember that night in—"

"Durh, not right now. And you're married. How about what I need you to talk about? What do you want me to do?" Gus asked.

There was a brief silence followed by a loud, single keyboard clack.

"Take her with you. I just told her captain what I'm going to do with her.

"She'll probably get a note form him in a minute, and one from me as well. Her time off is revoked and she's assigned to you as a temporary, and you're lead detective," Mark said. "And if she wants a tumble, don't say no. She'll still probably get blanked after this."

Gus closed his eyes and gritted his teeth. He had been hoping that somehow Mark would shut her down.

A soft chiming noise came from directly in front of him.

"Anyways. I need you to hit the DME, track down the Troll's mask. Far as we can tell, that's what made him go full berserker. It failed and took his mind with it.

"Then you'll need to hit his apartment and go from there. I bounced you all the relevant details in your office email," Mark said. "Update me when your shift's over, Gussy. Bye, dear."

Mark made several kissing noises and disconnected the line.

Growling, Gus stuffed his phone into his pocket and looked at Vanessa. She was reading something on her phone.

"I just got... reassigned to you as a junior detective," Vanessa said, her mouth curling in a slow smile.

Another chime that came from her phone. As she tapped at the screen, her eyes darted across the display.

"And my captain just revoked my time off, gave me my temporary assignment, and told me I'd be making quadruple my salary for a week," Vanessa said, raising her eyebrows. "You make that much?"

Gus shrugged his shoulders.

"Hazard pay," he said, digging back into his waffles. "Eat up, Ness. We're on the clock in three hours or so. We'll need to hit the armory first and get you kitted out."

Vanessa nodded her head rapidly, still grinning.

I really don't need to break in a rookie right now. If I'm right, this is way worse than anyone thinks it is.

Masks don't just fail. They don't make people go crazy.

Shit. Rookies are almost as bad as workin' with a fresh boot.

***

Getting out of Vanessa's car, Gus reached inside his coat and made sure his pistol was ready to be pulled. If a mask failed and made the wearer go insane, it meant the Enchanter who did it probably did it on purpose.

"Expecting trouble?" Vanessa asked, coming up beside him. She was fidgeting with her chest, pulling at what he assumed was her new shoulder holster. Her old one didn't fit the new pistol.

"Yeah… masks don't just go boom and make their users need to punch down walls," Gus said.

"Ah. So… this is more like a someone cut their brakes kind of situation?" she asked.

"Kinda, yeah. That's not a bad analogy."

"This looks like a DMV," Vanessa said, following Gus to the front of the building.

"It is. It's just a DME at the same time. Driver's licenses work great as a mask's enchantment anchor. Has to be with you almost all the time anyways. For Paras, it becomes more of the same," Gus said, pulling the door open and stepping to one side. "They just end up waiting longer here for an Enchanter after getting their license. There are some special cases for full enchantments where they have to do a house visit. Trolls and Ogres are good examples of that, if they're of the big variety."

Vanessa walked in, her head immediately doing a circuit as she surveyed the interior of the building.

"What are we looking for?" she asked when Gus stepped up next to her.

The layout looked like any other DMV one might walk into. Lots of chairs, glass partitions where employees worked, and a whole lot of people being bored to death as they waited.

"Whoever the floor manager is, we'll need to talk to them and get the Troll's record," Gus said.

"Michael Fitz," Vanessa said.

"Huh?"

"His name. That was the Troll's name. Michael Fitz."

"Oh. Right. Him then," Gus said. Then he pointed to a middle-aged woman in a blouse and long skirt. "Let's go ask her who the floor manager is."

Moving quickly to the entry point, a wooden half-door, Gus caught the attention of one of the two security guards. Gus was ready for the coming exchange.

He'd already pulled out his medallion and was holding it up in front of him when the guard came over.

He was, unfortunately, a normal human. This would go easier otherwise.

"Detective Hellström," Gus said, keeping the badge up.

"Detective Flores," Vanessa said from beside him.

"Could you please let the manager know we'd like to have a word with them? Preferably in private," Gus said. "That or I can step past this toddler gate and talk to them directly myself. Up to you."

The security guard didn't seem particularly happy with that.

"He won't see you," said the guard.

"Well, he doesn't really have a choice, and it sounds like I'll be stepping by to talk to him," Gus said, grabbing the wooden half-door's latch.

"You can't come back here," said the guard, grabbing the other side of the latch.

"Look—"

"Excuse me, Jordan?" Vanessa said. "We really do need to speak with the manager. If you could just tell them that two officers from the PID are here, I'm sure they'd be willing to speak with us."

The security guard turned his glare away from Gus to look to Vanessa, then back to Gus.

"I'll go tell 'em. Still won't see you," said Jordan, leaving them there.

"Any chance of the floor manager being a suspect?" Vanessa asked once the guard had walked away.

"No. Enchanters are assigned here but they don't work here. This is more of a training gig for most of them. Helps them build up their mana pools," Gus said.

"No reason for me to go cover the back door then? You don't think the manager will bolt?" Vanessa asked.

Gus frowned and briefly considered it. The guard was already talking to an older man who was apparently the manager.

He was a lanky fellow who looked to be in his mid-fifties. Balding, gray hair, and glasses that looked thicker than the bottom of an old soda bottle.

Gus cast about with his other senses. The abilities his parents had given him through the genetic lottery, so to speak.

He tasted fear here and there. Small bits of it, but nothing out of the ordinary. There was no fear of being caught here.

"I think we're fine," Gus said.

The man who was apparently the manager hurried over to the detectives in a strange, almost hopping walk.

"PID carries that much weight?" Vanessa asked.

"Yeah. Because if we can't solve it, we call in the Bureau, or the CDC. And they don't tolerate anything at all. They like to roll out the Para National Guard."

"Hi, I'm so sorry about that. Please, come in, come in," said the man, pulling open the latched door. "We can talk in my office."

With a nod, Gus indicated Vanessa to go first.

Might as well use her the right way. Everyone always does what a pretty lady asks.

"I'm Detective Flores," Vanessa said, introducing herself. "We were hoping to talk to you about a matter involving a… license and who put it together."

"Oh, of course, of course. I'm Blake Johnson, by the way," said the older man, leading them to the offices in the back of the building. "Is it Mrs. Flores or Miss?"

"Detective Flores is fine," Vanessa said.

Gus took the time to look around, giving the whole place a once-over. He could feel small flights of fear when he looked at people. But nothing that would draw his attention. Nothing that would signal him to stop and pay attention.

It looked like a normal work day. Here and there were Paras waiting for their new masks, people working the lines, and already a few Enchanters working with licenses.

Every day normality… at least as far as this goes.

Anything can be normal after a while.

Gus's thoughts flinched away from where his memories led him momentarily.

Putting his game face on, he stepped into Blake's office and moved to the corner. He didn't feel like sitting, and sometimes just standing in a corner could put people on edge.

"What can I do today for the PID?" Blake asked, looking from Vanessa to Gus as he sat behind his desk.

"First, I need a mask for detective Flores, general PID enchantment. She only needs it to see through other masks," Gus said, throwing a thumb toward Vanessa. "She's new. After that, I need to know who made a full enchantment mask for a… what was his name again?"

Vanessa had a small pad of paper in her hand he hadn't noticed.

"A Troll by the name of Michael Fitz, that's Foxtrot India Tango Zulu," Vanessa said, looking back up at the manager.

"Michael… Fitz," said Blake, typing something on a keyboard. "Alright. I should be able to get that. Let me just check the database real quick…"

Vanessa smiled politely, waiting quietly.

It's like looking at a damn different person. Where's the annoying feisty fucker from this morning? Or is that more of an on/off switch she controls?

As if sensing him and his thoughts, Vanessa threw him a glance and quirked a brow at him. Before he could respond, she was already looking back to Blake.

"Huh, that's strange. I can see Mr. Fitz's record. Nothing on file that would be a problem of any sort," Blake said, a massive frown covering his mouth. "But… there's no record of his enchantment. And that's not something that should be missing. Not for a Troll. It would have had to be done by a senior Enchanter."

Moving the mouse around, Blake seemed to be hunting for something.

"Is there any reason a record would be missing?" Gus asked.

"No. Not at all. In fact… it's almost impossible. Large Paranormal profiles will flag multiple warnings without a record. But… there's been no warning for Mr. Fitz," Blake said, shaking his head.

Alright. In other words… someone is covering their tracks, and they don't want us to know who did the mask.

Easing up a fraction of the control he kept in check at all times, Gus focused in on Blake. Slowly, a thin tendril of his telepathic ability snuck into the other man's mind.

It was full of rather interesting thoughts about Vanessa, and little else.

Which meant to Gus the man was telling the truth completely. There was no fear there, nothing being hidden, just unadulterated lust for the detective.

He couldn't be sure without tearing through the man's mind, but it wasn't worth the risk.

"Do you know when his mask was assigned, at least?" Gus asked, pulling back on his ability.

Vanessa cleared her throat, looking at her pad.

"His record at the DMV indicates his driver's license was assigned last year in May. Would that be matched to the mask date?" she asked Gus.

Huh. Well aren't you a little go-getter?

"Yeah, that'd match. Blake, can you get me a list of names of all your senior Enchanters since April of last year?" Gus said. At the same time, Vanessa was taking notes in her pad with a pen.

"Of course. Not a problem, Detective," said the manager, looking up from his screen. "I can probably get that to you by the end of the day. Where do you want me to send it, or…?"

"Yeah, just send it by email to GHellstrom at PID dot gov," Gus said with a shake of his head, pulling out his phone from his pocket. "Ness, get the address for Fitz, then go get your mask. I'm going to go update Mark."

Tapping and holding the speed-dial button for his boss, Gus left the office. He pressed the phone to his ear as he headed for the exit.

"Miss me, Gussy?" Mark asked when he picked up the line.

"Shut up, Durh. Got a problem here. Whoever did the FE backspaced the whole thing. All records of it are deleted," Gus said, pushing open the half door and heading for a section of empty seats. "Manager says that's not possible. I believe him."

"Huh. You're not wrong on those gut-checks, either. Alright. So we've got a dead Troll, a broken mask, and an Enchanter who did it and covered it up. That sum it up?" Mark asked.

"Yeah. Senior Enchanter, though. Gonna be a small list, and no matter what I do, it's gonna piss off a family," Gus said, dragging his free hand across his eyes.

Enchanters always came from magical families. Senior Enchanters almost always came from powerful magical families.

"Shit. No kiddin'? Alright. I'll get the chief involved now before it goes further. I'm sure he'll just yell at me and tell me to keep going, though."

"Yeah, he's a prick like that," Gus said.

"How's your boot doing?"

"Pretty good, actually. She took everything in stride so far and is actually being useful. Why, you doin' something stupid, Durh?"

"No, of course not. How could you ever say such a thing?"

"We didn't start calling you Durh without a reason, ya know."

"Yeah, yeah, go stare at your partner. I would. You coming over this weekend for dinner?" Mark asked. "Kelly would love to see you. So would Megan."

"Sorry, can't. Mom reminded me I have an appointment with them instead."

"Err… yeah. Alright. Cool. I'll see you later, Gussy. Keep me updated."

The line went dead before Gus could respond.

His mom tended to make people uncomfortable. Especially people who'd been in the shit. Mark had only met his mom once and had proceeded to avoid her forever afterward.

Stuffing his phone and his hands in his pockets, Gus slouched low in the chair. He let his mind wander, and he missed it when Vanessa walked right up on him.

"Gus! I have one," Vanessa said, holding up her driver's license. Her eyes were a bit wide and rounded out. It was obvious she hadn't expected to find herself face to face with everyday monsters today.

"Yep. I see that," Gus said. "Got the address?"

"Yeah, I do. That where we're going?"

Gus nodded and got to his feet.

***

Pulling up to a large apartment building in the heart of downtown, Gus felt apprehensive.

"This is the address?" he asked again.

"It's what Blake gave me. Considering how he was looking at me, I don't think he'd lie to me," Vanessa said, opening her door.

"About that—is that normal for you? To be a raging dickhead to me, then pull out the super-sweet, sexy detective for someone else?" Gus said, getting out of the car and closing the door.

Vanessa laughed at that and pointed a finger at him.

"Look, you, the only dickhead here is you. Everyone you meet seems to immediately dislike you. Me included. Though… maybe I was a bit short with you at first. I'm sorry for that.

"That's behind us now, right partner?" Vanessa asked, coming around to his side. "Though I don't think you should be calling your brand-new partner sexy. Probably bad etiquette. Should I tell our boss? Mark, is it?"

Gus snorted at that and walked to the door, where he quickly checked the front of the building for any cameras.

Cameras were a blessing. They'd helped solve far more Para crimes than anyone would ever want to know.

Eyewitness testimony was always questionable; cameras were far and away more reliable.

"Go for it. He told me to try and sleep with you since you'll forget anyways," Gus said.

"He did what?" she asked in a dangerous tone.

"Told me to plow you. Don't take it personally, we were in the service together. Filter is long gone," Gus said, pulling the door open and pointing to the mailbox on the inside. "Check for our vic."

"Oh, he's the one who walked out with you?" Vanessa asked, immediately scanning the last names on all the mailboxes.

"Yeah. One of 'em," Gus said as he looked around the interior of the entryway for cameras. There was one, but it looked old.

Very old.

"Got it. Definitely lives here," Vanessa said. "I'll find the landlord and get it o—"

Gus stepped forward to the mailbox and pulled out his carry knife. When he gave it a flick, the blade locked open and into place.

Not worrying about the knife—he'd had it reinforced eight ways from Sunday by a friend—he wedged it into the side of the mailbox where the latch would be and cranked it sideways.

With a dull pop, the door creaked open and a broken latch with a spring fell to the ground.

"No mail," Gus said, peering in.

"What the hell, Gus? Why'd you do that?" Vanessa asked, trying to close the postal box door.

"Because it won't matter. Landlord will get wiped of all memory about our vic; so will the neighbors. That way if anyone comes asking questions, this'll be a dead end," Gus said, closing his blade. "What number is it again?"

"Sixty-seven," Vanessa grumbled, turning toward the elevator. "So, sixth floor I guess."

Gus shrugged and slipped his knife back into his belt as he walked to the elevator. Flicking his hand to the side he pressed the elevator button with a finger.

"Are you always an ass?" Vanessa asked.

"Usually, I guess. My aunt always tells me I need to be more fluffy," Gus said with a yawn that made him feel anything but tired. "I only see her once every few years, though."

He felt nervous.

His anxiety about the situation was starting to creep up higher and higher. He could feel it.

"You ok?" Vanessa asked. For the first time, he felt just the barest hint of fear from her. But it wasn't directed at him.

"Yeah. This just… isn't adding up," Gus said, shaking his head. "It's feeling more and more like a murder charge. Or something else. And it's going to involve some powerful people."

The elevator dinged and the doors swung open. Getting in, Vanessa tapped the button they wanted.

"Got it. In other words, you think we're gonna get roadblocked real soon," she said.

"Probably," Gus said as the doors slid shut. Staring back at himself, he immediately looked to one side and saw Vanessa in the reflection. Who was staring back at him.

"For what it's worth… thanks. I know you could have shut me out if you really wanted to. It may only be for a day or two, but… thanks," she said.

Gus looked away from her, staring at the button panel instead.

"Yep," he said.

Nothing further was said as they exited the elevator and strolled down the hall.

When they reached the door numbered sixty-seven, Gus hesitated. A strange feeling of vague fear was coming from inside the apartment.

As if someone was in there and afraid of being discovered.

"Fitz lived alone?" Gus asked instead of acting.

"Yes. That's what was on the report Mark sent over in the email," Vanessa said.

Reaching into his coat, Gus pulled out his sidearm. Easing the slide back, he checked the breech and made sure a round was chambered. He pulled the safety down, then reached out with his other hand and touched the doorknob.

"Funny then, because I think someone is here," Gus murmured softly, looking at Vanessa. She was already pulling her own weapon from its holster and had it leveled at the door. "I'll take the left, you move right?"

Vanessa nodded.

Gus tried the door handle and found it was locked. Pulling his set of lock-picks from a coat pocket, he got down on one knee.

Carefully, methodically, he began to set the pins into position while pulling the cylinder with his tension wrench.

In little under two minutes, he'd gotten it unlocked. The lock wasn't anything exemplary. He could have just raked it, but that would have been louder.

Holding tight to the handle, he turned to Vanessa. She nodded her head at him.

Then Gus flung open the door.

Chapter 4 - Hunting

Storming into the dwelling, Gus and Vanessa passed through the entryway. They found nothing immediately there and slipped right into the kitchen.

"Police!" Gus shouted, his pistol drawn and held out in front of him. "PID!"

The kitchen was empty, and they cleared it in seconds.

Except Gus could hear someone down the hall now. It sounded like they were trying to open the window.

Keeping his weapon drawn and high, Gus charged around the corner as quick as he could while still clearing the way.

When he made it to the end of the hall, he found what he was looking for. At the window. The culprit had opened it and already shoved out the screen.

Not much good that'll do. We're way too high up.

The intruder turned to Gus, who found himself looking into the face of a woman. She had small, glowing blue sigils around the orbitals of her eyes. Almost like half circles. They sparkled and glowed in the faint light. It made her pitch-black eyes even darker by contrast.

A series of similar green markings traveled across her brow, down around her ears, and into her black hair that was pulled back behind her head in a tight braid.

Her ears weren't quite fully human, however, with just a hint of something else. She was also really pretty. Pretty to the point that Gus was momentarily distracted.

Dressed in a short coat, a blouse, and a pair of slacks, she looked like she could have walked into any office building she wanted to for an interview. There was a black choker around her neck, and a lovely necklace resting on her neckline and upper chest.

A Contractor. Damn me.

Her pupils widened slightly at the sight of him, and Gus got a momentary fear response from her. Which was instantly cut off, as if it had never existed.

"Hey," Gus said, the tip of his gun dipping down several inches. Then he came back to himself and lifted his gun back up. "Hold it right there, lady. This is a crime scene, and you're gonna go in for breaking and entering.

"How about you just lie down on the ground. We'll take this nice and slow, and you and I can play nice."

The woman giggled at that, lifting her hands up to the sides of her head.

"For you, handsome, I think I'd be more than willing to lie down on the ground. Doesn't really seem comfortable, though—maybe another time, somewhere else," she said with a tiny accent he couldn't place. Then she wiggled her gloved fingers. "I'm going to fall for you, Agent. Really hard. Watch me, okay?"

Closing her eyes, she fell out the window as if she were dropping off a boat to go scuba diving.

As the bottom of her black, strappy, high-heeled shoes slipped out of view, Gus rushed over to the window.

"Damn it," he cursed.

"She jumped?" Vanessa cried.

"No, she can probably fucking fly or something like that," Gus said, reaching the window.

The Contractor was no longer falling, and the marks on her face glowed brightly. The giant smile on her face when she saw him was unmistakable.

Meeting her eyes, Gus briefly considered what to do.

It's levitation, not flying. She probably doesn't have control over it.

Active magic, though, which means I can pull a trail. Just gotta be quick.

Then the Contractor blew him a kiss with her black-gloved hands.

Bitch.

Gus grinned, feeling his heartbeat racing along.

"We need to get to the car. I need to get a sniffer," Gus said, rushing away from the window.

"What about the apartment?" Vanessa asked.

"Lock it, we'll come back. Chances are she took anything useful anyways," Gus said.

When he reached the fire exit, Gus practically flew down the stairs, leaping from landing to landing. He slipped on some tiles and bounced off a wall, denting the plaster and drywall.

"What was she?" Vanessa shouted from a stairwell flight above him.

"Contractor! It's a type of spell user," Gus said as he reached the ground floor. Slamming through the doors, he didn't bother to look for the woman. Instead he rushed over to the trunk of Vanessa's car. He'd loaded her vehicle up the same way he had his own when they were at the armory.

Yanking at the latch, Gus cursed. It was locked and he didn't have the keys.

Then the car chirped, and the trunk clicked.

You're a fucking amazing partner, Ness!

Grabbing the handle, he opened the trunk and pulled over the bag of miscellaneous toys and gadgets agents could pick up.

He snatched up what looked like a small jewelry box from the bag and flipped it open.

Slamming the trunk closed, he ran to where he felt like the Contractor would have landed.

Except before he even had a chance to find her trail with the sniffer, he could taste a trace of fear. It was just a hint of it, but it was there.

When she'd landed, she'd had a fairly large fear response.

She knows I'm going to tail her.

Devouring that bit of fear, he could taste her.

It was sweet, with a hint of heat to it. It reminded him of spiced mint.

Gus leaned down at the exact spot he landed, then dragged the ball of his thumb across a small blade at the corner of the box. It was just enough to split the skin in a tiny slit.

Blood dripped down the blade, then seeped into the box itself. It glowed a faint red color and then snapped closed.

Looking at the top of the box, Gus could see a red glowing eye pointing away from the apartment building and down an alleyway.

"Got her, I'm going on foot. Follow with the car. I'll flip you a locational from my cell," Gus said, and he sprinted off after the trail.

"Wait, what!?" Vanessa screamed at his back.

Opening his cell as he ran, Gus pulled open her contact ID. Then he activated his "share location" feature in the messenger app and flipped it to her without any limit. He pushed his phone back into his pocket.

He didn't need the sniffer to follow the Contractor, though. Her fear was betraying her.

It was an active scent. Her essence was on the tip of his tongue. He could taste her.

Letting his inner-demon out of the cage and on to a leash, Gus sprinted after the Contractor.

At the end of the alley ahead of him, he could swear he saw her. Right as she turned the corner out of the alley and onto the sidewalk.

Ha! I've got you. You tasty little treat.

I'm going to devour your fear and fillet your soul.

I bet you taste amazing and –

Gus pulled back on his thoughts. Reigning in the monster he knew he was. It wasn't a separate part of him. It was him.

He was the Boogieman. His race was what had haunted mankind for millennia. From the beginning.

They were capable of inducing fear directly once they acquired someone's fear scent. Able to run them down in dreams and reality. To feast on their very soul if they were overwhelmed with fear.

So feared was his race, despite its unassuming name, that it had been hunted to near extinction. The race of the Boogieman was nearly gone.

Because of things just like this.

There was no escape once one caught your fear scent.

Taking the corner at full speed, Gus felt his shoes slip slightly out from under him. He took a stuttering step and bounced off of someone, then got his feet under himself.

Forcing his way through the crowded downtown sidewalks, he kept on after the Contractor.

He was getting closer. He could even see the top of her head now. She was walking, trying to blend in with the crowd around her.

I have her. When I catch her… maybe I'll just… maybe I'll just eat a little of her.

Just a little.

She tastes delicious.

As if she could sense him or hear his thoughts, her head turned around. Her eyes found him immediately. They widened, her mouth opened, and her pupils instantly dilated. In fact, Gus could see the vein in her neck pulse rapidly.

The immense spike of fear that rolled off her drove Gus into a frenzy.

I'm going to devour her!

Panting, Gus shoved someone out of the way trying to get closer.

The Contractor ducked low into the crowd and vanished. Breaking his line of sight.

Then several spells washed over him, and the sniffer failed. Losing its track outright. Not only that, but Gus was momentarily blinded, also losing his sense of smell and his hearing.

He pushed the sniffer into a coat pocket and stumbled off to one side to regain his bearings.

He didn't need the sniffer. Didn't need any of his senses.

Can't hide, pretty little thing. Can't hide.

I'll have you.

I'll eat you. Pull your soul out and eat it as you watch.

She'd taken several steps to break all the ways he could be tracking her. He had no way to find her at all. Not without exposing himself as something other than human.

Thankfully, it didn't matter.

Gus had the woman's fear scent. He knew exactly where she was.

If he thought about what he could see before he'd lost his vision, he guessed she'd tucked in close to a large van in a street-side parking space.

She was trying to let him pass by with the crowd. To be carried away while he tried to keep up, or get the effects of her spells to wear off.

Instead, Gus remained still, feeling with his hands until he managed to get between two parked vehicles.

Slowly, the Contractor made her way away from the position. Gus wasn't ready to follow yet. He could only just barely see, and it was mostly shapes and shadows. Nothing that would actually let him follow her.

Take this as a positive. A positive. I'm calm now. I'm calm. I'm in control again.

In control.

Gus was taking deep, calming breaths.

Still going to eat a little of her, though. Just a nibble.

Shaking his head once, Gus stepped back out into the pedestrian flow of traffic.

The Contractor was a considerable distance from him now. Perhaps half a block away.

But it didn't matter.

He had her.

Gus followed discreetly, making sure to remain out of eyesight. It took an hour, but she eventually seemed confident she'd lost him. Confident enough that she was going into a slightly run-down apartment building.

Pulling out his phone, Gus tapped in the address to Vanessa, who was parked at a coffee shop a few blocks away. She was running everything he sent her through the laptop to find out what they could.

She'd also already called in what had happened to Mark.

Waiting outside, wanting to give the woman all the time he could for her to get comfortable and let her guard down, Gus stared at his phone.

Even though it was his inbox, which had nothing to read yet.

People tended to ignore others, especially if they were tied up in their own social-media worlds. Standing around with your face in your phone was an acceptable thing to do now.

Then Gus's phone dinged, and Vanessa's picture floated down from the top along with a message.

"Found her. Melody Lark.

"Her address is listed as nine-thirty-three. She's a private investigator. Contracted and licensed locally, but also holds multiple licenses nationally," read Vanessa's text.

Of course it's a PI. They always get involved in things they shouldn't. Like it's their damn job to save the universe.

Half the time I have to clean up after their happy-horse shit.

The national licenses are different, though. Especially given the state of the building.

She must be lying low.

"Going in. Join me when you can, not going to wait just in case she bails," Gus sent back.

Without waiting for a response, Gus pushed his phone back into his pocket and went into the building.

He was immediately struck by how different it was on the inside. Immaculate, expensive, and everything looked new.

Then he realized what this was. A Para apartment building with an enchantment on the whole thing.

Unregistered since it didn't show up in Ness's record search. I'll need to let Durh know.

Gus headed up the stairs instead of using the elevator, trying to play it safe. He didn't want to be locked in a tiny metal box right now.

Getting off on the ninth floor, he felt energetic and ready. He could still taste her, though her fear was long since gone. It didn't matter, though. Not to him.

Finding the right door plate and feeling her inside, Gus hesitated for a moment on how to proceed.

Technically, he had no right to enter her home. Nor did he have his partner, or backup.

In every single way, doing anything right now was a bad idea.

But waiting felt like a worse idea. She could be inside right now destroying the very thing Gus needed.

Getting down on one knee again, Gus pulled out his lock-pick set and got to work.

It took four minutes this time, since there was a deadbolt in the door.

Taking hold of the handle, Gus drew his weapon with his right hand. Having already done this once, it felt strange.

He opened the door as quietly as he could and crept into the woman's apartment. He was in a tastefully decorated entryway.

Closing the door behind him, he continued on. He knew where she was. In a room at the other end of the apartment.

Gus cleared the bathroom and kitchen with only the barest of searches.

When he reached what he'd call the living room, he finally heard her. She was beyond an open doorway, the soft clicks of a keyboard audible to him. They sounded like gunshots with how quiet everything else was.

Easing up quietly, carefully, Gus snuck into her bedroom.

She was seated at a computer desk, rapidly filling in what looked like an email.

Aiming the weapon at the back of her head, Gus exhilarated in his successful chase. He hadn't felt like this since his mom had taken him out for his first hunt when he was twelve.

"Good afternoon, Melody," Gus said.

The woman froze, going absolutely still at her desk.

"Your carpet seems much more comfortable. I think we could finish our conversation here instead," Gus said, the corner of his mouth going up.

"Agent?" said the Contractor, her head slowly turning to one side. She only rotated her head far enough so she could lay her eyes on him. The Blue and Green contract markings on her face still glowed brightly. "It really is you."

"For what it's worth, the chase was fun," Gus said. "Now would you please put your hands on your head, get out of the chair, keep your back to me, and get down on your knees?"

Chuckling, she interlaced her fingers and put them behind her head. She got up out of her chair, turned to face him directly, and sank down to her knees. Her eyes fastened to him.

"Pretty sure I said to keep your back to me," Gus said, his gun still pointed at her.

"I wanted to see you," she said, a smile on her face. A dull, red, glowing symbol Gus had never seen before appeared between her eyes. It seemed to throb slowly. "You're impressive. I've never had someone run me down before. I was only teasing earlier, about falling for you. But I'm going to truly consider it now. If I haven't already."

"Why were you at that apartment?" Gus asked.

"Same reason you were, Agent. Just a different employer. Trying to figure out what happened the other day," Melody said, still smiling up at him from her kneeling position.

Taking a risk, and using as little of his telepathy as he could, Gus tried to snake a tendril into her thoughts. It was dangerous because there were a number of Paras that'd be able to feel the intrusion.

He found overwhelming and absolute lust in her mind. Enough to make a college party seem like a kindergarten daycare at nap time.

Flashes of desires, thoughts, and wishes were moving so fast through her thoughts that he couldn't keep up.

It was a literal tidal wave of erotica. All centered on him, and what she wanted him to do to her.

"Oh my goodness. I felt that. You're not human," she groaned. The symbol between her eyes became a bright cherry red. It sparked and hissed for a second before it took on a color like molten iron pulled from a furnace. The intensity of her desire became a raging torrent and it practically washed him away.

Breaking the contact, Gus shook his head with a sigh.

"I'm as human as they come, lady. As you can plainly see from the mask," Gus said, doing his best to play it off.

"No human could ever catch me. I'm the Lark. It's not possible," she breathed. "I felt you. What are you?"

"I'm annoyed, that's what I am. You're saying you were there to find out what was going on—did you take anything? Or find anything?" Gus asked, his left hand pulling a set of handcuffs out of their holster on his belt loop.

Her eyes tracked the handcuffs, and the red sigil dulled for a second before it became even brighter than before.

Oh my fucking god.

"I found a few things. I already sent them over to my employer, though. Mr. Fitz had visited C&C Marketing and Investments previously," said Melody. "After that, he went back to his normal, everyday life. Right up until he pulled the head off a PID agent. That was all I found."

Gus had the impression she was telling the complete truth. Even though there wasn't an ounce of fear in her.

Frowning and chewing at his lip, Gus hesitated. Then he put the handcuffs back in their holster and pulled out his phone. Holding it up in front of him, he took a picture of Melody and then began typing in what she'd just told him. All the while keeping the phone in front of him so he could keep an eye on the Contractor.

"I think I'd be willing for it to be on camera. But not the first time," Melody murmured, the red sigil of clear erotic magical origin between her eyes almost like a miniature sun now.

"Anyone ever tell you you're a little on the spooky side?" Gus asked, saving the note and closing his phone. "That or crazy."

"I'm aware. It's the contracts," Melody said with a shrug. "They have their prices. Though this is the first time since I received my Red contract that it called in its price immediately."

"Consider me flattered, lady," Gus said.

"You should be. I've had it for sixty years. I'm seventy-seven, by the way. I'm sure we can work through any type of age gap between us with a bit of understanding," Melody said.

"Uh huh. And who was your employer, by the way?" Gus asked.

Melody winced, her eyes finally turning away from him. The symbols on her face all instantly faded to little more than glowing embers.

"Ah… it was the Curator," she said.

Gus didn't react at first.

Finally, he let his gun fall to his side, and he pressed his left hand to his head.

"Did you say the Curator?" he asked.

"Yes. I did," she confirmed.

Great. Just… great. That's… no. Nope.

Done. I'm done here.

Done with this, done with the Contractor-sex-monster, done with Ness, done with Durh.

I'm going to quit, go home, and sleep.

"Yeah, uh. Breaking and entering is bad. Don't do it again," Gus said, holstering his weapon.

"You're letting me go?" Melody asked. "Not even a citation or a warning or anything?"

She sounded almost disappointed.

"Yep, letting you go. See ya," Gus said, going toward the exit of her home.

"You can't just leave," Melody said, following him.

"Sure, I can. Watch me go," Gus said.

Something jerked on his coat and pulled him off to one side. Melody was suddenly there, her hands pressed to his chest.

"No, you cannot leave. I need you to help—"

"Nope!" Gus said with a smile, and he pushed her to one side. "Don't want nothin' to do with you or the Curator."

Yanking open the door after he'd fumbled with the handle, Gus stormed out of her apartment and closed the door behind him.

Then he pulled out his phone and dialed up Mark.

Such a shit show. And she's probably already calling the Curator to warn him.

Chapter 5 - The Curator

"Gussy, you're so needy right now. That detective got you that hot and bo—"

"Durh, listen. How close has Ness been updating you?" Gus asked.

"Uh, I have a couple emails from her I haven't read. Why?"

"Ok, here's the dirty version then. I ran down the lady I found in the Fitz apartment and cornered her," Gus said, going down the stairs. "Apparently her name is Melody Lark."

"Melody Lark? As in the Lark? The Contractor? You ran her down? How? That's Lark. The Lark. No one runs her down or corners her," Mark said, his tone changing.

"That's not the best part, or I guess the worst part, which I'm going to tell you before I turn in my damn badge," Gus grumped, turning down the last stairwell to reach the ground floor. "She was working for the Curator. He wanted to know what happened."

There was no response on the line. Mark said absolutely nothing. Gus knew he was still there, as he could still hear the thrum of the fan in the corner of his home office.

Opening the front door, Gus stepped out of the apartment building and onto the street.

Vanessa was just closing the trunk to her car, and she turned toward him.

Pulling his phone down from his ear and covering the mouth piece with one hand, he shook his head at her.

"Done here," Gus said. "We need to head back to the precinct. I'm quitting and you need to get blanked ASAP."

"Wait, what?" Vanessa said, her tone turning incredulous.

Gus put the phone back to his ear and gestured at the car instead of replying.

"Durh, you there?" Gus asked.

"Huh? Uh, yeah. Sorry. Ok. The Curator. Ok. The Lark and the Curator are both involved, and a senior Enchanter from the DME," Mark said, assembling all the bullet points. "I already spoke to the boss; he was on board with chasing down the Enchanter. But I'll... I'll need to ask him how to handle the Curator and the Lark.

"As for you quitting, no. Not allowing it. I need you, Gussy."

Gus rolled his eyes as he got into the passenger seat of Vanessa's car.

"Yeah, and I don't really care, Durh. I've kept myself out of sight of everyone and everything," Gus said. Vanessa hadn't gotten in yet, so he could risk the statement. "You know why."

"Yeah, I do. And I get it. But I need you. This is too big for anyone else," Mark said, his tone and demeanor becoming drastically different from when the call had started.

"Yeah, well, this one is too much for me. Sorry. Can't," Gus said as Vanessa got in and turned the engine over on the car.

"Gussy... don't leave me behind here," Mark said.

Growling, Gus wanted to punch the dash in front of him. A moment of blind black rage threatened to overwhelm him.

It was the sudden and deep spike of fear from Vanessa next to him that brought him back to his senses.

Damn. I think I ate a bit too much fear from the Contractor. Not... fully in control right now.

Turning his head to Vanessa, he gave her a grimace and held up one hand asking for time.

"What do you want from me, Durh? This isn't something we normally run with. The Bureau deals with him," Gus said.

"Yeah, well, today that's you. I need you to go over there. Now. And talk to him. Ask him ever so nicely if he could help us out," Mark said. "If he won't, or if he's got nothing, haul it in. We'll figure out where to go from there."

"Already got that," Gus said, racking his brain for what Melody had said. "Apparently Fitz went to CCMI. Guess I'll be running that one down as well."

"CCMI? You mean C&C Marketing? The 'Pancakes!' people?" Mark asked.

"Yeah. Alright. I'm gone," Gus said, and he hung up the phone.

"So… you're not quitting?" Vanessa asked.

"Apparently not today, but we're both going to wish I had. We're going to go meet the Curator," Gus said, running a hand over his face.

"And who's that?" Vanessa asked. "And where am I going?"

"Head over to First and Main, next to the station on Second. There's an antique shop there along First. That's where we're going," Gus said, leaning his head into the headrest. "As for who the Curator is… as far as we know, he's one of the oldest beings on the planet. He doesn't get involved very often, but when he does, it's usually because everything is about to go really wrong. Sometimes he helps, sometimes he hinders."

"And you don't want to meet him," Vanessa said, pulling out of the parking space and into the flow of traffic.

"Damn me, no. No one wants to meet him. Mostly because no one wants him to know about them," Gus said.

"What happened with the woman?" Vanessa pressed.

"Let her go with a warning. She's just a damn PI who was hired by the Curator. Wouldn't have done me any good to deal any further with her. Dead end and little else after she gave up what she knew."

Gus closed his eyes, really reconsidering quitting again. This was about to get so much worse and he knew it.

Knew it and was walking into it with a rookie at his side.

"That it?" Vanessa asked.

Gus's eyes snapped open. He felt disoriented and lost.

He realized he'd drifted off and glanced over to see Vanessa was pointing at a building.

Following her arm, he saw the antique shop, Bygone Relic.

"Yep," Gus said and then started rubbing at his eyes with his palms. "That's the place."

Vanessa circled twice and managed to find a parking space in front of a breakfast diner.

Getting out of the car, Gus rubbed a hand at the back of his neck. It felt stiff. In fact, he felt somewhat sore all over.

Fucking Contractor hit me with a bigger whammy than I thought.

"What's the plan?" Vanessa said, coming up next to him.

"We go in, ask very nicely to please see the Curator if he has some time to talk. If he does, I ask him ever so politely if he can shed any light on Fitz. If he doesn't, we go to CCMI," Gus said.

"Got it," Vanessa said, the small pad of paper appearing in her hand along with her pen. "Treat him like a politician, full kid gloves."

"You're a great partner, you know that?" Gus said, walking toward the shop.

"Not till this moment. My girlfriend would agree with you though," Vanessa said with a shrug.

Taking a moment to look at the other woman, Gus reconfigured his view on her a tiny bit, then looked ahead again.

"Been together long?" he asked.

"Long enough to know we're at that point where we either move in together or walk away from one another," Vanessa said. Her tone was tense and had a bleakness to it. "It's starting to feel much more like the latter lately."

"Huh. Interesting of you to share that," Gus said, eying the door to the antique shop.

"She's unlikely to ever meet you, and if I can't be honest with you, how can you trust me as your partner?" she asked.

Yeah… trust. Sorry, not telling you I'm the thing that makes Paras frightened.

Vanessa grabbed the door and pulled it open for him.

Taking the cue, Gus walked into the shop and looked around.

It was exactly what you'd expect from an antique shop. Old-looking everything. Set about for viewing, and all with hand-written price tags attached to the displays.

"Five thousand dollars for a broken pot," Vanessa said next to him, looking down at a cracked piece of pottery.

"In the market for antiques?" Gus asked, sighting the store counter and a young woman standing behind it. She had a mask, but it didn't reveal anything out of the ordinary. Which meant she was an altered human rather than a creature.

"No. Apparently I'm not," Vanessa said.

Walking straight to the attendant, Gus pulled his PID medallion out from under his vest and held it out.

"Good afternoon. My name is agent Gustavus Hellström of the PID. Beside me is Detective Vanessa Flores," Gus said, indicating Vanessa, who was also proffering her badge to the woman. "I was wondering if the Curator could spare any time to speak with us?"

Looking from Gus's badge to Vanessa's, the woman raised her eyes back up. "I can ask."

"Thank you, miss," Gus said with a smile.

Nodding her head, the young woman left them standing there and walked deeper into the store.

"She's human?" Vanessa asked.

"I'm betting a magical type or something of that nature. Technically they're human, but they're not," Gus said.

"Can anyone become like that?"

"Kind of. Sorcerers are born. Magicians are taught, but they need talent for it. Contractors borrow power from elsewhere. Necromancers make deals with demons, spirits, and the dead. Wizards are somewhere between Magicians and Sorcerers. They turn up in the weirdest places," Gus said.

"Really? How so?"

"I met a Wizard back when I was deployed and didn't know it. For him it was all latent ability mixed with a dash of someone teaching him a trick, as best as I can figure," Gus said. "He could literally bend the probability of things to his will. If he really wanted to win that day at poker, he could stack the deck in a way that'd make it happen."

"That does sound like a weird in-between area. What happened to him?"

"He caught a round in the guts. Same place I lost most of my squad-mates. Died after two days. Not a damn thing we could do for him," Gus grumbled. "Odds are like that, right? Even if you work 'em, they can and will catch up with you."

"Ahem," said the young woman, coughing gently, getting their attention. "The Curator will see you, Agent Hellström, but he asks that the detective remain here."

"Right," Gus said, feeling nervous already.

"That's fine," Vanessa said, "I'll go see if I can get an appointment for us at our next stop."

"Ah, yeah. That's a good idea. Thanks, Ness," Gus said.

Vanessa gave him a grin and nodded, heading toward the exit.

"After me, Agent," said the woman, moving back toward the rear again.

Scratching at his forearm as he walked behind her, Gus had a feeling of pressure building up around him.

It was uncomfortable, but it wasn't going to stop him or turn him away.

"Just go on through here," said the attendant, gesturing to the door next to her.

"Thanks." Gus opened the door and stepped through it. On the other side was a comfortable-looking office.

It had a bookshelf, a TV with what looked like the weather channel on it, a computer desk, and a mini fridge. Considering what Gus knew of the man sitting at that desk, the office seemed almost too ordinary.

But then there was the man himself.

Sitting there at the computer desk was the man Gus assumed was the Curator, and he looked to be in his mid-thirties. He had light-brown hair and brown eyes with rings of bright blue in the middle of them. It was one of the strangest pairs of eyes he'd ever seen.

He was wearing a polo shirt and dark jeans, and he had slightly messy hair. There was absolutely nothing about the man that would give Gus warning signs.

"Agent Hellström, come in. Have a seat," said the Curator. "And before you start calling me by my moniker—and yes I am indeed the Curator—let us simply go with… Dave. It's easier."

"Alright, Dave," Gus said, taking the indicated seat across from him.

"It's been a while since I had a Bogey in front of me," Dave said. "Though I think the common nomenclature as of late is Boogieman."

Gus froze in his chair, his fingers locked together as he quickly considered his options.

"No reason to be nervous, Agent," Dave said. "I don't have the same concerns for your race that others do, despite your capabilities. Now, if you were a Bogeyman of old, attempting to build an empire of humans under you to feed on… well… then it'd be different.

"I wouldn't meet you in a million years."

Not knowing what to say, Gus scratched at the back of his neck instead, trying to figure out how to jump-start the conversation to where he was hoping to put it.

"Then there's Melody," Dave continued. "She contacted me as soon as you left her apartment. I'm sure you expected that."

Feeling completely off balance, at a loss, and without a way to bring the conversation back to him, Gus just sat there.

Waiting.

"She was shocked at the idea that you found her. Though now, in knowing what you are, that's not as surprising, I suppose. You fear-scented her?" Dave asked.

"Yeah… she tasted like spiced mint," Gus said, being a bit more honest than he wanted to be.

"Did she? I suppose that fits," Dave said with a chuckle. "Then again, not all Bogeys are created equal. You caught her on assignment, ran her down in downtown Saint Anthony in the middle of the day, and pursued her all the way back to her apartment. All with just a fear scent. You're rather powerful, aren't you?"

"I don't know," Gus said. "Mother doesn't know who her parents were, and we've never met any others. We can only compare to each other."

"Hm," Dave said, leaning to one side in his chair and propping his chin in his hand. "Thank you for not charging her with anything, by the way. Melody, that is. It can be a hassle to call in favors from the PID or the Bureau.

"So consider me owing you a minor favor. Though… you might come to regret meeting Melody in the way you did. She's very curious about you now. Don't underestimate her, by the way. She's a Contractor and carries all that entails with her, but she's also one of the smartest people I've had the pleasure to know."

Gus shrugged, not really sure how to respond.

"You said you owe me a favor?" Gus asked.

"Indeed. Though before you ask, I know just as much as you do about the dearly departed Mr. Fitz. His mask broke, it seemed to poison his mind in doing so, and he unfortunately was killed during his rage," Dave said. "I'm assuming you already went to the DME, so you've already found that the list of those who could have done the enchantment is missing. Which leaves only the lead Melody found."

Frowning, Gus nodded.

"Then we're at an impasse, for that's all I know as well. I don't think Leanne or Kat of C&C will see you today, however. They keep fairly tight to their office hours and..." Dave turned his wrist over and looked at his watch. "It's just a hair past five."

"Right," Gus said, looking off to one side. "Right. Ok."

"Call it a day, Agent, and maybe get some rest. I believe your day tomorrow will involve a good bit of detective work and running around," Dave said. Then he gestured to the door while holding out a card. "Take it. Keep me in mind. Otherwise, have a pleasant day, and don't be a stranger."

Getting up out of his seat, Gus took the card. He read it and flipped it over, then pulled out his wallet and stuffed it inside.

"Thanks, I'll do that," Gus said as he walked over to the door and stopped, the handle in his hand.

"Don't worry over it, Agent. Your secret is safe with me," Dave said. "Though I might poke around into your family. Just out of curiosity. See if I can't figure out who your grandparents were."

Gus grimaced. He really didn't know how he felt about that.

"I'll give you everything I find, and you can decide if you want to give it to your mother or not," Dave said.

"Thank you," Gus said. Then he pulled open the door and left the antique shop.

Vanessa was waiting for him in her car, typing something rapidly into the laptop.

Opening the door, Gus plopped into the seat next to her and turned to face her.

"He doesn't know anything else," Gus said. "He's at the exact same point we are."

Vanessa blinked once, then nodded. "That's good. It means we're not missing any pieces.

"I got ahold of the secretary for C&C. They're not willing to see us tonight, but they can see us tomorrow morning at ten am. I took it and made the appointment."

"Good job, Ness. Alright. I guess that's it for the day for what we can do. This is the only thing I'm working right now." Gus reached up to run his fingers through his short hair. "Drop me off at home, would ya? I'm going to start digging through witness statements from the scene, see if I can find anything. Then maybe go through Fitz's bank statements. See if anything jumps out at me."

"It's somewhat surprising," Vanessa said, closing the laptop and putting it in the backseat. She didn't have the same mounting bracket his own car did. "How much normal detective work seems to go into the PID."

"It's not like the Para world is any different. Not really, at least. Just need different tools to do the same thing as the normal detectives," Gus said.

Vanessa checked left and then pulled out into the street.

It took them an hour to get out of the city and into the suburb where Gus lived.

"Alright, I'll see you at the office tomorrow at seven, yeah?" he said, getting out of his seat.

"I'll be there." Vanessa waved a hand at him.

Shutting the car door, Gus walked up to the front of his house. He knew he needed to do some basic work on the case, but he was also considering taking a quick nap.

Pulling the keys out of his pocket, he unlocked his door and slipped inside, then closed it behind him.

Looking around the entry and the living room, Gus felt odd. Something didn't quite fit. He couldn't put his finger on it, but things weren't as they should be.

Something was wrong, and his Boogieman instincts were usually on point.

Pulling his pistol from his holster, Gus opened the door and peeked outside.

Vanessa was already gone, and there were no other unknown cars nearby.

Closing the door again, he got his phone out of his pocket and pulled up Vanessa's contact details.

While holding his gun out in front of him, Gus started to type in a message to the detective with his other hand.

Then he smelled it. He'd almost missed it. There was no fear attached to it, which made it really difficult to scent. But it was unmistakable to him now.

Spiced mint.

Gus briefly worried about why she was here, then holstered his weapon.

Once he focused on her, he knew exactly where she was in his home. The kitchen.

She's a friend of the Curator. Let's… take this as casually as possible.

As carefully as possible.

Chapter 6 - Uninvited

Moving through the living room to his bedroom, he passed by the hallway that led to the kitchen. Pausing there, he considered what to do.

Better to not... surprise her... right?

"I'm home, Melody," Gus called out.

"Oh? Oh! Welcome home, Gustavus!" came the shout from the kitchen. There was a clatter, and what sounded like cans dropping to the ground, and then Melody came skipping down the hall.

"You knew I was here?" she asked, a wild smile flashing across her face as she closed in on him.

"Yeah. Knew it as soon as I entered the house. What are you doing here, Melody? Pretty sure I gave you a warning about breaking and entering," Gus asked, untying his tie when she stopped three feet away from him.

"I wanted to see you. I stole one of your business cards before you sprinted away. Then I ran the information down and... here I am! I was going to just watch you tonight," she said with a fluttering of her fingers.

Contractors are usually a bit more unstable than this. She's remarkably well put together from a mental standpoint.

I wonder if she busted out of her old contracts and got new ones when she had enough power.

"Right, well, I'm going to go change," Gus said, pulling his tie out from the collar.

"Oh, ok. I already did a full sweep of your house with my Blue contract. You only had one listening device, but it wasn't functioning correctly," Melody said, the blue, starlike sigils around her eyes glowing for a second.

"Yeah, I know. You didn't remove it, did you?" Gus asked, walking into his bedroom and heading for his walk-in closet.

"No. I assumed you knew about it and had disabled it," Melody's voice trailing after him.

"Yeah. Someone got smart and stuck it in the wall itself. Inside an actual wall socket, and tied it in to the power. I just... did a bit of finagling and got it so that it only turns on when the light switch is engaged," Gus said, pulling his coat off and grabbing the hanger for it. "I got tired of constantly removing one bug and waiting for the next one to inevitably show up. I turn it on when I'm doing nothing interesting so they know it's working, then off when I don't want them to hear what I'm doing."

"Ah... that's rather clever," Melody said.

Glancing over his shoulder as he slipped his tie through the hanger for the coat, he found Melody standing in the doorway.

"If I was smart, I'd know who was doing it rather than just dealing with it as I have been," Gus said. Then he reached over and nudged the door to the walk-in closet closed.

Melody pushed the door open again immediately.

"Want me to find out for you? I could. Easily," she said, the green symbols across her brow starting to glow.

"No. Thanks, but no thanks, Melody," Gus said. Taking the door in hand, he closed it deliberately, maintaining eye contact with her the whole time. "I figure it's someone who just wants to keep an eye on me. So either the PID or the Feds. Easier to pretend I don't know about it."

Gus turned back to his shirt rack and quickly unbuttoned his shirt.

"That'd be my guess, too," Melody said, her voice suitably muffled by the door. "So, where are we going tomorrow? That was my last contract in the city. I have nothing to do for a few days."

"You? You're going to go home and do whatever it is you do. I'm going to keep working my case," Gus pulled the shirt over his head and then stuck a hanger through it.

"I'm going to work it with you," Melody said. "Pro bono, so to speak. I don't think you could afford my rates. I'm fully accredited and licensed for this type of work."

"Yeah, no thanks, Melody. I'm already dragging around a rookie with me. I don't need a freelancer as well," Gus said with a shake of his head. Unbuckling his belt, he pulled it out of his trousers.

"Gus… Gussy… don't make me play hardball. I'm going to be with you, whether you like it or not," Melody said. "I'll call the Curator if I have to. Or your boss if you prefer, Mark Ehrich. I believe you call him Durh from your enlisted days."

Gus frowned as he got the belt out of the pants, annoyed. Annoyed and frustrated.

He was quite fed up with people forcing him to do things.

"I understand. I do. I really get it. I'm the same way. I don't want anyone or anything holding me back. But I can't help it," Melody said. "I need to be near you. I have to know more about you."

"That's your contracts talking." Gus stepped out of his pants and flipped them over his shoulder. "We both know that's all it is. Look, I mean, if throwing you in the bed is going to be what it takes to get you to leave off me, I can think of worse ways to spend my evening."

She gave a light and joyful laugh in response to that.

"Oh, Gus. I'm so glad you said that, and flattered, and it makes my heart race, but… that would have worked back at my apartment. When the contract demanded it. But that was before, this is now. The contract isn't active at all," she said. "Take a look for yourself."

The last part she said wasn't muffled at all.

Looking over his shoulder, he found Melody staring back at him.

There was a three-foot-wide circular hole in his door, with her head directly on the other side.

She held up her hands in front of her mouth, and the Blue marks lit up again.

"See? No contract burning me to ride you like a stallion. This is pure interest on my part now," she said, her voice properly muffled. Then she let her hands fall back down and wrinkled her nose at him, her tongue sticking out between her teeth.

And winked at him.

"You're a lot of fun, you know that Gus?" she asked. "So, where are we going tomorrow?'

Running his tongue over his teeth and resisting the urge to let his Boogieman out, Gus managed a slow, deep breath.

Much more subtly this time, and with infinitely less energy, he threaded the absolute finest amount of telepathic power he could into Melody's mind.

Spinning off in every direction were wild thoughts, ideas, and random snatches of conversation.

It was a mind built for solving things. Figuring things out, working out what made them tick, and then setting them to one side.

Her choice of profession only mirrored that desire. For her, the world was a puzzle that was meant to be solved.

On top of all that, she was clearly much smarter than he was.

Ah. Got it. That's how we get rid of her.

Curator would probably tell her in time anyways.

Rather than retracting the power, Gus just let her mind absorb it and cut it loose. She'd never notice it, and it would be less noticeable than if he tried to pull it out.

"I'm a telepathic Boogieman," Gus said. "I'm not human. No one but my boss knows what I am, and that's because we walked out of the worst possible situation together. He saw me at my absolute worst, and he made sure I made it out.

"I was able to track you down because I fear-scented you. You smell like spiced mint, and from that I was able to follow you. And still could."

Taking a pause, Gus considered what to say next to get her to leave.

"I joined the PID because he asked me to. I have no plans, no goals, and I'm living day to day.

"My mother is a Boogieman, my father a Telepath, and they live on the other side of city. My sister is a Boogieman as well, but that's the extent of our family."

Finished, Gus waited. With any luck, that answered everything she wanted to know about him. It'd end her burning curiosity and get her to leave him alone.

And it cost him nothing she probably wouldn't have found out on her own given time.

Melody's delicate eyebrows came together, her eyes clouding over. There was definitely a sense of loss in her eyes, as if he'd ruined a surprise for her.

All along her jawline, curling up into her lower lip, yellow swirls and curves began to glow. A second set of orange symbols came to life above the yellow ones, except these went into her upper lip.

"Ah," she said as the symbols faded to nothing. "You read my mind and figured out how to get rid of me based on that reading and what I'd said."

Nodding her head, she gave him a wide smile.

"Very, very astute, and well done. There was a moment where I was so angry, I was going to leave. You ruined the surprise. Spoiled the fun." Melody's hands came up to hold to the hole she'd cut in his door. "But… that just makes it even more imperative for me. You can manipulate me!

"You know me. Know how my mind works and can poke around inside to figure out what I mean when I say the wrong thing. You can't misunderstand me."

Taking in a deep breath, she looked at him like she was going to swoon.

"You're amazing, Gustavus Hellström. Contract with me?" she asked. The red symbol between her eyes started to glow again.

Frowning, Gus pulled his pants off his shoulder and hung them over Melody's face.

"Go home, Miss Lark," Gus said. "I'll see you tomorrow morning. Be at my PID office at eight. I'll need to make sure to get you cleared. My partner will arrive at eight as well."

"Vanessa Flores, right?" Melody asked through his pants, not bothering to remove them.

"Yeah, her," Gus agreed, wondering if Melody had looked into her, too.

"She lives alone but is dating a Werewolf. She doesn't know. The girlfriend won't commit because she's afraid Vanessa would find out," Melody said. "From what I could tell, their relationship is over; neither one of them has broken up with the other, though."

"Great," Gus said, not wanting to get involved in that.

"I can smell you on this," Melody said, taking in a deep breath. "It sme—"

"Go-home-Melody," Gus hissed.

"Gone!" said the Contractor, and she literally vanished. Gus's pants landed squarely in the hole cut into his door.

***

Getting out of his car, Gus gave his coat a tug. Melody had flustered him yesterday. So much so that he'd ended up sending a long, bitter text to Mark, explaining the whole situation.

All he'd gotten in response was a laughing-crying emoji. Followed by a single line of text.

"Approved to hire one (1) vendor by the name of Melody Lark, licensed as 'the Lark' at no cost for one week.

"The Lark is to report to Senior Detective Hellström."

Rubbing his hand across his face, Gus went straight up to his desk, not bothering with anything else.

Only to find Melody and Vanessa sitting at the desk next to his, going over what looked like notes.

Vanessa was on time, though Melody was here an hour early.

Looking from one to the other, Gus said nothing. Instead he went to the coffee machine. Filling up the pot, he dumped it into the top and flicked the switch. While the water heated up, he dumped the used filter and grounds, put in a new one, filled it, and stuffed it back into the coffee machine.

"So, sleep ok without me?" Melody asked. "You tossed and turned, didn't you?"

Gus scoffed at that. Actually recognizing the line.

Considering he'd have to work with her, and that he knew how her mind worked, he decided to play with her.

"You're incredible," he said.

"Who told you?" Melody immediately replied, then started to chuckle to herself. "Gus, Gus, Gus, you're a winner in my book.

"So, since we're all here, should we go get breakfast together? You said our appointment was at ten, right? Lots of time."

Vanessa looked at Gus and gave him a knowing smile. Gus had the sneaking suspicion Melody had come early specifically to talk to Vanessa.

"Lots of time, let's go to breakfast. Your turn to pay, Gus," Vanessa said.

Rather than getting angry, since he was stuck with both of them for at least a week, Gus shook his head with a sigh.

"Fine. Let's go where we went yesterday," he said, and he turned off the coffee machine.

***

Gus set down his PID badge and ID in front of the secretary. She was manning the desk in the reception area of C&C. He could tell she was wearing a mask, but there seemed to be a second layer of magic on top of the first. It was thick enough that he couldn't punch through it with just his agent mask.

"Hello, my name is Detective Gustavus Hellström. With me are Detective Vanessa Flores and Agent Melody Lark," Gus said, smiling at the young woman. "We have a scheduled appointment for ten o'clock."

Melody and Vanessa also put down their credentials for the young woman.

"Ah, yes, I have you written in. Do you know if you're seeing Leanne or Kat?" said the woman, typing something into her computer and then turning to face Gus.

He turned his head to look at Vanessa.

"Both of them," she said with a smile. "I spoke with Kat, but she said she'd have Leanne sit in with us as well."

The young woman raised her eyebrows at that, seeming surprised. "I'll let them both know, thank you. Please have a seat."

"Thank you," Vanessa said, moving to sit down in the reception area.

Gus, on the other hand, gave the young woman his best smile.

"Excuse me, miss…?" he asked.

"Ashley," said the woman, returning the smile.

"Ashley… is there any chance you could tell me when Michael Fitz last came in?" Gus inquired.

"Oh, Mikey? Sure, one second," Ashley said, looking back to her computer and rapidly typing something in.

Checking over his shoulder, he saw Melody standing almost uncomfortably close to him. The yellow, orange, and red symbols were all lit up.

She was watching the secretary closely.

I'm betting on that being some type of truth-checking Contract spell.

I've personally seen five colors now. Blue, Green, Yellow, Orange, Red. That leaves… Indigo and Violet, right?

Those are typically much more personal contracts though. Indigo is marriage, love, and fidelity, right? Violet is… I can't remember what Violet is.

Giving up that train of thought, Gus turned back to Ashley.

Typing away at her keyboard, then moving the mouse, she spent perhaps a minute tracking down whatever it was she was looking for.

"Ah, here we are. His last appointment was four weeks ago. He met with Kat, but there's no listed subject item," Ashely said, turning back to Gus with a wide smile.

"Thank you, Ashley. You've been most helpful. If you can think of anything, would you call me?" Gus said, holding one of his business cards out to her. "The number with an M before it is my mobile number. It's my personal cell."

Ashley took the card from him and she nodded a bit, holding the card between her thumb and forefinger. "I'll do that, Gus."

Nodding back at her, Gus went and sat on the love seat in the lobby.

Melody sat next to him, crossing one leg over the other and giving him a flat stare.

"He treats everyone nicely," Vanessa said, reading something on her phone. "Or at least, he does it without anything behind it. He's been a detective too long and treats anyone and everything as a resource. He used me in a similar fashion back at the DME.

"Unless someone gets defensive or aggressive with him—then he becomes a real dickbag. Though… Judy was much nicer to him this morning than the other day."

Melody's mouth moved to one side as if she were sucking on something sour. Then she looked to Gus with a smile and wiggled her fingers at him.

"That was well done. I think she'll call you later with just a bit of information and try to talk you into something else," Melody said. The Yellow and Red contracts on her face started to glow faintly.

"Pity I'm not interested," Gus said honestly. "It'd never work, given my background."

"Need to stop thinking that way, Gus. Not everyone is going to back up because you were in the service, or the weird police department you're in now," Vanessa said, swiping her finger across her phone.

Melody was watching Gus. She didn't say anything right away, but the Yellow and Red contracts were fading.

They were replaced by her Blue contract, and what looked like a violet set of symbols that started where the blue ones ended. Creating a circle around her eyes.

Shit, six contracts? She's probably the strongest Contractor I've met.

Wrinkling her nose, she clicked her tongue.

"I don't like the way you make me feel," Melody muttered. "I can't keep my thoughts straight. With that in mind, I'm sorry."

Gus shrugged. The simple reality was that being a Boogieman was the single worst thing you could spring on someone for a relationship. If anyone ever found out, it meant a life of being on the run.

His father had decided his mom was worth all that, and he'd pursued her. Pursued her till she'd given up.

Which, given how his mother was with him, now seemed wrong and backward.

"Don't worry, I won't leave," Melody said. "I know all about you, but I'm ever more curious about how you think. I've already canceled all my jobs that would have taken me out of Saint Anthony."

"You did what?" Gus asked, very confused.

"I canceled my jobs," Melody said, leaning toward him. Her black eyes were wide, her pupils dilated, and she looked extremely excited.

None of her contracts glowed, though.

"They were silly little things. Two investigations and probably an extermination. A poltergeist or something," Melody said, casually waving her hand back and forth. "I sent my resume, a salary requirement, and a very tasteful cover letter to your boss. I'm sure I'll be hired on by the end of this week. I made sure he knew one of my requirements was being your partner. No offense to Vanessa over there, but I can be your equal."

Gus wasn't sure what to say.

And thankfully, he didn't have to say anything.

"Gus, Detective, Agent, they're ready for you," said the secretary, smiling at Gus from the front desk and making clear, direct eye contact with him.

Melody got his attention as the secretary turned away.

She bared her teeth at him, then started pushing her index finger back and forth through an "okay" signal with her other hand while shaking her head.

Yeah… got it. No sexing the secretary.

Great.

Might have been fun, too.

Chapter 7 - Cat and Mouse

Gus, Melody, and Vanessa were all directed into a large, tastefully decorated meeting room. There was a large television display on one side, a conference bridge built into the table, and an entire sound system that was apparently wired into the room itself.

The whole setup had clearly been built from the ground up to be exactly what it was.

And it spoke of money. Lots and lots of it.

It was also unfortunately empty.

"They'll be right in, just please have a seat," said the secretary, who closed the door as she left.

Taking up the middle seat of one side and putting his back to a window, Gus unbuttoned his coat and pulled out his phone.

He flipped it to his notes section and re-familiarized himself with some of the things he wanted to ask about.

"They're trying to impress us," Melody said, taking up a distant seat in the corner of the room at the furthest edge of Gus's side of the table. "And for a planned meeting, it's curious that they're 'ready' for us, but not here."

Glancing over to the Contractor, Gus saw there was a faint glow in her Orange and Violet contracts.

With how she acts, I forget she's an actual genius to begin with – and has some high-powered contracts to boot.

She's faster, stronger, smarter, and all around better than me in every way.

Don't underestimate her because she's pretty and weird.

Melody's eyes found him staring at her. Her cheeks reddened slowly, her Yellow contract starting to come to life, and the barest hint of her red contract blossoming as well.

Giving her a smile and then breaking eye contact as gently as he would with a predator, Gus turned to Vanessa.

"Alright, unchanged from what we discussed this morning. Fitz, what was he doing here, why was he here, and did they notice anything strange. Am I missing anything?" he asked.

"No, I think that's about it. Did you get the list of Enchanters yet?" she asked.

Gus grunted and looked back at his phone. Navigating to the email app, he opened it and flipped to the top. There wasn't anything from the DME yet.

"No. We might have to go pay them another visit. Need that list," Gus said.

There was a clack as the door opened.

Two women dressed in business attire stepped into the room.

On the left was a woman in her mid-to-late twenties, dressed quite stylishly. She had long black hair that fell straight as could be down her back and shoulders. There was an aura of power and confidence around her. Her eyes were as black as her hair, and her skin practically porcelain in color.

Sharp and elegant, she looked like she'd be more at home on a catwalk than as a successful business woman.

To her right was a woman in much more muted business clothes, though she was just as pretty.

Long dark-brown curls were gathered in a ponytail behind her head. Brown eyes and a smile made her pretty and gave her an easy-to-talk-to vibe. To Gus it almost seemed like she could stare right through his head and figure out all his secrets without having to ask for a single one.

They were both wearing masks, and of course the glow of the magic around them was obvious to anyone with a mask. But they appeared completely human.

As part of a general inspection, Gus had a habit of checking ring fingers.

Both women wore wedding rings. In fact, he'd swear they were wearing the same exact ring. He'd have to look closer later to make sure.

Interesting.

"Good morning," said the black-haired one. "I'm Leanne, and this is Kat. We're the co-founders and owners of C&C."

Kat closed the door behind her and nodded her head once. "Thank you for your patience."

"And for contacting us the way you did," Leanne said, moving to stand behind the seat directly across from Gus. "It was nice to be treated like citizens for once."

Gus gave them a smile and shrugged.

"I can't speak for anyone else, but I can assure you that we're here only to ask a few questions about someone who came to see you," Gus said, reaching across to shake Leanne's hand and then Kat's. "I'm Agent Gus Hellström of the PID. To my right is Detective Vanessa Flores. To my left is acting Agent Melody Lark."

Leanne looked to Melody as she took a seat across from Gus and raised her eyebrows at her.

"The Lark? What's the Lark doing here in Saint Anthony? And working for the PID?" Leanne asked, sounding genuinely curious. "Last I heard the PID wanted you for questioning in a number of cases, as well as the Feds."

Kat took the seat next to Leanne and politely turned to face Melody as well. Though she seemed almost uninterested in the conversation.

Looking from one woman to the other, Melody's eyes took in everything. Her Yellow, Green, Orange, and Violet contracts were all lit up.

As if someone had hit a light switch, they all suddenly turned off, and she smiled at the two women.

"I called in a number of favors, sent in emails, statements, and notices to several highly placed people," Melody said. "My record has been expunged and I'm working for the PID at this time."

Slowly, Indigo-colored symbols began to glow to life around the edge of her entire face. From her chin to the crown of her hairline. It was a single straight line that made her face look like a cutout.

Fuck me dead, she's a Rainbow Contractor. A contract for every color.

No wonder she's so damned strong.

"As for why I'm here… I'll answer that if you answer a question for me," she said.

Leanne was watching Melody quietly, a small smirk on her face. "I think I can already guess your answer, but I'll play the game. Ask your question."

"Did either of you already know why we were here, before we came?" Melody asked.

Leanne shook her head in the negative just as Kat did.

"No," they both said at the same time.

"Thank you for your answer. I'm here because I'm chasing Agent Gustavus. He's going to contract with me before the month is over," Melody said confidently.

Both women looked to Gus now.

Clearing his throat, Gus unlocked his phone and gave them a smile.

"Do either of you know a Michael Fitz?" he asked, ignoring everything that had just happened with Melody.

Leanne looked like her face clouded up in thought at the name. There was definite recognition, but also caution there.

"I believe so, yes," Kat said, not looking away from Gus. "He was a Troll, I think."

Curious. I didn't say anything about him being dead. In fact, I made sure to use present tense.

"Indeed. There was an unfortunate accident, and it seems his full enchantment failed. Failed and disastrously so. It ended up costing him his life as he went into a full berserker rage," Gus said. "We're attempting to run down everywhere he went before the accident."

"Ah. Yes, we did see him. He was here about securing an investment, and the possibility of taking something to market," Kat said, her placid, HR-friendly smile permanently attached to her face.

Leanne shook her head once, looking a bit upset.

"He's dead?" she asked.

"Yes. During his rage he killed a PID officer and was unresponsive to communication. Lethal force was used when he charged down two other officers," Gus supplied.

"Investigate them, then. Clearly they killed him on purpose," Leanne said with a flip of her hand.

"On purpose?" Vanessa asked, looking up from her notepad. "Could you explain that statement?"

Leanne clicked her tongue, looking from Vanessa to Gus. She was clearly upset about this. Something about Michael's death had unhinged her. More so than she had apparently realized herself.

"Are the officers involved in the shooting undergoing an investigation?" Kat asked, jumping the subject.

Gus wanted to run down the "on purpose" statement, but it seemed he wasn't going to be able to. Instead he took a note on his phone about it.

"The officers involved were justified in the shooting. There was a camera in the hallway that caught the entire situation.

"They were cleared the same night after it was revealed that Michael Fitz had killed the PID agent unprovoked. It was a non-confrontation situation that went from zero to a hundred," Gus said. He was providing more details than he wanted to, but he also didn't want them looking into things on their own. "The PID officer was doing a routine check-in with the teachers at the school for signs of unregistered Paras."

"You said he was here to discuss a loan and a business proposal. Could you share any of that?" Melody asked.

"It's confidential, but it had nothing to do with his mask, enchantment, or anything that would cause him to become enraged," Kat said. "Nothing that would cover a motive for certain, or a means for it to happen."

Leanne seemed to be coming out of her emotional distress, looking far more in control and calculated again.

"I think that'll be it for today as well, officers," Leanne said, getting to her feet. She was followed almost instantly by Kat, who looked like she'd had the same thought. "Please feel free to submit any other questions by email or letter."

"Of course," Gus said, standing up. There were a few things here they didn't want him poking into, and he wasn't sure what.

Yet.

He didn't think they had anything to do with his death, but they might be part of the cause.

"Can I just say," Vanessa said, "I love your books, Kat. I'm reading your latest, and I just… feel for the heroine. It's like I know her."

"My latest? Oh. Falling Far?" Kat asked, pausing in her exit. Leanne was already long gone.

"Yes. It's so bittersweet. I couldn't handle the ending very well, though. It was so… tragic," Vanessa said.

Kat gave the detective a genuine smile. Probably the first one Gus had seen during the entire time they were here.

"Yes. Unfortunately, that tends to be how life goes. Doesn't it? Thank you for being a reader," she said, then left.

Gus's phone vibrated softly as they filed out into the lobby again. It only made a vibration for two people in his life. Melody and Vanessa kept heading for the door.

Pulling it out, Gus gave it a quick look. It was from Mark. He unlocked his phone and checked the note.

"The senior Enchanter's name is Eric Mill. Part of the Mill family. DME contacted me rather than you when the information was found.

"One recently found alias, not reported in any systems. Eric LaMille. Handle all of this with care."

Great. That makes this a bit more problematic, but… I wonder.

The secretary was typing away at her keyboard, though with much less speed than he remembered her capable of.

Walking straight up to her, he gave her a smile.

"I'm sorry, could I ask you a favor, Ashley? Leanne and Kat had to go, but they directed me to you for help," Gus said.

Turning to face him, the secretary gave him a beatific smile. "They did?"

"Yeah. I was curious about a file, and they sent me your way. Eric LaMille. Could you check for me?" Gus asked.

"Eric... LaMille? That's spelled L A M I L E?" she asked, turning back to her computer. Melody was at the door, giving him a curious look.

He winked at her and held up a single finger as discreetly as he could. Melody tilted her head to one side, then left with Vanessa.

Several minutes passed as the secretary worked quietly at her keyboard.

"Found him," Ashley said. "You should have said he was an employee. Would have made it quicker. What do you want to know?"

"Oh, last address and contact would be great. Is he working today?" Gus asked.

"Not a problem, Gus. And, no. He quit about three weeks ago. He worked in facilities spell management out of the secondary office across town."

"Could you get me his boss's information as well then?"

"Of course," she said, writing down several things on a piece of paper. Then she held it out, making some serious eye contact with him. "I also put my number at the bottom."

Looking down, he found the hand-written information for Eric, and his boss. At the bottom was a much more cutely written "Ashley" along with her phone number next to it.

"I'll give you a call. Maybe coffee sometime?" Gus asked, looking back at her.

"Or dinner and dessert," Ashely suggested instead.

Smiling, Gus folded the paper and left the building.

Ok, that was a bit... unusual.

Now that I think about it, Judy responded differently this morning to me as well. No fear at all, just interest.

Scratching at his jaw, Gus made his way back to Vanessa's car. His two companions were waiting for him, talking between themselves.

"So," Gus said as he got close. "Apparently our senior Enchanter is one Eric Mill, of the Mill family."

"I'm afraid I don't know the significance. I'm not a local," Melody said with a shrug of her shoulders.

"And I'm the rookie," Vanessa said, equally as lost.

"Hm. Well. The Mill family isn't some all-powerful anything. But what they are is large. If you look hard enough at any Para institution, you can eventually find a Mill. Because of that, they've got a lot of connections. Running afoul of them is a quick way to end up hitting too many roadblocks to not want to hurt someone," Gus said. "Funny though, PID had him with a new alias. Eric LaMille."

"Let me guess," Melody said, shifting her weight to one leg and tilting her head. "You conned that poor little girl with a smile, and she gave you information. So, was he a client here, too?"

"Nope. He worked here." Gus pulled out the paper and handing it to her. "That's his information, and his old boss's info. Apparently he quit. About three weeks ago."

"That sounds like something we should run down. Fast," Vanessa said, typing into her phone as she read the sheet Melody was holding.

"I'd agree with that one. It's also a pretty solid lead," Gus said.

Grimacing, he realized Melody was probably going to be annoyed at the phone number at the bottom. He reached for the paper and tore Ashley's phone number off, then crumpled it up and tossed it into a trash can nearby.

The Contractor was staring into his face when he turned back around to her. Gus gave her a lopsided smile and shrugged one shoulder.

Just because he didn't want to dabble with a Contractor, which was the same as getting in bed with crazy, didn't mean he needed to provoke Melody.

Vanessa missed the exchange entirely and was still typing things into her phone. "Alright. Got it. I sent the info to Mark to run down for us. Should we go to the address on file first?

"No telling what the relationship with the old boss is. He might tip Eric off."

"Good call," Gus said, moving to the rear passenger door and opening it. "Let's go check his home address first and go from there."

Getting comfortable in the back, he shut the door and buckled himself in.

Once Melody and Vanessa got into the car, Gus pulled open his notes on his phone.

"Wasn't expecting them to stonewall like that," Gus said, typing in a few more notes. "They're definitely involved with Fitz. Far more than they want us to know about. Especially with how Leanne reacted."

"Yeah, that was a bit strange," Vanessa said, easing them out of the parking space and into traffic. "I got the impression that whatever they were working on with him wasn't a business venture in any way."

"Absolutely not," Melody said. "In addition to that, Kat has either telepathy or intuition. I believe she didn't know what we wanted to talk about before she walked in that door, but I also believe she knew what we wanted before we asked.

"I don't think anyone missed it when she used past tense for him. Then again, English is not my first language, so perhaps I misheard that."

"No, I heard it, too. It was more than enough for me to be curious about. You think she knew before we asked, then? Sure on that?" Gus asked. He hadn't tried to probe their thoughts for fear of creating a problem. They weren't quite suspects, but neither were they on the hook for anything.

"Positive," Melody said. "There's no doubt in my mind about that."

Gus had no reason to disbelieve her.

Not to mention she's been a PI longer than you've been alive. Maybe you could learn a thing or two.

"To recap… they knew Fitz. Ashley the secretary even had a nickname for him and recalled him out of hand.

"He had reasons for being there that Leanne and Kat didn't wish to discuss. It's unlikely they were responsible for his death, but they could be involved in a motive for someone else. Especially given that they think he would have been killed on purpose by officers of the PID.

"Eric Mill, the one responsible for Fitz's mask, just happened to work for C&C and was probably there when Fitz visited. Then promptly quit a week after Fitz came in."

The mood in the car was considerably more serious after all that had been laid out.

"In other words, Eric probably did it when Fitz came to visit C&C. Which means he knew about it and had planned for it? That's kinda farfetched. To get a job just to spike a mask?" Vanessa said.

"No, Fitz was a regular. It wasn't a question of knowing his appointment date, it was knowing that he visited often," Melody said, shaking her head. "That'd add back up with him deleting out his own records at the DME."

"Seems Mr. Mill is someone we really need to talk to. If we don't pick him up at the address on file for his checks, might want to put out a person-of-interest request. See if we can't reel him in," Gus said.

"I suddenly regret letting you feed my ego and throwing away that little girl's phone number," Melody muttered. "It could have been useful for if we have questions later."

"I wrote it down," Vanessa said. "Just in case. I'm surprised, though. I always heard the jokes about getting numbers from suspects and whatnot, but… never seen it happen."

Definitely was weird. And she was right earlier. Judy was really nice to me today.

Now that I think on it…

Gus reached into his wallet and opened it up to fish out the receipt from breakfast. There wasn't anything on the front, but when he flipped it over…

There was Judy's name with a horn coming up from both ends, followed by her phone number.

What in the world is going on?

Stuffing the receipt back into his wallet, Gus shook his head. He wasn't acting any differently. In fact, he was behaving the same as he always had.

The only thing that had changed was—

Melody. I hunted down Melody. An extremely powerful Rainbow Contractor. And fed on her while doing it.

Not much, but… a little. Is that it?

Dad always said Mom had a certain way about her that drew men in when she wanted.

He'd personally never seen it, of course. As far as he could tell, his mother got mad when other men gave her any attention at all.

Clearing his thoughts, Gus leaned his head back to the headrest and let his mind fall silent.

Vanessa and Melody started talking about whatever book Kat had just released.

Chapter 8 - Dead Dead-End

Getting out of the car, Gus did a quick survey of the area.

It looked like a slightly older but not quite run-down neighborhood. The type of place that had a lot of people living through rent-control laws. The moment a chunk of them died or moved, the area would get a face-lift. Getting itself ready for the next group of people to step in claim their own little piece of the city.

And that's why I live in the 'burbs. Got more than enough of my share of living in my tiny box. Right next to all the other tiny boxes.

Adjusting his coat, Gus looked to Vanessa and Melody.

"Seems normal enough," he said.

Melody's Blue and Orange contracts were lit up.

"Nothing I can tell out of the ordinary," she said.

Vanessa shook her head once.

"Nothing was in the database for this area either. Quiet neighborhood," she said.

Gus nodded, then headed for the building front.

"Ground floor here," Vanessa said. "Number seven."

"Huh. Don't people pay more to be higher up for a better view?" Gus asked.

"Depends on what you want and what the view is," Vanessa said. "I have an apartment in the middle of the building. Was the cheapest.

"How about you, Mel?" Vanessa asked, opening the door for the other two.

"Hmm?" Melody murmured, her contracts fading as she passed Vanessa.

"Gus lives in the 'burbs, I've got an apartment. How about you?" Vanessa repeated.

"I have multiple residences. Though I just sold one yesterday that I haven't visited in years," Melody said, eying the mail boxes to one side.

"Can't bust it open," Gus said, knowing where her mind was going. "He's a person of interest; nothing warrants that."

"Why sell it?" Vanessa asked, walking toward a hallway with 1-15 labeled on it.

"I'm buying a house. I put in an offer today," Melody said.

"That's exciting, where's the house?" Vanessa asked, reading the numbers on the doors as they walked.

Gus was already pretty sure what house she was trying to buy. He knew it without even needing to look at Melody. So much so that it made him sick. It matched the rest of her personality to a T, there was no way it couldn't be.

"Oh, just a quiet little place. Somewhere I can put my feet up and enjoy the view," Melody said.

Yep. House right next door. Damn her.

"You're buying a house in Gus's neighborhood," Vanessa said, stopping in front of door number seven.

"I did!" Melody giggling to herself. She started to swing back and forth excitedly, bouncing in place and holding her fists in front of her chest. She thoroughly looked like a toddler given candy.

"Probably the one next door," Gus said, sighing. "Who wants to go around the back just in case he tries to go out the window?"

"I'll go. My contracts need to be paid tonight and it's getting harder to sit still," Melody said, immediately walking back the way she'd come.

"She, uh..." Vanessa watched the Contractor leave the building. "Seems really interested in you."

"Yeah. Seems like she's giving me the full-court press," Gus said, then reached into his coat to check his weapon.

"To be fair, you're attractive, confident, and when you're not a dickhead, you're a nice guy," Vanessa said.

"You're not falling for me too, are ya?" Gus said with a smirk, looking at the shorter detective.

Vanessa shrugged at him.

"I'm… hopeful for my own relationship. I want to believe this is just a low point but we'll be fine.

"If I wasn't hopeful, I'd consider asking you out myself," Vanessa said, checking her own piece now inside her coat. "Doesn't mean I can't tell you that you've got some good points, though, and that Mel is way into you."

"Contractors are crazy. Their prices tend to take a toll," Gus said.

"She does seem different. But a fun kind of different. I'm sure Mark would tell you to, how did you put it, 'plow her'? Should be enough time for her to be in place," Vanessa said. Then she knocked hard on the door three times.

There was no response from inside.

Vanessa waited a beat, then hit the door three more times.

"This is Detective Flores. Could we please speak with you, Mr. LaMille?" she said, her tone changing rapidly to be more authoritative.

Gus thought about what to do next. There wasn't much in the way of leads outside of this one to go off right now. Other than going to the Mill family and asking about Eric.

But that was the last thing he wanted to do. That'd put them on to the fact that something was wrong.

Vanessa lifted her hand and slammed the door three more times.

"Eric LaMille, please open the door," she said.

Gus heard a creak of floorboards behind him. Checking over his shoulder, he saw door number eight.

Oh? Someone home? Maybe a curious neighbor? I love curious neighbors.

Turning around, he went to the door of apartment eight and gave it several hard knocks.

"This is Agent Gustavus Hellström," Gus said, staring into the peep hole. He could see the light behind it go dark as someone clearly looked through. He held up his medallion. "Could I ask you a few questions?"

The door creaked open several inches and went no further. An old man with wispy white hair appeared in the gap.

"What?" he asked.

"Sir, do you happen to know your neighbor, Eric LaMille?" Gus said, throwing a thumb back to door number seven. "Or if not know him, know when you saw or heard him last?"

The old man frowned, glaring at Gus.

"He was here yesterday. Had their damn television on as loud as possible. Some war movie," said the old man, looking more annoyed now after having remembered that. "Don't know nothing about him otherwise."

"Great. Thank you, sir," Gus said.

After nodding at Gus, the old man closed the door again and threw the dead bolt.

"Right. Yesterday, loud movie, not here today," Gus said, looking back to Eric's apartment. "I'm feeling like it's time to break a law."

Vanessa sighed and pressed a hand to her forehead. "Alright. Do it. I've already lied to Mark several times already. What's one more?"

Gus got down on one knee and went for his lock picks.

Only to have the door pulled open, and he found himself looking up at Melody.

"Yes, I do!" she said, clapping her hands together. Gus frowned. She must have been waiting on the other side of the door for this. "Can we contract one another tonight and make it official? Then make it really official?"

Unable to generate a response, Gus knelt there staring up at her.

"Ah, congratulations, Mel, Gus," Vanessa said, peering into the apartment. Then she winced and shook her head. "Oh… I know that smell."

Taking a whiff of the air, Gus smelled it then.

Death.

Nasty morning piss splashed with diarrhea and bad breath times a thousand.

"Yeah. Window was open," Melody said, moving away from the door. "I could smell it from the alleyway. I took a probable-cause angle and entered.

"Body's in the tub. Don't know him."

Gus had a sneaking suspicion he knew who it was before he'd even gone in. Getting up off his knee, he pulled out his phone and dialed up Mark.

It connected after the third ring.

"Agent Hellström," Mark said, sounding official.

"Captain Ehrich, who gave us the Eric Mill direction?" Gus asked, standing at the doorway to the apartment. He was watching for anyone wandering through, or perhaps Eric returning. After this went live, there was very little chance of Eric coming back here.

"It was a confidential informant," Mark said. "Why?"

"Never got the list from the DME manager, did we?" Gus asked, waiting for Vanessa to come back and confirm his suspicion.

"No. We didn't. Why?" Mark asked again, putting a bit more emphasis on the word.

"Gus," Vanessa said, coming up behind him. Pulling the phone away from his ear, he made eye contact with her. "It's Blake Johnson. From the DME."

Nodding at that, Gus brought the phone back up to his ear.

"Going to need a coroner out here at the LaMille address. Got a body in a tub. It's Blake Johnson, the DME manager," Gus said.

The silence on the other end of the line was palpable.

"I understand. I'll make the arrangements. Any sign of the POI?" Mark asked.

"Neighbor saw him yesterday. Said he had his TV real loud. Real, real loud. Action-movie loud. Hasn't been back since," Gus said. "Considering we saw the manager yesterday, it adds up in a bad way."

"Yeah. It does. Alright, I'll get things moving here. Take control of the locals I'm sending, do a canvas, and start working the scene. I'm not letting anyone else on the case," Mark said.

"You don't have a choice, sir. Going to need a second unit to get down to Blake's house, secure it, and start doing a run down. We need to know why he was even here," Gus said.

Knowing Mark as well as he did, Gus knew this would be the part where he would normally be cursing. If not hitting his desk.

"Right," Mark said instead. The whole situation made Gus incredibly nervous. "I'll take care of it." Then the line disconnected.

Shit. I wonder who he had in the room with him.

Walking into the apartment, he beckoned Vanessa over.

"Mark wants us working the scene. Officers are going to be on their way over. Local PD. I want you to arrange and organize them, and run a canvas. Doors, names, and statements from anyone we can. Get the landlord and see if there are any active cameras," Gus said.

"Got it," Vanessa said.

Gus walked into the bathroom and sighed. It was certainly Blake. He was still dressed in his work clothes. They were liberally smeared and coated with blood, but there didn't seem to be any obvious causes yet.

Getting down next to the body, Gus pulled a pen from his pocket. As gently as he was able, he lifted the flap of the coat lapel to see if he could get a look at anything else.

"There's splatter in the other room," Melody said, walking up next to him. "Looks like a couple of shots. Standing shooter, kneeling victim, or so it looks to me. Decent pool of blood, and drag marks this way."

"Great. I was hoping maybe they'd used magic so we could get a trace," Gus grumbled. Guns were a lot harder to track down than magic. Magic always left a calling card to whoever had used it. Especially a senior Enchanter.

"No such luck. Odd though, no head shot," Melody said, her tone curious. "A clear execution, but nothing to scramble the brain bits."

Unable to disagree, Gus looked at the toilet next to him. The seat was down, but the lid was up. "You're thinking whoever did it fucked it up and didn't want to risk another shot? Or they sat here and watched them bleed out and it was on purpose? Maybe even talked to them?"

"Para world feeds on blood, life, and death. Fear, too. Do you really think there isn't someone out there that doesn't feed off people dying?" Melody asked. "The question becomes: was it Eric and he botched it, or something worse and they were hungry?"

Gus felt like the whole case was rapidly spiraling further and further out of control, and he didn't like the odds of him getting out of this easily. At least not without more problems coming to make his life hell.

***

Exhausted, and unwilling to do anything more, Gus was spent. When he looked at the clock, he realized it was close to ten at night. Submitting the report to Mark on the murder of Blake Johnson, Gus leaned back in his chair. They'd found a number of receipts in the apartment. Both in the trash and in the pockets of the clothes left behind.

There was also a car in the parking lot they'd impounded and had taken apart.

Lots of small leads, nothing giving me a direction.

Eric was practically a slam dunk on the Blake murder. He'd been seen entering the apartment complex with Blake on camera, and by another tenant. Top that off with the old man in eight, and there wasn't much room for anything else here.

Especially when the name the DME manager was going to supply would be Eric's. The question now was why would Blake visit Eric? Or know how to contact him?

Blake's house had been locked down immediately, and a second PID unit had been sent to comb through it for anything of use. Everything they found was coming over tomorrow for Gus and his team to sort through.

"Is the day over yet?" Melody asked, her head down on the desk she was sitting in front of.

"Yep," Gus said, closing his eyes and leaning his head back to face the ceiling. "Now I'm kinda glad I sent Ness home. Would have been wasting her time."

"I would have had someone to talk to," Melody said.

"Yeah, but I told you to go home, too."

"Your home is my home. You have more than one bedroom; one of them is now mine. I didn't want to go without you," Melody said. "Would have looked weird. Your neighbors call the police a lot. I had to explain I was your fiancée from out of town the other day when I broke in."

Chuckling at that, Gus got out of his seat and locked his terminal. "Did you now? How'd that turn out for you?"

"I had to use a little contract magic, nothing terrible. Still annoying," Melody said, getting out of her chair as well. She grabbed her coat, pulled it on and then stretched, bringing all the attention in the world to her great physique. "Mm, that felt good. Not even going to fight me about staying with you?"

"No. If you really did already put in a buy option on the neighbor's house, I'd say I already lost any expectation of privacy I had," Gus said, pulling on his own coat. "You seem determined to run me down, and you're doing a fair job of cornering me—I'll give you that. But you're not forcing anything on me, either."

Gus picked up his mug and dropped it in the sink on the way out the door. Then he stopped when he got to the light switch. Looking back at his desk, he frowned. He hadn't been able to thank the cleaning lady in the last two days.

For whatever reason, he felt odd about that.

I'll get her something small on the way to work tomorrow as a thank you and an apology.

"Ready to go?" Melody asked, standing near the door.

"Yeah. Didn't you say you need to pay your contracts up?" Gus asked. "Should you go off and do that? Rather than stalk me home?"

"I'm going home with you so you can help me pay them," Melody said, walking to the elevator. "It'll be nice to have an assistant for once. I always manage to get blood and urine on everything."

Gus raised his eyebrows at that and got into the elevator.

"Sounds like a helluva party," he said.

"Wait till you see what I do with the turkey baster," she said, her curious accent surfacing a bit more on that one. The elevator doors closed shut with a swish. "Good thing you'll be there to take its place."

Unable to muster any type of conversation after that, Gus silently drove Melody to his home. For her part, she seemed quite content.

And terribly amused.

It made Gus wonder how much she was fucking around with him about her contracts. He'd heard some pretty ridiculous things people had to go through once they'd gotten a contract, but he'd never seen it.

Most Contractors were terribly guarded about it all, since it was the source of their power.

He handled it right up until the garage door was shutting behind him. The interior light illuminated the door leading into his house.

Turning the car off, Gus looked at Melody, who gave him a bright smile.

"Look, I'll help, but I could really use some direction here?" Gus asked.

"After all that, and your mind probably buzzing wildly with thoughts, that's what you came up with?" she asked him, opening the passenger door.

"You're a Contractor, and you enjoy messing with me," Gus said simply. "I can't tell which part is real and which isn't."

"Hmmm. Could you get me a towel, a good sharp knife, and four pairs of socks? The rest I can manage by myself," she said, closing the door to his car and heading for the house.

Gus shrugged and got out of the car, following her inside.

He collected the items while also pulling off his coat and work shirt, and then he went looking for her again. He found her in his bathroom, naked.

Her clothes were gone, and she was sitting in the tub.

"First things first…" She looked up at him, then gestured at her beautiful naked form. "I really didn't want you to see me naked until our first night. I'm a little disappointed that I'm breaking that, so please be appreciative of me."

"Ahh, yep. Definitely appreciative," Gus said quite honestly, looking at her from head to toe.

"Good. Thank you, Gus. You're a good listener," Melody said. "First, the easy contracts. Violet is fairly mundane."

Picking up the phone that was beside the tub, she unlocked it. She tapped through several screens, then let out a deep breath and hit a button.

"Ah… there we go," she said, the Violet symbols on her face flaring to life.

"What was that?" Gus asked, curious.

She smiled up at him, quirking a brow. "I donated money, and I made money. My Violet Contractor is now appeased. Next is Indigo, which is… going to be a little different for me this time."

Looking up at Gus, she wore the strange look she sometimes got when she was watching him. "I love you, Gus. I want to contract with you. Desperately so. You're the only man for me. My one male contract for my entire life. I can't stop thinking about you. It hurts me so to look at you and know you're not mine. I know it's been a very short period of time, but you're so wonderfully amazing."

Gus blinked several times, having no idea how to respond to that. He felt like his face was on fire all of a sudden.

Melody's Indigo contract snapped to life and glowed brightly. Brighter than the Violet contract.

"Oooh. Goodness. I don't think the Indigo contract has ever felt so fulfilled. Ok. Ah… what's the next easiest one," Melody said, looking down at herself in the tub. "Ah, Orange."

Picking up her phone again, she began to solve what looked like several crossword puzzles in a very rapid fashion. After she finished the third one, the Orange symbols were now visible.

"Yellow now, I suppose," Melody said, staring up at the ceiling. "Ah. We'll need to talk to Vanessa about her girlfriend before she finds out herself that she's a Were. It's only a matter of time before she checks the database. Her girlfriend is a listed Were.

"It would be the right thing to do, and would give her enough time to prepare herself. We should be good partners to her."

Almost immediately, her Yellow symbols came to life.

Empathy... I guess?

"Now the less pleasant ones, in an order I can't really change," Melody said with a sigh. Leaning over the side of the tub, she picked up Gus's carry knife. She'd asked for something sharp, and that was the sharpest thing he had in the house.

Unfolding the blade, she immediately went for her shoulder and began slicing down the length of her arm in one long, continuous cut.

Grimacing with her teeth locked together, Melody butchered herself. Carving two deep slices into her flesh from her shoulder down to her wrist. Then she brought the knife back up and cut a bit deeper into the top, bringing the two cuts together.

Panting, she stopped and laid her head down against the tub. "This is the crappy part."

"Can I help?" Gus asked.

"No, but thank you. I'm so flattered that you want to.

"It's a Contract, so I must perform it myself. Besides, you'll be helping me in a second," Melody said, giving him a sad smile and setting his bloody knife to one side. "Good knife, by the way."

Reaching up with her uncut arm, she grabbed hold of the top of flap she'd cut into her flesh. And jerked it down.

Screaming through her teeth, Melody kept pulling until she had a strip of ragged flesh at her wrist.

Melody had wet herself during the ordeal from the sheer pain of it, he imagined. He definitely understood now what she had meant earlier.

Gus had seen worse in his life, but he'd never seen someone do the like to themselves. He was surprised her flesh had come off so easily like that. It didn't seem quite normal.

"There... there's Green. And the pain... pain and suffering brings Blue," Melody said, her voice a bit quivery. A soft glow went up around the wound in her arm, and slowly, the skin flowed back up her arm and reknit itself together. As if there'd never been a problem. Though the blood remained.

"And now for the only fun part about this," Melody said, sounding very much relieved that her arm was whole again. Then she laid her right hand atop her stomach.

All of her contracts but the Red were lit up and glowing bright on her face.

Red is basically sex, isn't it? What's she going to – actually, I bet I know.

Melody turned her head toward him, and gave him a smile as her hand crept downward.

"Going to be much easier fantasizing about you," Melody said, her eyes widening slowly, "with you watching and right there."

Chapter 9 - Paper Trail

Melody was happily putting what looked like a breakfast burrito into a tinfoil wrapper, humming tunelessly all the while. At the same time, she was running his coffee machine into one of his traveler mugs. Another of the same mugs was already next to it, steam coming off the top.

Dressed in a long-sleeved white blouse, black slacks, and with a short black coat over one arm, she looked authoritative and very well put together.

Clearly sensing his presence, Melody's head turned toward him, and she smiled.

"Good morning, Gus. I was just finishing up a breakfast burrito, and then we can go. I'm always starving the day after I refill my contracts." She folded the top of the foil over the burrito. "I made you one as well, and some coffee."

Feeling a bit lost at the way his life was going right now, Gus only nodded and walked over to her.

"Thanks, Melody. I appreciate it," he said, spotting a foil-wrapped burrito sitting behind the already made coffee.

"Of course. Happy to do it. Having someone to help me out after… all of that was a real blessing. Thank you for washing me down and getting me into bed," Melody said, grabbing his car keys from the island. "I'll drive, you eat. Get your coffee and burrito."

Grabbing two paper towels, Gus followed Melody out of his house and into his garage. Melody closed the door and locked it behind him, picking the right key on the first try.

She tapped the fob, unlocked his car and got in. On top of that, without needing to be told, she tapped the appropriate button in his car that opened the garage door.

"Did you memorize everything about my life or something?" Gus asked, putting his coffee in the cup-holder.

"As much as I could. So far, at least, I'm still learning," Melody said, backing the car up out of the garage. She paused long enough to close the garage door, then got them on the road heading into the city. "I'm not just kidding when I say I want to Contract with you, Gus. This isn't me being a 'crazy contractor' or just looking for a one-night fling."

"Yeah, well, sorry. You're fun and all, but I'm just—"

"Emotionally closed off. I'd make a guess why, but I think I'd be right, and that'd only dredge up some demons you don't want to deal with," Melody said, taking a sip of her coffee.

Gus peeled the top layer of foil away from the burrito Melody had made, and he peered at it as he thought on her words.

"Don't worry. I'm very patient. I'll wear you down, but I do think I'll be in your heart in less than a month," Melody said as Gus started to dig into his breakfast. "That's not me bragging, I just know I'm the best woman for you."

Gus rolled his eyes at that and swallowed.

"Your contracts. Some of those seemed pretty rough, some seemed easy. Anything you can tell me? Share with me?" Gus asked.

"Normally this is the part where I tell someone to die." Melody took another sip of her coffee. "But I'm in the long run with you, so… my contracts are variable. Depending on the length of time since the I last fulfilled the requirements.

"I'm sure you've read about those Contractors with obscene or terrible things they have to do?"

"Yeah, thought that was the norm. By the way, this is delicious," Gus said, taking another bite.

"Thanks. I love you, too," Melody said, another of her frequent smiles on her face. "No, those contracts are bad contracts. Contracts made to favor the spirit who crafted it and make the Contractor subservient. Thankfully I had a mentor, so I never got stuck with one of those.

"Mine are very straightforward, and scalable. I try to keep up on most of them, but the Blue and Green contracts tend to go up quickly. I use them a lot," Melody said, veering onto the road that'd take them straight to work. "Picking up Vanessa. I need to have that talk with her today about her girlfriend.

It sounds pretentious, but I really do think it'd be best to help ease her into it. Best-case scenario, I can help her patch it up with her girlfriend."

Wincing at that, Gus finished the breakfast burrito in a massive gulp. He'd eaten it faster than he realized.

"Goodness, Gus, did you like it that much?" Melody said with a soft chuckle.

"Yeah, I did actually. It was amazing," Gus said honestly. By leaps and bounds, it was the best breakfast burrito he'd ever had.

"I cooked it full of love for you. Maybe a little something else, too," she said.

"Huh? What… else… did you cook it with?" he asked suspiciously.

"Fear! I did my very best to channel all of my fear from the last day or two into it. Did it work? I wasn't sure if you could put something like fear into food, but… it was worth a try," Melody said, pulling up to an apartment building. Turning the wheel a bit sharp, she bumped them up into a fire lane. She flicked the emergency blinkers into the on position, then picked up her phone and tapped something into it.

She put fear into it?

Pushing gently at his other senses, he found that the slightly hungry feeling he almost always felt was gone.

No, that's ridiculous. I'm sure this is just run-off from yesterday. You can't put fear in food. Still, it was delicious.

"She's on her way down. I need you to compliment her a few times today no matter what. Something about her clothing, her hair, or her eyes, alright?" Melody said, putting her phone back into her pocket. "Just something to build her confidence."

"What? Why?" Gus said.

"Because I think she's going to react badly to her girlfriend having hidden things from her when I tell her later today. React in a way where she thinks she's not worth being told." Melody looked out the passenger window. "If you're pushing up her confidence and it's on her mind, she's less likely to go try and sleep with another man or woman. Ruin her relationship with her girlfriend. You can string her along a bit and still let her down easy when she goes back to her girlfriend."

Gus shook his head, not entirely understanding what had just been said.

"Do it for me, Gus. Believe me, I'm always going to be jealous of other women in your life, but I need to make sure she gets through this at least as well as I can manage it. Contract, remember?" Melody said.

Sighing, Gus nodded. Looking out the window, he watched for Vanessa. "Fine, whatever. Just don't get mad at me later for it."

The door to the building opened, and Vanessa's head turned this way and that before she found Gus's car. She was dressed in a similar fashion to Melody, but with a bit more feminine appeal than Melody's outfit today. Which was the reverse from yesterday.

Getting into the car, Vanessa clicked her seatbelt in. "Thanks, I appreciate the lift. I could get used to being picked up."

Ah! There we go. That's an easy one.

"Considering how pretty you're looking today, Ness, I'm sure you could get picked up by anyone at any time, without a problem. No need to wait for a busted-down cop like me to do it," Gus said, taking a drink from his coffee. "If I were you and could get myself into a pair of pants the way you do, I think I'd be an awful nightmare for men."

Vanessa snorted at that, but he could practically hear the smile in the noise. Nor did she fight the words.

Glancing over at Melody, Gus saw just a hint of her Yellow contract, but it was almost invisible.

Huh, she's handling it well. Great. Good.

Maybe this isn't a terrible idea.

As she moved her head to look down the street for a turn, he saw her Red contract was a glowing ember between her eyes.

Ah… shit. Maybe not.

***

Gus spied the gift store next to the PID precinct as they pulled into the parking lot. He'd bought several gifts there and found that it usually had whatever he needed, or a version of it.

Shit, cleaning lady's present.

"Alright, I'll catch up with you two. I need to go get something," Gus said, getting out of the car.

"Cheating on me already?" Melody asked, closing the driver's side door.

"I mean, if it was Ness, maybe. You seen her without the coat on?" Gus said, playing back to Melody's earlier request.

"Stop it," Vanessa said as she shut her own door, but Gus couldn't help but spot the blush and faint smile on her face. "You two don't need me in between you."

"I don't know about that. I bet I could find a nice spot for you between us," Melody said.

To which Vanessa's face became a blazing crimson, and she put her hands over her ears.

"Not listening, not listening," she muttered, walking toward the front of the precinct.

Gus chuckled at that and turned to Melody. "I just need to pick up a small gift for the cleaning lady. She takes good care of my desk. I normally talk to her a little when the day's over. She seems to have a somewhat sad and lonely life."

Melody blinked, processing that, then nodded. "I'm going to head in and start prepping. Good work on Vanessa, by the way. Definitely hitting the right notes."

Turning, the Contractor left and followed after Vanessa.

Gus didn't waste any time and went straight to the gift shop. He was looking for something simple that could be given without anything behind it. He'd never seen her wear any rings or jewelry, but for all he knew, she was married with children.

He opened the door and entered the shop, going straight for all the jewelry off to one side.

She always has her hair up, though. Maybe a hair clip?

"...twenty years ago marks the anniversary of when they were first seen," said a news anchor on the TV above the cashier. "And haven't been seen since."

"Hey Gus, birthday this time?" asked Hermand.

"Haha, no." Gus waved at the man. "Just a gift."

Hermand owned and ran the shop. He was almost always here whenever Gus dropped in.

Then again, he's a damn zombie or something, isn't he?

"Showing up out of nowhere in military uniforms and rifles, they quickly and effectively knocked out communication to the city, penned up the local police, and shut down all broadcasts," continued the news anchor.

"Bah," said Hermand, and changed the channel. "They run the same damn thing every year. No one, not even terrorists claimed ownership. It's a mystery."

Gus didn't care. It was an incident that didn't concern him in any way and hadn't come back since.

It'd probably changed a number of views within governments, but it didn't impact the everyday people.

Stopping in his tracks, Gus stared at a green hairclip. It was a two-dimensional representation of a tree in an oval. Its roots went to the bottom with its branches going to the top.

Picking it up, he gave it a tap against the rack. It felt sturdy enough. He flipped it over and checked the price tag.

Huh. For thirty bucks, it better hold up.

"Hermand, these shit?" Gus said, walking over to the cashier.

"Nah. I got those on order from a friend back home," said Hermand as he typed something into his register.

"And where's home again?" Gus asked, looking at the man. His mask was clearly an enchantment as well. His flesh had a faint green coloring to it that looked sickly. His eyes were pale and colorless, and there was an open wound on his forehead.

"Haha, no, no, Agent. I'll never tell," said the man with a chuckle. "Twenty?"

Gus shook his head, pulled out two twenty dollar bills, and took the hair-clip. Hermand always tried to discount him whatever he bought.

Primarily because the first time they'd met, Hermand was being held at gunpoint.

Taking the two twenties, Hermand gave him back a ten. With a nod, Gus turned from the counter.

"Agent... ah... Gus," Hermand said before Gus reached the door.

Gus stopped and looked over his shoulder.

"You think the Fed is considering... considering making the Para world visible?" Hermand asked. "I'd really rather it not happen. I get enough problems from other Paras. Humans are my best customers."

Gus frowned, then shrugged his shoulders.

"Honestly Hermand, the day the Para world goes live is the day the next inquisition comes down," Gus said, and then he left.

***

He'd been expecting to spend the next three hours doing little more than paper-trail running, but even he was surprised at how achingly dull this one was.

Reading receipt after receipt, writing down the locations, and then figuring whether anything on the paper was worth trying to run down or if it was worthless. Mind-numbing, neck-ache-creating, tedious work.

Putting down another receipt for a burger joint, Gus looked at his tally paper. He'd already written down the address for this one. Picking up his pen, he made a small tick mark next to it.

"Who uses a credit card for a strip joint?" Melody said, sounding incredulous. "The whole point is to not leave a trail that you went. Cash is king."

"That a personal preference and a suggestion?" Vanessa asked as she read something over.

"I've been in more of them than I'd ever care to admit," Melody said. "Usually working a case. You end up with a lot of low-level spirit types in there that feed off men in one way or the other."

"Oh. I suppose that makes sense." Vanessa's eyebrows pressed together. "What're the more common jobs for Para people?"

"Really depends on the type," Mark Ehrich said, walking over. "Hey, folks."

He was dressed in his best "captain's got a meeting" navy suit, with matching tie. He looked like the typical depiction of a detective in a romance novel. Tall, dark haired, blue eyed, muscular, handsome, and with a bit of danger to him.

The squad had often given him shit for signing into the service on accident. Saying there was no way someone that good looking would join a military branch, and he must've been looking for the local lady's club to work at.

"Cap," Gus said, deciding to go for a more formal approach for now as he leaned back in his chair.

Melody and Vanessa were both staring at Mark, looking a bit surprised. Apparently this was their first meeting with him.

Smiling, Mark reached up and scratched at his jaw, his wedding ring quite visible.

Yeah, yeah. Make sure you show the ring.

"I've spent the last twenty-four hours assuring everyone under the sun that Eric Mill would be brought in alive," Mark said. "So if one of you ends up killing him, don't bother coming in the next day for work. In fact, do me a favor and just skip town.

"Any luck, by the way?"

"Nothing obvious, if that's what you're asking," Gus said. "Lot of receipts that show he really wasn't big on cooking for himself. I think I saw one grocery store in the bunch."

"A bunch of strip clubs," Melody added. "The sicko was using his credit card. Who uses a credit card?"

"I sure as shit don't," Mark said.

Vanessa opened her mouth, then closed it again.

"Spit it out, Ness. Your opinion is valued," Gus said, catching it.

"Huh? Oh, uh, thanks. It's just… well… it's just, if he's part of this big family, why does it look like he's on the run from them just as much?" Vanessa asked.

Gus nodded. He had started to barely wonder the same.

"It does seem odd," Mark said, "considering the mayor knows, my boss knows, and a number of powerful people, that the Mill family hasn't contacted me. I'm sure they've probably been told by now. Sounds like you have a visit to make."

"Yeah, sounds like it," Gus said. "Anything else?"

"Nothing at the moment. I really did come in just to tell you to bring in Eric alive or not at all.

"I'll keep you updated if I get anything. You sure about this weekend?" Mark said to Gus. "Kelly wanted me to ask again."

"Sorry. Same thing as last time. Tell her I said hi though. Megan, too," Gus said.

"Sure, sure. Say hi to your sister for me. If I wasn't married, I'd ask her out myself," Mark said and then left, closing the door behind him.

"He's full of himself," Vanessa said, looking back down at the paper she was reading.

"I'm sure he's gotten his way with his looks alone more times than not," Melody agreed, picking up another receipt. "Are you doing something with your sister this weekend?"

"Yeah." Gus picked up his list of addresses. Getting up, he walked over to Vanessa's desk and started combining the two bits of information onto a third piece of paper. "Dinner with the folks and my sister."

Once he was done, Gus made a small note on Vanessa's paper to mark where he'd stopped. Then he went over to the desk Melody was working from.

"I look forward to meeting them," Melody said without looking up from the receipt. "How formal is it? Should I wear a dress?"

Snorting at that, Gus picked up her address sheet.

"You're not going," he said.

"And why not? I'd be a great date for that. Is your sister bringing someone?" she asked, then laid down the receipt she'd been reading. Reaching over to the sheet he was reading from, she added a tick mark to it.

"Actually, she is. And there's no reason to bring you, Melody," Gus said.

"Of course there is. The sooner they meet me, the better. It'll be easier that way." Melody patted his forearm. "So, dress or casual? And is your mother more old fashioned or new age?"

"Melody, I really don't—" Gus stopped and hung his head.

"Wear a dress, nothing too formal. She's more new age and certainly liberal," he said, then dropped his volume significantly. "But she's just like me, so expect to walk up to an apex predator at the top of her game."

Melody wrinkled her nose and gave him a smile.

"Thanks. I look forward to it. Vanessa, you coming too?" Melody asked, looking back to her papers. "You can be my girlfriend and I'll be Gus's."

"Doesn't that just make me his girlfriend, too?" Vanessa grumbled, putting down another piece of paper.

When he was finished combining the addresses, Gus went to his desk and pulled up a mapping website on the left screen and a graphic editing program on the right.

"It does. Is that a problem?" Melody asked.

"Yeah, kinda dating someone. Remember?" Vanessa asked.

Gus marked down every location Eric had been to in the last four weeks, and he was a bit disappointed when he hit the halfway point. Everything was centered around the apartment he'd been living at.

Near the bottom of Gus's list, but halfway through Vanessa's section, he got an address that jumped across town.

"Ness, what was the receipt at… Fifty-six thirty-one Palm Street?" Gus asked.

Setting down the one she was looking at, Vanessa started to flip through the other receipts.

"Gas station," she said when she found it. "These receipts were all in his car, I think. A lot fewer of them, though, and a lot longer ago. Empty to full tank, it looks like. Unless his car holds more than eleven gallons."

"It doesn't." Melody was rapidly flipping through the receipts in front of her. "I have two more for that address here."

"That's different, then. It's in Saint Anthony still, but on the west side of the city," Gus said as he worked through more addresses on his sheet.

In other words, receipts from when he was out further are in the car. Possibly a spot he overlooked when he was cleaning it out.

Those receipts picked up closer to the apartment went into pockets, or a bag.

Vanessa and Melody were going through the paperwork in front of them faster now.

"I've got about… eight more in that area that I recognize," Vanessa said.

"I'm not familiar with the streets, but I think I'm seeing a few that stand out. Ah… Oak, Maple, Walnut, Heron, Trout… Trout? That's a funny name for a boulevard," Melody said.

"Those are all in the area, yeah." Vanessa turned her chair around to face Melody's desk.

Gus nodded and kept putting in addresses. Maybe they'd have a location or two to go look at after all. Like going to every single one of those addresses and finding out if they had any street-facing cameras.

Gonna be a lot of pavement pounding, isn't it? Might as well get ready now.

Realizing he was going to miss the cleaning lady again, Gus picked up the small gift he'd gotten her and set it on the edge of his desk. He pulled off a sticky note and simply wrote "Thanks for everything" on it, then put it next to the hair clip.

Grabbing his coat, he went over to Melody's desk to work out how they were going to do this.

Chapter 10 - Wrong Flavor

"Whose turn is it?" Gus asked, looking to Vanessa and Melody from the driver's seat. "I got out for the last one."

They'd been going address to address, showing a picture of Eric to employees and asking if anyone had seen him lately.

A few people had recognized him but said they hadn't seen him in a while.

"It's mine, but I did something I'm regretting," Melody said, leaning back in her seat next to him. "I wore shoes I haven't broken in yet, because they looked cute and I thought you'd like them."

Gus had indeed noticed her shoes. They looked nice enough, but without being able to see her legs, it was a bit of a miss for him.

"Would you do it for me, Gus?" Melody lifted a naked foot up. "I already took them off and I'm using as little contract magic as I can get away with to heal them."

She gave him a small, pathetic smile while wriggling her toes at the same time.

What the…? Ugh.

"Fine," Gus said, getting out of the car.

"Thank you, dear. I promise I'll make it up to you later," Melody called before he shut the door.

Adjusting his coat, Gus pulled out the reference picture he'd been using and walked into the convenience store.

Moving across the aisles, he walked straight up to the empty counter and the cashier.

"How can I help you?" asked the middle-aged woman.

"Officer Hellström," Gus said, holding his medallion out to the woman. She nodded after looking at it for a second. Then Gus held up the picture of Eric. "I'm looking for this man as a person of interest."

"Eh?" Leaning in, the woman peered at the picture. "Oh, him. He used to come here almost every darn day for a hotdog and a soda. He was gone for a while but showed up again yesterday, and today. Nice guy, always says have a good day.

"What'd he do?"

"Nothing," Gus said quickly with his best smile. "We just want to talk to him. His family has a problem and we're trying to run it down with him."

"Hah, yeah, family is like that. My brother stole my credit card three years ago and ran up a bill I couldn't believe. Would you believe he had the nerve to—"

Gus coughed once, loudly, and held up a hand in front of him. Then he coughed several more times.

"You ok there, kid?" asked the woman.

"Oh, yes, sorry. Just getting over a cold," Gus lied, glad he'd somehow stopped her from her story. "Know where I can find him, by the way? Eric, not your brother."

"Huh? Oh, yeah. He works in that warehouse right over there," said the attendant, pointing to the building across the way. "Apparently he works a night shift there. Comes in for food at the end of his shift."

Looking at her watch, the woman sighed. "Which is hours away for me. He already came in today though."

"Thanks much for your time," Gus said, tucking the picture away and heading back for the car.

Melody was engaged in what looked like a fairly in-depth conversation with Vanessa.

Which Vanessa wasn't handling very well at all. Violent hand gestures were being made on both sides of the conversation.

Werewolf talk. Great timing there, Mel.

Pulling out his phone, Gus hit Mark's speed-dial and pushed it up to his ear. He walked to the intersection, tapped the button for the crosswalk and waited.

Thankfully, Mark picked it up on the second ring.

"Let me guess, you talked them into a three-way, and now you're quitting to run away and elope in Melody's home country," Mark said. "Where she'll provide for you and Vanessa until you all die of old age."

"No. I think I found out where Eric's hiding, though," Gus said. "And you know where Melody is from?"

"No one knows where she's from. She's also older than my grandma, probably. What about Eric now?" Mark asked.

"Convenience-store worker pegs him at a warehouse. Mind if I read you off an address?" Gus asked as he crossed the street.

"You know, we need to get an analyst to work the swing shift with you. I'm your captain. I shouldn't be doing address checks for you," Mark complained.

"Then hire someone. Until you do, here you are," Gus said.

"You're in an awful mood, Gussy," Mark grumbled. "Did you eat lately?'

"Yeah. Melody. She tastes like spiced mint," Gus said, and then stopped in front of the warehouse like he was just having a normal conversation on the phone. "Ready?"

"You ate from Melody? Shit on a stick, man, that's ballsy. You don't want to know how many charges she's bought, bribed, or favored her way out of. Ready," Mark said.

"Eighty-four fifty-six seven, Rio Drive. Romeo India Oscar," Gus said, then started walking again.

"Got it. I'll give you a ring once I've got something," Mark said, then hung up.

Rather than hang up, Gus kept the phone to his ear, pretending to continue the conversation. Taking a turn down an alley that ran parallel to the warehouse, he kept his eyes to the ground.

While trying to look like he was having a very deep and meaningful talk with someone, he stopped in the middle of the alley. Tilting his head to one side, he held up a hand above his head and made a dismissive gesture as if he disagreed with someone.

"No, not at all. I won't do that," he said to absolutely no one. Taking the phone away from his ear, he made a show of rubbing at his neck and putting the phone to his other ear.

At the same time, he got a good look of the side of the warehouse.

It was brimming with magical wards and constructs. The air was practically humming with the power of it all. If they went off in a critical failure, the warehouse would be vaporized.

There was also no way someone was in there with all those security spells running. There was more there than what he'd seen on Fed buildings.

Turning around the way he'd come, Gus headed back to the car.

Stakeouts suck. And now I have to do it with an angry Norm finding out about her Para girlfriend.

Gus sighed, feeling much too tired and too old for this kind of crap. Then he felt weird for thinking that, since he was barely thirty years old.

Vanessa was moving her arms so much in the car that it was actually rocking back and forth.

"Damn, must have gone bad," Gus muttered, walking up to the car. He tried to do it from an angle where they'd see him coming, so they could stop before he got in.

He pulled open the door, then got in the car and shut it.

Looking to Melody and then Vanessa, he could tell Melody was a touch heated but holding her temper in check. Vanessa looked like a ball of fury, though.

"Gus," Vanessa said, her voice crackling with anger. "Melody says that Wendy is a Werewolf. Or a were of some type."

"Yeah, she told me the same thing," Gus said, meeting Vanessa's eyes squarely.

"Is she?" Vanessa asked.

"I don't know. Never met her," Gus said. He immediately discounted suggesting confirming what Melody already had in the database. Right now Vanessa could at least deny it. The Database check could come later. "Would be hard to see through her mask as well, since a were looks human when they're not shifted. Means the mask isn't even on until then. They hide well."

"Oh," Vanessa said, frowning. "How would you know otherwise? Are they allergic to silver like the books say?"

"Not really. More often than not, physical Paras aren't really that different than the physical world would think them," Gus said. "I mean, you can kill them with regular rounds. It takes more since they're made of pretty stern stuff, but you can do it."

"Ok, but how would you know?" Vanessa pressed.

"Without seeing?" Gus frowned and shook his head, looking down at the console. "They'd probably have a job that involves hunting, outdoors, or physical things. Like a trainer, bodybuilder, football player, things like that."

"Stripper," Melody added.

"Stripper," Gus agreed, nodding ruefully. "They tend to dress in things that can get pulled off quick and easy. Otherwise they go through clothes like no one's business. Beyond that… it's mostly mannerisms."

"Mannerisms?" Vanessa asked.

"Yeah. Weres tend to focus on smell. Scent. Or playing little games like sneaking up on you. They'll be possessive if they're a rogue, or have a very close knit group of friends if they're in a pack. You'll probably never meet the friends, but they'll take precedence over you every time. Sometimes it's family, sometimes friends.

"Big fondness for meat. Usually rare or barely cooked. They can put food away like no one's business but never gain a pound."

Gus shrugged and turned to face Melody.

"Got a hit, by the way," he said, changing the subject. "Worker inside said Eric comes in often for a hot dog, and he does so from that warehouse over yonder."

Gus pointed back to the building.

"Thing is loaded up with security spells. No one's home, I think. I figure we stake it out and wait for him to come back," Gus said. "Mark's running the address."

"Odd. Why a warehouse?" Melody asked.

"Dunno, but… at least there's a convenience store nearby," Gus muttered.

Snacks and coffee, and an easy-to-watch location.

Shame about the two pissed-off people I have to share a car with.

***

"I've caught her sniffing my underwear when she thinks I'm not looking. Or my clothes in general," Vanessa said suddenly. "She works at a gym. I've never met her family, and she often goes out with friends that I'm not ever able to meet or even know their names.

"She cooks a lot of meat, and it's almost always way too rare for me. Like… purple."

Melody didn't say anything.

Whatever argument Melody and Vanessa had gotten into before had turned Melody away from talking about the subject.

"That's nice," Gus said, watching the warehouse. They'd been sitting on it for six hours now. Mark had turned the information back to Gus as being owned by a corporation that went nowhere.

"You think she's a were, don't you?" Vanessa said.

"I have no idea, never met her. Do the details you provided line up to make her a were? Sure. But she could also just be weird," Gus said.

"Can I introduce you to her?" Vanessa asked.

"Rather not. Besides, if you've seen her since you got your mask, she already knows you got picked up by PID," Gus said.

"Oh. Yeah," Vanessa mumbled, her tone growing weak at the end

"She go radio silent on you after seeing you lately?" Gus asked.

"Yeah… she won't return my calls or texts since yesterday," Vanessa said, her voice soft. "I even tried to talk around what the PID was. She pretended to not know, I guess."

"Weres are cautious. They're pretty unhappy with the 'grand joke' as they call it," Gus said, his eyes fixing on two people walking toward the warehouse.

"Grand joke?" Vanessa repeated.

"It's what they call the fact that the government pretends Paras don't exist, and the Para world as a whole pretends they don't exist," Melody said. "Predominantly the vampires, goblins, and demons. They like it just the way it is."

"I think that's our guy. I think he's got the lady in the store backwards, though. He lives here and works somewhere else," Gus said, pointing at one of the pair of people. "Don't know who the other is."

"Other?" Melody asked. Her Blue contract sprang to life, and then her Orange as well. "It's a woman. I can't see her face."

Reaching up, Gus made sure to flick the switch off that would illuminate the car when doors were opened. Then he reached into his coat and checked his weapon. Then down to his belt to pull the taser free he'd loaded there.

He didn't have much faith in it. Tasers failed as often as they worked. Too often for anyone to feel comfortable relying on it or to want to risk their life in using it.

Except Mark made it clear we don't have a choice.

The man gave the woman a hug and then continued into the warehouse. Walking down the alley Gus had explored earlier, the woman vanished.

"We follow him?" Melody asked.

"Two of us do, one trails the woman," Gus said. "Ness, you're with me. Melody, you've got our surprise guest. I figure you're impossible to shake off."

"That I am. Give up yet?" Melody asked, getting out of the car.

"No. And I don't plan on it," Gus said, exiting the vehicle as well.

The three of them separated at the cross walk. Gus and Vanessa walked close to one another, like friends or a couple on their way somewhere. Melody had her phone out in a flash and started talking to someone in a foreign language.

"Does she have to be so pushy?" Vanessa asked.

Not the time for this.

"She cares about you, so yes. That's how her brain works. Contractors are a bit cracked. They deal with forces that aren't human and never were. Don't forget that," Gus said, looking at the warehouse.

The security was down and no longer operational. This was their chance to get the job done.

"She doesn't even know me," Vanessa grumbled.

"As if she knows me better? She wants to Contract with me. It's the way a Contractor marries. Why are you any less a likely target for her attention than I am?" Gus complained.

Reaching to his belt, he pulled out the taser and thumbed the non-lethal weapon to a live-fire position, then put it back in the holster.

"Security's down," he said. "Time to go in. You want front or back?"

"Front," she said. "Do you think she's a Were?"

"What, your girlfriend? I mean, sounds like it, but again, would need to see her. Get your damn head in the game, Ness," Gus growled. Then he flipped his wrist over and checked the time. "I'll announce at ten-oh-two. You do the same thing from your side. Hopefully he just… answers either door and we can bring him in for questioning. There's no warrant for arrest yet, after all."

Vanessa clicked her tongue. "This is almost as bad as my old job."

Not answering her, Gus walked off down the side of the warehouse toward the rear entry door.

Coming around the corner, he found it was more or less what he was expecting. A loading bay and dock with a single heavy commercial-grade door.

Stepping up to it, Gus checked his watch. He still had thirty seconds to go. Waiting quietly, he felt his nerves start to tick upward.

Like getting ready for a jump off.

Or out.

The clock ticked over to the appointed time, and Gus pushed the buzzer, then slammed his fist into the door three times.

"Eric Mill," Gus shouted, getting to one side of the door. "This is Agent Gustavus Hellström with the PID. Could I have a minute of your time?"

Not waiting for an answer, Gus immediately pressed the buzzer again twice more.

There was no response from inside.

Pressing the buzzer again, Gus pounded on the door three more times.

"Eric Mill, we're aware that you're inside the building. We just want to talk to you. If you'd be willing to give us some of your time, this'll go very quickly," Gus shouted again.

His other sense picked something up.

Fear.

A spike of pure, unadulterated fear. Followed by a single gunshot. Whipping out his sidearm, Gus aimed the handgun toward the deadbolt.

The ammo they used was heavy enough to punch a hole through some serious Para heavy hitters. A lock wasn't going to stand up to it.

Though the ammo itself could also be an issue.

Several more gunshots rang out, and then a short powerful blast of what sounded like an explosive. That was followed by two gunshots that were very clearly PID-issued rounds.

Fuck, please don't blow back toward me.

The fear he felt pouring out from the warehouse and beyond it was immense.

When he pulled the trigger, Gus saw the deadbolt explode inward toward the warehouse. Lowering his gun an inch or two, he drew the sight on the locking point for the handle and pulled the trigger again.

Part of the doorknob blew off into the warehouse, and another part splashed back into his hands. Instantly, blood began seeping out from a dozen small cuts.

Shit.

Crashing through the door, Gus entered the warehouse with his weapon drawn. It was a wide-open area with racks, aisles, machinery, and discarded hunks of iron all over. There was no rhyme or reason to it.

It was a rat warren.

The fear he felt spiked hard. Grabbing hold of it, Gus started to scent on it.

Pulling out his radio, he clicked it once, then spoke as softly as he could into it.

"Ness, you alright?" Gus asked, focusing in on the fear he felt and getting closer to a perfect fear scent on it. Trying to figure out where it was coming from. If he could identify Eric, he could track him.

Then the fear scent passed around behind him. It tasted like warmed chocolate. It was simple, rich, and deep.

Vanessa was the fear scent.

"I'm fine," she said over the radio. Her voice was a bit scratchy, and he could almost hear the rising panic in it. "He shot at me, then something exploded and the door got jammed. I fired back. I think I hit him. I'm sorry."

"It's ok. Hold the rear door and call for backup. Shots fired and medical required. I'm going to try and find Eric and render aid," Gus said. He couldn't leave Eric alone if he was down. Mark had made it clear.

"Eric Mill," Gus said loudly, putting his radio away. "This is Agent Hellström. Are you injured? Can you call out to me? I just want to help you."

There.

He felt it. The tiniest flicker of fear. It'd been lost in the tidal wave of fear from Vanessa, but now that he'd scented her, he could separate her out.

Moving toward it, Gus did his best to keep out of its line of sight. It wouldn't do to give Eric a clear shot on him. Injured or not, Eric had made it clear he was more than willing to fire on an officer.

Arguing with himself about putting away his sidearm and drawing the taser, Gus got closer and closer.

"Eric Mill, this is Agent Hellström. We just want to help you. Could you call out to me and let me know where you are?" Gus tried again, then immediately moved another aisle over to displace himself.

The fear coming from Eric was building. Getting stronger as Gus clearly got closer.

Pausing, Gus looked down at his feet when the floor popped. The wood looked rotten. Rotten and with holes in it that seemed to lead into a basement.

He was unhappy with the whole situation but unable to turn away, and there was only one real option.

Press on.

Peeking around the corner, he saw Eric. He was crouched low beside a table, his weapon pointed to where Gus had called out earlier.

Swinging the barrel around to aim at Gus, Eric didn't hesitate and immediately fired.

Having already long dodged back around the corner, Gus saw the round miss him and smash into the pillar next to him. The old rotten wood shattered and splintered, sheared in half, and collapsed.

Then the roof fell down.

And the basement, too.

Chapter 11 - True Fear

Coughing, Gus rolled to one side and looked up above him.

He could see the night sky and what looked like two floors, and where the roof had been. Somehow, he'd not just fallen from the floor he was on, but down into and then below the basement.

Gus watched as more of the roof started to collapse inward, creaking ominously.

Shit, it's still coming down. Going to need to be careful.

There was no way out of the hole he was in, and from what he could see around him, it looked like this was an emergency shelter.

That or a tunnel.

The walls were paved with slick tiles that looked thirty years out of date. Stained with dust, dirt, and long neglect.

Eric crawled out from the rubble nearby, lifted his gun, and fired two more shots. Both went well wide of Gus but sent him scrambling to the floor anyways.

Gus watched Eric vanish down a darkened hallway. Several seconds later, a soft mage-light appeared and kept bobbing down the tunnel.

When Gus thought on the situation, there really was no other option but to get up and follow him.

With a grumble under his breath, Gus reached for his radio. Feeling around at his belt, he realized he had not only lost his radio, but his cell phone and the taser as well.

He looked down to the darkened ground but couldn't see anything. The longer he delayed here, the further Eric would get from him.

Fuck it.

Still holding tight to his pistol, he sprinted after Eric, following the wobbling light far up ahead.

The heady scent of fear washed over Gus as he entered the tunnel. It was thick, real, and absolutely centered on Gus.

Eric was afraid of the agent chasing him.

Suddenly Gus could see in the dark as if the sun was out. His body didn't ache anymore. Catching his breath as if he'd rested for an hour, he chased after the man at a faster pace.

Without wanting to, Gus fear-scented Eric. He tasted like old leather. An old pair of leather dress shoes left in a box after being cleaned.

Gus took hold of his predator self. His Boogieman. The Bogey, as Dave had called him.

He began to work what his mother had always called her horror-magic. She'd taught him how to use it. Channel it.

Create it from fear.

But he'd never gotten into hunting humans the same way she and his sister had. The magic was more instinctive than casting spells, as he'd seen; it had everything to do with fear-scenting, and the hunt.

Along with a whole slew of things Gus didn't want to think about.

Latching onto Eric with his magic, Gus flipped a spell at him. One of the first ones his mother had taught him. Paranoia and panic.

The light in Eric's hand wavered, and Gus swore it looked like the man tripped. Screaming at the top of his lungs, Eric charged on, his voice breaking with the shout.

True fear flooded the tunnel. Like a crashing wave, it blasted Gus. Feeding him and nourishing him.

Gus built up another spell and flicked it ahead, the magical construct traveling along the fear scent toward Eric.

When it touched the Enchanter, what he sensed was fed back to Gus. Even his desires and his goal.

At the end of the tunnel, there was fork. One with several paths to take. Eric wanted to get into the left tunnel, desperately, as quickly as he could.

To leave the agent behind him in the dust.

Gus got the feeling he really didn't want Eric to take that path.

Once more calling up the horror-magic, Gus built an illusion and set it on Eric.

A monster was waiting for him up ahead. It was crouched in the dark, sitting at the mouth of the tunnels.

Waiting for Eric and his glowing ball of light. A foul thing that lived in the dark and delighted on eating the living. Especially those who could use magic.

But it was only a hint when compared to all that was in Eric's mind right now. A creeping fear coming up from the back of his skull that he was being watched. That his magic made him a visible and easy target.

A giant ray of bright fire lanced out from Eric and smashed into the darkness ahead of him. The hint of something in front of him had been more than he could handle. But it also broke Eric off the exit he'd been running for.

Taking a turn toward a door in the wall, Eric flung it open and vanished inside.

Gus could feel the Enchanter going up the steps to whatever was above. When he hit the door at the bottom of the stairwell, Gus started taking the steps as fast as he could. He'd been closing the distance the entire time, and Eric wasn't that far ahead of him anymore.

A door banging open and then slamming shut heralded that Eric had left the stairs.

Ten seconds later and Gus hit the same door, exiting out onto a street in what looked like a commercial district.

Eric was running down the sidewalk, bobbing and weaving amongst the few people who were out and about.

Chasing after the Enchanter once again, Gus had to be a bit more circumspect about what magic he used. Horror-magic could sometimes be visible.

Turning his head, the Enchanter looked over his shoulder. His eyes were wide, his face a mask of fear and shock. He saw Gus chasing him.

Throwing his left arm back, Eric launched a projectile of pure magic. It screamed down the sidewalk toward Gus. Gus side-stepped it with only a foot to spare, then lifted his weapon and pointed it at Eric.

Except he couldn't pull the trigger. There were civilians around, and Mark's warning resounded in his head.

Unfortunately, Eric didn't seem to have any of those concerns. About magic, citizens, or being taken alive.

Eric had to look ahead again or risk running into something or someone.

Feeding his horror-magic, Gus slipped in a fear that if Eric remained in the street or with citizens, the normal police would arrive. And shoot him on sight. That Eric needed to find an abandoned place to hunker down and hide from the PID agent.

Or turn himself in before he got hurt. Which was a much simpler and safer option. He'd probably only get off with a warning because of his family.

At least, that was the thought Gus stuck in there.

Getting off the sidewalk as if he'd had wings attached to his feet, Eric dashed into the road and across the street toward an empty parking lot.

He'd gotten across one side of traffic and was halfway through the other when he got clipped by a taxi-cab.

After getting thrown violently to the ground, Eric tumbled end over end and slid for at least ten feet.

Shit!

Scrambling after him, Gus holstered his gun, sliding it into place and locking the strap over the back of it. This was his one chance to grab Eric before this whole thing got worse.

Gus slammed into the Enchanter as he got up into a kneeling state, driving him back into the roadway. Latching his hands on the other man's wrists, Gus dumped horror-magic straight into him. An overwhelming fear that if he didn't cooperate, Gus might break his hands or arms on accident in trying to subdue him.

"I give up!" shrieked Eric. "I surrender, I surrender, I surrender!"

Cranking back on the other man's hands, Gus snatched his cuffs from his belt and clacked them shut around the Enchanter's wrists.

Letting out a slow, shuddering breath, Gus hung his head.

"Don't hurt me. I didn't do it. I'm innocent," Eric said, his voice sounding beyond panicked.

"Uh huh," Gus grumbled. "You wouldn't believe how often that's the first thing people say."

"Hey, is he ok?" asked the taxi cab driver. He'd stopped his car right there and had his emergency lights on.

"Yeah, he's fine. Hey, got a cell phone? Can I borrow it? I'm a cop but I lost my radio," Gus said, fishing out his medallion from under his coat and holding it out to the driver. "I need to make a call to get a squad car over here."

"Oh! Yeah, sure," the cab driver said, pulling out his phone and handing it over to Gus.

"Thanks," Gus said, then tapped seven-one-one into the phone. Pressing it up to his ear, he waited as the line rang.

With a pop, the line picked up and started up with an IVR service. Not even bothering to listen to it, Gus hit the pound sign, then tapped in his badge number followed by an asterisk.

Listening to the phone, and getting nervous at how many people were starting to come stare, Gus waited, the phone silent. It crackled for a second, and then the line started ringing again.

"PID non-emergency," said a woman over the line. "Agent Hellström, how can I help?"

"I need a pickup for myself and a suspect," Gus said into the line. "Ended a foot chase at—"

Gus paused to look around, trying to figure out what cross streets he was at. Finding a corner, he read the placards.

"Trout and sixth," Gus said, looking back at Eric. "Local will be fine if they're close."

Eric was more or less a gibbering ball of fear right now, and it was making it a little harder than normal for Gus to concentrate due to the constant power wash.

"Received. I have a local coming to your position now for transport," said the dispatcher.

"Thanks, I'll be at the corner itself," Gus said. "Please blank the records on this call with the provider."

"Of course," said the dispatcher, then ended the call.

Gus looked at the phone, then cleared the dialed call record out of the phone itself. Then he held it out to the driver.

"Thank you, sir. I appreciate your assistance. An officer is on his way here. Was there any damage to your vehicle?" Gus asked.

"Nah, he bounced right off the bumper. Not even a blemish. Little chicken-bone thing like him."

"Great. Then have a nice day, sir," Gus said, hauling Eric up to his feet. The adrenaline from the situation was starting to wear off, but the fear kept Gus way too keyed up.

Getting Eric to stand still in cuffs while waiting at the corner of a major intersection was an exercise in futility. Doubly so when Gus started to attract a lot of attention from everyone nearby.

Several minutes passed before a black-and-white rolled up on him. Sitting inside was a younger black officer, possibly in his twenties given his shaved head and youthful face.

"Thanks for coming, Officer. I'm Detective Hellström, out of the ninety-ninth. Just need a lift for myself and my friend here," Gus said.

"No problem, Detective," said the man. "I'm Wilson. Need a hand?"

"Nah, not if your car is anything like ours," Gus said, popping open the door behind Wilson. "Watch your head."

After easing Eric into the car, Gus shut the door and then took in a deep breath. He'd got him. Alive.

Moving around to the passenger side, Gus got in and looked to Wilson.

"Thanks for the assist," he said, slumping into his seat.

"Not a problem. Not the first time I've had to haul one of you ninety-nines around," said Wilson as he pulled the car into traffic.

"Yeah?" Gus asked, not entirely surprised. They were getting into the late hours of the day. Which meant the Para life was starting to spin up rapidly. The normal "day shift" for his precinct was probably already starting to arrive.

"Quite a few, actually. Seems like I'm always being asked to go pick someone up who suddenly doesn't have a way to contact anyone and lost their vehicle," Wilson said. "Doesn't seem like a normal precinct."

"It's not. Not by half. But hey, which one isn't?" Gus said, then closed his eyes.

***

Gus was sitting in Mark's office, feeling quite drawn out and worn down. He'd barely walked into the precinct before Eric was snatched away by someone else and Mark had brought him here.

"Can't believe you got him in alive, and only a fender bender with a citizen," Mark said.

"Well, there's the warehouse that collapsed. Gunfire was exchanged, a bomb went off," Gus said. "And he used magic in public, so that'll be fun to wipe from memories and cameras alike."

Mark waved a hand at the words, as if shooing them away. Leaning back in his chair, he folded his hands behind his head with a wide smile.

"It's going to feel so good to tell the chief about this," Mark said. "He's always such a dickhead. As if it's my fault he didn't get promoted because he's a Para."

"Really?" Gus asked.

"What, the promotion? That's what he says. I think it's because... well... he's a dickhead," Mark said with a shrug.

"You think everyone is a dickhead, including yourself," Gus said, slouching low in his chair.

"That's a good point. I do. And I am," Mark said. Then he sighed, looking at Gus. "Melody and Vanessa are on their way back. They found your cell phone, but your radio and taser are in that rubble somewhere.

"Melody was quite worried for you, apparently. I could hear her in the background while I was talking to Vanessa."

Not responding, Gus sat there and stared at Mark.

"Are you and Melody having fun, Gussy?" Mark asked, his smile getting wider.

Staring at his captain, Gus still said nothing.

"Gonna play house with her, maybe? Partners during the day, partners at night? She's definitely pretty. Way out of my league, personally. Yours too, actually," Mark said.

"Uh huh," Gus grumbled.

"Melody is your permanent partner. Every demand she made was met, and the brass is tickled pink with the idea that Melody Lark is working for a local PID. Can't say I'm unhappy about it; I got a massive raise for apparently convincing her to join," Mark said, his eyes tracking people outside his office as they worked. "I need a favor, Gus."

"What do you want, Durh?" Gus asked, sighing.

"Talk to me about Detective Flores. I have her scheduled for her blank tomorrow. What do I need to know and what do I tell her cap? He's aware of the Para world, but he's kinda unhappy we're going to hand her back with memories gone," Mark said, changing the subject.

"Oh. Yeah. Makes sense. With Eric in custody, there's no need to hang on to her," Gus said with a nod.

"Actually, I scheduled it before you caught Eric. Detective Flores knew about it, too," Mark said, his eyes jumping to Gus and sticking to him. "So? Detective Flores?"

Scratching at his jaw, Gus thought on it.

"Ness is... she's an excellent detective. She's driven, intelligent, determined, and will do what she has to. She'll meet force with force and politeness with politeness. She's versatile, adaptable, and dependable," Gus said honestly. "For the short time she was my partner, I was able to rely on her immediately. She knew how to anticipate me and did what needed to be done.

"I think she'll go far wherever she ends up."

Mark's eyebrows had gone up to the top of his head as soon as Gus started talking.

"Really?" Mark sounded a bit confused. "You'd put your name on her?"

"Yeah. I would. I think she'll outrank me in a couple years if she does even half as good a job back in her department as she did here," Gus said.

"I think I'm jealous, Gussy. You never praise me for anything, and here you're giving her compliments like you've spent the last three days turning her inside out in your car," Mark said, turning to face Gus head on now. "Are you sure?"

Chuckling at that, Gus stared up at the American flag in a shadow box behind Mark. Torn, burnt, and slashed in a few places.

Three soldiers and a flag were all that was left.

"Yeah," Gus said, letting his eyes drop back to Mark. "Mark, she's an amazing detective, and an equally amazing woman. She's young and optimistic. She'll go far."

Mark leaned back in his chair again and nodded. "I'll make sure I put that in my report for her.

"Shame she'll never hear about what you think of her."

Gus shrugged.

"What now? Am I running lead interviewer on Eric?" Gus asked, feeling tired and burnt out.

"No. Not tonight, at least. He's already asked for a lawyer. We've got him on more than a few charges, though I think attempted murder of an officer will keep him right where he is all on its own," Mark said. "For tonight, I think you're better off getting some rest and calling it a day."

Gus got up from the chair and stuffed his hands in his coat pockets. "Anything else then?"

"No, have a good night, Agent Hellström. I'm going to go gloat at the chief," Mark said.

Smirking at that, Gus waved a hand at Mark and left his office.

Only to find himself face to face with Vanessa.

"Oh, oops. Apparently Detective Flores did get to hear everything you thought of her. I didn't even see her standing there when I brought her up," Mark said. "Anyways, have a nice night Gus. Come on in, Detective Flores."

Feeling pretty damn awkward, Gus looked away from Vanessa and stepped around her, then stopped in his tracks.

"Uh… for what it's worth, I meant it," Gus said while looking at her shoes. "You won't know me from a hole in the wall, but I'll stop in just to see how you're doing. Take it easy, Ness."

Not waiting for a reply, Gus left Mark's office and closed the door behind him.

He went over to his desk and sat down at it.

Melody had his car keys and his phone. So until she showed up, he wouldn't be going anywhere.

Sitting in the space between his keyboard and his monitor was a white sticky note. One he had no memory of putting there.

Picking it up, he read it.

Thank you for the hair clip, Detective Hellström. It's very pretty.

~Trish

Smiling to himself, Gus took the note and stuck it to the bottom of his monitor. Then he took a piece of tape from its dispenser and ran it along the top of the sticky note so it wouldn't fall down and get lost.

All around him, people were working. Starting their shifts and pulling out cases from the previous day. Or new ones they'd just gotten. The sound of so many people in his office at the same time was momentarily disturbing to Gus. It was never this loud.

Putting his hands on his keyboard, Gus considered logging in. If only to look like he was working rather than sitting there.

"There you are," Melody said, walking into the open layout of the department.

A number of heads turned toward her.

"Oh, hello everyone. I'm Agent Lark." Melody waved to everyone, then sat down at the desk right next to Gus's. "I'm Agent Hellström's new partner. I look forward to working with you all."

Melody turned to Gus and gave him a bright smile, holding out his cell phone.

"Ready to go home? I can't wait to talk about today. I want to hear everything that happened. Maybe over dinner?" she asked.

More heads turned their way, watching the strange situation playing out. At this point, office gossip would have him banging Melody eight ways from Sunday no matter what he did.

"Yep," Gus said, not even bothering to try and do anything about it. "Why not."

Chapter 12 - New Partner

Opening his bedroom door, Gus found Melody in his kitchen once again. She was fussing with something in the toaster oven.

She was dressed in a short black coat, a white blouse, and a black dress that went to her ankles, with her hair once more pulled back into a single ponytail.

All in all, she looked professional and very tasteful, but her look was also a definite "call to arms" so to speak when it came to getting attention.

Taking a moment, Gus looked down at her feet. She had on a pair of black flats that looked well enough.

"No heels today," Melody said, apparently catching his look. "Why, did you like seeing me in them? Not intimidated by a woman who's taller than you?"

Now that he thought about it, she might be an inch taller than him normally. In heels she would tower over him.

"Not really," Gus said, moving into the kitchen. "I could always just eat you. Tall or not."

He'd said it casually, but it wasn't untrue.

Having fear-scented her, it was just a question of running her down till her body gave out, then eating her soul.

Melody gave him a strange smile. There was no fear coming from her, though. Not a single hint of it.

Realizing that she wasn't concerned about him, he went over to the coffee machine.

"Coffee?" he asked.

With a loud crack, she slapped him on the ass when he walked by her. Making Gus stand straight as a ramrod.

He'd never had someone be so forward with him.

"I like it when you're bold," she said. "Maybe later I can work up some fear and you can dig in a bit. Might be fun to watch you dine on me. Then maybe you can eat something else after that.

"And yes, coffee please. One sugar cube, enough creamer to make it brown. I'm finishing your breakfast right now. I filled it with all the fear I had for you yesterday. You'll have to tell me if it worked again."

Shaking his head, Gus pushed a traveler mug into the machine's spout, threw in a pod, and tapped the button.

"We never got around to talking about the woman from last night," Gus said, turning around to face Melody.

She was bent over, staring into the toaster oven. Unable to help himself, he took a minute to appreciate just how beautiful she was.

Especially from behind.

"Oh yeah, I forgot about that," Melody said. Then she opened the door to the appliance and pulled out what looked like a croissant. Stuffed with things between its two halves. "I was just happy to have dinner with you.

"As for the woman, I followed her for a while. She went a block away, got in a car, and they were gone in a flash. I didn't even have time to get a license plate. Just got in and boom." Melody stood up. Pulling off the top piece of the sandwich, she dipped a spoon into a small bowl nearby and smeared the contents all over the inside of the bread. "It was like they knew I was there and wanted to get her out quick. This is all starting to feel like a conspiracy."

Gus couldn't help but agree. Things weren't adding up in a normal way for him. This didn't feel like a murder or a normal crime. Everything was starting to feel much more like things were taking a decidedly planned-out-in-advance type of turn.

He was especially curious what they'd find in that warehouse. It wasn't as if Eric could have just gotten another apartment somewhere else. That warehouse had been chosen for some reason.

Nothing added up right now. Everything felt like it was missing bits and pieces.

"Ok. Check your internal Boogieman fear gauge, or whatever it is, and eat this," Melody said, turning toward him and holding up a small plate. Sitting atop it was the croissant sandwich.

He didn't feel like he needed any fear at the moment, but he wasn't "full" either. He'd probably end up having to find a source tonight or tomorrow morning.

Picking it up, he took a bite without hesitation. If Melody wanted to harm him, she'd had every chance to do so up to this point.

Immediately, he knew it was first and foremost delicious. Once again, she'd somehow made it absolutely amazing.

"Dunno about the fear yet," Gus said, unable to help himself even though he was still chewing. "But you make amazing food."

"Yeah? You should Contract with me. I'll make whatever food you want," Melody said, grinning at him.

Shaking his head at that, Gus continued to chew.

Ham, cheese, croissant, and the sauce tastes like…

Gus's eyebrows slowly went up. It tasted like spiced mint. And a hint of… copper. A coppery taste he knew instantly.

She'd actually managed to put her fear into the food. Though it seemed like she'd done it through her blood, or she was adding her blood to his food in some type of Contractor magic.

"Why not?" Melody asked.

Looking at her, Gus swallowed. "What?"

"Why not Contract with me? I'm beautiful, I'm smart, I'm funny, and I'm desperately in love with you. I want to make this work. I think you're amazing. You're so strong, so unique, and so humble," Melody said. "I've tracked down and killed men with half your talent who did ten times more damage. Do you have any idea how rare telepathy is? It's one in billions.

"Billions. The vast majority of people don't even worry about it because it's so rare. And that's telepathy. If you were trained to become a psyker, you'd… I don't even know."

Clearing his throat, Gus looked at the ground.

"First of all, you managed to do it. You definitely put your fear into the food. It's… I don't even know how to describe it. It's nice to be able to fill my stomach and my needs at the same time," Gus said. "Second, why are you putting your blood in it?

"Lastly… why not… because I honestly barely know you. For all the reasons you just listed as well. You are beautiful, and intelligent, and talented, and frightening as hell. You're also way more experienced then I am, and your bankroll is probably massive.

"You're just… everything. And that terrifies me."

"You can taste it? My blood?" Melody asked.

"Yeah," Gus said, then took another bite.

"Wait, because I'm so great you don't want to contract with me?"

"And, you know, because we just met. Contracting is a permanent thing, isn't it? But yeah, you're extremely intimidating. The idea of a woman like you being interested in me doesn't seem real," Gus said, not stopping at all in eating the food she'd made.

Melody nodded slowly, her eyes thoughtful. Then she looked at him with a bright smile.

"I love you, Gus. I only want to ever contract with one man, and you're him. You'll see. I'm flattered you ate the meal despite knowing my blood was in it," Melody said.

Gus shrugged, finishing the sandwich completely. "Was delicious. Your blood isn't bad tasting either. A little sweeter than normal, a nice addition. Makes me wonder what your heart would taste like."

Finally, Melody froze for a second, and just a whiff of fear trailed up from her.

You forgot what I truly am, didn't you? Thought I was teasing?

My kind eats everyone else. Soul, heart, blood, bones, whatever we can get, so long as it's through fear.

Giving her a smile, Gus picked up the coffee he'd made for her and held it out.

"Here's your coffee, hon," Gus said, feeling better for having put her off balance.

***

Rolling into the office right on time, Gus was surprised.

Mark was there with a packet of papers in his hand. Waiting for him.

"Morning Gus, Miss Lark," Mark said, nodding at the two of them. Then he held out the paperwork to Melody. "Here's your official paperwork for everything you requested, your job offer, and everything you'll need to know."

Mark patted the desk that faced straight at Gus's.

"And this is your desk. Your sidearm, locker key, and medallion are in the top drawer. Make sure you drop by the armory to collect everything else you'll need. I didn't assign you a car since you're partners with Gus and he has an official vehicle assigned," Mark said. "Everything alright with that, Miss Lark?"

Melody was beaming from ear to ear as she took the paperwork.

"Yes. Yes, it is, Mark," Melody said, flipping through the papers quickly. "This is so exciting. Was my request for permanency approved?"

"Yes. Gus is your permanent partner going forward, unless you ask to change it." Mark gave Gus an apologetic shrug.

"I won't. He's mine," Melody said, snapping the paperwork shut.

"But I do have one surprise for the two of you that I feel is non-negotiable," Mark said. "And there she is."

Mark pointed behind them, grinning.

Turning around, Gus found Vanessa standing there. She was dressed in her normal business wear and looked a bit nervous. Hanging around her neck was a medallion that looked just like Gus's.

"Mark? Did you make her an agent?" Melody asked.

"I did. She's going to be a partner to both of you. You're a three-person team now," Mark said, walking away from them. "Alright. I need to get over to the PID holding station. Eric's lawyer is coming in today, and I'm trying to arrange an interview today. I'll let you know when to be there if I get it."

The door closed, leaving the three of them alone in the office space.

"You uh… said you wanted a three-way," Vanessa said, sounding very unsure of herself. "Guess you got what you wanted?"

Melody laughed at that and then bounced over to her, holding out a hand.

"Congratulations, Agent Flores. Getting into PID isn't easy." Melody grabbed a hold of her hand. "Which desk is yours?"

"I'm right behind Gus, I guess," Vanessa said.

"Oh? Good. How'd things go last night?" Melody asked.

Ah. The Werewolf conversation part two. I think I'll start in on today's workload.

Pulling his coat off, Gus dropped it onto a hook on the hanger and went to his desk.

He logged in, then opened up his email and started reading through them. Doing everything in his power to not hear anything Melody and Vanessa were discussing.

It was none of his business, and he'd played his part yesterday per Melody's request.

***

"Who's the Fae?" Gus asked, pointing at the winged, suited man sitting next to Eric. "I mean, clearly it's his lawyer, so don't start with that. But I've never seen him before."

Mark shrugged.

"One Anthony Dao. He seems nitpicky to me already, and I've only had to talk to him for about two minutes," Mark said. "Alright, it's your case, and he's your collar. So it's your interview.

"Remember, we've got him more or less locked up on what you saw, and maybe the DME manager. Nothing on Fitz. I'd work backward if I were you."

"Not doing it," Gus said, then hooked a thumb at Vanessa. "She's going to interview him. I'm going to sit there and stare at him. Melody is going to play secondary to Vanessa."

Mark raised a brow at that, but said nothing. He knew everything Gus could do. He'd seen him at the absolute worst and lowest point in both of their lives.

"Your play," Mark said, then looked back to the monitor showing the interior of the room Eric was in.

Melody and Vanessa already knew the plan. He'd told them what he wanted on the way to the PID holding station.

All Paras suspected of a crime, awaiting transfer, or going through appeals in the area were housed here.

Thankfully, it wasn't over capacity or suffering a shortage of guards.

Mostly because it was all Paras housed here.

"Alright, let's go get this rolling then," Gus said to his two partners.

Vanessa nodded, then took in a quick breath and let it out again. Once it was obvious she'd gotten her thoughts together, she opened the door and left the surveillance room. Melody and Gus went in behind her.

Turning to the first door on the right, Vanessa knocked twice, then waited a second and opened it.

She stepped into the interviewing room and vanished.

"Good afternoon, I'm Agent Vanessa Flores," she said.

Melody went through the door next, quickly followed by Gus.

The interior of the room looked much the same as it had through the monitor.

Eric looked just as young and confident as Gus remembered. In fact, he'd almost say the prisoner looked arrogant somehow.

And Mr. Dao looked like every other Fae Gus had ever met. Pretty, winged, and snobby. Then again, Gus had only ever met Fae lawyers. They tended to come in one flavor.

Dickhead.

"These are Agents Melody Lark and Gustavus Hellström. How are you today, Mr. Mill?" Vanessa asked.

"Fine," Eric said, glaring up at the three officers.

"I was hoping to ask you some questions," Vanessa said to Eric before looking to the lawyer.

"Mr. Mill is prepared to answer some questions. Though he'll decline a formal statement at this time. Other than that, we're listening," said the lawyer.

In other words… unless we've got something, this is pointless. They'll hear us out on a deal, though.

Posting up in the corner, Gus crossed his arms and did his best impression of a framed picture.

"Why's that?" Melody asked, sitting down at the table across from Eric. Vanessa sat across from Mr. Dao.

"Why's what?" Eric asked.

"That you don't want to make a statement," Melody said. She put one elbow down on the table and put her chin in it, then slowly leaned forward. "It's your right, of course; it just seems weird."

Eric's eyes went down to Melody's chest. Gus couldn't see it from here, but he was sure she was giving him a good view. Probably hoping to trip him up or get him to answer her.

Taking this as his opportunity, Gus slipped a thread-thin piece of telepathy straight into Eric's skull. He could work more of his power in as time went on, but he'd have to start small.

Enchanters were tricky things when it came to telepathy.

"I just don't want to, that's all," Eric said before the lawyer could respond. Mr. Dao was starting to look frustrated.

"I mean, you know we've got you on some of this, right?" Melody asked.

"Mr. Mill isn't saying anything about that," Mr. Dao said.

Gus got the brief impression of anger, and flashes of the events from the previous day.

Seeing Vanessa outside and shooting at her, then shooting at Gus once he was inside. The resentment at being caught, and how it had all gone down.

Eric saw himself as the next master Enchanter. He thought all of this was beneath him.

"Certainly he has to have something to say about the fact that he used magic in public, attempted to kill an officer, and possessed an unlicensed and unregistered fire arm?" Vanessa asked, her pen stationary on the pad of paper she'd brought in with her.

Eric rolled his eyes and looked away. Not saying anything.

In his mind, though, he replayed all those events quickly. When he got to the gun, an attached memory bubbled up with the thought.

He'd stolen it from a cousin who'd left it behind on accident when he moved to another state, then filed off anything that would identify it. It was registered out of state with the cousin, which meant it wasn't legal here and probably wouldn't show up in a database search.

Loading up that small bit of information into a thought of his own, Gus gently pushed it into Melody's head without entering her mind.

Her body tensed for a split second, and then she sat upright.

"Where'd you get the gun?" Melody asked.

Eric still didn't say anything, preferring to inspect the light above them.

"Get it from a family member?" Melody asked. "Father?"

Eric still said nothing, didn't even look down.

"Mother, maybe? Brother? Sister? Your family is rather large," Melody said. She was clearly baiting him. Leading him to the memory Gus had put there. There was still no response from Eric. "A cousin, maybe?"

Eric's jaw flexed, but he still made no move or comment.

"Alright. A cousin. We'll start there. Probably out of state since there's nothing on file here?" Melody asked. "That's beside the point, though. Let's move to the next question of the day."

"You were seen entering your apartment building with Blake Johnson. How do you know him?" Vanessa asked, picking up from Melody.

Eric shook his head outright now, his arms tightening around his middle.

From inside his mind, Gus saw Blake meeting Eric for breakfast somewhere. He was loyal to the Mill family for something unrelated, and he was giving Eric a heads up. Warning him about the detectives who were after him.

Blake promised that he'd made sure to remove Eric's name from the only file that had been left on the computer.

Eric invited Blake back to his apartment at that point. He walked him into his apartment but didn't go in with him. Eric shut the door behind Blake.

Then he left. Before he made it to the end of the hallway, the TV turned on, the volume at max level. Followed by what Eric thought were gunshots.

He didn't know who had been in the room, but it was someone arranged to be there. To take care of Blake.

Eric had called in the problem to his handlers on a secure number on a burner phone. After the call was made, the phone was ditched.

Bundling all that up again into something manageable, Gus slipped it into Melody's mind once more.

All the while, Vanessa had been slowly asking Eric questions. Questions that had triggered more memories and thoughts that Gus had been following.

"Eric," Melody said, before Vanessa could ask the next question. "The camera has you walking in with Blake. No one can say otherwise. It's plain as day.

"Your neighbor saw you in the hallway, and then heard your TV playing very loud action movies.

"The camera never saw you leave."

Shit, that's a good point. If the camera never saw him leave, how'd he get out?

Waiting in Eric's brain for an answer, Gus was surprised. Nothing came up. It was as if Eric didn't know how he'd done it either.

"Then we find Blake in your bathtub, shot repeatedly, and you're gone. Help me out here, how does that happen?" Melody asked. "Maybe he attacked you? You had to defend yourself?"

The slugs they'd pulled out of the wall from behind where Blake had been shot revealed it'd been a heavy-caliber weapon. But they'd found no shell casings.

Either the shooter cleaned them up, or it was a revolver. For all this, though, it meant the gun he'd been found with wasn't the murder weapon.

"Or did someone else do it?" Melody finally asked.

A flash of eyes skidded through Eric's mind and then vanished. It was a partial memory, deep in his head. One that Gus wouldn't be able to get to without some time to pry at his thoughts.

Eric sighed, not saying anything.

Vanessa took that as her cue to continue.

"And what about Michael Fitz? Did you know him?" Vanessa asked.

"I'm sure you did," Melody immediately added, not waiting. "You deliberately messed up the enchantment on him for some reason. Maybe because he turned you down when you asked him out. Then you had Blake cover it up for you, which is why he had to die."

Eric's mind flashed with hatred for Melody, but he said and did nothing. As for thoughts of Michael Fitz, only a brief flash of memory about him being a Troll. And that a Troll was what Eric needed most.

But there was nothing about why that was so.

"I mean, unless you're just a garbage Enchanter," Melody said with a snicker, leaning further back in her chair. Away from Eric. "Maybe this is all just an accident that happened because you're so bad at your job. How many others did you screw up because of your incompetence?"

As he turned his head toward Melody, it was clear to anyone that Eric was enraged.

"What, lawyer got your tongue? Don't even have the balls to admit you just fucked up? Shit," Melody said, shaking her head. "You're just a little boy, running and hiding because you screwed everything up. Maybe we should call your daddy to come fix your life."

Melody sighed and looked at Mr. Dao.

"Let me guess, his daddy hired you. Not Eric. You're baby-boy Eric's bailout?" Melody said with a chuckle. "You wipe his ass and set up playdates for him, too?"

"I'm nobody's bailout!" Eric shouted. "And I didn't fuck up that damn Troll's enchantment. It must have just failed because he was messing with it. They're all as stupid as rocks anyways."

Vanessa coughed politely, then smiled at Eric.

"I never said it was a Troll, Eric. Could you elaborate on that?" Vanessa asked.

Mr. Dao stood up, laying a hand on Eric's shoulder. "I think that's all for my client today. He'll be invoking his right to remain silent at this time. Thank you, Agents."

Chapter 13 - Skewered

Gus didn't bother to leave the interview room. Both Vanessa and Melody took their direction from his own response to the statement from Mr. Dao.

"Great," Gus said. "We'll be sure to put your client back for you."

Mr. Dao looked flustered at the idea that he wouldn't get a chance to speak with his client.

"Say nothing," Dao said to Eric, then stood up and waited quietly. "I'll be here until—"

Two uniformed officers came in and collected Eric. Shackling his hands behind his back as they did so.

"Until?" Gus asked, looking at Dao, raising his eyebrows.

Clearing his throat, the lawyer said nothing and left the interview room quickly.

Moving to the other side of the table, Gus sat down where Dao had been.

"That was uneventful," Vanessa said with a glum look on her face. "It's never easy when they lawyer up."

Gus chuckled at that and looked to the door. He was figuring Mark would be joining them shortly. Probably give them some marching orders and send them on their way.

Technically speaking, the case of Michael Fitz's death was over. The culprit was apprehended, and he'd more than likely go down on a double murder and attempted murder.

Off to the great white north with you. Good luck, Eric.

Don't drop the soap. There's more in those prisons than those who want a go at you.

With a creak, the door opened and Mark stepped in. Hands in his pockets, he looked pleased with himself and rather happy.

"You look like Megan told you you're getting a special surprise you can record tonight," Gus said.

"I wish," Mark said and blew a raspberry. "No, but my day is going just as good, honestly. If not better than that."

"Do tell. Because I was in that interview just now and it felt like the prosecutor was going to have a long road to getting Eric convicted," Gus said.

"That? Hm. Yeah, but we knew that going in. You definitely poked some holes in there, and it sounds like there's some minor things to follow up on, but it's done," Mark said with a shrug. "They'll make a deal he can't refuse. Something like two counts of murder-two and forty years. Parole in twenty. He's an Enchanter so that's not much off his clock."

Melody made a harrumph-like noise, and Vanessa just nodded.

The court system was overloaded. If a deal could be reached, it almost always would be. Especially if a more powerful family was involved, like the Mills.

It wasn't any different than on the Norm side of the equation.

"No, I'm so damn happy because of you three," Mark said, grinning. "I've got Gus actually working cases. I never thought it'd happen.

"I 'somehow' managed to hire Melody Lark, a name that almost every Para law enforcement agency knows, and her requirements weren't terrible.

"Last, I've brought on a potential superstar rookie and got the Lark and my very own Gussy training her."

Mark paused and then laughed.

"And on top of that, the Curator sent a very nice note about an extremely professional agent in my employ who visited him. That he'd be more than happy to cooperate with the PID in the future as well if he could expect the same level of courtesy. And sent it to my boss. And his boss's boss." Mark leaned his head back and actually laughed for a few seconds before looking back at Gus. "My world is so damn positive right now, I can't wait to see what Troll bends me over a bench and manhandles me when my luck inevitably fails."

Gus snorted at that and shook his head.

"Just make sure you get the reach-around. What'd ya want?" Gus asked. "You seem like you have a need."

"I do," Mark said, and then he looked to Melody. "I've got some Contractors here today and would-bes. They're all local PID. Any chance I can convince you to give them friendly pointers? I wouldn't be averse to you making a Contract with them in exchange for whatever you offer them. Just make sure it's legal."

Melody's eyebrows went up slowly. "You want me to help Contractors in the PID?"

"Yep. It's not an order, obviously; it's a request. So… name your price," Mark said.

Melody immediately looked to Gus, then back to Mark. "I want to know how you know Gus."

Mark's face blanked at that, and his eyes became nothing more than reflective glass without life. It was obvious to anyone looking that Mark had gone straight to DEFCON 1.

"I'm afraid that isn't negotiable," Mark said, his tone having become quite cold.

Melody sensed the roadblock that'd come up.

"I'm sorry, I just thought I'd ask. You two are so close, and I want to be so much more to Gus, that I just… want to know more," Melody said sincerely. "I'll speak with the Contractors as a personal courtesy to you, Mark. Though if you can share any stories about Gus later, I'd be deeply appreciative of it."

The mask Mark had put on started to slowly give way as she spoke. Till finally it fell away and he was smiling at her genuinely again.

"You're a good lady, Miss Lark. I'll be happy to tell you about my sweet Gussy. Just later. And where I'm far enough away to run from him." Mark then looked to Vanessa. "As for you, Detective Flores, I think you should go say goodbye to your old precinct, collect your stuff, and settle in here. Today's Friday anyways, and you're working the Monday-through-Friday shift with Gussy. Consider that your end of day work."

In other words, he has nothing to give us, so it's clean up and get ready for next week.

Maybe it'll slow down and I can just… do my normal routine.

Rolling back into the office by himself, Gus rubbed a hand against the back of his neck. He just needed to close out a few files, clean up his inbox, and then he could go home and call it a day.

As he walked into the building, Gus's phone chimed.

He pulled his phone out and looked at the front of it even as his feet carried him onward on autopilot.

"Don't forget to be here tomorrow, sweetie. Or I'll send your sister out to go Hunt you," wrote his mom in a text.

Shit. Forgot about that. I'm sure Melody hasn't.

Dismissing the message, Gus stuffed the phone back into his pocket and looked at his desk.

Only to come face to face with Trish the cleaning lady.

She was standing in the aisle next to his desk. Her cap was pulled off, and the cleaning outfit she normally wore was gone. In its place was a brand-new uniform that fit her better and didn't make her look like a shapeless lump.

In fact, she had an extremely flattering and eye-catching figure. Like something out of one of the hundreds of magazines, pictures, and other terrible things he'd entertained himself with when he'd been deployed. Except she was better than that, too.

She smiled at him and Gus was immediately struck with how pretty she was on top of everything else. Her white hair was pulled back from her face and gathered behind her head. Her eyes were a vibrant green that practically glowed from within.

He'd known she was attractive; it was one of the reasons he'd been curious about her. But he hadn't really known she was this pretty.

"Hello Detective," said Trish, her left hand holding the large trash can she was wheeling around, a small bin in her other hand.

"Hey, Trish," Gus said. Slowly, he walked around her to his desk. "How's it going?"

"Not bad," she said. "It's Friday so… you know… yay. Friday."

Grinning to himself at the awkward exchange, Gus was flattered. He wasn't an idiot, nor a dense moron.

Trish was interested in him, or she wanted to be friends with him. Her entire demeanor had changed since he'd seen her last.

The only problem was she was far too pretty to be so awkward. Which meant she was probably a Para that didn't interact with humanity very well.

There was no mask around her to disguise her features, though. For all intents and purposes, she looked human.

"How about you, Detective?" she asked as she put the trash can back.

"As you said, it's Friday," Gus said, quickly working through the reports he needed to finish. "Looking forward to doing as little as I can. How about you?"

"Me? Oh, I'm meeting with a few friends. Going to maybe go out. Hang out with my cat," Trish said.

Grinning, Gus sent his last report, then clicked through the few emails he had.

Just in time, too—Trish was coming over to his desk.

Reaching under it, he picked up his trash can and held it out for her.

"Here you go, Trish. And it's Gus. Not Detective, or Detective Hellström," Gus said.

Trish smiled, took the trash can, and emptied it into the larger one. Then she held it back out to him. "Thanks, Gus."

Nodding his head, he took the can back from her and put it under his desk.

Trish continued on with her work, emptying cans at each desk.

"I'm out for the day. You have a good night, Trish," Gus said, locking his computer and getting up.

She gave him a glance over her shoulder and waved a gloved hand at him before she turned back to her work. "You too, Gus."

Pausing for a second, he realized she was wearing the hair clip he'd given her. Gus smiled to himself, then left and headed home.

***

Gus was driving toward his mom's house. Melody was sitting in the passenger seat, looking equal parts excited and nervous. Clutched between her hands was her cell phone.

"Are you sure the dress looks good?" Melody asked for perhaps the twelfth time. One of her hands smoothed down the lovely blue-and-white sundress she was wearing.

"Melody, you're beautiful. Ok? The dress only adds to that," Gus finally said, getting tired of her asking about the dress. He meant it too. She looked great in it.

He'd only told her it was fine up to this point.

"Really?" she asked, turning to him with a smile. "You mean that?"

"That you're beautiful or the dress?" Gus said.

"Both."

"Yes, I do mean what I said about both."

Melody made a funny humming noise and settled back into her seat. Looking much more pleased and confident all of a sudden.

Ok… next time… compliment her and the dress. Don't just tell her it's fine.

Melody's phone lit up, then started ringing.

"It's Vanessa," Melody said, a frown appearing on her pretty face. Accepting the call, she pressed the phone to her ear. "What's up, Vanessa?"

There was some chatter coming back to her from the other side of the phone. Gus couldn't make out a damn word and honestly wasn't that concerned. Vanessa wasn't his problem if they weren't at work.

Melody was mostly doing this as a charity case as part of her contract.

"That's… not surprising," Melody said.

There was an angry response. Followed immediately by what sounded like a much softer question.

"Somewhat. Going to Gus's parents' house for lunch," Melody said, turning to Gus and giving him a smile.

I wonder what's happening.

Melody didn't say anything for a bit as Vanessa talked steadily on the other end.

"No, that doesn't really sound like a healthy thing to do. One second. Let me see if I can sweet-talk Gus into something," Melody said, and then she tapped a button on her phone. "Gus? Honey? My love? Sweetie?"

Feeling like he was about to get hit with something he really didn't want, Gus decided the best course of action was to pull over.

Easing off to the side of the road, he pulled into a gas station and parked in front of the store.

"Yes, Melody?" Gus asked, turning to face her directly.

"I can promise to be a good or a bad girl, depending on whichever way you want it, if you do me a favor," Melody said, grinning at him.

Shaking his head with a soft sigh, Gus couldn't help but smile back at her. "What is it?"

"Let's go pick up Vanessa and take her to your parents. Her Were girlfriend just stormed off on her after she found out she formally joined the PID. I don't want to leave her alone. She's our partner," Melody said. "Besides, this is a good opportunity for me to try and get her into a three-way relationship with us. She's such a lovely woman, and I know she'll balance us perfectly."

"Melody, we're not even in a relationship ourselves," Gus said, flabbergasted. "And you said you were just trying to help her. Remember?"

"I know. But now I kinda want her for myself, and for you. And yes, we are in a relationship, honey. You just… keep denying it," Melody said, and one of her hands came up to gently brush something off his collar.

"Err, did I smudge it? It's from when I touched the garage door, isn't it?" Gus asked, tilting his head away but leaning towards Melody to look at it.

"Probably. Don't worry, it's nothing though, honey, one second," Melody said, licking a finger and gently dabbing at whatever it was. "There we are, I got it. Now, let's go pick up Vanessa. Ok?"

Gus sighed.

He was ultimately coming to the conclusion that Melody wasn't wrong. That he'd somewhere along the line surrendered to her being a massive part of his life. She'd forced her way in and was ever worming herself deeper.

He refused to Contract with her, though, until they were much further along in whatever this was. He needed to know a lot more about her and—

Melody leaned over the center console and hugged him tightly.

"Thank you, Gus. I love you," Melody said, and she gave him a quick peck on the lips before sitting back in her seat. "We're coming to pick you up. Put on a nice sundress. Something that shows off just a little skin, but not much. Gus will like it, and his mom isn't traditional so it'll be fine.

"Yes, he said it was fine. We pulled over to get gas real quick."

Gus sighed, shaking his head a bit, and pulled back onto the road with a tired smile. He wheeled the car around and pointed it back toward the city to get Vanessa.

It'd only take him an extra ten minutes, and they'd probably arrive earlier than when he said they'd be there anyways.

"We'll just say you're our girlfriend," Melody said, then fell silent at whatever response she got back.

"No, he can't hear me. He's getting something at the gas station," Melody lied. "Blue and white. Just a little cleavage. No heels, he likes your height just fine."

Gus rolled his eyes. Melody was maneuvering Vanessa as terrifyingly well as she'd probably manipulated him.

"Pin it back, nothing on your neck. It'll show off your complexion more. Gus will like it. He looks at your neck a lot.

"Mm? Uhm… I never asked," Melody said, looking over to Gus. "That's a tough one. I mean, how do you ask Gus 'Do you think Vanessa looks better with earrings or without?' without him getting suspicious? It was hard enough to get him to agree to dating me. It'll be harder still to get him to date you."

There was a loud response to that, which died off halfway through. Followed by a question.

Gus reached over and tapped the studs in Melody's ears, and then gave a thumbs up. Melody grinned at him, wrinkling her nose and sticking her tongue out.

"You're not wrong," she said, and paused again. "Yeah, he'd take you to bed in a heartbeat and show you, I'm sure. Ask him."

Gus wondered if he'd ever get back to normalcy.

"Hmm. Ok. Go with studs for your ears. Something simple," Melody said.

Forty minutes later, Gus rolled up to his parents' house on the other side of the city. In a different suburb. They owned a five-acre property at the end of the street, and a rather large house. They'd paid quite a bit to get it.

Gus opened the rear driver's side door for Vanessa, then closed it after she got out.

She was dressed up in a blue-and-white sundress that did exactly what Melody told her to do. Just a hint of cleavage, diamond stud earrings, nothing on her neck, and looking rather pretty with her hair pulled back.

Moving to the passenger side, Gus opened the door for Melody next.

"Oh my, this is such a cute home," Melody said, getting out and patting Gus's arm. "We should buy a house over here and be closer to them. Does your sister live around here?"

"Not far," Gus admitted.

"It's settled. Vanessa, we're going to buy a house over here and move in. How long do you have on your apartment?" Melody asked.

"Wha—? Mel! Stop it! We talked about this. I'm not… I'm not… No! This—"

"How long?" Melody asked, ignoring her.

"Four months," Vanessa said finally, coming over to stand next to Melody.

"Don't renew the contract, sweetie. We'll buy a house together over here," Melody said, not taking no for an answer and wrapping an arm around Vanessa. "It'll be our Contract present to each other. We can all chip in a third and make it ours."

"Mel, I don't have that kind of money," Vanessa said.

"Don't you worry. It'll work out. Your pay just skyrocketed with your promotion, remember?" Melody said.

She was rapidly nodding her head now, as if approving all her plans in her head. Then she held her arms out above her.

"I can't believe how lucky I am," she said to no one. "I never thought I'd be this lucky."

Rolling his eyes, having long gotten used to Melody by now, Gus started walking up the path to his parents' home. Vanessa fell in at his side while Melody did her thing behind them in the driveway.

"She's so pushy," Vanessa grumbled.

Gus shrugged his shoulders, walked up to the door and then knocked.

"It's part of what makes her—her. And… I kinda like it. Sometimes," Gus said with a smile at Vanessa. "Speaking of liking, you look wonderful. The earrings, the hair, the dress. It's just my family, you know; you didn't have to dress up so well for them. They won't believe what Melody says anyways."

Vanessa gave him a strange smile, then looked to the door as it opened.

Standing at a paltry five foot three was his mom, regarding him with a smile from the doorway.

Looking exactly as he remembered her. Her physical age looked like she was at the top of her twenties, even though Gus knew she was at least well into her late forties, early fifties. Her long, dark-red hair was swept back, and her light-brown eyes were without glasses today.

She was wearing a dress very similar to the ones Melody and Vanessa were wearing, just a bit longer, and darker in color.

His sister and his mom were beautiful, of course, and looked like sisters at this point. It was part of being a hunter. A predator had to draw in prey.

Looking young and pretty did that.

"Oh!" his mom said, turning her smile on Vanessa, then to Melody behind her. "I… didn't expect Gus to bring a lady, let alone two. Come in, come in."

Stepping to the side of the door, his mom got the three of them inside and shut the door.

"Mom, this is Vanessa Flores, an agent at the PID, and Melody Lark, also an agent at the PID," Gus said, introducing both women. "Ladies, this is my mother. Jennifer Hellström."

Clicking her tongue, his mom gave him a reproachful look.

"You got my hopes up. I thought you brought a lady friend for once," she said.

"He did," Melody said, and then stepped straight up to the smaller woman and held out a hand. "We're both his girlfriends. I'm a Contractor."

Melody's contracts flared to life in a brilliant haze of colors, as if to make sure she was being honest and direct.

His mom's face changed quickly from mother to something else, and she took Melody's hand in her own.

Gus felt a tiny fluttering of fear from Melody. The taste of it was strange, and Gus needed a moment to identify it.

He figured it out in short order, though. It even made sense, but he was mildly surprised. Her fear had nothing to do with his mother being what she was. But simply because it was his mom.

"Goodness," his mom said, releasing Melody's hand. Vanessa was there to immediately shake his mother's hand after that. "Two? And so suddenly? And a Rainbow Contractor no less. I love your dresses. You're both so lovely."

"I'm just a human," Vanessa said almost apologetically.

"So? Human is just fine," his mom said, immediately sensing that Vanessa didn't know what they were. "Now, let's go see the rest of the family. Right down the hall, dears."

Melody and Vanessa smiled, nodded, and started trooping down the hall.

His mom gave him a strange look and then a massive grin. She mouthed the word "Two" and shook her head.

She did look proud, though. Oddly enough.

Great.

Just great.

Chapter 14 - Herald

Walking into the family living room, Gus looked around. Melody and Vanessa were being led straight over to his sister, his mom already chatting with them as they went.

"Hey bud," said his father's voice in his mind. His father's telepathic control was scalpel sharp. Gus hadn't even felt him enter. Gus's power was significantly stronger, but he had nowhere near the same precision. *"Two girlfriends, huh?"*

"Not really. Well. Maybe. Melody is running me down and I think I realized I'd given up on the way over," Gus sent back as he walked up to where his mother was making introductions.

"I remember doing that to your mother. She may make it seem like it was mutual, but she ran away for a good while," said his father with a mental chuckle. *"I'm outside doing the grilling. Come say hi in a bit. I've got your sister's boyfriend out here. He seems nice.*

"Your girlfriends… Melody and Vanessa, right?"

"Yep. See you soon, Dad," Gus sent. Vanessa and Melody were done being introduced to his sister, so he walked up to his sister and hugged her.

"Hey," he said, crushing her as best as he could.

"Hi brother," Paris wheezed out. "Let go, you big oaf."

Grinning, Gus stepped back and looked at his sister. She was the same as ever. A mirror image of their mother, just taller.

Melody had somehow peeled his mom off to one side with Vanessa, and the three women were already deep in some discussion.

"I hear you brought your newest plaything," Gus said. His sister had a tendency to burn through men fast and furiously.

Shaking her head, Paris grinned at him.

"Nope, not a plaything. He's very nice, and I need you to help me with him. I want to keep him, so… please… make me look good?" his sister asked, looking up at him.

Holy fuck.

Gus's danger sense tripled, and he looked out the back door toward where he knew his father was.

"Gus, he really is nice. He's an anesthesiologist. He's also rather brave," Paris said. "I found him in a hospital parking garage. I was there for a quick snack."

His mom had taken him and his sister to hospitals when they were still kids.

"Let me guess, you decided to you wanted to fear-scent him and you got caught," Gus said.

Paris grinned up at him, ducking her head.

"Maybe? I put it in his head that there was a young woman around the corner being devoured by a monster. That he needed to run because it was coming for him," Paris said. She'd always tended toward the "help me" angle with her fear pushes. "Instead he came barreling around the corner looking to help."

Gus chuckled at that and raised his eyebrows.

"Aww, did you fall for someone without fear? Just like mom?" Gus asked. "Come on, I wanna introduce the girls to Dad."

"No, I didn't. He was full of fear. Reeked of it. But… he still came," Paris said with a smile. "And I like your girlfriends. They're pretty. The human, though… she doesn't know what we are yet?"

"Not yet. I'll probably end up telling her after today, though, if I don't miss my guess," Gus said, moving to where his mom was monopolizing Melody and Vanessa.

"Sorry Mom, but Dad's next," Gus said.

His mom clicked her tongue at him but waved a hand.

"Oh fine. I'll just come with you. He's probably set something on fire by now anyways just to watch it burn," she said.

"He's not that bad, Mom," Paris complained. "Besides, Stewart is there. He'd probably do something about it."

Vanessa came up beside Gus and gave him an odd look.

She suspects something is different. I guess this is the point where I put my trust in her.

That's if she didn't already suspect something before this point.

Hooking his arm through hers, he slowed her down as everyone began filing out into the backyard. Melody gave him a smile, as if she knew what he was doing, and kept walking.

Gently pulling the nervous-looking Vanessa to one side, he thought on how to say it. Then just went for the truth.

"So, clearly you're noticing something isn't normal about my mother. She never hid it very well. I figured you'd be finding out today. One, since you're my partner now, and two… well… you deserve to know. I trust you."

Gus sighed and shrugged his shoulders with a grin.

"Ness, I'm not human. I'm a Boogieman. So is my mother, and my sister. My father is a telepath," Gus said. "I trust you, Ness. And I cannot stress enough how scary that is for me. Because if you told anyone, my whole family would be hunted down and killed out of hand.

"Mark and Melody know; no one else does at work."

Vanessa was staring up at him. He knew her well enough now that he could spot when she was digesting information. Then she slowly nodded, and a smile broke out across her face.

"Thank you for trusting in me, Gus. I have a lot of questions to ask you later. But for now, let's go meet your dad," she said, and she pushed Gus out the door.

Wilhelm Hellström stood beside a closed barbecue. He was in every way Gus's dad, and shared all the same features. He just happened to be a bit heavier around the middle in his elder years, and a few inches taller.

Gus's mom had joined him and was leading him over to where Melody was standing.

Depositing Vanessa next to Melody, Gus stood to one side with a smile.

"Hi, hi, I'm Wilhelm, call me Will," said Gus's father, reaching out to shake Melody's hand.

"Hi! I'm Melody. I'll be your daughter-in-law soon. This is Vanessa—she'll be your daughter-in-law too," Melody said, shaking his hand.

Wilhelm blinked at that, then started to laugh.

"Good. Keep up the pressure. Gus is just like his mom. You have to run them down and tear their throat out before they get it in their heads to start running again," he said.

Rolling his eyes, Gus walked over to the other man in the back yard.

He was perhaps in his thirties, looked heavier than Gus was expecting, and seemed for all the world to be socially awkward. Brown hair in a very corporate-looking haircut, and soft blue eyes.

Grinning, Gus couldn't help shake the thought that his sister had picked more closely to how his mom had done it than she'd admitted.

Holding out his hand to the man his sister was dating, Gus smiled.

"I'm Gus, Paris's brother," he said.

"Stewart," said the other man, smiling back at him. The fear coming off the man was palpable, but none of it showed in his person or his bearing.

So much so that Gus couldn't not fear-scent the man.

He smelled like cotton candy.

Grinning wider, Gus chuckled.

"Good to meet you, Stewart. Paris was just telling me to talk her up to you. She's apparently terrified she's not good enough for you." Gus let the man's hand go. Getting straight to the older-brother shit he was good at.

Stewart looked confused for a second, then started to laugh softly. The fear left instantly from the man.

"Did she now?" Stewart said, his eyes moving to somewhere behind Gus. There was a silly grin on his face. It was obvious he was very much in love with Paris.

"Oh yes. It was the first thing she said to me. So do me a favor and pretend I talked her up like crazy to you and you don't know how you functioned without her up to this point," Gus said.

Stewart started laughing harder at that, looking back to Gus. "I can do that. Thanks. Paris tells me you're a cop?"

Heh. I like him.

***

As they pulled into Vanessa's apartment building, she sighed, her hands in her lap clasping one another. Her head turned, and she looked up at the building outside the window.

"Vanessa, can I use your restroom real quick?" Melody asked. "It'll just be a minute, I promise."

She wants to take her upstairs and make sure she's ok.

Not for the first time, Gus was appreciative of how much Melody did seem to care for him and Vanessa.

"Sure, that's fine," Vanessa said, looking bright at Melody's request. "Come on up. Gus? You staying here?"

Gus started to nod, then stopped himself.

I should go with them. If only to show my support. Vanessa had a rough morning. Sending her back to an empty apartment seems like a punishment.

"No, I'll come up too," he said.

"Great. You can hide under her bed and be the Boogieman," Melody said, giggling at her own joke and opening her car door.

"Ha, ha." Gus rolled his eyes and got out of the car as well. "Maybe I should."

There'd been a long talk about what he was on the way to Vanessa's place.

"I think it's neat," Vanessa said, walking to the front of her apartment.

"You just like that he shared his darkest, most personal secret with you," Melody said, wrapping an arm around Vanessa's shoulders. "And introduced you to his family. If I had any family nearby, I'd introduce you to them. But I'd want to kiss you a few times in front of them to make sure they knew you were my girl."

Ah. Melody has the right of it, I suppose. Vanessa had no intimacy at all with her girlfriend. Between me and Melody, Vanessa just got drowned in it.

Vanessa elbowed Melody once but didn't actually push her away.

The trio made their way to the elevator and took it up. Vanessa and Melody were talking about a movie, and Gus just trailed along.

"…just there to add color," Vanessa said. Pulling her keys out of her small handbag, she pushed one of them into the lock and popped the door open.

"Huh. Yeah, ok, yeah. But that's no different than Gus. He's only coming along because he's worried about you. That'd be 'for color,' wouldn't it?" Melody asked.

The door swung open, and at the same time, Gus felt a massive thump in his feet. It made his guts vibrate.

A bare second after that, it sounded like all the glass shattered at the same time as an extremely loud rumbling noise took over.

"What the hell?" Gus said.

Melody was over to the window in a flash, staring out of it.

"I can't see anything," she said. "But that felt like an explosion."

"I've been in explosions. This was more than that," Gus said. He'd felt similar things during his service, but nothing as large as what had just happened.

Pulling his phone out and shutting the door to Vanessa's apartment at the same time, Gus hit Mark's number.

Vanessa had gone straight to the TV in her living room and turned it on.

None of them were bothering with the glass or cleanup. Figuring out what had just happened was top priority.

Mark picked it up on the first ring.

"Don't know, call you back," Mark said and hung up.

Gus nodded and putting his phone away.

"Mark doesn't know yet, but he'll keep us updated," Gus said, moving over next to Vanessa and sitting down on the couch.

Melody was still staring out the window, looking for anything.

Vanessa flipped through the channels that would normally have information, and she found nothing. Nothing at all.

Despite the explosion big enough to break the windows in an apartment building, and probably every building nearby.

"It's something Para related, that's for sure," Gus said, shaking his head. "A media blackout, even though we clearly know something is happening, means it's being crushed."

"What are we supposed to do in a situation like this?" Vanessa asked.

Gus didn't have a good answer to that, so he shrugged his shoulders. "Normally it's assemble at the precinct and go from there. But that's only if we know it's Para related. Until Mark calls and gives us news… we're in neutral, I guess."

Vanessa looked at her broken windows, and then at the TV.

"I think the city is about to get problematic," she said. "There's no way they can cover that up, can they?"

"Bigger things have been hidden, and in worse situations," Melody said.

"Can I wait for word with you two?" Vanessa asked. "I really don't want to sit alone in my apartment."

"Yeah. Grab a bag and stuff it with a week's worth of things. Pretend you're going to a hotel," Gus said and got up. "Melody, help her. I'm going to do what I can for these windows."

Melody skirted past Gus, dragging a hand along his middle as she did so. The she grabbed Vanessa and corralled her off into her bedroom.

Gus didn't want to say what he was feeling right now.

Out in the streets, he could sense an overwhelming and utter panic. Fear.

Fear the likes of which he hadn't felt or tasted since he'd gone to a high school on the first day of school for a courtesy check.

It was intense, and almost sickening. The city was terrified to its core.

And he wanted to be anywhere else.

***

Melody had been making phone calls the entire way back to Gus's place, and Vanessa had been calling around to her old co-workers.

Gus had kept his phone open, waiting for Mark.

He trusted Mark. There was no one else on this planet he'd put at his back before Mark.

Not even his own mother.

When they trooped back into Gus's house, Melody immediately went into his bedroom and came back out with his laptop.

"It's not just here," she said, sitting down on the couch and putting her phone down on the coffee table in front of her. "It's everywhere. It's an actual terrorist attack. Every single Fed building had a bomb dumped into it, in front of it, or on it."

Gus was standing in the kitchen, which looked out into his living room.

Vanessa had vanished into one of his guest rooms, putting her stuff away.

"They bombed the Fed offices?" Gus asked, shocked.

"Yeah. It's… everywhere. Every state. Bombed," Melody said as she clicked through multiple web pages. "They didn't touch a single PID building, though. Nothing local.

"No one's taking ownership of the attack either, which… doesn't feel right."

"No." Gus shook his head. "Not at all. That's one of the first things they fight over. Claiming who actually did it."

With a sigh, Gus went to his bedroom. He figured he might as well get dressed for work. It was likely he'd either be working nonstop or living at the precinct itself.

Gus dressed like it was a race, taking only minutes.

"My turn?" Melody asked without looking up from the laptop. She was watching a board as people responded to a thread.

"Yeah, even though you look amazing in that, I don't think you can work in it," Gus said, deciding to go with another compliment. "Go on, Miss Amazing, I'll man the computer."

Melody lifted her head up and looked at him, her face containing a bit of confusion, her Orange contract bright and glowing.

Slowly, her Indigo and Red contracts started to glow, and she gave him a smile.

"Thank you, Gus," Melody said. "I know I'm the Lark… I'm a notorious criminal or hero depending on who you ask. One of the best freelance investigators out there as well, not even including my Contractor powers. I'm intelligent to the point that I intimidate most people, and I have more than enough power to scare the rest.

"It's… nice… that you treat me just as you do."

"Uh huh," Gus said. "Get movin'. I'll flatter you later if you want."

Melody got up and handed him the computer, then left. All of her contracts faded but the Indigo.

Dropping into the couch, Gus started to flip through what she'd been reading. Which was a much longer version of the same thing she'd already told him. She'd boiled it down to a point where it was useful for him. Far quicker than he could have figured it out, too.

Good thing I'm not intimidated by smart women.

Gus's phone started to ring in his pocket. Setting aside the computer, he looked at the screen after he fished it out. It was Mark.

Pushing the accept button, he put the phone to his ear.

"Mark," Gus said.

"Hey. I'm sure you're already aware to a degree, but the Bureau got blowed up. It's almost every Fed building whoever did this could find," Mark said. "Federal government is putting out a state of emergency and is pulling in a massive amount of PID resources to help cover the gap that just got created."

"Got it. What do you need from me?" Gus asked.

"Nothing," Mark said. "In fact, that's the same orders I got. Our department is being asked to remain on standby, but not activated.

"Best I can figure is it's all emergency workers and patrol PID officers getting pulled right now. I'm sure we'll start getting leads from nowhere, information to run down, and people to ask questions."

"Great," Gus said. "In other words… sit here with my thumb up my ass, come in to work Monday. They have all the help they want on board because they don't know what's going on, and this is way worse than anyone ever thought."

Mark was absolutely silent for a time.

"Yeah, that about sums it up. But… Gus, I think we're walking back into something that's possibly even worse," Mark said. "And I honestly don't know where the hell any of this is going to fall out. Keep your head down, and try not to get too many people looking at you. Someone was asking questions about certain types of Paras."

Damn.

"Got it. Thanks for the heads up, will do what I can. You going to call Vanessa and Melody and tell them the same?" Gus asked.

"No, you tell them. They're yours anyways," Mark sighed. "Remind me when we're through with this one why we're working this job."

"Money. And it's easier than going full civie," Gus admitted, then hung up his phone.

Vanessa was seated in a recliner across from him.

"Anything new?" she asked.

"Nope. Exactly what Melody said. We're going to hunker down and wait till our shift. You staying here with us, or do you want to head back home?" Gus asked. "If you stay here, you can look forward to Melody trying to talk you into her bed. Or my bed. Who knows."

Snorting at that, Vanessa closed her eyes and sank into his recliner.

"I'll stay. Mel can try. I'm just as strong willed as she is," she muttered.

Good luck with that. I thought the same thing.

"Honey?" Melody called from the other room. "Can you help me with this zipper? I don't want to rip the fabric and I think it's stuck."

Sighing, Gus got up off the couch and went to check on Melody.

Chapter 15 - Missing It

Gus could still feel the fear in the city. It'd been two days, but the fear was the same, if not worse.

"The fear is pretty bad," Gus said as they drove deeper into the city. "Feels the same as Friday or worse."

"Really?" Vanessa asked from the passenger seat. "That makes me wonder if the street's saying something different."

"Probably," Gus said.

"I'm not a cop." Melody leaned forward, putting herself between the two of them. "Explain for me, honey? Sweetie? My loves? My destined bookends?"

Shaking his head, Gus only grinned.

Melody hadn't stopped going after Vanessa since she'd come over on Saturday. There'd been a brief conversation about the possibility of her going back home.

Which Vanessa herself had ended after only about twenty seconds. She didn't want to be in the city, nor alone.

"A lot of the time the street knows something we don't. Often, in fact," Vanessa said, turning to speak to Melody. "If there's still a lot of fear, and not the normal blasé response to something or the jaded disbelief, then it's still ongoing. It's not over, and the street knows what's coming next, or what happened."

"Ah, yes. I now understand what you mean. I often find that criminals do tend to know more than the police," Melody said. Then she grimaced. "Except I'm now the police, and I know less than the criminals. We should go poke around, ask questions, and see what we can dig up."

"Sure, if we get assigned the case," Gus said, to which Vanessa nodded.

"What?" Melody asked.

"We may not get the case. It's quite likely we'll be assigned something else. We don't really pick what we work on, you know." Gus gave Melody a quick glance.

"Oh. Yes. I didn't think about that," Melody said and then sighed, laying her head on Gus's shoulder. "The things I've done just to be near my beloved. Though, this is fine. I'm happy. I sowed all my oats, as they say, and now I must settle down."

Feeling weird about the whole thing but having spent the weekend just enjoying being with Melody and Vanessa, Gus was unsure.

About everything.

But he knew beyond a doubt, Melody did genuinely care for him in her own Contractor crazy way. It made him feel warm. Warm and protective of her.

Reaching up, he gently ran his fingers through Melody's hairline, smoothing it back with careful fingers.

"That's how life goes when you get a career and a job," Gus said. "You work what you're given. Though I'm fairly certain Mark will put us on it eventually. He's going to herald us as his 'crack team' or 'ace in the hole,' or some other stupid thing. But he won't do that till he gets some pressure from someone.

"After all... he's got the Lark on his payroll."

Melody was nuzzling Gus's shoulder, basking in the attention he was giving her. Putting both hands back on the wheel, Gus put his mind back to his task.

"I'm finding that my career life so far has been very good to me," Melody said. "I found my loves, I'm working a very similar job, and my paycheck is steady."

"Wait until we hit a lull or a boring case; you might change your mind," Vanessa said with a snort.

"It'll be fine," Melody said, then reached across Vanessa and hugged her. Melody laid her head down on Vanessa's shoulder.

"Mel..." Vanessa said softly without any heat.

Melody only tightened her hold on Vanessa. After several seconds, Vanessa laid her hand on Melody's arm and began petting it.

***

"Aaaaaand?" Melody asked, sitting on her assigned desk and watching Gus.

"High-value break-in," Gus said, closing the email Mark had sent him. "A lead detective already did the interview with the owner, and everything else with first steps. We have a written statement, a statement from the patrolman, and a statement from the detective as well. Not to mention the whole thing is itemized."

"Huh." Melody's face turned into a pout. "How high value?"

"Something like four hundred thousand in mechanic-shop equipment. Valuations seem strange to me, but I don't know much about mechanic equipment.

"Was someone else's case after all, so… this one's odd all the way around. Getting shuffled to us since they're working the bombing." Gus leaned back in his chair and looked at Melody.

Vanessa spun around in her chair to face Gus. With her back to him, she was his "space-mate," as the force called it.

"Definitely doesn't feel quite right," Vanessa said. "If you read over the equipment list, it's everything you'd need to strip a car but also run diagnostics on one. It's not normal. It's not like you can't just buy the equipment. It's not something that needs any type of license or registration."

"Which leaves a lack of funds, a lack of time, or a lack of planning." Gus shook his head. "Suppose we could hit the normal spots and ask some questions. Sometimes just the fact that we're poking around can turn up CIs with information."

"Wait, why are we working a case that seems a lot like something for the normal police?" Melody asked.

"Were claws on the lock, fur found at the scene for several unidentified Weres, and the camera shows a number of eastern timber wolves breaking in," Gus said. "This is a fairly standard case, it's just that the valuation of the stolen property is high."

"Don't they have different departments for different types of crimes?" Melody asked. "Aren't we a homicide department?"

"That's true for most normal police agencies," Gus said, standing up and pushing in his chair. "Not for us. Not enough of us and too much work.

"Alright, let's go. We need to ask around a bit and see what's going on. Since it's Wolves, we can bug-fuck the Lions and Bears."

"Could we just ask a different pack of Wolves? Would they be in competition with one another?" Vanessa asked, getting up and pushing her chair in as well.

"Yep. And we'll get to that. But Wolf pack clans tend to try to stir up trouble for their enemies, regardless of who you're looking for," Gus said.

"I'll drive," Melody said, hopping off the desk. "I need to keep learning the streets. This is going to be my home, after all."

"Did you end up buying that house?" Vanessa asked as she walked to the coat rack.

"No. No reason to. I just moved in with Gus," Melody said. "Speaking of, should we swing by your apartment and get more of your stuff today after work?"

"Probably should. Otherwise it'll just— " Vanessa paused, shaking her head. "No. I don't live with you and Gus. I don't have any— "

"Good. I'll buy you some luggage if you don't have any and we'll load that up. Just leave the furniture for now." Melody took her coat from the rack while adjusting her holster and the weapon there. "Is there anything else you need before we turn your keys in?"

"Mel, I really don't think this is a good idea," Vanessa said. She looked very uncertain.

"It'll be fine, sweetie. We should stop on the way home so I can buy some ingredients for dinner tonight. How do you feel about lasagna?" Melody asked as she guided Vanessa from the office.

Gus shrugged his coat on, checked his weapon, and followed the two women out. "Lasagna sounds great."

Melody lifted her head, looking at him with a wide smile.

***

"Is this the place?" Melody asking, pointing to the mechanic sign in front of them. It read, "Bear-ake Check" and had a picture of a bear in a car.

"Yeah," Gus said. "Owned by a larger family of Weres. Black bears. I popped their kid a while back for boosting a car. I gave 'em a warning and sent the dumb asshat home, red eyed and snot nosed. Parents were grateful obviously. I check in now and again and sometimes they've got info for me."

"Should we come in?" Vanessa asked. "Does your CI get quiet if others are there?"

"Nah. You can come in or stay, up to you," Gus said.

"I'll come," Melody said.

"I'll stay. I've been reading through stuff on the share-drive. Lots of information floating around right now about the bombings. I'm curious about it all," Vanessa said.

Getting out of the car, Gus gave his surroundings a quick once-over.

Elf, Goblin, Troll… and a whole lot of people that look absolutely human with masks.

Gotta be Weres. A lot of Weres out and about if that line of thought is true.

Why so many?

Stashing that thought away for later, Gus wandered into the storefront. No one was in the front, and it sounded like there were people working in the attached garage.

Melody's Orange and Blue contracts glowed faintly as her eyes combed over the side wall of the store.

Hm. She find a trace of something?

Contractors could be grab bags of interesting abilities and techniques. Once more, Gus found himself impressed. Melody had apparently really built in her contracts to fit her desires. They weren't just random power grabs.

"Gus?"

Looking toward the voice, Gus found the owner, and exactly who he was looking for. A young woman who looked like she was in college, in her early twenties. Dressed in overalls and a cap, she was clearly working today.

Black hair pulled back into a tight ponytail and a set of blue eyes in a pretty face ran counter to the "mechanic" expectation most people probably had. She was also only five foot four.

He'd seen her in her bear/human hybrid form, though. She was bigger than all but the biggest he'd met. Were forms had different sizes than their respective human forms.

"Hey there, Hailey," Gus said with a grin.

She smiled at him and then looked off to one side, the smile locked into place.

"This is my new partner, Melody. And before you ask… she's a Para. A Contractor. I trust her," Gus said, laying everything out for the young woman.

"Yeah?" Hailey asked as she pulled the cap from her head.

Melody came over and held her hand out to the other woman.

"As my partner said, I'm Melody." She shook the mechanic's hand.

Hailey nodded at the Contractor, then looked to Gus. "Hey… those explosions…"

"Someone attacked all the Fed buildings they could across the country. Haven't heard a damn thing otherwise and no one's claiming responsibility," Gus said, being direct and honest with her. "But that's for you and your family, no further."

Hailey looked a bit shocked, shaking her head slowly. "I… I didn't realize… it's serious then?"

"Very, but that's all I got. My turn?" Gus asked her, putting his elbow on the countertop between them and leaning onto it.

Hailey gave him a small smile and leaned up against the same countertop.

"Sure, your turn. What do you want?" she asked.

"I got a pack of Wolves, it looks like, that stole a bunch of equipment from a mechanic shop." Gus pulled the inventory list out and handed it to her. "You hear anything at all?"

Hailey was already shaking her head before she even got the list.

"Haven't heard a thing. So they're not reselling it and… wow. This is a lot of gear to take," she said. "How'd they even manage it? They would have needed a truck. Big truck."

"Big truck. Ok. Any ideas on what packs are in the area that might be in for something like this?" Gus asked. "Eastern timber wolf markings."

"Eastern…?" Hailey asked, still reading the list. "There's that newer group down by the old dog-food plant on the outskirts of the city. They work out of a warehouse there. They've mostly kept to themselves, but they're an eastern timber wolf pack."

"And you think they'd be likely?" Melody asked.

Hailey looked up from the list to Melody.

"They're not showing up to Were-meets. Nor are they showing any respect to the local pack lord for the Wolves," Hailey said.

"Means I can ask them about their involvement, or who they think might be involved, since they have no clan feuds," Gus said with a nod.

Hailey looked back at him and smiled. "Exactly. Hey… you're looking a lot better today. You finally start eating right like I told you?"

"You could say that," Gus said, taking the list back from Hailey. "Thanks. Tell your folks I said hi."

"You do it. Come back around dinner time. They'll be here then," Hailey said.

Gus only smiled at her and waved a hand, leaving the shop.

As the door closed shut behind them, Gus tapped the paper against his palm.

"Guess that means we're going for a long drive," he said to Melody. "Want me to take the wheel?"

"No, I want to. I need to learn and I'll do that best by driving. Remember?

"Besides, I can always punch the address into the dashboard PID computer," Melody said.

Gus shrugged and got into the car.

"Anything?" Vanessa asked after both of them had gotten in.

"Some weird hints of magic in the front, but nothing I'd try to run down," Melody said. "That and his CI is in love with him."

Gus snorted at that, buckling his seatbelt.

"She's in college," Gus said, looking out the window.

"And in love with him. See? This is why we need to get him locked into a three-way with us as soon as possible," Melody said.

"Mel, really. I don't—"

"I mean, come on, don't tell me you don't look at him with hungry eyes," Melody said as she put the car in reverse.

"I do not—"

Melody whipped the car around and pulled it into drive, sliding into the street smoothly.

Feeling his asshole pucker to the tension of a snare drum, Gus glared at the back of Melody's head. Vanessa seemed equally freaked out.

"Yes, you do. You look at him like he's a damn candy bar sometimes," Melody said. "I mean, so do I, but I'd eat him. You just look at him like a fat kid on a diet."

Vanessa shook her head angrily and busied herself with whatever she'd downloaded from the drive.

An hour later, they were in the approximate area Hailey had described. It was full of run-down warehouses, down-on-its-luck industry, and the remains of a very large dog-food manufacturing plant.

"Am I the only one amused by a Were pack of Wolves living next to a dog-food plant?" Melody said, putting the car in park after she'd pulled into a parking space.

It was funny to Gus, but he wasn't about to say that. Vanessa still looked angry, and he didn't want to test it.

"I can't find a damn thing on Weres being in this area," Vanessa grumbled. She'd been in a bad mood the entire ride over. Melody had finally pushed her over the edge today.

"I'll get out and take a peek. Seeing a PID officer with their mask usually sends people into fear spikes. I can typically find what I'm looking for with that alone," Gus said, and he got out of the car.

"We'll be right there." Melody unbuckled her seat belt and leaned over the center console toward Vanessa as Gus closed his door.

Adjusting his collar, Gus started walking toward the nearest warehouse.

When he glanced over his shoulder into the car, he saw Melody holding Vanessa, saying something to her.

Vanessa shook her head at first, then nodded once. At which point Melody kissed her cheek and pulled her in closer.

The hell is wrong with her?

Gus looked back to the warehouse, peering at the windows.

This isn't her just trying to get Vanessa over her Were girlfriend. She really is trying to get Vanessa into a relationship with us.

Wait, us?

Gus's thoughts stopped dead when he felt a stab of fear coming from further down the road he was walking. It was sharp, distinct, and he knew exactly what it was.

The single epithet shared by criminals everywhere.

It's the cops!

Turning around, Gus made a show of looking at his phone. As if he wasn't interested in the warehouses at all.

He tapped in a note to Melody, Gus playing the part of a bored person with nothing to hide.

He hit send, then looked up at the other side of the dog-food manufacturer. Sitting there was a small, abandoned two-story office building that looked like it'd been in a fire. Flickering in and out around it was a half-demolished set of wards and security spells.

I'll need to let the decontamination teams know about that to take care of it. Spells are meant to be removed when a building is gutted like that.

It's just an accident waiting to happen.

Shaking his head, Gus looked at his phone and saw no response from Melody.

When he looked at the car, he saw why—Vanessa's face was pressed into Melody's neck.

Vanessa was clearly crying, with giant shoulder-quivering sobs. Melody was patting the smaller woman on the back, rubbing it gently. Her cheek pressed to the top of Vanessa's head.

She locked eyes with Gus and gave him a small smile.

Or maybe it really was all part of an attempt to help Vanessa move past the girlfriend.

Whatever.

Deciding he could wait a bit for them to compose themselves, Gus pulled open the games part of his phone and started working through a new game of Minesweeper. He didn't have to rush them, and their happiness and comfort was worth more than running over to someone who was afraid of the cops.

A lot of people were afraid for no other reason than they were the police.

After finishing the first level quickly, Gus opened up another one and started to tap his way through that.

Leaning up against the side of the car, Gus settled in to wait. At least he had something he could keep himself mildly entertained with.

Chapter 16 - Werehouse

The sound of a car door opening pulled Gus from his minesweeping.

Vanessa was getting out of the car. She looked infinitely more composed than she had a short time ago.

For some people the break is instant, for others it's much later. I wonder how long she was with her girlfriend, and how long ago the end was before it actually happened.

Maybe Melody will lay off now.

Closing his game and locking it, Gus dropped his phone into his pocket. Standing up straight, he brushed his hands off on his pants.

"So. I got a fear sense from up ahead," Gus said, trying to keep things moving along when it seemed like she was going to start apologizing. "At that warehouse over there. I'd like to wander over that way and ask some questions. I'm betting it's where the Weres are anyways."

"Heh, where the warehouse is full of Weres, we should call it a Werehouse," Melody said, closing the car door.

Gus had a particularly stupid thought pop into his head.

"Let's hope the warehouse full of Weres don't catch you unaware since you know where they are," Gus said with a smirk.

Vanessa closed her eyes tightly together, but she was clearly fighting a smile.

"You two can be so stupid at times," she said after a few seconds, shaking her head. Except then she opened her eyes and smiled at Gus. "It's hard to… hard to take all of this seriously."

"It's stress humor," Melody said. "If we were uptight all the time like you normally are, we'd break. Not all of us are as mentally strong.

"Now, honey, is it that one at the end there?"

"Yeah. That's where I got the fear hit. It died off pretty quick when I started messing with my phone," Gus said.

"You do kinda look like a cop. It's like the moment anyone sees you, too. It's not like you could hide in plain sight," Melody said.

Gus shrugged. "Vanessa, take the rear. If anyone comes out, see if they'll respond to questioning without a detain. Melody, you come with me to see if we can't get someone to answer the front door."

"Me at the top, Vanessa at the bottom. I'm down to make a wobbly-triangle out of Gus. Didn't think I'd get to be the one queening him though," Melody said, getting back into the car.

"Wobbly-triangle?" Vanessa asked, also getting back in. "Queening?"

"Yeah, it's—" The door shutting cut off the conversation.

Sighing, Gus closed his eyes and counted to five. Then he opened the driver's-side door and got in.

"…his face. Then I lean over and kiss you," Melody said, finishing her explanation.

"Mel! I swear I'm going to actually hit you. Is sex all you ever think about?" Vanessa asked.

Gus flipped the car into position and drove them all to the warehouse at the end of the lane.

"Lately? Yeah. Kinda hard not to. Gus makes me wild," Melody said. "My Red Contract is being very demanding about it, too."

"Oh. I see. Sorry," Vanessa said.

"It is what it is," Melody said. "It's ok though. Gus is actually coming around."

Pointedly ignoring the whole conversation, Gus got back out of the car after he turned it off and headed straight for the warehouse.

Vanessa went by at a light jog, her coat flapping behind her as she headed toward the rear of the warehouse.

Melody caught up to Gus right when he reached the front door.

"Why'd you send her over that way?" Melody asked. "I could have done it."

"You sure could have, but I don't think you've memorized all the things you can and can't do as a police officer, have you?

"Do you know the dos and don'ts of questioning without a detain? What constitutes a legal search and what doesn't?" Gus asked. "I'm not doubting your intelligence," he said, looking at the Contractor. "You're a brilliant woman. Smarter than I am, I have no doubt of that. But it just hasn't been long enough, enough time in general really, for you to learn all the basic stuff yet. You got hired on without basic training, the academy, or even doing the normal coursework."

Melody's Orange contract lit up for two seconds, then faded instantly.

"Yes… you're right. I'm reading through everything Mark sent over, and doing the coursework in the book, but I'm nowhere near done." Melody smiled at him. Then she leaned in close, practically hovering over him. "Thank you for watching out for me, honey."

Gus pressed a hand to her chest and eased her back, then knocked hard on the door three times.

Melody turned toward the door, and the strange and sweet Contractor vanished. There in an instant was a woman who would happily turn someone else into paste if they were in her way.

She's the Lark after all. Pretty sure there were some murder charges in there.

"Who is it?" called a muffled voice from behind the door.

"My name is Agent Gustavus Hellström, from the PID. I would like to ask you a few questions," Gus said.

This was the tricky part, of course. Technically, they didn't have to answer the door. Most people would simply do so because that was the natural inclination when police were at your door.

"What's this about?" called the voice from beyond the door.

"There was a crime recently that involved some Weres. I wanted to ask you some questions to see if you could perhaps help me go in the right direction," Gus said.

There was no response from whoever was on the other side of the door.

"Sir?" Gus asked after five seconds had gone by.

"One second," responded the other person. It was followed by the heavy door opening, a man stepping out, and then closing the door behind him. He looked fairly average in all regards and stood at about five foot six with brown hair and blue eyes. Gus wasn't fooled, though. There was an aura of strength around the man and his mask was obvious. He looked absolutely human. Which made him most likely a Were. And a Were going into his hybrid form could be much bigger than his human phase. "Badge?"

It was a common request. There was, of course, a small bit of magic in the badge that'd make anyone who saw it know it was real. Counterfeit PID officers had been a problem some years ago.

Gus pulled out his detective medallion and held it up. While he was doing that, he also threaded a small filament of his telepathic power into the other man's mind and began to slowly grow it.

Melody had done the same thing at the same time.

"Who's she?" the man asked Gus.

"I'm Agent Melody Lark," Melody said, her presence seeming to loom over the other man. At the same time, her Blue, Green, and Red contracts began to gently glow.

The Were looked at Melody, a hint of fear showing up in his eyes.

"There was a theft recently of some fairly expensive equipment," Melody said, taking the lead. "Have you heard anything about doing a large job?"

Gus was thankful for her stepping in like that. It was hard to question someone while simultaneously hunting for thoughts in their head.

Especially when they were trying hard to pull a poker face.

Gus got brief flashes and images of several small crimes and even some narcotics work, all flooding through the man's mind.

"No. Not really. We're a new pack to the area and still trying to figure out our place in the territories," the man said.

That'd be true, too. A new pack would have to take some time to figure out where they could expand into, and what they could work. More often than not, Weres would have to ask permission from other packs to work a job in a different territory.

Except permission was almost always given, as their own people would have to do the same for their jobs.

A new pack could threaten the balance quickly.

"I see. What if I said it was a timber wolf breed we were looking for," Melody said, tilting her head to one side as she stared into the Were's face. "Would that make any difference to you? And what breed are you?"

In a flash, the man's mind snapped to the break-in Gus was looking for. This man and his pack were the ones directly responsible for the theft. He watched as the man loaded up a truck full of all the missing equipment and other Weres came and went with more.

"Wouldn't make any difference to me," said the man. "And I'm a Gray. Don't want anything to do with those Coyote fuckers."

Gus saw a number of men and women cursing at this very same man for being a "Coyote fucker" in their last home.

Timbers tended to breed with Coyotes as often as they did with their own kind. Gray wolf Weres kept to their own kind and looked down on their eastern cousins, while also happily killing any Coyote they could.

"Your name?" Melody asked, putting some weight into her words by maintaining heavy eye contact. She didn't want to be lied to.

"Sean. Sean Smith," said the man, looking quite cowed.

Gus got the impression he was telling the truth there. Then the man's thoughts flashed to his driver's license being in his back pocket, and that it matched.

Melody squinted at him.

"I'll be in touch, Sean," she said. "And if you happen to hear anything about a large theft of equipment, or who might be involved in the hiring or arranging of such a job, let me know."

Melody held out a card to the man while his thoughts rapidly went through the faces of everyone involved in the job.

There was one that stood out to Gus in that convoluted nightmare. A woman working downtown. Working downtown at a shop that dealt in storage.

Trailing that thought as long as he could, Gus got the name of the store and the woman's face squared away in his memory.

As well as the number eighty-three. A white painted number on a blue placard.

"Of course. I'll keep you in mind," Sean said with the card in his hand.

"By the way, would you mind if we searched your warehouse?" Gus asked.

"I… what?" Sean replied.

"Can I search your warehouse? I'm formally asking for consent," Gus said.

There was a flash of wild, uncontrolled fear. Followed by thoughts of the equipment in question being found right in the middle of the warehouse along with a car they'd been working on.

Most of the fear was coming from the car being discovered, though.

"No," Sean said. "I-I don't consent to a search."

"I understand, thanks," Gus said, and he walked away from the door.

Pulling out his phone, he tapped in a message telling Vanessa to stay there for a minute, but that they were done.

Walking to the curb, Gus turned around and stared straight back at Sean. He dialed in to the local dispatch for PID officers, then waited.

"PID non-emergency," said a woman over the line. "Agent Hellström, how can I help?"

"I need a building put under surveillance. I know for a fact that they have stolen goods at their facility, but I can't do a search yet. I think they'll try to move it before I can get a warrant," Gus said. He was lying a bit, since he had nothing at all to go on to get a warrant. He'd never get one with what he had right now.

"I understand," said the woman. "Is this a Para matter or can a local resource be assigned?"

"Local is fine. It's a bunch of Weres who stole some mechanic equipment," Gus said.

"Understood. I'll have some local resources assigned. Is it from the location your vehicle is at?" asked the dispatcher.

"Yeah… building seventeen," Gus said, checking the number on the building. All throughout the conversation, Sean had been standing there in front of the warehouse door, staring at Gus.

And Gus stared back.

He wanted it to be very clear he didn't believe Sean and that any attempt to move anything would be caught. It was likely the Were pack wouldn't do a darn thing with the equipment.

"Just looking for them to watch, be obvious, and see if anyone who comes out responds to questioning," Gus said.

"Understood. Is there anything else, Agent Hellström?" asked the woman.

"Nope, take it easy," Gus said and hung up the line, smiling at Sean. He was prepared to wait for his local resources to arrive.

"I think I now understand why Mark said you were his best detective. Questioning for you is considerably easier due to your abilities," Melody said. "People can't really hide from you, can they?"

"No. Nothing can hide from the Boogieman." Gus turned to Melody with a grin.

A tiny twitch of fear wafted out from Melody, and it was like he'd been doused with a bucket full of caffeine and stimulants.

Damn. Why does she have to taste so good?

Now that he was actively thinking about it, since she'd started cooking for him, he felt different. Considerably so. Everything was just easier.

On top of that, he hadn't eaten from anyone in days, other than Vanessa and Melody.

Need to talk to Mom.

***

Wandering into the "Stop and Drop" location he'd found in Sean's mind, Gus looked around.

Vanessa and Melody had slipped into the lot itself when a truck had driven up to the gate and gone through. They were going to go see if there was a unit numbered eighty-three with a blue placard.

Pulling open the front door and stepping through, Gus heard the "bing-bong" of an entry notification sound in a back room.

Smirking, he walked over to a line of flattened boxes on one wall and began to poke around at them. There wasn't much he could do till someone came out from the back.

Huh. I wonder if these are the same prices around Christmas time.

"Hello, welcome to Stop and Drop," said a female voice.

Turning to the side, Gus found the woman from Sean's memory standing there. She was young, perhaps in her late twenties. Pretty. Light-brown hair and light-brown eyes.

She was clearly a Were to Gus's eye. Taking a tiny piece of his power, he slipped it right into her mind, just as he had for Sean.

He hadn't done this much mind-reading in a long time.

Then again, when was the last time you let Mark give you casework like this?

It was in the way she carried herself, the magic from a mask surrounding her, and the general aura from her.

He picked up a flash of animalistic fear from her when she focused on him.

"Hello," Gus said, then looked at her name tag. "How are you today, Wendy?"

"I'm well. What can I do for you?" she asked, a plastic smile etched on her face.

"Wendy, my name is Gustavus Hellström. I'm an agent with the PID. You're a Were, right?" Gus walked up to the counter slowly as he spoke.

Fear started to ooze out of Wendy. In an ever-increasing amount with every step he took toward her.

"Ye-yeah. I'm a Were," Wendy said, the smile still frozen on her face. "You said PID? Could I see your badge?"

"Of course you can, Wendy the Were." Gus came to a stop in front of her. Pulling out his medallion, he held it out to her. "Would you happen to be a Wolf?"

Wendy's neck twitched as if she were fighting the urge to swallow, and she leaned over his badge.

"I'm a Wolf, yes," Wendy said.

"Eastern? A timber?" Gus prodded. Her thoughts were bland and gave him nothing much of anything. Which didn't match her fear.

"Ah... yes. Yes, I am," Wendy said, a massive wave of fear flooding out of her. Standing upright, she looked him in the eyes, even as she put out enough fear to match an emergency room.

"What pack would you happen to be a part of?" Gus asked, tucking his medallion back into his shirt.

"It's a pack of timbers. They've been around here for a while," she said.

"Ah... that makes sense. I'm here because I was hoping to ask you a few questions about a particular storage unit for an individual," Gus said. All of her thoughts had matched her words, and there wasn't much out of the ordinary there. Which meant it was time to change the questions up. "Could you perhaps lead me to the unit and open it for me?"

Some of the fear died off from Wendy when his line of questioning changed. Moved away from her directly.

"I can get you the information, but to search the unit, you'd need a warrant I'm afraid," Wendy said.

"That's fair. It's more or less what I was expecting," Gus said.

Resting his arm on the countertop, he smiled at Wendy.

"I need you to tell me the storage-unit number of one Sean Smith," Gus said.

Wendy blinked, and her fear skyrocketed through the roof. Images of Sean flickered and flashed through her mind faster than he could keep up.

"Sean? I can search for the name for you, but it doesn't sound familiar," Wendy said, starting to type into the keyboard nearby.

"Storage unit number eighty-three. Who rents it?" Gus asked, interrupting her.

Wendy's fingers froze on the keyboard, her face turning toward him.

Gus smiled at her, waiting.

Wendy's thoughts were slowing down, and one thing was coming to her crystal clear. The PID officer already knew, and knew she was a part of it. It wasn't a question of *if* he knew but *how much*.

Rapidly, thoughts began to spill out of her about the entire thing. That Sean Smith was his real name. That he'd come to her asking for information on where he could get a hold of some equipment. She hadn't thought anything of selling him information about a mechanic who'd just pulled a whole bunch of equipment out of storage for his shop.

Sean had paid her well, and was paying her still to keep him updated on a list of other items he was looking for.

"So... who has eighty-three, Wendy?" Gus asked.

The door behind him opened, and the "bing-bong" sounded again.

Glancing over his shoulder, Gus saw Melody and Vanessa heading his way.

A tsunami wave of fear blew out of Wendy as if she were facing down a weapon. Fear the likes of which Gus hadn't seen or felt since his deployment.

He looked back at Wendy, absolutely confused. Wendy was staring at Vanessa.

"Wendy?" Vanessa asked suddenly.

Gus watched as memories and thoughts of Vanessa ripped through Wendy's mind. Through it all was a constant state of fear that she'd find out she was a Were. From images of Vanessa naked in bed to her going to work.

Then, when Vanessa made PID, it was fear and anger. A lot of anger. And fear of discovery that she was a Para criminal. That her entire pack was full of Para criminals.

Melody hooked an arm into Vanessa's and immediately took her right back outside.

Gus sighed and looked at Wendy.

"Well, Wendy, looks like this just got a lot more complicated for you. You can come clean and help me figure out this mess, or we get to pick your life apart with Vanessa watching the entire time,"

Gus said, deciding to apply some pressure. "Because I already know about everything. I'm just getting the detail work done as I figure out who did what."

Chapter 17 - Warranted

"Hey," Gus said into his phone. "I just got a lead, some evidence, and a witness as well as a culprit."

"Gussy, it's only your second case of coming to active duty. You don't have to solve it in one day just so you have nothing to do for the rest of the day," Mark said.

"I'll need a warrant on the address I texted you, Durh, as well as the rental space here," Gus said, ignoring him to a degree.

"Yeah. I already kicked both over to the DA. He managed to get ahold of a judge, and that should come back to me soon," Mark said.

"Great. I'm going to see if I can get a statement out of the witness-slash-culprit," Gus said. "Any concerns?"

"No. Just let me know if you need anything else. We're swamped with this bombing case. Not a whole lot to go on yet," Mark said.

"Yup," Gus said, and hung up the line. Lifting his head, he saw Vanessa sitting in the car, typing away at the laptop.

Melody was inside keeping an eye on Wendy.

Unsure what to do for Vanessa, Gus stared at her for several seconds.

When he'd made up his mind, he went over to the passenger side and knocked on the window twice.

Vanessa's head came up, giving him a chance to see her eyes. They were moist, but not panicked or too upset. It looked like she was putting the job ahead for the moment.

Good girl.

Smiling weakly, she rolled down the window.

"Yeah… three cheeseburgers, two large fries. Two chocolate shakes, and one large coke," Vanessa said, then paused. "Too early for flapjacks?"

Snickering to himself, Gus sighed.

"Sorry. I didn't think she'd make you watch it four times in three days," Gus said. "I never would have told her I owned a digital copy of it otherwise."

Vanessa shrugged.

"Good movie. It was funny watching it with Mel just for being with her." She took a deep breath. "So, what's up?"

"Wendy in there is a Were. A wolf. Timber wolf. I was poking through her thoughts while I talked to her," Gus said, going for pure honesty. "She's going to be going to prison for a bit, probably. She's definitely part of this. Also explains why she suddenly broke away from you. I'm going to question her and get to the bottom of it."

Vanessa closed her eyes and shook her head slightly.

"I warned her over and over about getting involved with people or things that seemed too good to be true," Vanessa muttered. "And she ends up working here, while she was telling me all along she had a good job as a fitness instructor. Just how much of it all was a lie?"

"No idea. Not sure I really want to find out either. Personally? I think you're great," Gus said. "You can do better. And she did herself a lot worse.

"For now, I want you to keep an eye on my email account. I put in a couple warrant requests so I can search Sean's warehouse."

"I can do that," Vanessa said. Then she grimaced and looked back down at the laptop. "I just believed everything she told me."

"Happens to the best of us, Ness. Don't let it get to you. Alright, I'm heading in. Thanks for being you," Gus said, and he headed back inside the store. He needed to grill Wendy for information.

On top of that, he already didn't care for her. Gus suspected this would be a great way to burn off some annoyance.

When he opened the door, he found someone else standing behind the desk.

"Uh… can I… oh. You're the other detective. Your partner is in the back in the break room with Wendy," said the man.

Gus nodded and went into the back room. Opening the door, he saw Melody and Wendy off to one side, pushed up into the corner.

Melody made eye contact with him for a brief second, then looked back at Wendy.

The other woman was unresponsive, staring at the table between the two of them.

Taking a seat, Gus pulled out his phone and set it down on the table. He thumbed it open to the "record" setting. He sometimes used it if he wasn't at the station and needed to conduct a field interview. It was easier than taking notes for him, if he could manage it.

"Wendy. I'd like to ask you some questions and record your answers. I'm not detaining you, nor am I holding you in any way at this time," Gus said. "But I think if you cooperate now, it'd be in your best interest in the long run."

"You're not arresting me?" Wendy asked.

"No, I'm here just to ask you some questions for the time being."

"Ok," Wendy said, looking back at the table.

"First off, this is Agent Gustavus Hellström and Agent Melody Lark. We're interviewing Wendy," Gus paused and looked to the woman.

"Hills," said Wendy.

"Wendy Hills in a case relating to the theft of mechanic equipment. Do I have your permission to record this, Wendy?"

"Yes," she said.

"Are you willing to answer some questions?"

"Yes."

"Great. First, do you know Sean Smith?" Gus asked.

"Yeah. He has a storage unit here. He comes in every now and then. Usually likes to flirt with me, asks some questions about things, and then leaves," Wendy said.

"Alright. What kind of questions does he ask you?" Gus prompted. At the same time, he listened to and watched her thoughts.

"Uhm. What people have stored. If there's anything valuable in them. He usually pays me for the information. Sometimes he comes back and pays me more later for no reason," Wendy said. She had multiple flashes of memories of just that. Sean walking in, paying her, and leaving. Many times.

"Ok. And do you believe that money was directly proportional to whatever Sean stole?" Gus asked.

"Yeah. I do," Wendy said, crossing her arms. "Especially after the mechanic stuff. He came in and gave me four thousand dollars."

"That'd certainly be a hefty amount of money to drop off for no reason," Melody said. "Did he say anything during that drop?"

"No. Just to keep my eyes and ears open for anything I think he'd like," Wendy said, her face screwing up in a bitter scowl. "I mean, it didn't start like this, I thought I was just giving him information and he was like… a divorce detective or something. Trying to assess value."

"Is that the story he gave you?" Melody pushed.

"No. He never said anything about that or like that," Wendy said.

Alright, so she made up that theory in her head to help soothe her conscience. That makes sense. People do that all the time.

"Did Sean ask you about the equipment, or did you volunteer it?" Gus asked.

"He came in asking about cars," Wendy said. "So I mentioned the equipment."

"Cars?" Gus asked. "Just… cars in general, or a specific type of car?"

"Cars in general. Actually, no—he said he wanted cars that were long," Wendy said.

"Right. Long cars," Gus said, feeling rather confused with that request. It seemed almost arbitrary. It didn't feel right. "And you believe he has some of those stolen goods in his storage unit?"

"I know he does," Wendy said, grimacing again. "He… paid me to let him know if anyone came around asking about him or his unit. He didn't say anything about cops, though."

"And did anyone come looking?" Gus asked.

"No. No one did," Wendy said.

So far all of her thoughts had matched what she said. There didn't seem to be anything she was holding back about the theft.

Gus still had a feeling she was keeping something in reserve, though. As if there was a subject she didn't want to talk about under any circumstances. Unfortunately, he had no idea what that subject was or how he could trigger thoughts about it. Nor did he want to go deep diving through her memories just to figure out what she wouldn't talk about. It'd come up eventually given enough time.

"Alright. I think that's everything we need for now," Gus said, then reached over and tapped the phone off.

Almost at the same time, his phone started to buzz and vibrate. It was Mark calling him.

Getting up, Gus put the phone to his ear and started to walk away.

"Hey," he said.

"Wendy Hills, you're under arrest for accessory after the fact, theft—" Melody's voice faded out as Gus got further away. He didn't need to hear the charges Melody was putting on Wendy. It would be more than enough to put the young woman away for some years.

Unfortunately for her, in PID, Weres tended to go to max-security prisons due to their nature.

Maybe they'll throw her a deal to join the Para-National Guard. They don't normally take convicts, but Weres are always welcome.

"I got your warrant for the rental property, but nothing on the warehouse," Mark said, his keyboard clacking away in the background. "They won't let you move on it yet. Find something in the garage to make it stick and the judge will grant it."

"Got it, I'll go check the garage immediately," Gus said and hung up. He marched out to the front counter, hoping the unit would have something.

Anything.

He'd love to be able to close this case up before the day was out. Especially when he already knew everything that had happened with the equipment and cars.

"I need access to unit number eighty-three," Gus said.

"Eighty-three," said the clerk, dropping down behind the counter. Gus heard the man sorting through keys under the register. Finally, he popped back up and held out a key for Gus. "Here you go, Officer."

Gus didn't bother to correct him and took the key. Stopping at the door, he hesitated. He'd planned on just going and checking the unit immediately.

But if Melody was leading Wendy out the front, it was likely Vanessa would see her. And that was if a squad car was already here to pick her up and take her away.

Going out the front door, Gus headed over to the car and got in the driver's seat. Vanessa looked at him as he sat down, the question open on her face.

"Going to drive over to the unit; I've got the key," Gus said, starting the car. "Mind going for a drive with me?"

"Sure," Vanessa said, and she closed the laptop.

Driving up to the metal gate, Gus went to lean out and tap the intercom button. Only for the whole thing to start opening before he had a chance to do so.

"Must be watching," Gus muttered. "We should pull the video recordings as well."

"I already put in a request for it. A tech should be out a bit later to get it all. I figured we wouldn't have time for it ourselves," Vanessa said.

"Great. You really are a great partner, you know," Gus said as he drove along the alley.

"You've said that a few times now. Straight to the end, it's on the left," Vanessa said.

"Me saying it more than once makes it more true rather than less," Gus said.

No response was forthcoming from Vanessa. She just sat there, looking like a Hispanic statue more than anything.

Pulling up to the unit labeled eighty-three, Gus killed the engine. It looked just like it had in Sean's memory.

Getting out, Gus pulled out the key and fit it straight into the padlock. When the lock popped open after a second, Gus had a weird thought.

Most places didn't supply locks or keys. You had to bring and maintain your own. What made this place different?

After a few seconds, he figured it out.

Hah, this whole place could be cleared out in a weekend and the owner would be gone in a flash. I wonder if this is a violation of some law.

Makes me wonder if this place doubles as something else.

Pulling the lock free of the bracket, Gus grabbed the bottom of the garage door and shoved it upward. It rattled and clanged into place above him.

From one wall of the unit to the other, it was filled with a vast sundry of items.

"Huh… I have no idea how I'm going to prove any of this is stolen," Gus muttered.

"There's a rifle right there," Vanessa said, pointing. "Let's run the serial on it. If it comes back clean, we'll have to try something else. But honestly… I'm betting it's not his, and if it's reported as stolen, that's even better."

"Good plan," Gus said. Picking up the rifle, he looked at the frame. "Filed off completely. That's as good as stolen. Want to call it in yourself?"

"Sure," Vanessa said, pulling her phone out of her pocket.

Gus laid the rifle to one side and started looking for any other firearms. It wasn't illegal to have guns, of course, but it was sure as hellfire illegal to get rid of serial numbers.

"You know," Vanessa said, looming over his shoulder. "Before I joined PID, I wasn't viewed very well. People thought I wasn't a good detective."

"Huh? How so? I think you're a pretty solid detective, and you anticipate a lot of my needs. As a junior partner, you're impressive," Gus said.

"I was viewed as hotheaded, too eager, too quick, hard to get along with. I think in general I just… rubbed people wrong. I'm pretty young for a detective," Vanessa said. "Remember how we met?"

"Mm, yeah, you're definitely young. Don't see how that has any bearing on your ability to do your job," Gus said. "As for how we met, I just figured that was me."

"Maybe. Maybe my… my reputation was my own fault. Maybe I really was all of those things. Maybe… maybe finding out the world I knew was only half of what was out there hit me harder than I thought," Vanessa said. "Maybe I'm slowing down to jump at things and not so positive all the time about what I should do."

Snorting, Gus pulled out a pistol from a drawer and checked the frame below the cylinder. The serial number was filed off there too.

"After I walked out of the desert and realized even if I was the biggest, baddest sonuvabitch on the planet that I couldn't save people, I definitely slowed down," Gus said, handing the revolver to Vanessa. "Another one with no serial. Anyways. I think you're a good detective and a great partner. Couldn't have asked for a better one."

"I know. I was there when you told Mark what you thought of me," Vanessa said.

"Ugh, don't remind me. The dickhead did that on purpose. He likes to push my buttons," Gus said.

A chirp came from Vanessa's phone, causing Gus to stop in his search.

"Got it," Vanessa said. "We can move on the warehouse. I'm going to call the locals out in front of it. See what they say."

Gus nodded.

Guess I get to wrap this up quick after all.

***

The PID SWAT officer blasted the door open with the battering ram, and their team charged inside. Gus heard follow-up shouts and challenges as the SWAT team stormed inside the warehouse.

Several minutes passed before someone came out and nodded at Gus.

"Definitely found your equipment, but no suspects," said the man, still wearing his helmet, goggles, and balaclava.

"Thanks. Appreciate you all coming out," Gus said, nodding at the SWAT commander.

With a nod in return, the SWAT team leader walked off. Turning to Melody, he held up his hands in futility.

"Got the equipment at least, and we know who's responsible. Just have to throw out a BOLO for their pack and call it a day, I guess," Gus said.

Melody grinned at him, looking surprised.

"Really? That's it?" she asked.

"Yeah. We found the equipment, tagged the baddies who did it, and executed the warrant," Gus said. "Our part's donezo."

"How fun. I was thinking we'd have to track them down now and bring them in," Melody said.

"Nope, that's for others to do. We just had to figure out the case," Gus said, then headed off for the interior of the warehouse.

"Great! We can hit a grocery store on the way home tonight, and I can cook for us," Melody said. "How you feel about me making enchiladas instead tonight, and lasagna tomorrow, Vanessa?"

"Honestly, I don't think I sho—actually, you know what, yeah. Make 'em, Mel. I'm going to eat as many as I can, get drunk, and pass out," Vanessa said. "Today sucked."

"Awww, I promise to only get a little touchy-feely with you when you're unconscious. Maybe a kiss or two," Melody said.

"Just make sure you don't go too far, or I'll have to tell Gus to punish you," Vanessa said.

"You wouldn't," Melody said.

"I would. I can't stop you, but I know you'll stop on a dime for him," Vanessa threatened. "And he'll listen to me."

"Fine, fine," Melody said. "Red or green sauce?"

"Red please," Vanessa said.

Gus was ignoring them completely. He was also ignoring the SWAT team members, and he wasn't looking for the equipment anymore.

He was staring at the car set up in the middle of the warehouse.

This was the same vehicle he'd seen in Sean's memories over and over. They'd spent a considerable amount of time on this thing.

Except whatever it was they were doing with it had ended. They'd just left it here.

In those memories, Gus had seen Sean get in the driver's seat, turn the radio to the on position with full volume, and then start the vehicle with the keyless ignition.

Moving around to the driver's side, Gus imitated everything he'd seen Sean do.

When the car turned over, a shield of glowing bright runes came to life and encircled the entirety of the car.

Getting out carefully, Gus looked them over.

Everyone nearby was also staring at the car that'd suddenly become a giant, glowing, flashing brick of magical runescript.

Except Gus was already beyond the runescript as a whole; he was focused on the spells themselves. They felt familiar to him. He'd seen very similar things on a warehouse.

Familiar, and they made his stomach tilt in a very sickening way.

"I think…" Gus started. "I think Eric Mill made these runes. Or at least designed how they should be written out, and someone else did the work."

"Wait, Eric? Our Eric?" Melody asked.

"Yeah. Our Eric. Which makes me feel a lot worse all of a sudden about this case. A whole hell of a lot worse," Gus grumbled.

Glancing at his watch, he suddenly didn't care. The amount of time it had taken to get the PID SWAT team assembled, the warrant validated, and then to serve it, had put them right up to the end of his shift.

"Fuck that," Gus said. "Shift's over, case closed. I'm logging this shit to Mark and he can handle it during his shift. I'm hungry and tired."

Chapter 18 - Self-Licking Ice Cream

The phone chirped happily and annoyingly next to Gus's bed. Unendingly, unceasingly, it reminded him joyously that the night was over and it was time to get up.

Even if he just wanted to remain in bed and do little else.

Rolling over, he found a messy and rough-looking Vanessa. Unsurprised, and thankfully knowing exactly what had happened, Gus groaned and got out of bed.

At some point in the night she'd gotten tired of Melody and whatever she'd been doing. Vanessa had stumbled into Gus's bedroom, complained about Melody, locked the door, and then passed out immediately in his bed.

Opening his bedside table, Gus pulled out four ibuprofen pills from the bottle he kept there and set them down on the table on her side. Then he put the cup of water he always took to bed on her side as well.

Let's see how you do with a hangover.

Grabbing Vanessa by a shoulder, he shook her gently.

"Nnnnuuuughh," she moaned.

"Ness. Water and pain meds on the bedside," Gus said. "Take 'em and drink it down."

"Nnnnnnnn," she mumbled.

"Come on. Take the pills, drink the water, or I'll let Melody in," Gus said.

One eye opened amongst the dark, messy hair over her face and looked up at him. Slowly, she brushed her hair out of her face, and her eyes focused on him.

There was a strange question in her face that only took Gus a second to understand.

"You just came in here when I assume Melody wouldn't leave you alone," Gus said. "You literally just slept next to me. Take the pills, drink the water. Then drink as much water as you can. Till your bladder pops."

Vanessa licked her lips, and then her cheeks puffed out suddenly.

"No, no, no!" Gus said, scurrying to the bathroom. Grabbing the trash can, he made it back just in time. He held it out to the side of the bed and Vanessa turned, upending everything in her stomach into it.

It reeked of hard liquor and enchiladas.

Petting her gently on the back of the head, Gus got down on one knee next to her and held the trash can. The smell was intense, but he'd handled much worse.

"Oh my god," she said, followed immediately by another round of vomit.

"Yeah. You went pretty hard last night." Gus held her hair back from her face. "For what it's worth, you only cuddled with Melody. She seemed to realize how drunk you were and made you play Scrabble instead.

"You have an interesting… dictionary… when drunk."

"I remember," Vanessa said, and then threw up again.

"Do you? That's impressive. Anything you don't remember?" Gus asked when she finished with the current round.

"Just how I got here. I remember waking up here in the middle of night, but not how I got here. Melody put me to bed and went into her own room, I thought," Vanessa said. "I think… I think I'm empty."

"Great. Let's get you into my shower then, and you can clean up. Soon as you're feeling able, take the pills and the water," Gus said.

Vanessa sat up, grabbed all four pills, and popped them into her mouth. Then she drained the entire glass of water.

Uh… ok. I mean, won't she just throw that up again?

"Not my first night finding the bottom of a bottle," she said, shivering and making a strange face. "I'll be alright. Just… get me in the shower."

"Uhh, yup," Gus said. Reaching into the bed, he scooped her up out of it and carried her bodily into his bathroom. After sitting her down on the toilet seat next to the shower, he turned it on and then left. Shutting the door behind him.

He grabbed the puke-filled trash can and walked it out to the kitchen.

Guess I'm taking a shower second today. That or risking Melody's bathroom.

"Actually… I need to talk to Mark," Gus said aloud to no one. Pulling out the trash-bag, he flipped the whole thing into the much larger kitchen trash can, then closed the lid to it. Thankfully, it did a fair job of immediately cutting off the puke stench. He promised himself he'd throw it out later this morning.

Grabbing his phone, he went back into his bedroom and flopped into his bed. He dialed Mark, then let out a breath.

Smells like flowers.

Frowning, Gus sniffed the air twice. Then he leaned over to where Vanessa had been sleeping and smelled the spot.

It smelled of melted chocolate and flowers.

Why was she afraid?

"Fuck me, man," Mark said when the line picked up. "I haven't even ended my shift yet. What do you want now?"

That wasn't a normal response from Mark.

"Hey. Sorry bud," Gus said. "Wanted to catch up with you and see what you thought about that car from yesterday. Can I bring you some coffee? Donuts? Breakfast sandwich?"

Gus could hear background noise of keyboards clicking and people chatting as Mark processed that.

"I love you, Gussy. You're such a good office husband," Mark said. "Please bring me coffee, donuts, and a breakfast sandwich? I'm so hungry and empty. I promise I'll love you so good later."

Shaking his head with a grin, Gus sighed.

"I swear to god, Durh. Yeah, I'll bring it all. Where are ya?"

"Only Fed building left in town. Somehow the old Fed building from the seventies out by the old industrial section wasn't hit. Don't think you've ever been here," Mark said. "Third floor for me, I'm in an office that was occupied by an analyst. He's very mad he got kicked out for me to work out of it and assist with the investigation."

"Got it. We'll head there first. I'll bring you those stupid hard chocolates you like, too," Gus said.

"Really? I'm going to blow y—"

Gus hung up the phone before Mark could finish the statement.

***

Staring up at the building, Gus was amazed. It was a massive construct of complex security runes and symbols, all tied together and functioning as a whole. There wasn't anything about it that acted by itself.

The entire building was one massive security defensive grid. He'd never seen the like on this scale.

Closest I've seen was that warehouse Eric was in, but it was nothing like this. Nothing at all. That was child's play and simplistic in comparison.

As he pulled into the parking garage under the building, the glowing security shield vanished. Rolling up to the booth, Gus held out his PID badge as well as Vanessa's and Melody's to the officer.

"Agents Hellström, Flores, and Lark," Gus said.

Taking all three badges, the officer checked each one, holding them up to look at the faces of the owners, then went into the booth.

"Anyone else notice the rifle-wielding, angry-looking man on the right?" Vanessa asked.

"Yes, I did. I'm also not making eye contact with him. He's an Ogre," Melody said. "Ogres love the Feds. The Fed loves Ogres. They hire as many as they can all the time. Ogres literally move from other countries to come here to get jobs."

"What? Why?" Vanessa asked.

"Thank you," Gus said as the officer returned the badges.

"Captain Ehrich is waiting for you on the third floor," said the officer, buzzing the heavy gate open. "Be sure to check in at the reception desk for your visitor badges first."

"Because Ogres are given positions they can handle and enjoy. SWAT teams usually. Good gear, training, and high pay. It's actually rather progressive for Ogres," Melody said as the car rolled past the gate. "Honey, do you think I should wait in the car? There are people up there who probably don't like that I joined the PID."

Huh. That's a good point.

"Yeah… that's not a bad thought. Maybe you should. Sorry," Gus said.

"Oh, I don't mind," Melody said from the rear passenger seat. "I wanted to catch up on our email anyway and see if anything new has been reported in the forums. I still can't believe they got away with calling it all a terrorist attack."

Gus pulled into a visitor parking space and turned off the car.

"Terrorist attack is easier than saying a bunch of paranormal federal buildings exploded by bombs that weren't mechanical," Gus said, then looked at Melody. "You need anything?"

"A kiss?" Melody said with an enchanting smile for him. She was dressed immaculately again, in a black suit, and had pulled her hair back.

Gus frowned at the request. She'd managed to weasel her way into sitting next to him constantly, and she'd even started snuggling with him last night after Vanessa had gone to bed. Though it hadn't progressed beyond that, despite her continued and repeated attempts to get there.

Vanessa opened the car door and got out, immediately shutting it.

"I've been a good girl," Melody said, not one of her contracts glowing. "I'm playing by all your rules and showing you I'm in it for the long run.

"I even texted your mom last night to let her know what was going on with the bombings."

Gus had noticed she'd done that. His mom had made a point to text him in return that Melody had done so. And to expressly state she liked his girlfriends.

Plural.

Because apparently Vanessa had texted his sister the same information, which had circulated back to his mom.

"Fine," Gus said. "But—"

Melody shot forward, grabbing him by the tie, and kissed him hungrily. Her lips pressed hard to his own. The kiss lasted only a couple seconds before Melody pulled back.

"Oh, that was quite nice," Melody said and pulled a tissue from somewhere. She lightly began to brush it over Gus's lips. "Sorry, just a little bit of pink there."

Before he could respond, she adjusted his tie once and pulled on his collar.

"There, all fixed," Melody said, sitting back down in her seat. Slowly, her red contract began to glow. Before it became a burning bright spot on her face. "Me oh my, apparently all it takes is one kiss for me. I feel like such a child."

Gus slowly grinned, coming out of his stupor. It'd been a hell of a kiss, to be certain. But nothing had happened. She hadn't tried to force more, or push a Contract on him—nothing.

"Remind me to kiss you again later," Gus said, feeling odd about it all. Melody blinked and then stared at him, her eyebrows rising slightly.

"Oh, and by the way, you look great today," Gus said, getting out of the car while grabbing the bag of stuff for Mark.

Catching up with Vanessa, who was waiting by the door, Gus gave her a lopsided grin.

"She get one?" she asked.

"Yeah," Gus grumbled, pulling the door open for Vanessa.

"Huh. Surprising," Vanessa said, holding Mark's personal carrier of coffee and sandwich.

"Why, you want one too?" Gus asked.

"Got mine last night," Vanessa said as she walked into the building.

Huh?

Gus was unable to ask her anything further as the visitor's desk was right there. Then they were escorted up to Mark's office personally.

Sitting behind a rather large desk, in an office bigger than the one he had down at PID, Mark looked like he was drowning under an endless pile of folders and papers.

Looking up from his computer, he smiled when he saw the two of them.

"Gus, Vanessa, and… oh my… is that… is that all for me?" Mark said, lifting his hands toward the coffee carrier. He briefly opened and closed his hands at it.

"Yep," Gus said, stepping into the office. Their escort vanished and Gus closed the door. "Vanessa made it up for you, just the way you like it."

"You're a beautiful woman, Agent Flores, even if you're Gus's girlfriend," Mark said, taking the carrier directly from Vanessa.

Opening the front of the cardboard box made to hold enough coffee for twelve people, Mark began drinking from it directly.

Vanessa set down the breakfast sandwich next to Mark's keyboard and then took a seat in one of the two chairs. She was dressed almost exactly like Melody, just with a bit more color.

Letting out a massive breath, Mark set down the coffee carrier next to him. Then he picked up the sandwich, tore open the wrapper and started eating immediately.

Lifting up the bag that contained two cardboard rectangles of donuts and a large pack of candy, Gus set it down on Mark's desk.

Laughing with his mouth closed, Mark nodded his head rapidly.

"Oh yes, pay raises for all three of you. Your whole messy love triangle," Mark mumbled with his mouth full. "Pay raises."

"About the car, Eric say or do anything?" Gus asked, trying to change the subject before Mark could get off on a tangent.

Shaking his head, Mark took another giant bite.

"No. He won't say anything at all anymore. He refuses to talk and his lawyer won't give us anything," Mark said, chewing. "I had someone from the Enchanter's guild take a look at it, though. He agrees with your initial thought, but a bit differently. Eric didn't do them."

Gus raised his eyebrows and waited.

"He didn't do them, but he wrote it out so someone could copy it?" Vanessa asked.

"Exactly!" Mark pointed at Vanessa. "Oh, I'm so lucky. I have three great detectives closing out my shifts now. This is gonna be a good year, I think, for my year-end review.

"Guild thinks Eric wrote out directions for someone else to do it. Apparently it doesn't take a great talent to copy work, just a steady hand and a decent mind."

"That's… odd, right?" Gus asked.

Mark shrugged, swallowing hard. "Maybe. Maybe not. Eric was literally doing merc work out of that warehouse. We've been running down his finances.

"Best we can figure is that he was on the out with his family until he got caught. Doing whatever he could to make ends meet. For all we know, he got hired to do the job for the Weres."

"Maybe," Gus said, still not feeling quite right about it.

Picking up the coffee carrier, Mark began to chug from the mouth of it. Large gulping noises were the only thing Gus could hear as he drank and drank.

Finally, he set it back down and then went straight to the bag Gus had put down for him.

"Kelly is going to kill me," Mark said, pulling open a box and immediately yanking out a donut. Tearing into it, Mark leaned back in his chair and sighed as he chewed. "Surprise, you're working on the bombing case now. Getting some heavy pushing from above to make progress; Feds gave me a blank check on overtime and pulling in anyone I want."

"Ok," Gus said with a shrug. He'd been expecting that.

"What do we have so far?" Vanessa asked, pulling out a pad of paper and a pen from a coat pocket.

"Nothing," Mark said, smiling widely at her. "In fact, less than nothing. The Feds are ruling the case, and they haven't even let my detectives onto the scene. You three are going to be the first ones to get a chance to look.

"Honestly? I reassigned all my people back to normal cases last night. It'd become apparent the PID was being shut out.

"I figure the Fed dick in charge got broken in half once someone higher up found out. Now he's begging me to use my resources to help."

"And you're sending us in?" Vanessa asked.

"Honestly, Gus is the best detective I've got. But you three also finished your case first, so… happy coincidence," Mark said with a shrug, reaching for a second donut. "Your Fed contact is… eh, I forgot their name. It's in an email I sent you as soon as I was notified you checked in. Has all the details and your official assignment."

Gus nodded as he scratched at his stomach. That sounded about right for Mark. He was a good officer. In the end, the squad had been able to hold out for so long because Mark stepped up.

Goofy as he was, strange as he was, he had most things on lock and under control.

"… probably be waiting for you in the lobby as soon as you're done here. Can't say I'm real happy about working with them, but we do what we're ordered," Mark said. "Charge of the Light Brigade and all that."

"What?" Vanessa asked.

"Orders are orders," Gus said, getting to his feet. "Theirs not to make reply, theirs not to reason why, theirs but to do and die. Which means we get to go run a shit show, improvise, adapt, and overcome."

Vanessa got to her feet, tucking away the paper and pen.

"Anything else?" Gus asked Mark.

"No. You've breathed life back into me," Mark said, licking his fingers. "Just play nice with the Fed while you work the bombing, don't worry about who runs the show, and let them have all the credit if they want it.

"Honestly? I don't want any part of this. PID doesn't need to get involved. Whoever did this didn't target us. That speaks to a political nature to me, more than anything else. Beyond that, make sure you keep your head down. No need for the Feds to start poking around.

"On top of all that, everything is running as it always has. No changes. It's as if the Fed didn't really do anything anyways. Damn ice-cream cone."

In other words, they've already asked a few questions about me, and they want to know more. Give them nothing, allow no hints to anything, and keep them guessing.

Be defensive, keep the security up.

Gus nodded and went to the door.

"Oh, that reminds me, the light show going on around the building," Gus said. "That's a lot of increased security. Do they really think this building will be a target?"

"Huh? Oh. Oh. No. That security is what's normally there. One of the wards failed and the system became visible," Mark said.

"Failed?" Gus asked.

"When the bombs went off, a number of people went a bit… stupid. Panic, fear, whatever you wanna call it. A lot of old people just gassed their cars into anything or hit the brakes harder than a senior's special dinner," Mark said. "Some old man popped the curb and smashed into the corner of the building. He's lucky they just let him go with a warning since it wasn't his fault. Not really, at least.

"Anyways. Old building has had the same wards since the nineties. Apparently they were a bit different than the normal ones. The car managed to trigger only a couple with the impact. All the normal ones fixed themselves, but the cloaking rune failed."

"Huh. And it's not related to the bombings?" Gus asked, suspicious.

"Nope. Really was just an old man. A Norm. No mask, no relations to Paras. Was a transit worker his whole life. Retired. Car was clean, no runes, no bombs, no substances or traces of anything.

Completely and utterly unrelated. They even called in one of the few trained telepaths in the known world to check—an actual psyker," Mark said.

Mm. That's...rather thorough. Ok... so... unrelated.

Shrugging, Gus dismissed it. There was no way the car or the old man was related to the bombing if they used a psyker.

Vanessa already had her phone out as they left the floor Mark was working on.

"Got it," she said. "The name of the Fed is Justin Bird."

"The fuck kind of name is that?" Gus muttered as the elevator doors closed.

When they opened again, a pudgy man in his early thirties was standing there. He had a goatee, a mustache, and a receding hairline that matched his expanding middle.

Great.

He's literally the definition of a Fed, isn't he?

Next he's going to either insult me for being a Para or Vanessa for being a Norm.

"There you are," said the man as Gus and Vanessa walked toward him. "Here. Your badges. Head on down to the main Fed building blast site. Update me when you get a chance."

After handing the badges to Gus and Vanessa, the man waddled off.

"Uh," Gus said, turning to Vanessa. "That wasn't what I was expecting."

"Or me," Vanessa said as she looked at her badge. "And he spelled my name wrong. It's with an S, not a Z."

"Right," Gus said, "Let's go get Melody and head over."

"Yeah." Vanessa shook her head. "This is going to suck, isn't it?"

"Yep."

Chapter 19 - Blasted

Getting out of the back of the car, Gus looked around. They were parked in a small lot next to the ruined federal building. They'd made it past the security barrier easy enough with their badges and their visitor badges.

"Damn," Vanessa said, stepping out the passenger side. "It… it's gone. It's like it never existed. Just a mound of rubble."

Melody shut the driver's side door.

"I've seen some destruction. Made plenty of things go boom myself, mind you," Gus said, running his tongue over his teeth. "But uh… this looks odd. Bombs tend to make things fly outward. Explode outward, really.

"But if you look around, nothing is damaged in the nearby buildings. They're way too close for there to be anything but giant chunks ripped out of the sides of them, given the look of the Fed building. It doesn't make sense. Even just looking at it from here."

"Huh," Vanessa said, starting to walk toward a small group of tents out in front of the Fed building.

Rescue workers had long since left. The survivors, bodies, and otherwise had all been pulled out rapidly through magical means in the first two days.

Now it was all investigation and bomb squad duty.

"You're right," Melody said, walking next to Vanessa. "The blast wasn't just localized, it was only the Fed building itself. There wasn't a single brick or stone that blew out of the building's perimeter. How's that even possible?"

"It isn't," Gus grumbled. "It isn't on any level. I know what a shield can withstand, and if the blast was big enough to do that to the building, the shield used would have had to be massive. Equal or bigger to the shielding we saw back where we met Mark.

"But to be that big and heavy, a shield takes time. Years. Constantly building and rebuilding wards and runes to a set location."

Melody's Orange and Blue contracts were glowing brighter and dimmer in alternating patterns. "It doesn't make sense at all."

Right. She's the one most likely to figure out the puzzle here. And Vanessa is most likely the one to get information out of anyone here.

That means I'm a third wheel and a problem. Maybe I could see if there's any video footage to review.

There have to be cameras nearby that saw it, right?

Gus cleared his throat.

"Melody, you handle the blast and figuring it out. Vanessa, you take care of the contacts and start working them over for information. I'm not as good at either of those tasks as you two," Gus said. "I'll see about finding if there's any footage of the blast."

Both women nodded. They'd heard him and agreed, but they were both tied up in in this new case already.

Clicking his tongue, Gus stuck his hands in his pockets and wandered off to the ever spot-able techie truck. A massive modified bread truck that usually was just a plain flat white with a few pieces of whatnot sticking out the top.

Rather than set up in a field base or a location, it was just easier to have everything loaded into a specific vehicle. Outfit it to hold three techs, a driver and all their gear, and you had a stinky, smelly, fast food-smelling tiny space that resembled little better than a spider hole.

Personally, it made Gus feel a bit uneasy, but the techs never seemed to complain about it.

The question was: was it a Fed truck or a PID truck? If it was a Fed truck, it was unlikely Gus was going to get anything.

And if it was a PID truck…

Tapping on the rear metal door of the big bread truck, Gus waited.

There was a clatter inside, and then the door lock clacked into place.

Ah shit.

When the door swung open, Gus stared up into the wide-framed glasses of Michael Noble. He was a mousy looking man, thin, and narrow. He looked like he was made out of bones and tendons, and little else. His brown hair was lank and light colored, his eyes a similar color.

"Gustavus," Michael said, pushing up the glasses on his nose. "You here to work the case?"

"Yup," Gus said with a smirk. "How you doing, Mike?"

"Michael. Not Mike," he said. "I'm fine. What do you want?"

"I'm sure you already went door to door to see if there were any cameras nearby? You're a thorough guy, Michael, but I do have to ask. Just to make sure," Gus said.

Michael grinned, suddenly looking like a rat. "Yeah. Got everything I could. Nothing to see though. Nothing on the main approach, nothing facing the front of the Fed building, and not a security camera along the road either.

"Feds did a good job of making sure there weren't any cameras looking at a Para thoroughfare."

"Yeah. Too good a job it seems. I take it the internal cameras lost their feed with the blast? Nothing to recover?" Gus asked.

"Nothing. Everything was shredded beyond possibility of recovery. Almost seemed like it had a self-termination protocol on the drives." Michael frowned. "Whatever. None of my concern what the Feds do. That it, Gustavus?"

"Yeah. Suppose that's it," Gus said and sighed, looking around. It left him without a direction to head in. Which meant he had to make one of his own.

"Your sister won't return my calls," Michael said.

Ugh. Really?

"Considering she's dating a very nice man, I'm not surprised, Michael. Besides, you only ever went on one date," Gus said, regretting bringing her to the PID office party last year. "Take it easy."

Wandering along the sidewalk, Gus looked across the street. Everything had been cordoned off, which left people having to cross the street to go around.

It created an unhealthy amount of interest in the whole situation. A lot of lookie-loos who could easily have something to do with the attack.

Then again, trying to pick someone out returning to the scene of the crime would be pointless. It was days after the fact, and it'd be terribly unlikely.

Gus was staring at the sidewalk in front of him.

He could see the exact place where the explosion had been cut off. There were black char marks on one side of the cement, and on the other it was pristine. Fairly extreme, to say the least.

How'd they manage that? Was it just a giant spell? Not even a bomb? Is that why they can't figure anything out or find anything?

Walking back, Gus headed for the center tent. He could see Melody scrambling up and amongst the debris ahead. She was moving through the rubble with most of her contracts lit up, clearly processing everything she could see and touch of the situation.

Vanessa was off to one side, speaking to an older man who seemed more than willing to give her anything she asked for. She was taking notes down as he spoke.

Fuck this.

Gus reached for his wallet and pulled out a card nestled there. There was no name on the card now that he read it again. Just a telephone number.

Digging his phone out of his pocket, Gus tapped in the number and held it up to his ear.

It rang three times and then connected.

"Agent Hellström," Dave the Curator said over the line. "To what do I owe the pleasure?"

"The bombings. Anything you can tell me? I'd like that little favor you said you owed me," Gus said, deciding to dive straight in without preamble.

"Ha. I suppose I might have guessed," Dave said and then sighed. "I'm afraid you can't call in that favor, because I know exactly as much as your dear Feds do. If not, perhaps less, if that were believable."

"What…?" Gus asked, not really understanding. "You're the Curator."

Laughing on the other end of the line, Dave seemed rather amused.

"I am! And yet, there it is. I know absolutely nothing, if not less than you do. I'm afraid all my sources went to ground. All of them," Dave said. "There isn't a single one I can contact at any level."

That's… not good. Is it?

When all the rats go running, it means there's more coming.

He's also being rather friendly, isn't he?

"And yes, if your thought just now was 'that's bad,' then I'd agree. I've been packing up my belongings just in case, and have made arrangements for my shop," Dave said. "I don't actually think anything will happen, but I'm not going to sit idly by and let another riot roll over me."

"Riot?" Gus asked.

"Yes, agent. A Riot. There's been a large amount of resentment and tension building in the Para community as of late," Dave said. "Them being shoved into a media blackout over the bombing of some essential federal buildings isn't endearing anyone to anyone.

"I mean, let's speak for what that is. If you were a citizen and suddenly all the buildings you believed kept you safe and secure at night from humans go ka-boom, would you be feeling particularly safe?"

"No," Gus said, licking his lips. Dave was making a really good point. In all the mess and fuss of the situation, Gus had forgotten that he was himself a Para. Just one in hiding, and unregistered as such.

If he were part of the normal Para population, he'd definitely be nervous.

The Federal Department for Paras had been established primarily to keep the two worlds separate, and to keep Paras safe by doing that.

"Now, throw in a blackout of all media, information, and coverage. Drop a whole lot of mojo on the humans to keep them unaware, and add 'terrorist attack' to that mix," Dave said. "What do you think the normal citizen is thinking?"

"Yeah. Yeah, I hear ya. But I mean, they're probably working on this. That, I mean," Gus said.

"Who?" Dave asked.

"The Fed. I'm sure they're aware of the problem and are working on it," Gus said.

"No… Agent. Who? I don't have hard numbers, only speculation, but I think… I think the Fed has been gutted. I don't think there's the manpower or the numbers for anyone to be worrying about the common citizen right now. Everyone seems to think the Fed has some buildings that weren't hit. Secret offices that are still perfectly fine. What if there aren't? What if there are less than twelve operating buildings in the entire country?

"Have you seen any casualty lists? Numbers? Names? Or is it all mum's the word? Much like a number of operations you were involved in where any losses were counterproductive to morale," Dave said.

Which was almost always because when someone died, whole teams did. There really wasn't an in between, was there?

Damn.

"You think they suffered catastrophic levels of fatalities, are hiding it all, and are a step away from collapsing," Gus paraphrased.

"Roughly," Dave said. "Hence, the packing."

"Yeah. Got it," Gus said, running a hand through his hair. This call wasn't going the way he wanted it to. At all.

"No results on your family, by the way," Dave said.

"Huh? Oh. Oh, yeah. No worries," Gus said, feeling very unsettled. "Not a problem. Just, uh… update me and… yeah."

"Though I did hear some interesting news," Dave said.

"Yeah?" Gus asked, walking toward the perimeter. There was a human Fed agent there looking bored, but watching the crowds for any issues.

"I hear Melody Lark moved in with you. That she canceled all her contracts, called in an ungodly number of favors, got her record wiped clean, and settled down in your guest bedroom. You're playing house just outside the city," Dave said.

"Yeah. I guess that all happened," Gus said. "She's living with me, I guess."
"And your other partner, Vanessa, as well," Dave said.
"Uh, yeah. That one is only temporary; she's supposed to head back… actually, I guess that's tonight, but—" Gus frowned. He stopped in his tracks, halfway to the agent. Melody had already said what she was planning for dinner tonight, lasagna. Vanessa had already said she wanted to watch a movie as well after dinner. They were both acting like she wasn't leaving.
"I see Melody has captured her as well. Has she contracted either of you, yet?" Dave asked.
"No. Well, not me, at least. I don't think she contracted Vanessa. She's just being friendly with her to help her get over her girlfriend," Gus said. The words sounded stupid the moment he said them.
He knew they were false.
Melody wanted both him and Vanessa, then wanted him and Vanessa to be together as well.
One happy harem for Melody.
"Hm. I won't even bother to respond to that bit of fluff. So, where shall I send the Contract gifts to? Your house?" Dave asked. "Because let's be honest. This is Melody Lark we're talking about. She isn't going to veer away from you at this point. Nor is she going to relent."
Closing his eyes, Gus pressed a hand to his face. He'd remembered kissing her this morning, and he didn't want any part of that thought at the moment.
"Melody wants to buy a house after we're all contracted," Gus said finally. Stupidly.
As if he'd given up.
"Ah, smart girl. Send me the address once it's all taken care of, and I'll send some presents," Dave said.
"Yeah. I'll do that," Gus mumbled.
"For what it's worth, I believe she's genuinely happy, and beyond interested in you. The inquiries she sent to me and my people were… numerous, when she was looking into you," Dave said. "Congratulations in advance."
"Yeah, thanks," Gus said. "See ya, Dave."
"Goodbye for now, Agent."
Ending the call and locking his phone, Gus felt like his whole world had suddenly come apart at the seams.
Keep it together. Been through worse. Right?
Right. Been through worse.
Lots worse. So much worse that I could write a book about it.
Marching up to the agent nearby, Gus stuck a fine sliver of his ability into the man's thoughts. They were unguarded, blessedly non-complex, and purely human.
They were also focused squarely on Melody's rear end.
Those thoughts rapidly cleared up when the young man noticed Gus was within fifteen feet.
He looked young. Young enough that Gus wondered if he was still in college. A standard Fed dress suit, Fed sunglasses, and a blank Fed face.
"Agent," said the young man.
"Agent," Gus said, and held out his hand. "Gustavus Hellström. On loan from the PID."
"Oh, yeah," said the Fed, not giving his name.
"I was wondering if I could bug you a bit?" Gus asked.
"Yeah, but I wasn't here when this happened," said the Fed. In his mind, there were sudden flashes of memory. It was the federal training academy for agents. They had been going through another course when the news came to evacuate.
Evacuate and head for immediate safety and shelter.
It was hours before someone came back and released all the students back to their classes and dorms. Then it was revealed what had happened.
And that they were all graduated ahead of schedule.
As were the four classes after them.
Gus managed to keep a tight leash on his emotions as the thoughts coming out of the man confirmed his worst suspicions. The fear Gus actually had about the situation was real.

Fear didn't come easy to him, as he was a master of it. He dined on it regularly. It took some work to make him afraid.

This was a special case.

"Got it. Actually, I was wondering if you could tell me how many made it out of this building? Trying to get an idea of the lethality of the detonation. Might help us narrow down what it was," Gus said.

"Three," said the agent immediately.

Except it wasn't three. It was one. Two of those three had died at the hospital; every single other person in the building had perished as well. It meant that of the roughly six hundred and twenty people working in the building at the time of detonation, less than one percent survived.

The agent's memories moved from the fact that almost no one had survived here to the fact that this was common for the disaster sites. The casualty list of the Federal Department for Paras was a staggering ninety-five percent of everyone who was working out of an office building.

The federal agency was gutted, and it almost didn't exist anymore

Smiling, Gus nodded and waved a hand at the agent.

"Thank you for your time," he said, leaving at as easy a pace as he could manage. Sweating under his coat, and feeling like he'd just discovered the worst possible situation, Gus didn't know what to do.

He took out his phone and dialed Mark up. Mark was the only person who would understand how bad this situation could get.

Almost immediately, the line picked up.

"Hey the—"

"Mark," Gus said, interrupting him. "Are you alone?"

"Uh, yeah. Why, what's up?" Mark asked. There was the click of a door shutting.

"Who are you reporting to right now?" Gus asked.

"Huh? Uh, the local Fed commander. My boss got shipped to the capital on orders to help out there," Mark said. "Gus, what's going on?"

"Have you talked to the commander? What's his name? Her name?"

"I mean, I talked to them in an email this morning and a few text messages," Mark said.

"No, talked to them. In person, or over the phone so you could confirm it was them," Gus asked.

Mark was silent.

Gus heard the slow creak of a chair as Mark probably leaned back into it.

"Now that you mention it," Mark said. "Never have. Never had a face-to-face or a hand-off. Just got my orders handed to me and was told what to do."

"Yeah. Yeah, that might be the problem." Gus grimaced. "I was poking around. I know, you said not to in your own way, but I had to. I also called the Curator."

"You did what?" Mark asked, his volume going up.

"I called Dave. The Curator. He gave me his card. Told me to call him. So I did," Gus said. "Curator thinks the Fed is gutted. Toast. Donezo. Beyond KIA. Exterminated. End of fucking watch.

"Beyond ninety-percent casualty rate at this building. Almost every building is like this. I've got some young fucking agent here who looks like he might be able to buy me a beer, but he'd get carded four times trying to do it," Gus said. "He got graduated early. Forced recruitment."

"Gus," Mark said, drawing out the name.

"Mark, if I don't miss it, you're the head asshole in charge of the state right now by virtue that everyone else is dead," Gus said. "And so you wanting to play nice-nice is probably not going to work, because there's no one to fucking play nice-nice with."

Mark audibly sighed.

"Yeah. Got that," Mark muttered. "I'm gonna… gonna tell Kelly and Megan to head out of the city for a while."

"Always welcome at my place, or my mom's. Mom likes Megan," Gus said.

Megan, Kelly, and his mom all got along perfectly well. Then again, they didn't know what Gus and Jennifer were.

"Maybe," Mark said. "Maybe… for now… do what you can. I'm going to start doing what I think I need to. Try not to piss off anyone if you can help it. Not sure if there's anyone here to bail us out if you manage to piss off the wrong people."

"I hear ya," Gus said.

"Right, see ya later," Mark said, and disconnected the line.

Chapter 20 - Wrong Fit

Pushing his phone in his pocket, Gus really wasn't sure what to do with himself. They were operating beyond having no safety net. There wasn't even a tight rope.

Most people just thought the Federal Department for Paras was there and did its own thing. Gus had a different view, mostly borne of his debrief from his time killing Elves. One he didn't share with people.

With anyone, really.

Not even his own family knew what the Fed really was. Mark was the one who probably understood the most, but that was because of his own position and how much more closely he worked with them. He knew what they were about.

And that was protection for the entirety of the Para world.

The Fed was what operated between the Para world and the Norm world. It interfaced between the government, and operated as a de facto government for the Para world. It was the government, the health system, the police, the finances, the everything. Everything was what the Fed was.

To the PID, the Fed was their version of the FBI. To a Para citizen it could be the DME, record depository, and social security offices.

And someone hadn't just attacked it, they'd ended it.

There were precious few people right now acting on behalf of the Para world to interface with the Norms.

Pressing a hand to his face, Gus took a deep breath. He held it in, focusing on what he could do for the time being. He couldn't fix what had happened to the Fed. He couldn't rebuild it or help it.

What he could do was figure out who had done it. Or maybe at least how.

If he could figure out how it had happened, there was the distinct possibility he could prevent it from ever happening again.

Letting out his held breath, Gus felt his thoughts crystallize on that goal.

Figure out how it had happened.

He looked at Melody and saw her standing off to one side now, staring at the wreck that had once been a large office building.

Let's see what she's got and go from there.

Stuffing his hands in his pockets, Gus wandered over to Melody.

She was facing the ruin, and she didn't turn toward him. She was acting like she didn't even know he was there.

Coming to stand beside her, he leaned forward and saw her face clearly.

Her Blue, Green, Orange and Violet contracts were all blazing and bright. She wasn't just working on this, she was burning her own power to put her entire self against it.

Tentatively, he connected back to the fiber of power he'd left in her mind. Her thoughts were chasing one another wildly. Dodging over clues, hints, and small things she was trying to piece together in a mad hodge-podge of screaming and shouting Melodys.

She had nothing, and she was trying to put it all together.

"Hey," Gus said, figuring this would be a good time to interrupt her. She seemed like the type of person to fall way too deep.

Melody didn't respond, but her head marginally turned toward him.

"If you drop your contracts and chat with me, I'll give you another kiss later," Gus bargained. He really did think it'd be better for her to stop. If she hadn't figured it out at this moment, standing here and spinning her wheels wasn't going to do it.

All of her contracts came to a screeching halt. At the same time, her Red, Yellow, and Indigo contracts lit up.

"You will?" Melody said, her head turning toward him completely. Smiling, she seemed very interested in him right now. "I'll take that bargain, but I want my kiss now."

Gus was going to decline, but then he realized it didn't matter. If Dave was right, it wasn't really a question of if anymore, but more a question of when. He'd already relented and let Melody in.

Laying a hand on Melody's shoulder, Gus leaned in, tilted his head to one side and kissed her.

It was a tender and innocent thing that lasted only a few seconds. Moving away from her when it ended, he smiled and raised his eyebrows.

"There. Contract complete," Gus said with a chuckle.

Melody opened her eyes and gazed at him with a sappy and sleepy-looking smile. "Yeah."

"So, I took a poke into your head. Looks like you're as stumped as the rest of everyone on the planet. It seemed like you were running in circles. Figured you could use a break," Gus said.

Melody's Indigo and Yellow contracts glowed white and then faded away, her Red contract simply fading.

"I think… you're right," she said, looking back at the mound of rubble. "There isn't much to go on. The blast itself seems to have removed a goodly amount of whatever traces you would expect to find. It's just… all gone. There isn't even a magical imprint of whatever spell was used to cause the explosion. There's no bomb or explosive fragments either. It's as if there was no explosion at all."

"Hm. That's curious. Alright, let's go get Ness and then see about taking a break. I have some news as well. News I don't think is going to go over well once I explain some backstory," Gus said. He wasn't looking forward to this conversation, but his talk with Dave had made him realize how important these two women were to him.

And that meant cluing them in to how bad it actually was that the Fed was gone.

***

Standing with Vanessa and Melody, Gus pulled down the tinfoil a bit further on his hot dog. They'd found a food truck and Gus had filled them in on the problem. With the noise of the busy street behind the truck, and everyone rushing around in every direction, it was a conversation that was safe to have.

Vanessa and Melody looked appropriately afraid now.

"Part of me thinks we should just move," Melody said, and shook her head. "Pack up Gus's family, sell the house, and move. I have several countries I can get us a visa for without much of a problem."

Vanessa shook her head slightly.

"I know," Melody said before Vanessa could shoot it down. "We're not leaving. It's not really a valid option, but it's something we can fall back on if things get bad."

Sighing, Vanessa pressed a hand to the side of her head, her hot dog forgotten in the other.

"I mean, here's the reality," Gus said after swallowing. "It doesn't change anything for us. It doesn't really alter what we're doing or how we're going about it. We also can't fix it, or even help it along to recovery.

"Best I can figure is we determine how it happened, so it doesn't happen again. The Fed has gone through some bad times before—it'll limp through this and make it through."

Melody nodded and then systematically destroyed her hot dog. Eating it faster than the eye could practically blink. It was as if she didn't even taste it.

Coughing, she wiped at her mouth with her napkin and tossed her trash into the can.

"You're right," she said to Gus. There was a strong sense of determination there. "You're right. All we can do is soldier on and do what we can to make it so this doesn't happen again. The Fed will do for itself what it needs to and has to. Mark will do what he can for us in the PID."

Nodding her head, Melody started marching back to the blast site.

Gus laid a hand on Vanessa's back and started leading the detective back as well, though at a much more sedate pace.

"Hey, you got family in the city?" Gus asked.

"Huh? Oh. Not in the major part of it," Vanessa said. "Somewhat in an offshoot neighborhood."

"Good. Was there anything else you needed from your apartment?" Gus prompted, trying to get Vanessa to keep with the thought. She seemed the most disturbed by the news for some reason.

"No. Mel and I hired movers. All my stuff is in storage now. I broke the lease and turned over my key by mail," Vanessa said. Then she looked at him, her eyes slightly widening. "Wait, you didn't know? Mel swore up and down she told you and that you knew."

Gus waved it away with a hand.

"I knew she was trying to get you into my house. I just didn't know she succeeded. Her next goal is to get the three of us into a bed together," Gus said. "Don't tell her, but I already surrendered to her. I'm just going to play hard to get for a while. It's fun to make her chase. She likes it anyways."

"Huh. I want… to talk more about this, but I need to ask you a question," Vanessa said.

"Hit me." Gus came to a stop at the intersection across from the toppled Fed building. Melody was already back on the scene clambering up a twisted chunk of steel.

"This is actually a terrorist attack. If the Fed is everything you said, we're fighting an organized, well thought out, planned in the extreme, and likely armed and dangerous force of people," Vanessa said. "Do we really think they won't hit the PID now that we're working in place of the Fed?"

Gus blinked, thinking. He'd known everything she'd said, but he hadn't put it all together in such a simple way yet.

And it was frightening.

They were fighting what was essentially a terrorist faction, or an insurgency. He'd already fought against both and hadn't liked it one whit.

Worst of all, the enemy would be an almost entirely Para force. They could be anything at all so long as they matched up ideal wise. It was a truly terrifying thought.

"Yeah. I mean, you're not wrong. The problem is that until we get an idea of who it is or how they did it, we're operating in the dark. To find out who they are, we paint ourselves as a target. Damned if we do, damned if we don't."

"I figured," Vanessa said, then sighed. "And my life was really starting to look up."

Chuckling, Gus finished off his hot dog and crumpled up his trash.

"Your life is still looking up," Gus said. "It's just… complicated."

"That's putting it mildly. I'm living with a man who is apparently going to become my boyfriend at some point, and a woman who is already more or less my girlfriend. All while discovering a new world and breaking up with a Werewolf. Been an interesting month," Vanessa said. "Talk about rebounding hard in the other direction."

Gus's phone vibrated in his pocket.

Frowning, he reached in and pulled it out, then unlocked it when he realized it was listed as a PID officer on the ID but he didn't recognize the name.

"This is Gus," Gus said.

"Agent Hellström," said a man into the line. "This is Captain Vard at precinct six. I've got someone here that I think I need you to take a look at."

"Oh? I have a BOLO out for—"

"No. No one you were expecting, I'm afraid," said Vard. "I've got an Elf that is losing her mind here and—"

There was a screeching howl in the background that sounded like something out of a nightmare. In fact, Gus had heard it many times when he'd been on deployment, and in his nightmares since he'd gotten home.

Elven warhowl. What the fuck?

"And yeah, I was wondering if you could come down and take a look at her. Someone reminded me that there had been a similar case with a Troll," Vard said. "I can't pull up anything on the database since everything we had was hosted by the Fed. Someone knew your name around here and flipped it to me."

Hosted by the Fed… oh shit. How much information has been lost? Michael is a paranoid bastard and I know he kept a local, and illegal, copy of most of the databases we use.

But is that true for everyone? Do they have their own Michaels? Doesn't seem like it.

"Right, ah… you said six?" Gus asked.

"Yeah, six. You willin' to come over and take a look?" Vard asked.

"Uh-huh. I'll bring my partner and we'll head over to your location. Do me a favor. See if you can locate their driver's license to see if their mask is there. If it's intact, don't touch it or disturb it. If it's not, we need to figure out where it was assigned," Gus said.

"Got it. Thank you, Agent," Vard said, and hung up the line.

"We going on a trip?" Vanessa asked.

"Apparently we've got another Fitz," Gus said, putting his phone back into his pocket. "An Elf this time. We'll need to let Melody know, then head out. She can keep working the site for now. It's probably what she'd enjoy most anyways."

"That's fair. I'd rather do something else anyways. I'm not any good for something like this," Vanessa said. "All the lead investigator wanted was my phone number in the end."

"Huh. You get that a lot?" Gus asked, walking across the street when it finally turned green.

"Often enough in the past. I told him you were my boyfriend, though. He left it alone after that," Vanessa said.

***

Standing across from the Elven woman, Gus wasn't quite sure what to make of the situation.

Her arms were bound behind her back in full transport chains, which were locked into the leg irons and shackles she was wearing. She was completely bound and weighed down. On top of that, the whole thing was locked into an eye loop bolted into the ground specifically made for Paras like Ogres.

And still the Elf stood there, her entire body bent forward toward him in a vain attempt to reach him. Reach him and likely murder him.

Her eyes were almond shaped and slanted. Bright blue, they were filled with an insanity Gus had never seen before.

Her tipped ears stuck up from the wild mess of brown hair that covered her head. She was also almost naked, having apparently torn her clothes apart in her maddened fury.

"We found her atop a dead Norm she'd mauled. Was sitting on top of his chest and apparently trying to scoop the eyes out or something," said Captain Vard. He was a large older man in his fifties and probably pushing retirement. Black hair, black skin, and dark-brown eyes. He looked like he could still bench more than Gus could, even during his military days when he'd had daily PT.

"Elves have a thing about eyes," Gus said, frowning. "A number of the old generations believe the eyes aren't just windows to the soul, but where the soul itself resides. After all, how you interpret the world is all your own. I could say her eyes are an ice blue, and you might think they're a winter blue.

"We just call that perspective; they call it filtering through the soul."

"And trying to rip the eyes out of a dead man?" Vard asked.

"Trying to get his soul and probably eat it," Gus said. "Like I said. Older generations. Though… she's a Meadow Elf, I think. Has the coloring for it."

"Right, well, leave you to it. I got things need doing," Vard said. He flipped a hand at Gus and left the interview room.

"How old is she?" Vanessa asked.

"Her? Hm," Gus said. Reaching out carefully, he waited for a second and then lashed out, grabbing her jaw when she moved her head to one side.

Thrashing wildly against his hand, the Elven woman began to speak at him in Elvish.

Gus forced her head to one side and brushed the hair away from her ear.

"Length determines age up to a point. After that, they tend to put in earrings for each century," Gus said. "She's… old enough to be your great-great-great-grandma. Somewhere between two hundred and three hundred."

"You'd need a few more greats. My family bred early and often," Vanessa said.

Gus let go of the woman's jaw and sighed.

Her license wasn't her mask, or the mask was well and truly shattered. Unrecoverable.

In either case, this felt exactly like Fitz all over again.

"Her name is Misha Trent," Vanessa said, holding the license in her hand.

Misha's head turned to Vanessa, and she began to speak in Elvish again.

"What… what is that?" Vanessa asked. "Is it Elvish?"

"Yeah. She said you're a nasty-looking mud worm," Gus said. Clearing his throat, he tried to say one of the only things that tended to work on the Desert Elves he'd fought. He'd befriended a number of them to learn how to hunt them better.

"Will you share your story with me?" Gus asked in Elvish.

Snapping her eyes back to Gus, Misha blinked, and the madness seemed to recede.

"Help me," she whispered huskily in Elvish. Then her eyes flashed and the crazed light appeared there again. "I'll murder you, mud worm. I'll take your soul from you and use it to see your world. Then burn that to the ground!"

Taking a step away, Gus was at a complete loss.

"She said help me," Gus said to Vanessa. "Which makes me think she's still in there, but there's something else keeping her like this."

"Is that even possible?" Vanessa asked.

"I mean, anything is possible with magic. Given enough time, runes, spell-crafting, and a good mind, you could do anything," Gus said with a sigh. "I've seen enterprising young kids straight out of a nightmare neighborhood turning cats and dogs into bombs with some rune-crafting, time, a smidgen of talent, and a book on beginner glyphs."

"That's awful. So… she could still be in there watching all of this happen, and not be able to do anything about it," Vanessa said. "Do you think Eric did it? Did he do her mask, too?"

"That'd be pretty impossible, given her license should be from out of state. That's what Vard said, right? The stuff in her purse made it seem like she was just passing through," Gus said. Then he rubbed a hand against the back of his neck. "In other words, a copycat, a coincidence, or a concerted effort."

"But what'd be the point of this being a concerted effort? That doesn't add up," Vanessa said.

"It doesn't," Gus said. "We should check in on that car we had pulled out. Maybe the rune analyst can tell us something we missed."

Gus walked over to the door, opened it and went looking for Captain Vard.

He found him sitting behind a desk and working through a number of case files by hand with a pen.

"What?" Vard asked without looking up.

"The Elf is awake in there, under all the crazy," Gus said.

"Huh? Oh, sorry Agent," Vard said, looking up and giving Gus his full attention. "She's… in there?"

"She's in there. The rational Elf known as Misha is in there, watching all of this happen, and she can't do anything about it," Gus said.

"Bullshit," Vard replied immediately.

"No, really. She is. We figure there's some type of madness spell on her. Lock her down, keep her safe, let's hope it wears off. Maybe she can tell us where her mask is," Gus said. "I'll keep working the case and update you if I find out anything."

Not wanting to wait around, Gus waved a hand at Vard and left immediately.

"Should we get Mel?" Vanessa asked.

"Probably, yeah. Call her and see if she wants to go with us," Gus said. "Let's hope she found something. Cause I sure as shit don't have any other ideas."

Chapter 21 - The Forest

Pulling into the motor-pool parking lot for PID, Gus found a space and killed the engine. No one had said much on the way here.

The mood in the car was rather somber.

Melody had ended up coming with them. The blast site for the local Fed building was barren of evidence. The next closest building was a half a day's drive away.

"Gus, I don't think I have enough to figure out what happened with the bombings," Melody said. "I haven't figured out anything new since we last talked about it."

"Yeah. I know. Honestly, I'd be surprised if you had," Gus said. He made no move to leave the car immediately. "I just don't know what to do next. I mean… if the Fed were honest about what had happened, I'd feel like they knew more. The fact that they're quiet… that they're hiding that they got wiped out… makes it seem like they don't know what's going on.

"That they don't even know who to trust. For all we know, the PID could be involved."

"It's a pretty bad situation," Vanessa said. "I think I'm still puzzled by the motivation. What did it accomplish? Anything?"

Gus frowned and nodded. The motivation was a good lead to look into.

"Going to hit my CIs. See if they know anything." Gus pulled out his phone and started texting all his confidential informants. Asking them what they knew about the situation, if they'd be willing to talk either by text or in person, and if they did know about the bombing, could they spare any details on why they thought it had happened.

"I already spoke with all my contacts," Melody said. "Nobody knows anything more than we do. Intelligence agencies, even those from my homeland, know nothing. Not a whisper or a hint."

Shaking his head, Gus put his phone back into his pocket.

"Alright. Let's switch gears for a bit then. Focus in on this new mask rage, and see what we can do about it," Gus said. "In the meantime, we see what my CIs have, and if that fails… I don't know. I know everyone with a criminal history in explosives has already been questioned, and by a psyker. Everything has been coming up blank."

"They pulled a psyker?" Melody said, her tone shocked.

"Yeah. They did. So don't feel bad about not finding anything. Anyways, focus. Focus on Misha, and what we can do for her. She's alive and needs a hand," Gus said.

Opening his car door, he got out.

Vanessa and Melody followed suit, and the three of them trooped toward the garage where Sean's runed car had probably been pulled into.

After knocking on the front office door, Gus waited for a second and then opened it.

"Hey," Gus said, looking around for anyone inside. There was no one.

He entered the office and clicked his tongue.

"Hello?" he called.

There was no response.

Walking around through the back into the attached garage, Gus found a pair of legs sticking out from below Sean's car. The feet were happily moving, so Gus wasn't afraid of the person being dead.

"The runes are off," Melody said, walking around to the front of the car. "I wonder why."

"No idea," Gus said, then leaned down and tapped the pair of feet roughly.

Flinching away from him, the mechanic rolled out from under the car. It was a middle-aged man with a pair of small earphones in his ears.

Pulling them out, the brown-haired man sat up.

"Hey, sorry. Couldn't hear anything. What can I do for ya?" asked the man.

"Agent Hellström, PID," Gus said.

"Oh! Yeah, you're the guy who found this thing," said the mechanic, hooking a thumb at the car. "It's a weird one, man. Real wild."

Pulling off his goggles, the man rubbed at his brown eyes for a second.

"Name's Bob," he said. "What can I do for ya?"

"You figure anything out? Trying to get an idea of what the car was meant to be for," Gus said. "It's related to a case we're working."

"What, the bombing? I mean, that's what I thought this would be, too," Bob said and shook his head. "But it's not a bomb, that's for sure. The runes are weird, and I've been trying to figure them out, but… honestly… without an idea of what it's for, it's a lot harder.

"Definitely not a bomb, though, or even a primer, catalyst, or anything like that. Only bit I've figured out is that it interfaces with something else."

A phone rang in the office nearby.

"Shit. Uh… I'll be right back," Bob said, and got up to go get the phone.

"He thought this might be a bomb?" Vanessa asked, hovering near the trunk of the car.

"I mean…" Gus started, staring at the car. "You can definitely turn anything into a bomb. But the runes on the Fed building would probably be tuned to stop that. Wouldn't they?"

"They would," Melody said. "I got out and looked at the runes when I didn't go up with you two. Those runes are very intense, and very rigid. They'd stop anyone up to something that would destroy the city first.

"They're also clearly not meant for any specific building. So long as it fits inside the rune-structure, it'd work."

A strange thought occurred to Gus.

"We went right back to the bombing," he said. "We're here to work for Misha."

"Ugh," Melody said, and then sighed. "Yeah. Sorry. It's because Bob thought this might be related."

"But that's just it. It might be. When I was poking around in Sean's head, I saw meetings with others. Several of them, but I never caught a name. Just flashes of faces," Gus said. "On top of that, Michael Fitz had a meeting with C&C and they didn't want to talk about it. Then there was the PID officer who was meeting with Michael when the mask shattered.

"Beyond that, why did an outfit like Sean's steal an entire set of tools to do… whatever this is, only to abandon it and the warehouse as if it wasn't theirs?"

"You don't think it's related to the bombing, do you?" Vanessa asked.

Getting into the car, Gus fired up the rune structure again. Just as he'd done the first time.

"When I spoke to someone about it, they said Michael didn't do the rune-work. But that apparently he'd written down how to do it and someone connected the dots, so to speak," Gus said, getting out of the car.

Staring at the car again, Gus could actually see the unfinished part now. It was at the front bumper. The furthest point forward.

Thinking back to the last couple times he'd seen runes, Gus racked his brain to figure out what could go there.

The warehouse Eric was working out of. The Fed building. This car. Two had a similar hand in their making, the last probably being made before I was even born.

Gus blinked when a new thought popped into his head.

The partially burned-down building near the warehouse Sean had been in.

"We need to go," Gus said, turning back toward the exit. "I need to see Sean's warehouse."

A short while later, Gus pulled them around to the partially destroyed building he'd seen before. He'd been further away the first time he'd seen it, and he'd misjudged it's size.

It was much bigger than he'd thought.

Flaring and fading intermittently, the runes sat there. Stern as a warning.

Getting out of the car once more, he stared up at the building. The runes were familiar. But it was hard for him to figure out where he'd seen them before.

Maybe Eric's?

"Oh shit," Melody said. "They're the runes for the Fed building. It's a little sloppy, but… that's what they are. They're just barely functioning, though. Makes it hard to see the resemblance."

Now that she'd said it, Gus saw it too. They were Fed-building wards.

"Ok… so we've got a car with runes being built over there," Gus said, pointing back to Sean's warehouse. "Across from a building that looks like it was partially exploded, or set on fire, with runes that look eerily like a Fed building's.

"All of this in an unconnected case involving a pack of Weres from out of town."

"It adds up on that angle," Vanessa said. "But it still doesn't make sense for the rest. Especially when you try to factor in the masks, and Michael and Misha losing their minds."

"There are tire tracks," Melody said, walking up to the front of the building. "They drive right up to where the boundary is for the runes and—"

Melody paused, lifting her eyes to the front of the building. Moving forward, she clambered through some rubble and a collapsed wall. Several minutes passed as she clearly worked her way deeper.

"There's a car in here. It's pretty mangled, but it's a car alright," she shouted from the rubble.

"Huh. Ok, so… the car itself isn't a bomb, the runes aren't a bomb, and the building goes kaboom nonetheless," Gus said.

"Wait, wait," Vanessa said, looking extremely excited. "Are we not seeing the forest for the trees? We keep focusing on the individual parts here, but we're not thinking of it as a whole.

"Yes, the car isn't a bomb, and neither are the runes, and maybe this is my inexperience here, but… if the runes on the car collide with the runes on the building, could you turn the whole thing into a bomb as it passed through?"

Gus's mind blanked out as he considered her point.

"You're saying," Melody said, crawling back out of the rubble. "You're saying that the car is like a key? When the car goes through the rune, the building, uh… interfaces with the runes on the car, and the whole thing becomes the bomb?"

"Yeah. Is that possible?" Vanessa asked. "We keep going round and round on the same details, but we're not considering how it all functions when you put it together."

"I mean… I'm not a rune-wright, but it's definitely possible. Melody?" Gus asked, turning to the Contractor.

Her Orange contract was blazing like the sun, as well as her Violet one. The smile on her face was iridescent.

"I think Ness just figured it out," she said. "Or at least, how the buildings went up in a ball of fire that stayed exactly within the runes themselves."

"Let's not rush this. We're not sure of that, but we definitely need to investigate it. Ness, you see if Eric is willing to meet with you. Maybe he'll give you the time of day if he remembers that pretty smile of yours. Let me know if he agrees; I'll be there so I can pick his thoughts.

"Melody, know any rune-wrights—or smiths or whatever title they go by—you trust? Preferably out of country. Not really keen on handing out information in country right now. For all I know we could be feeding information to an enemy," Gus said.

"I know a few." Melody looked thoughtful. "I'll start calling them and see if there's anything they can tell me. You just want me to run the idea by them and see what they say, right?"

"Yeah, exactly. See if it's even something to consider. I like the idea, but for all we know it's just gonna fall flat after we look into it," Gus said.

"I can do that," Melody said, walking toward the car. "I'll make my calls while we're on the way to where Eric is being held."

Gus nodded at that and then went to the passenger side.

"I'm going to call Mark and update him with where we are," he said. "Can you drive, Ness?"

"No worries," she said and went over to the driver's side.

Everyone got in with a renewed sense of determination. They'd maybe made headway. Now it was a matter of tracking it down to see if they could get some traction.

Sinking into his seat, Gus dialed up Mark quickly.

It rang several times before it picked up.

"Captain Ehrich," Mark said.

Shit. Uh.

"This is Agent Hellström," Gus said. "I'd like to update you on where we are, Captain."

"Ah. Alright. Give me a second, Agent," Mark said. Then the line was muted.

Gus pulled the phone away from his ear and muted the line as well.

"That's weird," Vanessa said, giving him a look as she pulled away from the warehouse.

"I think he's got someone in his office that doesn't do well with informality," Gus said. "That or they're such a high rank that Mark isn't going to risk it. Can never tell until it's too late."

"Ah, yes. I've unfortunately had that experience before. My first lieutenant when I got my badge. She was a real bitch," Vanessa said, a frown on her face. "Now that I think about it, I'm sure she's one of the reasons my file doesn't read as well as I wish it did."

"She didn't like it that you were batting for the home team?" Gus asked.

"Didn't like me because I was Hispanic. She didn't care that I had a girlfriend," Vanessa said and then laughed. "Though I wonder. Is Hispanic even a worry anymore? Should I be more worried about people being speciesist? Is that a word?"

"Yes, you should, and I have no idea. Elves typically hate humans. They see us as the ugly kid brother they never wanted," Gus said. "As a whole, though, humanity wouldn't do well mixing with Paras."

"It's happened before?" Vanessa asked.

"Inquisition comes to mind for me," Gus said. "But then—"

"Ok, Gussy, I'm all yours," Mark said, the line picking back up.

"One second," Gus said, smiling at Vanessa. Then he unmuted his phone and put it back to his ear. "Hey. Had a bigwig?"

"Unfortunately. You were right, of course. The moment I asked for an in-person meeting, all hell broke loose. I got six different emails from people I've never heard of, two phone calls, and a general dropping in just to say hi," Mark said.

"In other words, yeah, Fed government is toast and we're the second string," Gus finished. "The only string."

"Oh yes. The general told me his expectations, and then asked me why my family has suddenly gone on an unexpected holiday," Mark said. "Thanks for the heads up. When I explained it to Kelly, she and Megan hightailed it out of town."

"Yeah, no worries," Gus said. "But I have something else to throw at you that may help."

"Hit me."

"Eric Mill and Sean Smith. They were working together in some strange way, right?"

"Yeah."

"Well, that car I found, Vanessa put a theory together about it," Gus said.

"Ok, but I told you to work the bombing," Mark said.

"We are, and this is where it ties in. Vanessa thinks maybe the car is acting as like a trip-sensor when it hits the runes on the Fed building. The front of the car being 'toward enemy' and the rear being the explosive sensor," Gus said.

"What…?" Mark said. "Wait, no. I get it. I get it. I think. Rather than the car being the bomb, the car turns the runes themselves into a bomb. They explode, get hemmed in by the runes themselves, and localize the whole thing. That's why there is no bomb, no detonator, no spell. It was the runes themselves, which went away after exploding."

"Yeah, exactly. Now, down by where we found Sean and the car, there's a building off to one side. The runes on it are Fed-building runes. The place is a wreck, like it blew up or caught fire. There's a car on the inside of the building," Gus said. "It looks like Sean got nervous and tried to do a test before actually committing to the whole thing.

"Maybe doing that test, they sacrificed their working car and ended up with a car that wasn't finished by the time it was go time. Hence the Fed building not exploding," Gus said.

"Meaning… it's still a target right now," Mark said, sounding nervous. "And the runes protecting the building are what blew it up."

"Uh… yeah. Maybe you should not go into that office for a while," Gus said.

Mark coughed twice. "Yes, I suddenly feel quite sick. I think I have some medicine back at my PID office. I'll need to go get that.

"Ok, good work. What else ya got? That's an interesting theory, but you haven't proven anything yet."

"Vanessa is going to see if Eric will see her. She's got that pretty latina thing going for her, so we're going to use it," Gus said. "At the same time, Melody is working through her rolodex for rune-smiths out of country to get their opinion on if it's even possible."

"Great," Mark said. It sounded like he was walking around his office. "I'm going to go head over to my PID office. I'm also going to put the Sean Smith BOLO severity to a national-security level. If what you're saying is true, then we have a link to the rest through him.

"I'll also see about that little Wolf girl you brought in who got him the stuff. Maybe she knows how to contact him."

"Oh. Oh yeah, that'd help. About the PID office, you think it'll be safe there? I mean, they could do the same thing with those runes, couldn't they?" Gus asked.

"Nah. PID is paranoid. As a whole, we're way more jumpy than the Feds, and a lot less confident," Mark said. "Our runes get recycled and updated every year. We don't renew the old ones, we get a new build. Fed runes haven't changed in years.

"Remember when I was complaining about having to hire new building maintenance Enchanters like a year ago? That's them. That's what they do."

"Huh. I don't remember that. I remember you complaining about something like that, but the department name doesn't ring a bell," Gus said.

"I mean, I could have used the fancy name they like to throw around. Facility spell management, or something like that," Mark grumbled. "If it's a duck, it's a duck. Doesn't need a fancy name like mallard."

Gus wasn't listening, though. He'd heard that name recently. That department name.

Then he remembered.

Eric Mill had been working in facilities spell management for C&C.

Oh. Shit.

Chapter 22 - Catching up to Be Behind

Gus was tapping through his call history to try and find the number for C&C. He felt like he owed them a warning about what Eric had been up to. If their hunch was right, apparently the C&C building was a target for some reason.

Finding it, he hit the number and then pulled the phone up to his ear.

"C&C, Ashley speaking," said the secretary.

"Hello Ashley, this is Detective Gustavus Hellström," Gus said. He caught a strange movement out of the corner of his eye and turned his head.

Melody was glaring daggers at him, her own phone pressed up to her ear.

Smiling, he rolled his eyes at her and held up a finger.

Melody immediately looked askance at him, but she seemed calm.

"Ah! Hello, Detective. I was just thinking about you," Ashley said.

"I'm afraid this is a bit of an emergency. I need to speak with Leanne or Kat. Immediately. It's a matter of life and death. Can you see if they'll take my call?" Gus asked.

"Goodness. Of course, one second, Gus," Ashley said, and then the line went quiet.

Melody stuck her tongue out at him and looked rather pouty. Especially when she was a Contractor old enough to be his grandma.

Really? Actually, might be my fault. Maybe I'm playing too hard to get.

Especially now that I've given in.

Reaching out, he grabbed her by the collar and dragged her forward to the center console. Then he kissed her without an explanation.

Melody sat there as he did so, unmoving. When he finally released her, he pressed his lips to her ear.

"Knock it off, I don't like the jealousy," he said. "Have some faith in me."

Then he pushed on her shoulder and sent her back into her seat. Where she stared at him wide eyed.

"I'm sorry, Gus," she said, then smiled at him. Then she looked surprised. "Sorry, not you. No, I'm listening. Okay, yeah, exactly."

Sitting back in his own seat, Gus looked at Vanessa, who had a grin on her face.

"You need one, too?" he asked her. "Not going to go jealous crazy on me later and hit me with a shoe?"

"Only if you need to be hit. And no, I'm good right now. Driving," Vanessa said, tapping the steering wheel.

"Hello, Gus? Leanne said she'll speak with you. One moment," Ashley said, and then the line popped before he could say anything.

"Hello Agent," Leanne said. "Ashley said this was life or death."

"Yes, it is. I was looking into the death of Mr. Fitz, and while I was doing that, I identified a suspect. That suspect happened to work for your company."

"A lot of people work for us. That doesn't—"

"Wait, please," Gus said. "He worked for your company in a position where I believe he was maintaining the runes and spells that protect your building. Or one of your buildings at least.

"There was an attack recently that distinctly didn't make the news. I'm sure you're aware?"

"Yes," Leanne said after a brief silence. "Yes, I am. And I'm listening."

"I can't give you the details, but I can tell you it's suspected the runes of the buildings themselves were weaponized. I'm calling to let you know that I think you should change the runes on your building. Immediately. Today."

"Thank you. I'm going to do just that," Leanne said.

"I'm looking into this whole thing, but I'm really starting to suspect a lot of this is tied together. Is there anything you can tell me about it? Anything you might know that would help me out here?" Gus asked. It didn't hurt to see if she knew anything.

"Honestly, Agent, if I knew anything. I'd tell you. Our work with Mr. Fitz was entirely innocent, and it had more to do with shaping perceptions on 'what Trolls really are' more than anything else. That and some backyard scientist work that is entirely unrelated.

"We're a pro-Para organization, but we don't really agree with the worlds merging. That's it. There's not much else to tell."

Gus believed her. Trolls really did have a terrible image, even amongst Paras. The simple fact that C&C was a marketing firm built on simple products, brand names, and building others wasn't just a coincidence either.

"Alright, thank you for your time, Leanne," Gus said.

"Not a problem. Good day, Agent," Leanne said, then ended the call.

Gus set his phone down in his lap. He didn't have anyone else to call.

"That was nice of you," Vanessa said, pulling the car onto a freeway. "I'd forgotten all about that. Though… why would he be interested in them? C&C is as staunchly conservative as you could be. They may be about getting attention on brands, but you couldn't find more than a couple photos of Leanne or Kat online if you tried."

Gus only nodded. He wasn't sure what the connection there was, but he was sure there was one. He just had to find it.

The problem seemed to be that Leanne and Kat weren't the originators of the connection, which made them targets and victims.

Someone who would target the government, and apparently conservatives.

"Ok, yes I'm going to put you on speakerphone," Melody said, and then leaned forward. She held her phone out between everyone in the middle of the car.

"Ok!" said a man on the other end. His accent was like Melody's, just far more pronounced. "Am I on now?"

"Yes, you are," Melody said, looking a bit nervous.

"Oh good. Er, yes, helloooo Aodie's boyfriend and girlfriend. I am—"

"Please proceed, yes?" Melody asked, cutting the man off.

"Yes, yes, ok, yes. I have done a mockup of some runes I think will do what we would like. It's very rushed, though, so… eh," said the man. "And I'm going to now try pushing it through a teeny, tiny version of the runes Aodie described."

"Aodie?" Gus murmured, looking at Melody.

She made a shooing gesture with her hand but looked mildly embarrassed.

"And we are pushing it into the box," said the man. Immediately afterward there was a crash, followed by a whump-like noise.

Over all of that, Gus heard a manly screeching sound.

After several seconds, the noise died way. Melody was staring at her phone as if she had no idea what to do.

"It would seem," said the man. "That it is indeed quite possible to make the runes themselves explode. With a very energetic reaction, might I add.

"Though, I think one must know each and every quirk of the runes to do this. When it traveled back up and through, it was almost as if any deviation would cause it to fail.

"Now, Aodie said you were her—"

Melody immediately tapped a button on her phone and held it back up to her ear. She gave Gus a tight smile and pointed forward toward the dash.

"Right," Gus said, looking over at Vanessa.

She caught his eye and mouthed a single word: "Dad." Then she shrugged. Her guess was as good as his.

Ah.

***

Eric was willing to see Vanessa.

Alone.

Without cameras, recording, or anything else. None of it would be recorded or on record.

Vanessa of course agreed to all of this, since she knew very well that Gus would be sitting there reading his mind as he went along.

Except there wasn't anything there.

Gus picked his mind apart for every thought that came up, but he found nothing. Trying to push any deeper would give the game away, since the man was an Enchanter. He was attuned to things like psykers and spells.

Through it all, Gus got the sense that Eric had just wanted to talk to someone. Apparently he'd been locked away in solitary confinement since he'd been brought in. He'd been starved for entertainment of any sort. Even if it was talking to cops.

Defeated, and without a lead, Gus closed his eyes and pressed his hands to his face. They'd presumably figured out how the Fed buildings had been blown apart so efficiently, identified a cell that had been working on said plan, and had even managed to finger someone who had made the runes that did it.

Except they didn't have the grounds to rip into Eric's mind, couldn't find Sean, and had nothing to go on beyond their suspicions.

Melody sat down next to him at the same time as Vanessa did on his other side. They were in the holding facilities break room, sitting around a small circular table.

"So, we know how they did it, a few of the people who did it, and how to prevent it," Vanessa said, holding up three fingers. "But we don't know the why."

"And we haven't caught Sean," Melody grumbled.

"And Sean. But honestly, that isn't our job," Vanessa said, and it rang true for Gus when she said it. It wasn't their job to catch the bad guy. It was their job to figure out what had happened. "For all intents and purposes, we completed the case and did our job."

"Then why does it feel so… anti-climactic," Melody said, a frown on her face.

"Because you're used to walking something from start to finish," Gus said. "I feel you, Mel, and I even agree with you. It feels… bad. But Ness is absolutely right. We did everything we were supposed to do.

"We even found out how it was done, and provided everybody with a clear idea of how to prevent it. We did more than the entire PID and the Fed combined."

"Uhm, what do we do now then?" Melody asked.

"Normally we'd have other cases to work. Hell, normally I'd be working three or four at the same time. I'd be drowning in the paperwork afterwards as well. That or running around to get a sign-off from a judge, paperwork from clerks, bullshit from other detectives when I got their case, or hell knows what else," Gus said, shaking his head. "Honestly, it feels like most of my day is paperwork. All day paperwork and catching up with it. Then other days I'm never at my desk. It's all just random. I'm just thankful that Mark doesn't call me in during the middle of the night. He already has more than enough people on staff that calling in his late night doesn't help."

Melody sighed, her face falling and her eyes dropping to the desk.

"Being a PI was a lot more fun than this," Melody said. "But this is the price I'm paying to be with the two of you. I don't want to be a housewife while you two run around."

"It is what it is," Gus said with a shrug. "The only other thing I had planned was—"

He paused, looking at Vanessa, then decided it didn't matter. She was a strong woman—she didn't need him pussyfooting around it.

"I'd planned on interviewing Wendy. See if she knows anything more about the situation. She was involved, after all. There's always the possibility she knew more than she realized, or was holding back," Gus said.

Vanessa groaned and pressed a hand to her head.

"Yes, that'd make sense, wouldn't it?" she said. "It's who I'd go back to re-question in this situation. Is she here as well?"

"Should be. I haven't asked about it yet, but… Mark was going to put it in for me," Gus said. "Hell, Mark's been running a lot of our paperwork lately. I'm really not looking forward to when he gets over it and just throws it all back at us."

"Won't be so bad," Melody said, reaching out and grabbing Gus's hand. Then she grabbed Vanessa's as well. "There's three of us in this together. We'll all be swapping around with one another in the bedroom soon enough, laughing about when we were worried about paperwork."

Closing his eyes, Gus couldn't help but let out a soft chuckle, and he smiled.

She's been burning herself out, hasn't she? Probably need to refill her powers.

"Contract?" Gus asked, not really needing to but wanting to confirm it.

"I'm fighting it pretty hard. I really want you to line me up from behind while you shove my face into Vanessa's p—"

"Yep, got it, thanks," Gus said, holding up his free hand. "No need to elaborate. We'll hit up Wendy, plow out paperwork, and call it a day. It'll be contract night, which means pizza and beer while we take care of your needs."

Opening his eyes, he looked at Melody for confirmation.

Vanessa was nodding her head. "Sounds like a plan to me. I could go for that. I'll pick out a movie. My turn anyways."

Melody was smiling at him, her eyes hooded, and looked really pleased with herself.

"I love you, Gus. Thank you so much for knowing me and my needs," Melody said, squeezing his hand. Her head turned to Vanessa. "I love you, Ness. Thank you for being so understanding. I'm so lucky to have my wobbly triangle. My bookends."

"Yeah, yeah. Alright, come on then," Gus said, getting up. He was feeling really self-conscious having these conversations and displays of affection on the clock. He was pretty sure there was a massive "no fraternization" policy for the PID.

Walking out of the break room, he adjusted his coat.

As he headed for the reception area, he did his best to shake the out weirdness out of his head. He might have mentally accepted the fact that he was probably already in a relationship with a Contractor who was pretty far from sane, but his heart still quailed at the idea of it.

If he was completely honest with himself, Gus wasn't over his last relationship. And it wasn't something he'd ever be able to find a resolution for, considering she was dead. Lost in the same place he'd lost all the rest of his friends.

The rest of his family that wasn't family.

Those he saw in the quiet moments in the night when he stared up at the ceiling, wondering if he was awake or asleep.

Shaking his head, Gus stepped up to the counter and smiled at the officer there. It was a middle-aged man who looked like he'd lost the ability to run a Para patrol officer route with a missing eye. Prison guards were police, and there was no private company running them. It was simply too much to risk to the lowest bidder.

"Hi, we're also here to see one Wendy Hills. All done with Eric," Gus said. "The arrangement was probably made by a Mark Ehrich."

"Wendy?" asked the man behind the glass. "Wendy Hills? Huh. I didn't see that on the list, but I'll take a look. One second."

Vanessa and Melody were chatting to one side. He had no idea what it was about, but it sounded like they were talking about a movie.

Probably trying to figure out what to watch after Melody pays her dues.

I wonder what they're thinking.

Turning his head toward them, he started to follow the conversation.

"Sorry, Agent," said the officer, getting Gus's attention before he could even figure out which movie they were talking about. "Wendy was released a day or two ago. Someone bailed her out. Had a quick overnight arraignment, apparently. One… Francis Dern footed the bill. Listed only as a friend. Fifty grand was the total. She got out with five from Francis, the rest picked up by a bail bondsman."

Gus frowned and nodded.

"Thanks," he said, then headed over to Melody and Vanessa.

"What's up?" Melody asked, noticing instantly that something was off.

"Wendy's out on bail," Gus said. "She got arraigned and bailed out. Kinda quick. Bail wasn't high, though. Only fifty grand."

"She bailed out?" Vanessa asked, looking extremely confused. "There's no way. She could barely afford her rent. It's why… why it didn't make any sense that she didn't want to live together."

"You're right there. It was one Francis Dern who got her out for the ten percent needed for a bondsman," Gus said. "Name ring a bell?"

Vanessa frowned, clearly thinking. Then her face fell and she closed her eyes.

"Ex-girlfriend. No idea where she lives or anything about her. Other than Wendy swore up and down she hadn't seen her in years and didn't even know her number. Guess that was a lie, too."

Gus blew out a breath, then laid a hand on Vanessa's shoulder. Her small shoulders shook once and she looked away to one side.

"It'll be alright. It's done and you can move on. You can think it out and get your head in the right space. You have a home now and—"

Vanessa moved into him, hugging him tightly. Her hands pressed into his back.

Awkwardly, Gus laid his arms around her shoulders and hugged her back.

Only for Melody to slam into both of them from one side, wrapping her arms around them.

"Oh, my destined ones, my bookends, how I love you both. My honey, my sweetie.

"Let's play in the bed tonight. I'll take care of both of you at the same time," Melody said, far too loud for Gus's personal wishes.

Glaring at the Contractor before she could continue, Gus caught her just as she opened her mouth.

Then she gave him a smile and laid her cheek on Vanessa's head.

"Can we call out sick for a few days?" Melody asked. "I don't want to do paperwork, and I don't want to go to work tomorrow."

"I mean… uh… we could, but Mark kinda needs us," Gus said.

Melody clicked her tongue but nodded her head.

"We can just work from home," Gus offered as an alternative. "It's paperwork anyways. You two should have laptops back at the home PID office now. We could pick them up, go home, and just work out of the house for a while.

"Mark won't care, and we've got a lot of stuff to put together."

"Really?" Melody asked, pushing closer to Gus and smooshing Vanessa closer as well.

"Yeah, Mark won't mind, I'm sure. We really do have a boat load of paperwork to do. We never did finish up all the crap from the warrant we served on Sean," Gus said.

"Yes, please," Vanessa said against Gus's chest.

Right. Wind-down time.

"Let's go tell Mark then, and head home," Gus said.

Chapter 23 - Hood Watch

Vanessa's phone started ringing.

Which was surprising considering he'd never heard it go off. Vanessa pulled her phone out and immediately put it to her ear. "Hello?"

"I'm really glad Mark said we could just… do paperwork," Melody said. "This job is easier and more difficult than my old one at the same time."

"Can definitely understand that. From being your own boss to having multiple bosses," Gus said. He was sitting up front and Melody was driving. Vanessa was sitting in the back this time, and she hadn't even gone into their precinct with him and Melody.

She was clearly still dealing with her own issues, which was understandable. He couldn't blame her either. Her entire world and life as she'd known it had been turned on its head and spun around.

"It's ok though," Melody said. "I have my bookends, a steady paycheck, and I'm not on the run from the law."

Gus chuckled and looked over at her. She'd said that a few times now, as if to reassure herself. Looking at her hand on the center console, Gus reached down and slipped his fingers into hers.

"You do indeed have your bookends. Everything else is changeable," Gus said. She'd done a lot just to put herself in a position to be near him. He was flattered. Flattered and afraid. But he also knew beyond a doubt that she wasn't messing around with his head. "Maybe… maybe later you can convince me to change professions. Maybe being a PI would be easier for me. Or safer."

Melody's hand clamped tight to his.

"Really?" she asked.

"Yeah. I was really only doing the job for Mark and a paycheck. I've been kinda just living day to day," Gus said. It felt stupid to say it, to admit it, but it was real. Real and honest. "I haven't… really… left the desert. I'm still there sometimes."

"I know. I've heard you wake up in the middle of the night," Melody said.

"Yeah. That, too," Gus mumbled.

"Can I ask what happened?" Melody asked softly. "If not, I—"

"Got trapped," Gus said. "Everyone I knew and was close to got trapped in what essentially was a run-down stone fort. Taking cover from a sandstorm.

"Ended up walking into the middle of the real war going on out there. I'm sure you know about it."

Glancing over his shoulder, he saw Vanessa was still on her phone. She was talking quietly with someone in what sounded like Spanish.

"Yeah. I know," Melody said. "Elf on Elf, and dragging most of the normal world along for the ride."

"Yeah. Well, we were just grunts. I'd accidentally led everyone into a Desert Elf haven. Apparently we Boogiemen can see right through magic even without a mask," Gus said. The guilt came back in a massive punch to his gut. "I walked everyone into it since I was the one who saw the fort. And for the next month, we fought off Desert Elves.

"Only three of us walked out. Me, Mark, and Olsen. Olsen ate his gun when we got back state-side. Mark flourished in the Para world and smashed his way up into the PID ranks."

"You held out against Desert Elves for a month?" Melody asked.

"Well… I did… really. Most of my team just hunkered down and played fire-base. After the second day, the fear started to overwhelm me. I had to get up. Get out. So I went out," Gus said. "I started hunting and killing Elves every day. Every night. It all blended together after a while. I'd come back every now and then. Mark was always the one who found me. Got me cleaned up, patched me together, and got me a bed. Then I'd go back out. Do it again."

Melody's eyebrows were crawling up to the top of her head, her eyes on the road.

"You hunted Desert Elves in the desert?" she asked.

"Yeah. It isn't so hard. Honestly, tracking and hunting is easy. I just have to let the good part of myself go quiet to get into that space," Gus said. "I'm not human. It's not like I'm letting something out of a cage, or anything like that. I'm just… relaxing my control over myself.

"It was easy. Half the time, more Elves would come looking for whoever was missing. They value their own numbers quite deeply. I'd just pull one's eyes out, rip out the tongue, and break their arms and legs. Leave them there in the middle of someplace visible," Gus said, his mind oozing backward in time. "They'd be brave about it for a while. Lie there. Not making a sound. Not wanting to call others to their position. Eventually they'd break, though. They always did."

He could vividly remember figuring out what tactics worked. Through trial and error, unfortunately.

Even the last outing he'd gone out on. Before the Elves had finally let him, Mark, and Olsen leave. It'd been the day after Emily died when he'd set out.

"No one wants to die. After a day just lying there in pain, in the burning sun, they'd start calling out. Or trying magic," Gus said. "Either way, more Elves always came. You never wanted to hit them when they arrived, though. That'd just spook them. You let them get their comrade. Then you take a few of the rear guard as they leave. Two or three will do it. Your investment just paid off.

"You take one and repeat the process, stow the others for later. Just in case you need more bait. A few more will come back looking for the ones they lost. You hit that group up front, take a few more of their number."

He could remember staring into his makeshift cage at the large number of Elves he'd captured and stuck in there.

They'd viewed him and his people as normal humans, beneath notice. They'd not bothered to even to try and talk. The one time an attempt had been made, they'd killed the messenger Mark had sent.

"After a while, they'll stop coming to investigate. That's when you just… kill some of your bait. Scalping them, and making sure you get the ears, is a pretty great way to get them all sorts of riled up.

"Then you just put out more bait again, and repeat the process," Gus said. "They're much more likely to try and save their comrades when you leave out scalped bodies."

Blinking several times, Gus came back to himself and looked over at Melody.

They were pulled over to one side of the road now, and she was staring at him. There was no judgment in her eyes. No pity, no regret.

Just understanding.

She gave him a smile and patted his hand.

Vanessa cleared her throat from the backseat.

"That was my mom. She says there's someone hanging around her house. Can we stop by and take a look?" she asked. "She wouldn't call me unless it was something of an issue. She lives in… well, a neighborhood that handles its own problems."

"Of course," Melody said. Her eyes promised to talk more about this later with Gus, but for now, she grabbed the steering wheel. "Where'm I going?"

"And does she know about the Para?" Gus asked.

"I… told her a little bit. The rules said I could. I haven't told her everything yet," Vanessa said.

***

Walking up to the door, Gus looked around. It was the type of place he would meet a CI. A back alley that ran along the rear of a series of small ranch houses. These were how people came and went more often than not, rather than the front door.

Front doors ended up watched by people you didn't want to see you.

It amused him that Vanessa had deliberately parked at the end of the alley and had them walk all the way in.

Gotta let the local boys know we're here, and we mean no harm.

Not cops, just detectives.

Most neighborhoods didn't like detectives, but they also knew how to deal with them.

Don't say anything.

Vanessa walked right up to a door and knocked on it several times. It was a very normal knock.

The door opened immediately, and an older, heavier version of Vanessa stood there in the doorway.

She said something to Vanessa in Spanish, looked at Gus and Melody, then stepped to one side and opened the door.

Vanessa nodded and walked into the home, waving behind for them to follow.

Walking in, Gus couldn't stop himself from doing a visual check for things "in the open" that he could work off. It was just normal for him now.

The house was decorated in a style that seemed thirty years out of date. There were small knick-knacks that looked like they'd come from another life. A porcelain angel with a medallion hanging from its hand. A small wooden box with several medals and a name tag in it. Next to it was a flag folded into a triangle, only the blue and stars showing.

Live on, friend.

Gus turned away from the reminder of too many ceremonies where he'd been the one to assist in folding the flag.

Looking at the older woman, Gus decided he'd get ahead of this one, and he pushed a fiber of his telepathy into her mind. He was also low on patience.

Immediately, he got an impression that this woman was suspicious of him. In fact, she was staring at him right now.

"El Coco," muttered the woman, her brows coming down as she looked at him. The mental translation came across to him. A monster that lurked in the shadows and stole children away.

There were a few people in the world who, through the events of their life, could identify non-humans. Gus knew that if he told her, she would tell her husband, but that it would go no further than that. Not even to her sons.

From what he could gather of her husband, he would tell no one as well.

"Yes. Yes, I am," Gus said to her. "And that's a secret your daughter knows, and that I trusted her with. I'd be killed out of hand if you told anyone."

Vanessa's mother's head turned toward her daughter, and she asked her a question. Once more the mental translation came over, and this time she was asking if he spoke Spanish.

"No, mother, he doesn't. But you can't just say stuff like that and not expect a response. Now, tell me again what's going on," Vanessa said.

Gus walked over to the front door and tilted a blind slat as minutely as he could. Across the street, he could see a number of cars parked. There was no one out and about.

Things seemed odd to him, though. Tense.

"...sitting there in his car. He's watching my door, I know it," said the older woman. "It's the green one."

Gus saw the car. It was a newer sedan. He couldn't quite make out who it was in the driver's seat, but he could definitely see him.

"He's a skinny white boy," said the woman. "One of the boys went over to talk to him, and then he ran away."

"Ran away?" Gus asked.

"It's Sean," Melody said. She was standing next to Gus, peering out the same slat. Her Blue contract was glowing. "What the hell is Sean doing here?"

"No idea, but last I saw, he's got everyone in the country wanting a piece of him," Gus said. "He's probably the single highest-value target out there for us right now. Let's get this one called in and see if we can't get a PID patroller to collar him."

"Ha... collar a Were," Melody said, even as she pulled the radio at her belt up to her mouth.

Leaving her to that, Gus looked back at Vanessa and her mother.

"We'll take care of it, Mrs. Flores," he said. "Thank you for telling us. That's a criminal out there we've been on the lookout for. No idea why he's staking out your house, but... you weren't wrong. He's definitely watching your door."

Mrs. Flores was giving Gus an evil eye, her mouth turned down in a frown.

"How long have you been dating my daughter?" she asked out of nowhere.

Blinking in surprise, Gus had no idea how to respond to that. He could see Vanessa grimacing out of the corner of his eye, looking like she was ready to run out of the house.

From the mental fiber he had in her mother's mind, he could tell she felt positive that Gus was dating Vanessa. She wasn't quite happy with it, either, but there was a strange feeling of "better than" attached to it.

Ah. That'd be it. She'll approve of Vanessa dating me more than Wendy. I'm not a woman.

"About a week," Gus said, breaking the mind reading he had going on in her head. He'd learned what he wanted to. Now he felt like he was just intruding. "Your daughter is an amazing woman, and I consider myself quite fortunate. You raised her very well, and she's accomplished much. Would it be too much to ask if we could have dinner sometime at your table?"

The frown dropped away to a degree, and much of the hostility faded from Mrs. Flores's face.

"I know it. She was very difficult, but worth it. We eat dinner early in this house, but that's fine," she said. Then she looked at Vanessa and said something rapidly in Spanish.

Vanessa's face turned a bright red and she responded in Spanish for the first time, with an angry chop of her hand.

"Gus, Sean's heading this way," Melody said.

"What? Shit," Gus said, and turned to the window. Sean was indeed heading this way. He was already on the sidewalk, in fact. Gus turned to Mrs. Flores. "Are there any windows open in the house? Quick."

"No," she said, then shook her head. "Wait, yes. The kitchen window is open. The oven makes the house too hot sometimes."

"Quick, out the back door," Gus said. "We need to get to the car. He's going to bolt in a few seconds when he scents us."

I really fucking hope he doesn't run on foot. I already got my foot chase in for the month.

Then again, is a car chase any better?

Where's that damn backup?

Finding the back door, Gus ran out of it at a dead sprint for the car.

Melody blurred past him, making him look like he was walking.

Damn, her contracts really are out of this world.

Glancing over his shoulder, he found Vanessa only a step behind him, running full out as well.

They hit the car just as Melody slammed it into gear. Before they could get their seat belts on, she was peeling out of the parking space and wheeling the car around.

She floored it. The car lurched forward and they sped off toward the front of the house. Just in time to see Sean in his green sedan blast by them.

"Damnit, we're not really the high speed ch—"

Melody yanked the steering wheel, mashed the pedal, and they were off. Racing after Sean.

Reaching to the center dash, Gus flicked on the built-in lights in the grill and headlamps, then turned on the siren.

He could hear Vanessa radioing in the whole thing in the rear seat.

"Oh my heavens—I'm in a high speed chase, but I'm not the one on the run!" Melody said with a high-pitched giggle. "This is so insane! I love it!"

Shit, shit, shit.

You're not girlfriend material, you're a damn criminal.

Melody shot him a glance while laughing all the while. Her eyes were wide open, her Blue, Green, Red, Orange, and Violet contracts all lit up.

"I love you," she said in a breathy rush as she looked forward again, zooming in and around people. Her Indigo contract exploded with bright light.

Out ahead of them, Sean was racing ahead, dodging through traffic.

"Oh my fuck, someone is going to die," Gus said. "We're going to have to call this one off. This is just too risky to civilians."

"Mark just said not to break off under any circumstances," Vanessa said, putting her radio down. "He also said turn on the car radio."

Oh. Oh yeah.

Gus flicked on the radio and then grabbed the handset.

"This is Agent Hellström. Please confirm orders," Gus said.

"Do not break off pursuit for any reason, that's an order," Mark said over the radio.

Rolling his eyes, Gus reached back and gave the handset to Vanessa. He didn't want to deal with Mark right now.

Besides, he could try to use some of his horror-magic to impact Sean. If he got close enough, that was.

Sean took a turn at speeds beyond unsafe. Bouncing up the curb and onto the sidewalk, he wiped out a mailbox and two parking meters before he got his car under control and back on the road.

Melody jammed the wheel to the left and grabbed the hand brake. Yanking it up, she sent them into a drifting turn.

Gus closed his eyes and gripped the side door and his knee. He didn't let go until he felt them pull out of the turn. They were right behind Sean now.

He could actually taste the fear coming off the Were. It tasted like soggy french fries.

"He's heading for the freeway," Melody said. "What a damn amateur. Sure, you can really open it up, but you're not going to lose anyone like that. Tiny urban streets with lots of turns and hills are best. Break line of sight and ditch the car."

Sean bounced up and off the road for a second as he hit the on-ramp and flew up it. He also hit two cars as he did so, sending them skidding into the center divider.

Melody flew by them, managing to avoid hitting the now-crashed vehicles. Gus had a brief view of deployed airbags and shattered windows as they sped up the on-ramp.

Damn. This is getting more and more dangerous by the second.

Someone's going to end up dead at the end of this.

Chapter 24 - Supersonic

Melody practically fish-tailed the car as they came flying out of the on-ramp and onto the freeway.

"Holy shit," Gus said as their rear end swung around and actually hit another vehicle.

"Fuck, sorry. This thing steers like a damn boat," Melody said, her foot dropping down on the pedal and speeding them on after Sean. "I promise I'll get your car fixed, Gus."

"Not my car," he replied. "Department owns it. I don't have my own vehicle. I never drove it, so I sold it."

"Oh. Okay," Melody said. "Now I don't feel as bad about trashing this thing if I need to."

I regret this already.

"Ok! Shoot his wheels out," Melody said.

"What? No!" Gus said emphatically. "That only works in movies and TV shows. You're more likely to cause a ricochet and hurt a civilian. Besides, I'm a good shot, but even an expert would have problems with hitting a tire. Handguns are pretty rough beyond fifteen feet, even with a lot of time on a range."

"Huh? Then what are we going to do?" Melody asked.

"Run him down, wear him out," Gus said. "Hopefully we get some backup here soon, or a chopper, and we can fall back. No reason for us to be the lead car.

"Best case, we cycle out with vehicles better equipped for this."

"That doesn't make any sense," Melody said. "We've got him right here and now—why don't we just take him down?"

"Because that's more likely to endanger citizens," Gus said. "We're the police, not a gang or vigilantes or PIs. We have protocol and procedures to follow."

Melody snorted at that, staying right behind Sean.

Gus wasn't about to tell her she really should ease up on how close she was. Being this close was more likely to make Sean increase his speed than decrease it. Policy was to do everything possible to deescalate a chase rather than bring it up in danger.

He was close enough to try out some horror-magic, but in the same breath, it was more likely to send Sean careening into the divider and possibly oncoming traffic.

"They're deploying spike strips up ahead," Vanessa said. At some point she'd returned the hand mic to the holder and was using her personal radio again. Apparently Mark didn't care for the fact that Melody and Gus had tuned him out completely.

"Crap, alright. Did he say what kind?" Gus asked.

"No, he didn't," Vanessa replied, then started talking into her radio again.

"Ease up, Melody. They need time to pull 'em out of the way after they get Sean's tires," Gus said.

Melody grimaced but did as instructed. She slowed the vehicle down until they were several car lengths back.

"Should be enough right there. We just need to give our people time to yank 'em back to the side," Gus said.

"Yeah, I know. Spike strips aren't immediate, though, and not guaranteed," Melody said. "I only look at ambush-resistant cars, if I need to buy a car. Let's just say a spike strip wouldn't stop me. I'd lose some performance, but that's it. If this is as well organized an operation as we seem to think, it's possible they reinforced their vehicles. No?"

Chewing at his lower lip, Gus didn't know what to say to that. There was a definite possibility she was right. But there was an equal possibility she was wrong. Sean may not be high enough up to warrant such a thing. It was obvious to Gus that Sean had already failed at a number of different tasks his bosses had wanted him to do.

No. There's no way he'd be worth it.

"Gus, Mel, Mark just said we have permission to perform a PIT after the spike strip. Freeway is clear up ahead. Only if we get the chance, though. He'd rather have this end sooner rather than later," Vanessa said. "He doesn't want to wait for the tires to deflate. He thinks doing a PIT on top of the spikes will put the car out of order."

"Shit, shit," Gus muttered, then reached down under his seat. He kept a lockbox there with different magazines for his service weapon. "Sean isn't going to surrender, he's going to go Were-stare and then attack."

"Were-stare?" Vanessa asked.

"Weres get a bit weird in their hybrid form. Not human, not animal," Gus said. "Their thinking changes. They tend to go into staring matches. You can almost always bet on it, and things either get better or worse right after."

Opening the lockbox after he put in the combination, he grabbed the normal-round magazines. What he had in right now would just explode Sean to bits. They needed him alive.

Which meant he was going to have to stand up to a Were with just a handgun and rounds designed for humans. Somehow get him to stand down, or knock him out for long enough to get the PID cuffs on him.

"Can you fist-fight a Were, Mel?" Gus asked.

"I've done it before. It isn't fun or pretty, but… if I push my contracts, I can do it. Going to hit my limit, though. Won't be fun for any of us if I do," Melody said. "Suppose I won't have a choice if we're bringing him in alive."

"We are. We need him. He's our only link to whoever did any of this. Eric isn't talking, and he has a powerful family behind him. Makes it hard to put pressure on him," Gus said, thumbing the magazine release on his weapon. Grabbing it, he pulled back the slide slowly and fished out the chambered round. After pushing the round back into the magazine, he dropped it into the case. Then he picked up one of the several regular-loaded magazines and pushed it into his pistol.

"Sean, though… Sean is a Were, a terrorist, and has no backing," Gus said, chambering a round after the magazine clicked into place. "He's going to vanish into a holding cell that would make third-world countries wince. We'll be lucky if we ever see a photo of him again."

"Charming," Vanessa said.

"But true," Melody offered. "I had to break out of one once. Also into two of them. They're rather bleak and horrid."

"Anyways," Gus muttered. "Here's some mags with standard ammo. Make sure you load your weapon appropriately. Pull your chambered round as well. It won't take much to make a Were pop with PID rounds."

Up ahead, Gus could see a small rise in the road.

"Spike strip will probably be right over that there. On the other side. That way the deploying officer can get out of the way and not be visible the entire way up," Gus said.

"Got it," Melody said.

She eased up on the gas for a moment as they crested the small rise.

Sure enough, on the other side, they could see the patrol officer reeling in the spike strip. As soon as Melody figured she'd clear it, she gunned the car ahead again.

Sean's tires were clearly hit. Gus could tell at a glance. Bright silver spikes were visible in the treads of both rear tires.

"Don't drive behind him. Those things can pop out sometimes and come flying like little missiles," Gus muttered.

Melody took the advice, and she still had the pedal pushed down. They were roaring up to the side of Sean's vehicle at an incredible speed.

"Good thing he's a Were," Melody said. "Cause I bet this would kill a Norm."

"Wait, do you know how to do a PIT?" Gus asked, checking his seat belt.

"I've had more than enough done on me that I think I've got the idea. But you never know. I guess we're gonna find—"

Melody cut herself off and brought the front right of their vehicle into the rear quarter panel of Sean's car. Right behind the tire.

There was a grinding shudder through the car, and Gus watched as Sean's car started wildly veering left in front of them.

Thankfully Melody was already breaking their vehicle, and Sean passed in front of them without another hit. Sliding sideways until he was facing backward, Sean slammed into the center divider.

Rapidly bringing their car to a stop, they came up alongside Sean practically. As if realizing this wasn't ideal for them, Melody hit them into reverse and scooted them back some thirty feet.

Getting out of the vehicle, Gus stood behind the door with his handgun drawn. Sean's car looked like a pillow factory and shattered glass. All the airbags had deployed and were now slowly deflating.

"Driver, get out of the vehicle with your hands raised above your head," Gus called out. "Do not attempt to shift into any form or make any sudden movements. Doing so will be interpreted as hostile intent!"

"Can he even hear you?" Melody asked, standing behind the driver's side door, her pistol leveled. "I mean, he just smacked his head on the airbag, yeah?"

"He's a Were, probably didn't even feel it," Gus said. "Driver, get out of the vehicle with your hands raised. Do you hear me?"

"I can see him," Melody said. "He's just sitting there. He's not moving, and it doesn't look like he's even paying attention. I don't think he knows what to do."

Frowning, Gus stepped out from behind the door and started to walk up toward Sean's car.

As he did so, he took a thread of power and stabbed it into Sean's mind. At this point, he didn't really care what Sean thought he knew. No one would believe him anyways, or they'd treat it as a head injury.

"Driver, get out of the car!" Gus shouted. Pushing and pulling at the thoughts he found, Gus was doing his best to sort through everything Sean was thinking about as fast as he could.

He probably wouldn't get another chance after this, and he had to make the best of it. Sean was going to get shipped off to a holding cell smaller than a bathroom stall.

"Sean, get your ass out here!" Gus shouted.

That got his attention. He could feel the anger bubbling up inside of Sean's mind. Slowly, his thoughts trailed back to when he'd met Gus. When they'd been trying to get rid of the car and the equipment.

In fact, the car itself had indeed been what Gus had surmised. A second build because Sean had wanted to test out what it would do on a building. Except he hadn't counted on the runes going away after use.

Sean had failed spectacularly on almost every level. Originally, the car and rune equipment was going to be supplied to him by his handler, except Sean had messed that up and gotten it stolen. He'd left it out behind the warehouse and someone had seen it as a crime of opportunity they couldn't pass up.

He'd involved Wendy after that, as she'd been a contact for him. Apparently she was a well-placed informant who had connections to the local police force.

Which led him back to Vanessa's mom's house. He'd been there to use her to get at Vanessa and find out what the PID knew.

Oh, they meant Vanessa, didn't they? She was the connection.

"Sean, come on out. It's over. We already know everything, and it's just a matter of putting the cuffs on you. You're not getting away from this," Gus said.

In the distance, he could hear a helicopter speeding their way.

Good, good. That'll help.

Sean's mind went rampaging around at the sheer frustration of the entire situation. He'd been left out to dry by the rest of his pack. They'd all fled north to the border and vanished into the wilds. Leaving him to pick up the pieces and figure out how to do what he'd been charged to do.

On top of all that, Wendy hadn't responded to his texts or calls since he'd been made. As far as Sean could tell, he'd been cut loose and they were pretending he didn't exist.

"Even if you make it out of here, we'll be all over your fallback point instantly," Gus said, trying to guide Sean's thoughts.

Instantly, a picture of a run-down house on the far edge of the city came to mind. So far out east it was practically in another city. Gus memorized the address. There was also a small storage shed on the property, hidden in a small grouping of trees Sean wanted to get to.

"We can work this out, Sean," Gus said. "All you have to do is surrender, and the PID will help you get through this."

"You don't get it," Sean shouted from his car. At the same time, Gus picked up images of some very scary-looking people in a large room. It was only a single flash of a memory, and there was no context. Sean was absolutely terrified of it though. If he ever had to go to that room, or had anyone come for him from that room, he'd rather be dead. "There's no going back. None. This is it. We're all going to swing for it. My whole pack, but that's just how it is. That's just how it is… I guess."

What? That's a red flag if I ever heard one.

The thoughts streaming to Gus now were exactly what he didn't want to see on top of that. Thoughts of simply dying at Gus's hands and letting it end.

Sean and his entire pack were part of an organization as well. One that would kill them for their failures. An organization that was seeking to expose the world to the fact that Paras existed. To push everyone into the fact that the world was infinitely larger than they thought. Whether they wanted to or not.

No. No, no. This isn't a good thing. This is a terrible idea.

The Para world doesn't want to be known, because every time it is, we get hunted practically to extinction. What are you fools doing?

"Sean, let's just talk this through, alright? Everything will—"

Getting out of the car in his mixed phase, Sean tore the car door from its hinge point. Tossing it to one side, he stood upright and stared at Gus.

It was a full Were-stare, one that promised as soon as it ended, he was going to charge. Sean had already decided this was where he was going to die.

Taking several steps back, Gus pointed his weapon at Sean's chest. His best bet was to explode the heart or lungs.

Normal rounds would do absolutely fuck-all to a Were. But without a heart or lungs, he'd get dropped until he could regenerate them.

"Sean, just… take it easy and lie down. We can get through this nice and easy, alright?" Gus said. "We can just—"

Sean's head exploded in a bright-red, pulpy, gooey mess. Bits of brain and flesh flew in every direction.

A second later and Gus heard the boom of a long rifle.

Diving to one side, Gus started crawling on the ground to get behind the car.

"Down!" he shouted. The ground where he'd been standing exploded, and the sound of another rifle cracked a second later.

There were a few more pops and cracks as rounds struck the car and ground around them. The booms of the rifle coming seconds later.

"You two ok?" Gus called out.

"I'm alright," Vanessa said, crawling around to Gus's side of the car.

"I got winged in the leg, but it's a through-and-through flesh wound. It'll heal up tonight when we fix my contracts," Melody said, wriggling up next to Vanessa. She had her hands pressed to the outside of her thigh on both sides.

There was a crash, followed by the engine of the car sputtering. Then it died outright.

"I think they just shot the engine," Gus muttered.

"Yeah, they really don't want us going anywhere," Melody said with a grimace. "Did you get anything out of him?"

"Yeah. I know where he was hunkered down, and what's going on," Gus said. "It's… an organization alright. I even found out their goal. It's actually rather simple.

"They want the Norm world to know about the Para world. They don't want to hide in the shadows. They think that by destroying the Fed, no one will be able to prevent them from going live about Paras being real."

"That's stupid," Melody said with some heat. "The mixing of worlds never works out. Ever. It always ends in bloodshed.

"It doesn't make any sense. Why would anyone want to do that? It's stupid!"

"For the same reason so many people follow and believe in stupid things," Vanessa said in response. "Do you really need an excuse to account for the stupidity of others? Or that someone much smarter than them has conned them into believing something?"

"No," Gus said, knowing full well he'd seen his share of idiotic things. "Not at all. Hey, Ness, did you radio this in?"

"Yeah, shouted active shooter, sniper. Lost my radio though when a round blew up part of the wheel well next to my head," Vanessa said. "Sorry."

"Ptff, you did better than Gus and I, sweetie," Melody said, laying her head on Vanessa's back. "Neither of us was even wearing our radio."

Vanessa looked at Gus, then smiled slowly.

"That's our wobbly triangle, isn't it? We cover for each other's faults," Vanessa said, and then she laid her head down on the pavement. "Among other things."

"Awww, I love you, too, Ness," Melody said, snuggling up closer to Vanessa's back. "Sweetie, can you help me out here?"

"Sorry, Mel. My brain… isn't working very well right now. You think they killed him?" Vanessa asked, turning around and tending to Melody's gunshot wound. "The organization he was working for?"

"I'd certainly bet on it," Gus said. "The harder question to ask, though, is… how'd they get a shooter out here so fast? It wouldn't have been posted to any news channels. Not really.

"Nor would it be circling the Internet that quickly. It really only leaves one source of information—PID radio—which, honestly, is kind of impossible. There's a lot of backend magic I don't even pretend to understand that makes it impossible to pick up for anyone not on a PID radio."

"That leaves someone in the PID leaking information," Melody said, pulling her hands away so Vanessa could get to her leg.

"Or the Fed. Suddenly I'd be very curious to see who's left in the Fed," Gus muttered.

Overhead, a helicopter was circling from far above. They were clearly looking for the shooter. Gus just hoped the shooter had gotten spooked and fled.

Instead of flanking around to get a shot at him and his partners.

Especially since there wouldn't be a damn thing they could do about it.

Chapter 25 - Clock Out

Melody was seated on the edge of an ambulance. The medics were arguing with her about whether or not she should go to a hospital.

Holding his phone to his ear, Gus walked away from the loud argument. He couldn't hear Mark very well over the volume Melody was putting out.

"Damn, she's really angry," Mark said.

"Yeah, well, she got shot. Medics think she needs to go in, she doesn't want to. She just wants to go home and activate her contracts," Gus said.

"Huh, well, whatever. Contractors are Contractors. Nuttier than squirrel shit. Though to be fair, she's one of the more mentally apt ones I've seen so far," Mark said.

"Likewise," Gus agreed. "Anyways. Do you want me to head in for a debrief?"

"No, just tell me over the phone. I'll record this one for my notes," Mark said. "Starting now. Keep it informal. This is just for me. Too much going on, my memory is shit."

Gus chuckled and then sighed.

"I got Sean to start thinking after we got his car stopped and—"

"Why was he at Vanessa's mom's?" Mark asked.

"Oh, he wanted to hold her hostage and get Vanessa to come over, then take her and find out what we knew. He was operating in the dark," Gus said. "Even his own higher-ups wanted nothing to do with him."

"Yeah, they cut him loose once he went off the field," Mark said. "Ok. So you got him stopped and...?"

"Got him stopped and read his mind. Asked him lots of questions. The gist of it is pretty scary and simple," Gus said. "They're an organization that wants the Para world to interface with the human world. That's all they want. They want it to merge and become one. They're tired of hiding in the shadows."

"Don't they fucking pay attention to history?" Mark asked. "Every time the two worlds get close, an inquisition or a plague happens. Whole nations get wiped off the face of the map. There's no secret to where the missing civilizations went—they all got Human'd."

"Yeah, well, we've seen stupider shit and crazier before, so it's not hard to believe people would get behind an organization like this. Feeling like they're somehow oppressed into being silent, rather than protected," Gus said. He agreed with Mark completely. Humans outnumbered Paras. Every time it came down to it, the Para population got wrecked.

And without hesitation, apologies, or a prelude to war. Just a sudden and ugly purge.

"I mean, you're not wrong, but come on. This seems patently obvious, doesn't it?" Mark asked.

"Whatever. Anyways, that's what's behind it all. They cut off from him pretty quick after we figured out what he was about and what he'd been up to," Gus said. "He was dead to them before they killed him."

"Yeah, does really feel like they killed him. No one else would want to do it at that point. We all wanted him alive," Mark said. "Does make a lot of people nervous though. That information was recent, critical, and it wasn't shared far. There's a leak. A big one."

"Yeah, we thought the same. You runnin' that one down since it's more likely the Feds are the leak?" Gus asked.

"No. They yanked that shit so fast from under my feet it gave me rug burns. Fuck 'em. If this goes any further wrong, I'm quitting and moving past the border," Mark muttered. "I'm all for doing my job and the duty behind it. But it's just a job. I'm only paid up to a certain point of caring. Not military anymore."

Gus could really identify with that sentiment. Almost too well. He briefly considered telling Mark about his reservations, and that he was considering getting out of the line of work, but he kept it to himself.

For now.

"Anyways," Gus said, drawing the conversation back. "Sean has a rally point. I texted you the address earlier. Only send people you trust to it. There's a shack to watch out for as well, in the middle of a bunch of trees you'll need to have them check."

"Got it. I was wondering what that was, came back to a Francis Dern as the owner," Mark said. "Know the name?"

"I do actually. And that's the next bit of information to talk about. Wendy? Wendy Hills? She's in on this whole thing. She was a point of contact for the organization and was operating as an information pump for the local Norms," Gus said. He didn't want to drag Vanessa into this, but he didn't have much choice.

"What? Oh. Oh, I see. She was the one bangin' your new girlfriend, right?" Mark asked.

"Yeah, she's a Were. We'll need a check-in from her bail officer. If she doesn't come to that, a BOLO or a warrant for her," Gus said.

"Huh? Bail officer? We have her in custody, don't we?" Mark asked.

"Nope. Made bail, and she's out and about. The one who paid her the ten percent is Francis Dern, an ex-girlfriend apparently," Gus said. "Or so Vanessa told me."

Looking over to the ambulance, he realized it was gone now. He turned toward their car, where he found Vanessa and Melody talking. The medics had apparently given up on Melody entirely.

A tow-truck was nearby, getting ready to tow away Gus's ruined car.

"Got it," Mark said, the sound of a pen scribbling across paper audible. "Damn, this is just getting more and more convoluted. Mills still won't talk to us. He just sits there now. As if he knows a whole lot of bad went down."

"Yeah, well, I'm hoping this is the darkest before the dawn because this shit is pretty bad," Gus grumbled.

"Mm. Alright, that it? Anything else of interest?" Mark asked.

Gus racked his mind for whatever might be of use to Mark. After several seconds, he couldn't think of anything new he hadn't told him.

"Nah, sorry. Got nothing else," Gus said finally. "Actually, I have one last thought. We never found that woman Eric was with. Any chance on offering him part of a deal to find out who she was? Or maybe hint he could play it off on that person instead of himself?"

"Huh, I'll talk to Richard. He's the one the DA assigned to work Mills. Richard London," Mark said. "Not bad for a Fae lawyer. I call him Dick. He doesn't care."

"Course you do. I'm not sure why that surprises me," Gus said. "Alright, I'm done. I'm going home. So are Melody and Vanessa. We're probably calling out sick for a few days, so… whatever."

"Yeah, I figured. I put all three of you on leave with pay for the shooting death of Sean. Mostly because the Feds are involved, but also because you could use a touch of downtime. All your paperwork is already being handled by others," Mark said.

"Mm. Okay. Oh, and Mark? I told Melody about what happened out there. With our team," Gus said. "Vanessa heard it all, too."

The silence on the other end of the line was deafening.

"You did?" Mark finally asked.

"Yeah. I did. Just giving you a heads up that it's an ok topic if it comes up," Gus said.

"I'm… surprised. I'm also happy, Gus," Mark said. "I'm very happy. Make sure you give 'em a chance to ask questions. Can't say for sure if I'm envious of you having two girlfriends, or if I pity you."

"Both, maybe. Okay, I'm gone. Need to find a ride home. See ya, Durh," Gus said.

"Bye, Gussy. Smoochies smoochies," Mark said, then killed the line.

Smirking, Gus slipped his phone into his pocket and walked over to Melody and Vanessa.

It was time to go home.

***

"Gus, it's so good to be home," Melody said, walking through the front door. "I know I said I wanted to buy a house near your mom, but I really like this house right now."

"You're just saying that because you're home. You'll change your mind again when we start looking," Vanessa said.

Melody laughed softly to herself, then nuzzled Vanessa who was helping her walk through the living room.

"You said 'when' we look. Have you surrendered? Will you be mine?" Melody asked.

"Yeah, shut up. I'm willing to see where it goes for now with both of you," Vanessa said. "Just don't rush me."

"Oh, oh—Gus, you're in too, right? We're... we're in a three-way relationship now? My harem?" Melody asked.

Closing the door, Gus shook his head and sighed.

"Yeah, just... like Ness said. I'll see where it goes, just don't rush me," Gus said.

"Best day ever. Best... best day ever. I love you both. You're both so amazing to me in your own ways. I can't wait till we have our first three-way together," Melody said. "Ness, I want to just devour you and—"

"Aaaand off to the bathroom with you, Melody," Gus said, walking up to the Contractor and wrapping an arm around her hips. "Time to go fix your contracts so you don't sound like a horny teenager all day."

"Yeah... thanks. That'd be nice," Melody said. Most of her contracts were glowing in one way or another right now. "I admit I want to do those things with you two, but it's hard not to talk about it right now. Been pushing my contracts a bit hard lately."

"Yeah," Gus said. Reaching into her pocket, he pulled out her phone and put it in his own pocket. Getting her into the bathroom, he set her down on the toilet. "You get undressed. I'm going to make sure Ness is ok, and I'll be right back. I have your phone, so you can just dump your clothes, ok?"

"Mmhmm," Melody said, starting to unbutton her blouse.

Walking out, he almost ran over Vanessa, and he had to grab her instead of bowling her over.

"Ah, sorry," Vanessa said, patting his chest. "Do you want me to start getting things ready for dinner? Melody said she wanted to cook."

Gus was still holding Vanessa, staring down into her face.

"Yeah, you should do that. That'd help. I'm going to take care of Melody and get her fixed up," Gus said.

"Good. Take care of our girlfriend," Vanessa said, peering up at him with a small smile. "Mom wants us to come over for dinner sometime. Doesn't like that you're white, but better than me dating a woman. She'll come around quickly; she just thinks you might be using me is all."

Gus snorted at that, not knowing what to do. He hadn't been intimate in a long time with anyone. Romantically or emotionally.

Sex was usually one-night stands from a bar or elsewhere.

And emotionally, he was just shut off.

He had a strange warm bubbling sensation in his guts whenever he was around Vanessa or Melody. It was worse outside work, and more so if he was close to them.

"Going to kiss me or let me go?" Vanessa asked suddenly.

At first he didn't know what to say or do. Then he leaned down and kissed Vanessa. It lasted only a moment.

Easing away from her while she was still smiling at him, he wanted to run away.

"Go take care of our girlfriend. I'll get things moving for dinner and pick a movie," she said, giving him a chance to leave.

Taking it, he walked back into the bathroom.

Melody was naked, and just now lying down in the tub.

"Ness is going to start getting everything out. She said you still wanted to make dinner?" Gus said.

"Yup, I need to cook for my loves. It'll just take me twenty minutes to recover afterward," Melody said, growing still in the tub. "I hate that it's always so cold."

"Can't do it with the water running?" Gus asked.

"It's too hard to turn it off after. And it gets cold if I wait till I'm better. It… oh… yeah. I have you now," Melody said, smiling up at him. "Douse me, beloved. In whatever way you see fit."

"Your contract really hits you right in the pheromones, doesn't it?" Gus said, standing up and turning on the hot water. Grabbing the drain, he pulled it open and started to adjust the temperature. He wanted her warm, not boiling.

"You have no idea. I get a bit too honest with the darker things I want," Melody said. Gus wanted to ask more about that, but this didn't seem like the right time. Especially considering the fact that she'd said it was something she wanted.

Getting the temperature right, he pushed the stopper into the tub and let it start to fill.

"That's lovely. You'll have to help me out with a lot of this, though. Little things, but not actually doing the contract itself," Melody said as the water starting rising. "I overdrew on them. A lot. I'm… not doing very well right now. Getting shot hurts, on top of that. I'm going to have to do them outside of my normal order. I need to start with the Red contract, unfortunately. I can barely think straight. It's all sex, sex, sex, right now."

Gus nodded his head and walked over to the bathroom door, and shut it. Unbuttoning the cuff on his right arm, he started to roll it back from his wrist.

"Now… how about you just lie back and let me take care of that Red contract," Gus said, getting down next to the tub and trailing his right hand up along the inside of her knee. "Like I said, I'm… in this with you. Don't rush me, but I'm not going to drag my feet."

"Oh… I like this. Best day ever, even if I was shot," Melody said, her Red contract blazing like the sun as she smiled at him. "Please… help me, Gustavus Hellström."

***

Sitting on the edge of his bed, Gus wasn't sure what to do with himself.

It was two in the morning, and he couldn't fall back asleep.

Melody had normalized pretty quick once her contracts were taken care of. Apparently, half of the insanity one saw in a Contractor was from over-usage. It tended to burn them up from the inside out, and quickly.

Dinner had gone well, and then they'd all sat there and watched a movie. Vanessa had picked something he'd never seen before. The girls had enjoyed it, but Gus had only watched it partially. Most of the night, he'd spent doting on both of them and trying to do whatever he could to help them unwind. Finally Melody shoved him down between her and Vanessa and gripped his hand like a vice.

Gus didn't feel stress like normal people. Or fear. He hadn't since he'd gone on deployment. Sometimes he never felt it, only for everything to come crashing down months later. He'd wanted only to give those two a chance to get rid of their own stress, since his wasn't going anywhere anytime soon.

As he stared at his hands, he felt like tonight was going to be a bad one. He'd already woken up with some rather ugly nightmares. Since talking about the whole incident today, he'd figured it was going to happen. It always did.

Realizing what he wanted to do, and not having done it in a long time, Gus picked up his phone. Before he knew what he was doing, he'd dialed his mom's number.

It picked up on the second ring.

"Hello dear," his mother said on the line. "Is everything ok?"

"Yeah, everything's ok," Gus said.

"He's fine, honey. Go back to bed," his mom said to what he assumed was his dad, who responded with something Gus couldn't hear.

"What's up?" his mom asked after several seconds.

She must have left the bedroom.

"I can't sleep. Had a bad day. Told Melody and Vanessa what happened out there in the desert," Gus said. "Had dreams."

"Ah… I see. I'm proud of you, though. You haven't really opened up to anyone since… well, then," his mom said. "What'd they think?"

"Nothing. Melody accepted it as it was and left it alone," Gus said. "Vanessa changed the subject."

"Good. Both of them are good girls. I like them. Their fear tastes lovely as well. Melody reminded me of a mint with cinnamon or something like that," his mom said.

Gus chuckled at that.

"And Vanessa was like chocolate. Both very delicious," his mother continued.

"Mom, stop it," Gus said, laughing a bit harder.

"Son, we're predators. It's what we are," she said. "I won't lie; I scented them just in case I needed to kill them later. Nothing permanent, just a good scenting. But clearly that's not needed. They're both living with you now?"

"Yeah," Gus said, feeling really weird about this whole thing. "We're not... really doing anything yet though."

"Oh? That's fine. That'll come with time once you loosen up a bit, I'm sure. Did I mention how glad I am you called? I don't think you've called like this in a long while," his mom said. There was a whumpf-like noise. It sounded like she'd just dropped into his father's easy chair in the living room. "Those girls are doing very good things for you. You even looked happy at the barbecue."

Thinking about that, Gus realized he had indeed been happy. In fact, even with everything that had been happening lately, his days had felt... good.

Great, even.

"Mom, I'd been avoiding feeding on people directly for a while. A long while," Gus said.

"I know. It was obvious. I figured it was just a phase. Did that change?"

"Yeah. I fed from Melody. A lot. I had her to the point that I fear-scented her. Permanently. Her and Vanessa both," Gus said.

"Goodness. I've only ever done that to your father," his mom admitted. "Let me guess. The moment you did it, women started paying attention to you?"

"Huh? How'd you know?" Gus asked. It was almost comical how often he'd been getting looks from women now. It had started with the secretary, and the waitress at the restaurant.

"Mm, from my own experience obviously. After I chose your father, I had countless men after me. It was rather frustrating. When I feed off him, it draws them in again," she said. "It seems the more you take in, the more appealing you are to opposite sex. I get the impression it's a hunting thing. Draw the prey to you."

That makes sense. But it's also rather disconcerting.

"I briefly considered having a harem of men," his mom said in a muted voice. "But then I realized I only wanted your dad. Your sister seems to be following in my footsteps. Only you became the hussy."

His mom started to laugh as soon as she said it.

"Ugh," Gus groaned, then started to laugh as well. "Yeah. Guess you're right. Your son is a hussy. Sorry Mom."

His mom laughed again.

"It's alright. They're good women. Now, talk to me. What's going on lately? How was your day?" she asked, her tone changing.

Sitting there on his bed, for the first time in a long while, he unloaded his soul to the one person who had always loved him no matter what.

Even when he'd come back a broken shell of a man from his first real job with a bag full of Elven scalps.

Chapter 26 - Milk Weed

Gus cleared his throat and let out a short breath.

"Thank you for coming with me, Gus," Vanessa said from the passenger seat.

"I mean… I did tell your mom I was your boyfriend. It'd be kinda weird if I didn't show up after that," Gus said.

"Yes, well, still. Thank you," Vanessa said. "I really do appreciate it."

"Uh huh," Gus said, and checked himself in the rear-view mirror.

He looked exactly as Vanessa had dressed him and styled his hair. Nothing was different in any way.

"I'm sad Melody didn't get to come," Vanessa said. "I know my mom doesn't really approve of me, well, having a girlfriend, but I do want her to meet Melody."

"I get that," Gus said, easing them through the intersection once the light turned green. "She'll be back soon enough. She said she'd only be gone for the weekend."

"I know, still. Though I'm glad she went to see her family," Vanessa said. "Sounded like they were very curious about where she was in her life."

"You sure it was her dad?" Gus asked, pulling the wheel to the side and turning into Vanessa's mom's neighborhood.

"Sounded like her dad to me. Sounds like my own dad when I call him, at least. I could be wrong," Vanessa said, her hand creeping over the center console to grip Gus's right hand. "I'm a little nervous."

"Huh? Why? I already met your mom," Gus said. "I mean, she called me El Coco, which was amusing, but hey, I've been called worse."

"You're going to meet my brothers. And I don't think they'll be as friendly as my mom was. They weren't even nice to friends I brought over," Vanessa said.

"I think I can handle 'em. There's very little in the world that would give me pause," Gus said, his mind drifting for a moment. "How do you want me to act? Be myself? Be aggressive? Be passive?"

"Could you… actually, just be yourself," Vanessa said, seeming to change her mind from her original direction. "If this is what Melody wants, and it seems to be going that way, I think we'll be tied to each other for a long while. Better you just be yourself."

"Contracting with a Contractor puts you into their version of marriage," Gus said. "And it also ties your life-span to theirs, but not your life. If they're immortal, you're immortal. Far as I can tell, Melody is immortal, and the single strongest Contractor I've ever met."

"Wouldn't that mean her father is immortal, too?" Vanessa asked, lifting her other hand and pointing at a driveway.

"That's a good point. He probably would be," Gus said, and turned toward the driveway. They were parking out in front of the house this time. Along both sides of the street in front of Mrs. Flores's house were trucks. Four of them.

"My brothers are here," Vanessa said. "Nice of them to keep the driveway open for me."

"Older or younger?" Gus said, unfastening his seatbelt.

"Three older, one younger."

Nodding at her remark, Gus got out, walked over to Vanessa's door and opened it.

Neither she nor Melody often gave him the chance to open doors for them, but every now and then, they let him.

See, Dad? I paid attention.

Just not always.

"Thank you," Vanessa said, getting out. She was dressed in a light-blue summer dress, her hair pulled back, and wearing simple stud earrings. To Gus she looked great, and she wasn't even that dressed up.

Closing the door to the new car Melody had bought them, a mid-market sedan, Gus turned and followed Vanessa up the walkway to the house.

Not even bothering to knock or ring the doorbell, Vanessa just opened the door and walked in.

The sound of men talking over a broadcast of what sounded like football came from the right. Up ahead in the kitchen, Gus could see Mrs. Flores along with an older man Gus hadn't met before.

"There's Dad," Vanessa said, and she walked forward toward the kitchen.

Gus pulled off his light coat and his holster at the same time. He hung both on the coat rack in the corner.

He still had his concealed carry at his ankle, though. That never came off.

Following after Vanessa, he got there just as she turned to hold a hand out to Gus.

"...my boyfriend, Gustavus. He goes by Gus. Gus, this is my father, George," Vanessa said.

Her father was around the same age as her mother, with dark hair that was starting to gray, a clean-shaven face, and dark-brown eyes. He didn't look as world weary as Vanessa's mom, but he definitely didn't seem to have a lot of optimism in his face either.

"Sir," Gus said, holding out his hand to the man.

There was a slight pause, and then George reached out and shook Gus's hand. Releasing it, he nodded at Gus.

"You work with my daughter, then?" George asked. His accent was a little rougher than his wife's, but it wasn't bad.

"I do. I'm her partner, sir. She's an amazing woman," Gus said. "Much as I said to your wife, she's a joy to be around, and I consider myself quite fortunate."

As if summoned by those words, Mrs. Flores came out from around the corner, a small smile on her face. She immediately walked over to Gus and pulled him into the kitchen.

She was speaking to him in Spanish, and he didn't catch a word of it. As gently as he could, he picked up the tiny fiber of power he'd left in her mind and connected it back to himself.

A second of reading her current thoughts, and he realized she was asking if he wanted anything to drink or eat. Letting the power fade to a dull pulse, Gus decided he'd have to intrude a bit on everyone in this house.

English wasn't their first language, after all, and if it was easier for them, he'd play along. He'd just have to be polite about not reading their thoughts.

"No, I'm fine, thank you Mrs. Flores," Gus said, giving her a smile. Vanessa had just been talking to her mom in Spanish, trying to explain once again that Gus didn't speak Spanish. "And no, I don't speak Spanish, but I have my own way of understanding."

Mrs. Flores nodded and pointed a finger at her husband, then the table. As if realizing he was fighting an uphill battle if he said no, George came over and sat down.

"My wife tells me that you're..." George paused, seeming to consider how to say it. Gus took a moment to repeat the same thing he'd done to Vanessa's mother, dropping a tiny speck of power there. He needed to know George could be trusted.

"A Boogieman?" Gus offered after confirming the man would say nothing to no one. "I believe she said El Coco, which isn't wrong. To answer that, yes. I am. And that's a family secret that would get me executed faster than you would expect. I ask for your trust in that."

George frowned, but nodded his head. "What does that mean?"

"Means I'm human, but I have other things I need than just food and water. For me, it's fear," Gus said. "I eat fear."

All three members of the Flores family were watching him right now.

Vanessa seemed shocked that he was sharing this information with her parents. And her parents seemed unsurprised at his statement.

"But you do eat?" Mrs. Flores asked in Spanish.

"Yes, I do eat. Your daughter has a fair hand at cooking; did she get that from you?" Gus asked.

Mrs. Flores's chin raised up, and she nodded her head sharply.

"Always a pain, my little one. Never did what I wanted until she suffered for not listening, but she was worth it," Mrs. Flores said still in Spanish, busying herself with the oven.

George was smirking now, watching Gus. "Come on, I'll introduce you to the rest of my life. Sounds like those two are going to get into it anyways. Good time to escape."

Vanessa and her mother were arguing now in Spanish, much as George had predicted only a second before.

Must be a normal state.

George nodded his head to the side and escorted Gus into the family living room. Four men were sitting around on couches, talking about something Gus couldn't figure out since it was in Spanish and he wasn't reading their minds yet.

He quickly tied off multiple strings of power so he could follow along, just in case.

Across the other side of the room were three women and four children. Two looked to be about seven, the other two much closer to two. They were happily playing together, and the women were talking amongst themselves.

Strange division. But maybe that's just how it is here.

Gus immediately dropped more lines of his telepathy into the women. It was starting to drain him a bit, keeping so many minds on a line at the same time.

George walked up to the men and put a hand on Gus's shoulder.

"This is Vanessa's boyfriend," George said to the four men. They were all variations of George himself. "He works with her. His name is Gus. These are my boys. Ricky, Tony, Martin, and George Junior."

Gus got the impression that, by and large, they didn't seem impressed with him.

The youngest, George Junior, who looked to be just out of high school, muttered something under his breath. Gus got the mental translation of it as "white bread." And it was rather derogatory.

"I mean, sure, I guess. White bread fits," Gus said, jumping straight in. He'd never backed down from a challenge. He stared straight into the younger man's eyes. "Pig fits, too. Or cop, or whatever else you like."

All four men froze on the spot, and George glared at his youngest.

"Uh… I—" said George Junior.

"You, what, didn't think I'd hear you? That you could just say it and not give a shit? I've killed people for less when I was running around with a rifle and kicking down doors in the desert," Gus said, heat rapidly coloring his voice. The beast that was Gus's temper gave itself a sudden shake when he had a stray thought about Vanessa. Then it settled back down. He didn't need to prove anything to this kid, and it would only bother Vanessa. "So if you wanna start this one off on that foot, sure, we can do that. I came here because I care for your sister and wanted to meet her family. So I'll give you the benefit of acting like this never happened."

There was a pall of fear coming up from all five men around Gus, and he could feel it creeping into the women on the other side of the room. They didn't know what was going on, but they could sense that there was a massive problem looming in the room.

George Junior looked like a child scolded.

"You… you served?" asked Tony, who seemed to be the oldest.

"Seven years," Gus said, turning to the other man and finally breaking eye contact with George Junior. "All out of country. Was contracted for eight, came back on an honorable discharge after wounds suffered."

"Our brother served," Martin said, looking sad and confused at the same time.

"I saw. My respects to the fallen," Gus said.

Vanessa appeared in the doorway then, looking concerned. She was looking straight at him, apparently expecting some sort of trouble.

Checking himself, Gus found the aura he kept in check was still expanding around him. It was something he'd learned to do on deployment. Something he'd never been able to turn off since, and he usually kept it bottled up unless he needed to threaten someone.

Stuffing it down back where it had come from, Gus gave Vanessa a smile.

"Hey, Ness, we were just talking about my service history," Gus said. "Your dad just introduced me."

For his part, George was looking at Gus in a very different light right now. Like a man who had a bear in a cage and wasn't sure what to do with it.

"Oh," Vanessa said, then looked at George Junior. Her eyes hardened by whatever she saw there. The young man looked further chastised, if that was possible.

Ah, this isn't the first time he's been the stupid one.

Great.

Dinner is going to be fun.

***

Gus stepped outside, pulling on his coat and holster. He couldn't really handle anymore conversation right now. He needed a break, so he'd made an excuse about making a call.

Realistically, he was just tired of doing telepathic translations for so many people while also trying to be pleasant.

Dinner had gone fairly well, with only a few weird spots. Mostly caused by Vanessa's mother asking questions that weren't appropriate for a dinner table. Let alone the children at the other end.

With any luck, they could leave in an hour or so.

And not come back for a damn long while.

Shaking his head, Gus walked down the stone-lined walkway toward the sidewalk. When he got there, he looked around.

Everything looked fairly normal.

Street lookouts were at both sides, watching for anything that might be heading into the neighborhood. They didn't seem to be doing anything, and Gus didn't see any obvious signs of crime or problems.

Hood watch.

Gus decided it might be good to make contact.

Directly across from him was a younger man in his twenties. Shaved head, street clothes, and tatted-up arms. He looked fairly normal, other than the mask magic that was fluttering around him. He looked entirely human, however.

Local Were pack?

Gus checked the street in both directions, then hopped off the curb and started walking toward the other man.

Noticing Gus immediately, the man looked like he might just up and bolt.

"Hey, I'm not a cop," Gus said by way of introduction. "I'm not here on the job either. I'm just a detective, visiting my girlfriend's parents."

The Were seemed to hear that and believe it, and decided not to run. He still looked incredibly nervous to Gus, though Perhaps to anyone else, he would seem to be full of bluster and pride. People had a hard time hiding things from Gus.

Stepping up to the man, Gus pulled his medallion out from under his dress shirt.

"I'm Gus, Gustavus Hellström, PID, out of the ninety-ninth," he said. "Just a detective. Like I said, I'm visiting my girlfriend's parents."

After looking at the badge and then at Gus, the man turned to the Flores house behind Gus. "You're dating Vanessa?"

"Yeah, I am. She joined the PID recently as well. You part of the local pack?" Gus asked.

Nodding his head, the man squared his shoulders. "What about it?"

"Nothin' about it. I was going to ask you for a favor, though," Gus said. "You keep an eye on the Flores place, and I'll owe you a favor. That's it."

"Favor? Like what kind of favor?" said the man.

"Can't get anything with violence or gang elevation bounced, but I can probably make other things vanish," Gus said, being completely honest. He had a certain amount of leeway he could work when it came to getting things out. Claiming a CI went a long way, and it usually paid itself off the next time Gus needed something. "All for keeping an eye on a nice family of Norms."

"Can't speak for the pack, but I think our leader won't argue. I bet she'll say yes," said the man. "That and she used to run with Vanessa when they were in high school."

Gus chuckled at that. "Let me guess, you were already watching the house then. Probably because of what happened the other day."

The man grinned and shrugged. "Maybe."

"Whatever," Gus said and shook his head. "Pitch it up to your boss. And feel free to tell them I handled that situation with the Were who was in your neighborhood. They won't be coming back either."

"Huh. I'll let her know. Hey, actually... you said you'd do us a favor. What if I wanted it right now?" said the man.

"Kinda depends. Just did dinner with her parents, not really on duty. What's the favor?" Gus asked.

"We uh... well... one of our pack went crazy yesterday," said the man, sounding unsure, but desperate. "He just... attacks everyone who comes close. He won't settle down and he just screams at us. You think maybe... maybe you could get a doc over that won't ask questions?"

Shit. Another one? I sure as hell hope this is just a Were disease. Please don't let this be another Mask Madness thing.

"Let me... go talk to Vanessa. Think you could take me to see your pack member? I think I might have an idea of what's going on," Gus said, not really believing for an instant that his luck would hold out. That it wasn't another mask break.

"You're in luck, they're watching from the window," said the man. "She'll probably meet you at the door."

Clicking his tongue, Gus stuffed his hands in his pockets.

"Hey, George Junior doing anything I need to be aware of?" Gus asked, changing the subject.

The man frowned at that, giving Gus a strange look.

"Nah. Nothing that would land him a cell. Stupid shit, sure. Nothing terrible though," he said.

"Great. Want my card or you got the info for me?" Gus asked.

"I got it. Gus Hellstorm, ninety-ninth. PID," said the man.

Close enough.

"Great. Be right back then," Gus said, then turned and checked the street, crossed it, and walked back up to the Flores house.

Vanessa was practically on the doorstep waiting for him when he came back in.

"Everything alright?" she asked.

"Yeah, just checking in with the local Were pack," Gus said. "Asked him to keep an eye on your folks house and I'd do him a favor."

Gus stamped his feet on the floor mat. Then he walked back into the house. Vanessa's parents were walking away from her. The fleeting image he got from them was they had overheard what he'd said to Vanessa.

And were feeling guilty for some reason.

"They thought you were telling him to take a hike," Vanessa said. "He's a... neighborhood boy, as they call him."

"He's a Were, from the local pack. He also asked me for a favor for watching your folks' place. Sounds like they got a pack member that's got a mask break, like Misha and Fitz," Gus said with a grimace. "That makes three we know of."

"Another?" Vanessa asked, looking troubled. "What'd—"

"He didn't say anything," Gus said interrupting her. "But he asked if we could help. I told him we'd go take a look. If you feel like we can leave, that is."

"Oh, yeah, we can go. I was just telling everyone we were going to head out anyways," Vanessa said, gently shoving him out the door. "We'll go now."

"Right, ok, yeah, I don't need to say goodbye or anything?" Gus asked, letting her move him.

"No. I already did for you," Vanessa said.

Doesn't sound good. I'm s—

"I'll tell you about it later," Vanessa said, as if plucking his thoughts from the air. "Let's go."

Chapter 27 - Scope

"Any chance you'd be willing to tell me what you told your parents yet?" Gus asked, looking over to Vanessa as they slowly drove through the neighborhood. They were tailing along behind the Were Gus had spoken to.

"I'd really rather not. At least not right now. I feel like we're walking into a trap," Vanessa muttered. She'd taken over driving as soon as they'd determined what they were doing.

Gus wasn't about to disagree with her, but he also knew better. He'd been listening to the man's thoughts the moment he agreed to take them back to their pack house.

A pack house was more or less the den where they did all important pack activities out of. In some of the larger packs, it also served as a den where they kept their children.

Rather than press for more information and probably just make Vanessa angry, Gus let it lie. It wasn't worth finding out what was going on with her family.

Flipping open his phone, Gus typed up a message to Melody and then sent it. He wanted to make sure he kept her in the loop on what was going on with their case.

With Eric being involved in the mask problem of Michael Fitz and a separate case involving an Elf from another state, Gus was starting to worry that this was part of a larger problem.

A much larger problem, if he didn't miss his guess and fear.

But he'd find out more information shortly, he imagined. Once he found out what was going on with the pack member.

"He said I used to run with her? Their pack leader?" Vanessa asked.

"I mean, that's what he said. He didn't name her or anything, though it was mildly amusing to find out he was there to partially watch over your parents.

"Got any high-school exes I should be worried about?"

"No, actually," Vanessa said, sounding somewhat sad. "I looked really awkward all through high school. I didn't start fitting my face until senior year."

"And boy do you fit it now," Gus said more to himself, staring out his window.

"What's with the flattery?" Vanessa said.

"Huh? Flattery? What, you mean saying you fit your face? I mean, you yourself said I was handsome. Why aren't I allowed to be honest about you being pretty?" Gus asked.

"Because it's... you know what, fine. I'll just take it," Vanessa said. "What the fuck... is he going into there?"

Gus looked at the man they were tailing. He was going up the walkway to a liquor store.

"Mm. Probably. A lot of packs end up buying stores like that. Convenience stores, gas stations, liquor stores, smoke shops. Things that just require a couple licenses and a bunch of people to take turns at a counter," Gus said. "Money is shared and pooled, which means employees are free if they're pack."

"Oh. Huh," Vanessa said, pulling into the parking lot. "There's just... a lot I never really thought about. I mean, you see all those movies where they secretly run the city and night clubs and all that nonsense. So far it's just... way more normal than I expected."

"I mean, I'm sure there are Paras who own nightclubs. And probably some Vampires and Werewolves who do. But it's not like they really have to go to that extreme," Gus said, unbuckling his seatbelt as Vanessa put the car in park. "It doesn't take much for Norms to promise away their blood in the hopes of joining the ranks. That's usually how it goes. Much like Weres, though, Vampires work in a similar way. Covens instead."

Getting out of the car, Gus adjusted his coat, reached into his holster, and thumbed the catch open. Turning away from the front window, he eased his weapon out and pulled the slide a fraction to make sure it was chambered.

Satisfied, he pushed it back into the holster and disengaged the safety.

"Expecting a problem?" Vanessa asked, coming over to stand with him. She was still in her dress, though she was wearing a sweater now.

"No, but I expect to always need to be aware," Gus said. "After you. This is your neighborhood. I'm just the white guy who's ruining you."

Vanessa scoffed at that, then walked up to the liquor store and opened the door. They both went inside, immediately getting waved toward the back room by the same man.

"In the back. We locked him down as quick as we could," said the man. "Bunch of fuckin' Norms were all around us. Damn near gave me a heart attack. Last thing we need is the Feds coming in to mind-wipe the neighborhood."

Shit. And there it is.

It's really as simple as that, isn't it?

If a bunch of masks fail in a relatively short period of time, it'd hit the news one way or another. Either through the Internet or an actual station.

And without the Fed to crush it, blot it out, and make it vanish… it'd happen.

Following Vanessa, Gus pulled his phone back out and fired off a quick note to Michael. He wanted to know if he had a backup of the database for the DME, for all states, and if he could access who'd had their masks updated in the last six months.

No sooner had he sent that message off, another came in.

It was from Melody.

Tapping it open, he read it.

That's not good. It sounds like it's worse than we all thought. I'll be home soon, my love. I miss you quite badly.

Oh, and my mother wants to meet you at some point, so we'll need to plan a trip out.

Other than that, nothing to report.

Except I'm really wishing I was home with you and Nessa. Don't do any sexy things with her without me. I want our first time to be a three-way together.

I LOVE YOU DESPERATELY, GUSTAVUS HELLSTROM!

Huh, I can't get the little o thing with the dots.

Stupid phone.

Rolling his eyes, he closed the message and shoved his phone back in his pocket. When he looked up, he realized they'd entered another room and gone down a flight of stairs as well.

Apparently the Were lookout had told his packmates what to expect, though. No one stopped them, and in fact, they seemed to be herding them somewhere.

Opening another door ahead of them, Vanessa and Gus walked into it.

Off to one side, bound in heavy chains, handcuffs, a steel muzzle, and locked up with multiple padlocks, was a Were in its hybrid phase.

It was screaming, roaring, and thrashing wildly against the bindings. The room was empty otherwise.

"Oh," Vanessa said, stepping to one side and freezing up.

Gus doubted she'd ever been around a Were in a full-on frenzy. Because that was what this was. A Were completely lost in a frenzy that would happily kill anything and anyone in front of it.

Even its own pack.

"Yeah, that's… not good," Gus said, walking over to the Were. "Coyote. Big one, too."

"That's a Were… coyote?" Vanessa asked.

"Yep. Honestly, it's possible to be a Were anything, really. It just takes a mutated virus. It's kinda like rabies. Add a bit of magic and a bite, and voila.

"It's why you almost only ever see predators, though. It's always transmitted through bites," Gus said. "Coyotes are actually pretty reasonable. They're not as territorial as Wolves, or as hyper aggressive as Bears can get."

Squatting down next to the Coyote, Gus grabbed an eyelid and peeled it back.

The eye was fully dilated and red rimmed. There was no humanity there at all.

Just like the Elf.

"He's been like that for a couple days," said a voice from behind him.

Turning his head, Gus looked to the door.

A young woman stood there. She had similar features as Vanessa, though she was a touch thicker in almost every way, and a head taller.

"Elise?" Vanessa asked, sounding confused.

"Hi cousin," said the woman, walking over. "Surprised you joined the PID. Dad said Uncle didn't want anything to do with him or our world."

Vanessa shook her head. "Wait, my dad knows?"

"Course he does," Elise said, sounding rather annoyed. "He was there when my dad got bit ten years ago. It's the same year I got turned."

"I... I never knew. As far as joining the PID, I had an encounter with a Troll. Was recruited after that... Ah... this is Gus," Vanessa said, turning toward Gus. "He's my boyfriend and partner at the PID."

"Hello, Gus the boyfriend," Elise said. "I'm Elise the Were cousin."

"Hi Elise. You said he's been like this a few days?" Gus asked, looking back at the Were.

"Yeah. We were going through a checkpoint to watch a game," Elise said, walking over to stand next to Gus. "He just started screaming. Acting like a fool. Two of my people knocked him down, and we dragged him out before he could start to shift. Acted like he was drunk and we were taking him home."

"No sign of it going away at all?" Gus asked. "No change from the onset?"

"Not at all," Elise said, gesturing at the bound Were. "He just... screams and yells and... does all this."

"Hm. I should I check in with Vard and see how Misha's doing. She's been locked in for a while too by this point. I was hoping this whatever-it-is would fade after a while, but that doesn't seem to be the case," Gus said. Looking up to Elise, he cleared his throat. "You, uh... know where his mask is? Or where it went? On top of that, do you know when he last got it updated?"

"It was his driver's license," Elise said. "Wasn't on him though. Couldn't find it. He got it updated six months ago or something."

Shaking his head, Gus looked at the Were with a frown.

Ok. So. This has all been people who had their mask updated in the last year so far. The mask is gone after the madness sets in, and there isn't an end to it.

Rubbing at his jaw and chin, Gus was unnerved.

If even a fraction of the Para population went on wild killing sprees, and whatever else they could do, there was likely no possible way at all to stop the whole thing from going wrong.

This wasn't the middle of a plan. The opening moves of this attack had been set into motion a long time previously. They were in the end stages of the game now, and Gus had no idea how far behind the PID and Fed were.

"Register this one with the PID ninety-ninth precinct. It's where we're out of. Make sure you flag it for one Mark Ehrich, he's our captain. He'll know what to do with it and maybe be able to offer some help," Gus said and sighed.

"You don't know what's going on," Elise said.

"Oh, I know what's going on. I even have a pretty damn good guess on the what, who, and the why. The when and the how escape me.

"Get it logged, we'll do what we can and update you with news," Gus said, then stood up. "For now, keep an eye on anyone who had their mask updated in the last year. Beyond that, I got nothing at the moment. Thanks for your time and your trust."

Elise nodded at Gus, then at Vanessa. She didn't say anything though.

It was a dismissal, and the end of the conversation if ever there was one.

Walking back the way they'd come, Gus and Vanessa got back to the car without a word. Vanessa had elected to drive again, walking over to the driver's side and getting in.

When they were finally in the car with the doors shut, Gus took a shaky breath.

"Their goal is to just have as many Paras go insane as possible at the same time, isn't it?" Vanessa asked.

"That'd be my guess. And for some reason, a few people are having it happen early," Gus said. "I mean, it's a nice break for us, but in the same breath, I have no idea how it's happening. Which means about fuck-all. We know what the hell is going on, and the plan, but no idea on how to stop or fix it."

"What do you think we should do?" Vanessa asked. "We're on leave, but we were assigned the case."

"I already pitched a message over to our tech. See if he has the databases for the DME. I don't think he does, but it's worth a shot. The problem is that the Fed is toast. Which means all their databases are probably scrapped," Gus said and ran a hand through his hair. "On top of making it impossible for them to stop this from going live should all those masks break, they probably lost every scrap of information on who got their mask updated."

"Damn, I didn't even think about that," Vanessa muttered. "We're not just playing catch-up then. We're getting lapped."

"Uh huh. Let's go home and regroup for now. I want to call Melody and let her know all the details, then call Mark as well," Gus said. "It'll be good to make sure they're aware and Mark rescinds our leave."

"Yeah, as much as I want those days off, I can't really sit on the sidelines for this one right now," Vanessa said.

"Me either. Now, did you want to talk about your family here, or when we get home?" Gus said. "Cause I imagine it'll come up at some point. Which would you prefer?"

"Ergh, here is fine. On the way home, in fact. Driving will help. Let's me feel like I'm getting away from the problem," Vanessa said, then started the car and put it in reverse.

"Honestly, I didn't think I did too badly with your folks. Your dad was pretty wary of me, but considering what happened, that's not entirely unsurprising," Gus said. Then he shrugged his shoulders. "Your mom likes me though."

Vanessa snorted at that, her hands tightening on the steering wheel as she got them onto the street.

"She likes you alright. In fact, I got a pretty heavy-handed lecture about how I need to make sure you don't get away. Even if that means I should make sure to not use birth control," Vanessa growled. "I mean, really Mom?"

"Hah. I'm flattered," Gus said. "Speaking of, Melody told me you're off limits until she's back. Apparently our first time is going to be a three-way.

"I can't remember agreeing to that. You?"

"No, but she made me promise it to her," Vanessa said, shaking her head. "I can't deny I care for her in a way, but she's so fucking crazy sometimes."

"Comes with the territory, I'm afraid. You could always back out. I think she'd let you escape if you really pushed," Gus said.

"She would… and I should… but… I kinda like it. It's a little crazy and a lot of warmth. Reminds me of my parents when they were younger," Vanessa said. "Besides, I'm curious to see how it goes. Anyways… yeah, Mom likes you."

"And your dad?" Gus asked.

"Thinks you're dangerous, to which my mom agrees, but she sees that as a good thing. What'd my brother do? They wouldn't tell me," Vanessa said.

"Called me white bread. I told him he can call me whatever he wants, and if that's how he wanted it, that'd be how it is," Gus said. "I did offer to let it drop, though, if he wanted. Left it at that."

Vanessa started to curse under her breath in Spanish.

"I'm going to wring his neck," she said. "This is the first damn time I've brought someone home and he starts with that shit?"

"Not a big deal, Ness. I've heard worse. First, huh?" Gus asked, looking over to her. "Are we that serious?"

Vanessa pursed her lips, then nodded. "We are. I mean, come on, Gus. I'm attracted to you, you're attracted to me, we're both willing to go for Melody together. We've been talking about buying a house together, but at the same time, we all live with one another already.

"I know I said I didn't want to get rushed, and I don't, but in the same breath… am I dragging my feet?"

"If it makes you feel better, I'm having the same thoughts and reservations," Gus said. Then he reached over and put his left hand behind Vanessa's head and started to lightly tickle her neck with his fingertips. He just wanted to touch her right now. "And maybe we're dragging our heels a bit. But Mel can be so fucking pushy sometimes."

"Tell me about it. She came in my room the night before she left and said she wanted to snuggle naked," Vanessa said, not mentioning Gus's hand.

"Oh? Did you?" Gus said.

Vanessa turned a faint red, then looked at him with a smile. It faded after a second, though.

"You're not going to get jealous if… I mean… when… Mel and I err, play without you?" Vanessa asked.

"No. Just as I hope you wouldn't or Mel wouldn't get jealous when it's just us, or just me and her," Gus said. "Though that's going to be a conversation we probably should have in advance, isn't it?"

"Probably," Vanessa said. "Mel really wanted to invite you into the room so you could join us. Sorry but I told her no, I was just too tired and was afraid of where it would go. Mel kept her hands to herself thankfully."

"Pity I missed out," Gus said, continuing to stroke Vanessa's neck.

"An-anyways. I told my family to be nice and treat this seriously. Because it is serious. Then they saw you talking to the neighborhood boy and were afraid you were going full cop on them," Vanessa said. "I know they heard what you said when you came back, so I'm going to be calling them and reaming them both out for that later."

"Leave it alone," Gus said, lifting his fingers to scratch at the base of Vanessa's head. "Not worth it. Let's just… go home, make our calls, and have a nice dinner. You up for a movie tonight? You can pick it."

"Yeah? Alright, let's do that then. Can we order pizza, though? Melody is a good cook, and I'm not bad myself, but I just really want some pizza and beer," Vanessa said. "Pizza, beer, and snuggle on the couch."

"Sure, no worries," Gus said with a chuckle. It was surprising to him sometimes with how pretty Vanessa was, how down to earth she was at the same time.

Chapter 28 - Abnormal Para

Gus stuffed his hands in his coat pockets and exited the back door of the PID building. Taking in a slow breath, he wasn't sure what to do with himself.

Go sit at the tree. Catch a breath or two.

As he walked into the private garden and patio that had been built as part of the "lunch and break" area for the building, Gus felt strange. He used to come back here almost every day at some point during his shift.

Usually just to catch a glimpse of Trish when she emptied her trash cans into the dumpster back here.

He'd been low-key keeping track of her for around seven months. She'd been a curiosity at first. Someone that pretty cleaning out the trash didn't fit with his view of the world.

If I were a woman and as pretty as Trish, I'd probably be an awful bitch and climbing my way up a company ladder.

Chuckling at the strange thought, Gus sat down at a bench off to one corner of the area. It wasn't the main seating area most people went to. This was truly out of the way, and it didn't offer much shade. The tree down here looked to be still growing. The trunk wasn't much thicker than Gus's thigh.

When he'd first taken the job, the tree had been little more than a poor, twisted thing getting blown about by the wind.

Letting out a sigh, Gus reached out and pulled on one of the supports he'd put in back then. The tree probably didn't need them anymore, but he just hadn't gotten around to removing them.

It'll grow out of them on its own, doesn't need me to do it.

Closing his eyes, he just sat there.

Melody wasn't home yet. Her "weekend" visit seemed to be growing longer.

She'd promised as soon as she finished up what she was doing, she'd come back as soon as she was able. But that was still a couple days away, apparently.

Michael Noble had confirmed he didn't have any of the DME databases. But he did say he was working through recovering data. He'd put that in his critical not-critical pile of work to do, as he called it.

Vanessa was currently going through everything the teams had been sent that they'd found at the address Gus had given Mark. All the links, hints, clues, and anything of relevance.

In the short time they'd been off, Wendy had a BOLO and a warrant, as well as Francis.

Except that was it. There was a wealth of hints, clues, and small bits of information, but it ended with that. Nothing led to anyone outside of Wendy and Francis.

Even the shack Sean had been worried about had really just contained everything the man would need to escape in the end.

They were mostly back to square one, just with a better idea of what they were facing.

The quiet rattle of wheels over sectioned pavement woke him from his thoughts.

Opening his eyes and turning his head, Gus found Trish wheeling her set of trash cans over to the dumpster. She was dressed in a clean, new uniform today. Her hair was pulled back, the hair clip he'd gotten her resting firmly at the top of her ponytail. Her hat was off, the cap back slid through a belt loop.

After dumping her trash cans out into the dumpster, she set them back on the trolley she used to cart them around the building.

Dragging her wrist across her brow, Trish leaned back, stretching. Unconsciously, Gus's eyes were immediately dragged down to her impressive figure when she did so. Even in her uniform, she was great to look at.

As if sensing his eyes on her, her head whipped around to where he was sitting.

Lifting his eyes, and a hand to wave at her, Gus didn't look away or move.

Trish froze, staring at him, and then she waved back at him. Popping her latex gloves off, she flicked them into the dumpster, then pulled off her uniform coat. She was wearing a tight undershirt that really only made it harder to keep his eyes on her face.

She tied her coat around her waist and started walking in his direction.

Uh… ok. Right. Uh. Beautiful woman coming this way.

Not a good time for this. I have two girlfriends. Bad thoughts go away.

Come on, Gus. Get it squared away.

Shoo. Shoo thoughts, shoo.

Trish meandered over to him.

"Seat taken?" she asked, indicating the bench he was on.

"Nope, feel free," Gus said. "Was just taking a break. Been hitting my head against a wall all day. Kinda tired of it. Decided I wanted to take a break from it. Wall's not going anywhere."

Trish smiled at him, and Gus felt his heart start to race. It was strange, but it almost didn't feel right for someone to be as pretty as Trish was.

Sitting down next to him, she sighed and leaned back into the bench.

"Must be fun to be a detective," she said. "Probably better than being a cleaning lady at least."

"We all have our problems," Gus said, looking at the tree again. "Some are easier than others."

"I suppose," Trish said. "At least I'm not constantly hit on here. The last PID building I worked at, it was a never-ending turnstile of come-ons. Then again, I was working at night and most of them were around."

"Yeah, well, I'm sorry?" Gus asked, not really sure how to respond to that. He couldn't really fathom what it'd be like to be an attractive woman. "Can't deny you're beautiful and eye-catching, but in the same breath it probably gets old being asked out constantly."

I bet she gets hit on a lot. After a while, it's got to be tiring. It's not like she's asking for it either. Especially at work.

"Don't be sorry, that's just how it goes," Trish said. "For me, it gets old, yes. I'm sure there are women out there who enjoy the constant attention. I don't."

Gus only nodded his head.

"Most people don't come over this way," Trish said. "But I see you often enough over here."

"Gotta see my tree," Gus said, pointing at the tree in front of him. "When I first got hired on, it wasn't doing so well. I put in some stakes, tied it off, got it straightened out."

He'd actually done much more for the tree than just that, but it felt weird talking about it.

"You did that?" Trish asked, her head turning toward him now.

"Yeah," Gus said with a shrug. "Seemed like the gardening crew that handles this area didn't really care about it. So I did."

Ok, let's… let's make sure this is clean and fair and –

"Though with two girlfriends, I'm not sure I'll have as much time to look after it," Gus said, spring-boarding from his own thought. "Good thing the tree seems to be fine all on its own now."

Trish was still looking at him. Gus could see it out of the corner of his eye.

"Two?" she asked.

"Yep," Gus said, assuming she meant the two girlfriends comment. "One's a Contractor, the other is a Norm."

"Ohh. Contractor. Yes. They tend to end up with as many wives and husbands as they do contracts," Trish said.

Yeah. Good thing Melody already told me she only wanted one man in her contracts. Though I never really asked her why she suddenly chose Vanessa.

Or… or if she'll try to get us more girlfriends.

Hm.

That's unnerving.

"Thankfully I'm the only guy, and the only one planned," Gus said with a chuckle.

"Yes, you're far too much of an ideal man to be wasted on anything other than a harem full of women," Trish said. "Your Contractor sounds like a smart woman."

Huh?

Looking to his side, he found Trish was still watching him. Her green eyes almost glowed with an inner light.

"You. You're an ideal man. You'd be wasted to not have your genes spread further," Trish said. The amount of eye contact she was making was a bit uncomfortable now.

"Yeah, well, we'll see. Two girlfriends already sounds like one too many," Gus said, feeling like Trish was somehow pulling him into her eyes themselves. There was a strange pressure building around his mind as well.

Then Trish blinked and broke eye contact with him, looking down towards his lap. Shifting sideways, she turned herself more towards him. Her shirt twisted with her torso and bunched up around her middle.

Keeping his eyes up top with the utmost control, Gus smiled at her.

Now that he was staring at her—and that he felt allowed to without being rude or creepy—Gus noticed her ears weren't quite human. Not really, at least.

"What kind of Para are you?" Gus asked. The question could be considered rude, but in the same breath, he felt like they'd crossed that bridge a moment ago when she'd talked about him "spreading his seed" wider.

"Oh, uhm, I'm partially Elven," Trish said, one hand going up toward her ear, stopping halfway, and then lying back down in her lap. "It's my ears, isn't it? I had my mask updated three months ago. I had a few minor enchantments that made my ears look normal under the previous mask, but they're not working on the new mask."

Frowning, Gus wasn't sure what to say to that. He knew some people often used minor enchantments for stuff like that. It wasn't quite legal, but it wasn't really illegal either.

"Can I see it?" Gus asked.

"What… my ears?" Trish asked, smiling at him. She reached up and pulled her hair more firmly behind her ears, then tilted her head toward him. "See? They have little tips to them. My father was Elven."

"Ah… no, I'm sorry. Your mask, could I see it?"

"Oh, sure," Trish said with a soft laugh. She pulled out a wallet from her back pocket, then flipped it open and pulled out her driver's license.

Weird. She uses a wallet.

Gus leaned over to look at the license.

Patricia Ash.

It looked fairly normal to him. Nothing out of the ordinary at all. Reaching out to take it from her, he stopped. His hand was inches from taking it, but he didn't want to.

In fact, his internal senses were screaming at him to not touch it at all.

"That's odd," Trish said, peering at her own license.

"What is?" Gus said, putting his hand back in his lap and deciding not to take the license.

"What? Oh, nothing, it just looked odd, sorry," Trish said, hastily tucking her license back into her wallet.

No. She saw something. What was it?

Taking a thread of his telepathy, he slid it into Trish's mind.

And found nothing but a wall. A very firm mental wall and that he'd been caught doing it.

Trish was staring at him, and Gus could feel that she'd not only sensed what he was doing and blocked it, but was now reversing it back toward him.

Her mind was suddenly atop his, peering into his thoughts.

"Oh," Trish said, breaking the contact. Her voice became incredibly delicate and soft. "I'm so sorry. I didn't know what you were doing and I just… matched it. I'm sorry. Please don't arrest me. I'm so sorry."

Giving his head a shake, not having expected any of that, Gus pressed a hand to his temple. He felt lightheaded.

And incredibly tired all of a sudden.

"Ohhh… I'm sorry," Trish said. She was practically on top of him now. Cool fingers were pressed to his throat. Then her hands were on his face, thumbing down his eyelids and looking into his eyes. "Everything looks ok. You just weren't expecting it, maybe? Oh! I used your own power source to do all the work. That's it."

Gus blinked. He was really at a loss right now.

"You'll be alright in a minute or two," Trish said. She was still holding his face in her hands, her thumbs lightly brushing along his cheek bones. "Sorry. I let my curiosity get the better of me. I wanted to know what you were trying to do to me."

"I wanted to read your thoughts. I wanted to know what you saw," Gus said. Trish was dangerous. Extremely dangerous. If she'd wanted to crush him in that instant, she could have. He also got the impression that in that split second, she'd read his mind almost top to bottom. Not just his thoughts, but a good portion of his memories.

"Yes. I know. The runes on the mask don't look right. They were reacting to your hand, but were still passive," Trish said. She was looking into his eyes, and not moving away from him at all. It was rather intimidating to him.

The whole thing was.

Melody didn't scare Gus. Few things did.

Trish had pushed a grain of fear into him, though.

"I had no idea you were a Boogieman and a telepath," Trish said, her head tilting to one side. "It's impressive how well you blend in. And on top of that, you don't even use your powers for your benefit."

That grain of fear just exploded into a ripe field of it.

"Shhh, it's alright," Trish said, one of her hands stroking the side of his face. "I'll keep your secret if you keep mine. I'm not just Elven, I'm a Sorceress. Without any training, a mentor, or even accreditation."

There was more to it than that, though. Gus knew it. Things didn't add up.

Except a lot of that he needed to set aside. She'd said something that made sense in a different way to him.

"Your license was reacting to me?" Gus asked.

"Yes. The runes on it were shifting toward you. I can't read them, as I don't understand the magical language used, but I could see what they were doing," Trish said.

"What are you doing?"

Trish turned her head and looked off to Gus's right. The voice had sounded like Vanessa.

"Nothing," Trish said. "He tried to read my mind, and I noticed. I copied what he did and followed it back into his own mind. I ended up wearing him out in doing it. I accidentally used his own power source.

"Are you his girlfriend?"

"Yes, I'm Vanessa," Vanessa said, coming over to stand next to Gus. He felt Vanessa put her hands to his head and take him away from Trish. "What did you do to him?"

"As I said, I wore him out. It was an accident. I'm so sorry," Trish said, sounding incredibly apologetic and sincere.

"Who are you?" Vanessa asked, tipping Gus' head into her stomach, one hand on the top of his head and the other stroking his hair.

"Oh, I'm sorry. I'm Patricia, but I go by Trish. I clean the building. We were talking about my mask and my license and… well, one thing led to another and here we are," Trish said. "The runes of my mask were reacting to him."

"Trish, can you pull it out and show it to Vanessa?" Gus asked. "Don't touch it, though, Ness."

Trish quickly opened her wallet again and pulled out her license.

It looked just like a driver's license to Gus. Holding it up, she moved it close to Vanessa.

"It's reacting the same way. But it doesn't seem to be her directly," Trish said. Moving her license close to Gus, then Vanessa, the beautiful cleaning lady looked confused. "Can you two start pulling everything out of your pockets?"

Vanessa seemed reluctant to let go of Gus, but eventually did so.

By this point, Gus felt rather normal, but he'd been enjoying the attention. It'd felt amazing to be touched by both of them. It made him feel warm all over. Like rain falling on a desert.

I crave being touched, apparently. That or just… affection.

Sitting up normally, Gus began emptying his pockets.

Trish brought her license close to each object, and then did the same with Vanessa as she dumped out her belongings.

"No… none of any of that is what it's reacting to," Trish said. "Anything else on your person that could be a source of magic, mana, or enchantments? What about your own masks?"

Gus reached into his shirt and pulled out his medallion.

Trish brought her license close to the medallion, then jerked it away.

"Yes, that's what it is," she said. "My mask is reacting to yours. And it almost seemed… violently so. It almost looked like the runes were going to explode or mutate for a moment."

Explode or mutate?

Oh… oh no.

Her mask is sabotaged. Just like Misha's, Michael's, and the pack member's.

If her mask pops, she'll go crazy.

But wait, is that what happened?

Michael or Misha's mask got too close to a PID or Fed mask?

"Didn't the Were say something about going through a checkpoint?" Vanessa asked.

Strange way to refer to her cousin, but… they did, yes. They went through a checkpoint to watch a game.

"We'll need to find out what game it was, and if there was a PID officer or a Fed at the gate," Gus said. "Then we need to run down Misha and see if she had a similar encounter."

"What about Michael?" Vanessa asked.

"PID member was on the scene and killed. Remember? That's the starting point then. Michael might have handed his license over to the officer," Gus said.

Trish was holding her license now, cupping it against her chest as if to protect it.

"Alright, so… we head over to precinct six and check on Misha," Gus said.

"Good place to start," Vanessa said.

Then they both looked at Trish, who seemed somewhat lost and confused now.

"Uhm, I'll just… go back to work now," she said.

"No. You're coming with us," Vanessa said. "You can see the runes, so you'll need to tell us if you see anything else as well. Gus and I can't see them."

Gus nodded at that. Trish would be useful.

"I'm… I'm not really suited for that kind of thing," Trish said, sounding almost panicky now. "I think I should just—"

"Trish, please. I know you work for the PID maintenance department. I'll call them, tell them we're borrowing you against your will and that we'll return you when we're done. That you're not in trouble at all," Gus said. "I could use your help. Will you help me?"

Trish was looking at Gus, her face troubled. Then she sighed, and her head dipped down fractionally.

"Ok, Gus. I'll help you," she murmured. "I'll… go change then."

"Meet us on the PID office floor. We'll wait for you there," Vanessa said.

Trish nodded and went back to the dumpsters quietly. She grabbed her trash cans and wheeled them back into the building.

"I don't… think I've ever seen a swimsuit model empty trash before," Vanessa said. "She's beautiful. If I had a pair as big as that, I don't think I'd be cleaning trash."

Gus only nodded. He didn't know what to say.

"Beautiful and seems like she's got a crush on you," Vanessa said, looking down at Gus with a small smile. "You putting out those Boogieman vibes again?"

Gus shrugged. He didn't know what to say to that, either.

"I'm a little hungry. Haven't had a fear meal from Melody in a while," Gus said. It was true. He hadn't hunted at all for a few days. The hunger he used to feel was crawling its way back to the top.

On top of that, last night they'd had pizza, beer, and snuggled on the couch. Which had quickly become getting really drunk together and sloppily making out with a lot of fondling, then passing out on the couch atop one another.

Vanessa snorted at that, her right hand coming out to lightly card through his hair.

"You can feed from me tonight then. Melody told me how she's been doing it," Vanessa said. "Looks like we need to keep you topped off or you end up pulling in little helpless maidens."

"She wasn't helpless," Gus said honestly. "She could have snapped my mind in half if she wanted to. She had me cornered."

"Oh?" Vanessa asked, still not breaking eye contact from him. Then she stepped forward and brought his head to her midsection, her fingers playing with his hair.

"Shouldn't we—"

"Hush," Vanessa said, interrupting him. She continued to toy with his hair and neck.

Gus said nothing.

Chapter 29 - Running Cold

Gus, Vanessa, and Trish all got out of the car.

"This is ok? Really?" Trish asked for perhaps the fourth time.

Looking over at the woman, Gus sighed and tilted his head partially to one side.

"Yes, Trish. It's ok. You were there when I talked to your boss. You heard me tell him I'm borrowing you to work on a case as a consultant. You heard him say it was fine. You saw me write an email to my boss about you," Gus said. "There really isn't much more to 'being ok' than that, I imagine. Or did you expect something else?"

Trish hunched her shoulders and ducked her head. Her bright green eyes dulled and she looked off to one side.

She was dressed in casual clothes, as that was what she'd worn to work today. She certainly wasn't within the normal PID dress code, but she didn't look unsuited for the work either. She was in a simple blouse and dark jeans with ankle boots, and her black patterned sweater she wore over the blouse helped give her a more business look.

She was unfortunately very eye-catching in her street clothes, and men seemed to eye her wherever she went. No one approached her, though, thankfully. Gus and Vanessa hovering around her seemed to deter people.

"I'm sorry, Gus. I'm just… nervous," Trish said, her eyes slowly moving back to him. She looked like a kicked dog. "I'm just a cleaning lady."

"Well, today you're a consultant to the PID as a Sorceress," Gus said. "So… just trust in that, alright? It's fine. And thanks for hanging on to your bad mask. I know it's a little unnerving, but we need it till we can figure it out."

"It's fine. It's the smart play. Having it replaced out of hand would just be… silly," Trish said.

Vanessa seemed uninterested in the conversation; she was reading something over on her phone.

Trish nodded her head mutely, chewing on her lower lip. Her eyes darted to Vanessa and then back to Gus. Then she gave him a small smile. "Ok, Gus."

"Great. Now, let's go in and see Misha," Gus said, then turned and headed toward the hospital entrance.

"Hard to believe they transferred her here," Vanessa said, slipping her phone back into her pocket after typing into it.

"I dunno. Seems like a logical place to put her once we figured out it was against her will," Gus said. "I'm more curious to see what condition she's in. Is she still raging? Is she awake? Is she medicated?"

"Hmph, suppose so," Vanessa said, then gave her body a small shake. "Sorry, hospitals give me the creeps. I don't like them."

Gus nodded. He could definitely understand her distaste. It was why he'd hunted at hospitals for so long. People hated and feared them.

"They're not so bad," Trish said softly behind them. "They usually have a lot of plants and trees in and around the buildings. It helps liven things up."

Not for the first time, Gus thought Trish was a little strange. But then again, so was he.

Opening the door, Gus ignored the reception nurse and walked to the elevator. He knew where they were going. Stabbing the button with a finger, Gus stuck his hands in his pockets and waited.

"Uhm… so… have you been a detective long, Miss Flores?" Trish asked.

Vanessa looked at Trish as if she didn't know how to respond, and then she let out a breath with a small smile.

"I was a regular detective for a few years. Just made it to PID," Vanessa said. Then she rolled her eyes. "And it's Vanessa, Trish."

"Vanessa, ok," Trish said, smiling. She was nodding her head rapidly now. "Do you like the PID?"

"It's pretty good so far. It's... well, honestly it's no different than being a regular detective so far. Just new tools to use to find people, and different ways the perps hide," Vanessa said.

The elevator dinged, and all three of them went in.

"Fourth floor," Gus said when Trish looked to him for direction. She'd ended up next to the buttons.

Tapping the button, Trish tucked her hands behind her back.

Before the door could close, several men in casual clothes got in the elevator. They took one look at Vanessa's flat stare, then at Trish and her slightly widened eyes, and they crowded her instead. They were practically pressed up next to her.

Gus reached out and took Trish by an arm, and he pushed her back behind him into the corner. Then he pressed himself up against the man who had gotten closest to Trish, practically pushing his crotch into the man's rear end.

When the man turned to stare at Gus, Gus gave him a teeth-baring grin.

"Hey there," Gus said. Suddenly the three men made room and moved to the front of the elevator. "What, don't wanna get so friendly cause I'm not a woman?"

Shifting his left shoulder back, Gus stuck his hand into his belt loop, making his shoulder holster and the butt of his pistol obvious.

"Uh," said the main in a smart tone. "I didn't—"

"Get off on the next floor and take the stairs," Gus said, a hint of anger coloring his voice. "Or I'm gonna get curious and make your life hell for no reason."

One of the other two men hit the button for the second floor a few times.

"Yeah, got it," said the third. When the doors opened, all three got out quickly.

"Thank you," Trish murmured from behind him. "That happens more than I'd like, but thankfully it doesn't get worse than that. The few times it has, I ended up having to use some magic."

"Scum," Vanessa muttered. "And as for you, Gustavus Hellström, you need to rein that in. They're gone. There's no reason to be in full evil-Gus mode."

Gus shook his head once, as if to shake off the situation, and pulled back on his aura. It'd slipped his hold when he'd gotten angry.

Then the door opened for the fourth floor. Walking out the doors, Gus went straight to the nurses' station, pulling out his medallion.

"Gustavus Hellström," he said, his voice sounding normal now. He could faintly hear Vanessa and Trish talking behind him. "PID. I need to see Misha Trent."

The nurse, who looked to be some type of demonic Para, gave him a once-over and then his badge, then finally looked back at her computer.

"Room forty-two," she said, not bothering with him any further.

Nodding his head, Gus left the station and headed down the hall toward the indicated room. He stopped to knock twice on the door, waited for a second, then went in.

Misha was lying in a hospital bed, clearly unconscious. There were padded straps at her wrists and ankles, and one across her middle.

Frowning, Gus walked in and stepped over to the side of the bed. Leaning in close to her, he gently shook her shoulder.

There was no response. The monitor behind her showed that her heart rate was stable and normal.

"Looks like they're keeping her medicated," Vanessa said, peering at the chart at the foot of the bed. "Can't say I blame them, given what we've seen of those affected by the Mask Madness."

Trish was directly across from Gus on the other side of the bed. She was looking at Misha's face.

"I can see... a construct around her head," Trish said, lifting a hand and pointing a delicate finger at Misha's temple. "It's encircling her brow and goes all the way around. I can't read it, but... it looks angry. It feels confused and malevolent."

"You can't read rune-script, right?" Gus asked.

"No, I'm not trained," Trish said, focusing on the runes. "But you don't have to be able to read them to get a sense of what they're doing. Magic is magic, after all."

"Does it show any signs of aging, breaking, or going away?" Gus asked.

"No. It's directly feeding off her. As long as she lives, this will remain," Trish said. "I could break it. It isn't that strong, just hard to see."

"And why can you see it?" Vanessa asked.

"Because I'm an Elven Sorceress," Trish said simply. "Should I break it?"

Trish looked to Gus for direction.

Part of him wanted to leave Misha like this because it gave them a point of reference. Another part of him was concerned that giving her permission to do something like this would violate a slew of departmental procedures.

If something went wrong, it'd be his ass on the line.

"Break it," Gus said. He needed answers. If Misha woke up and was normal, she could tell him what happened. What he really needed was her able to tell him if she'd given her mask to someone with a badge. If she had, that was all they needed.

Nodding her head, Trish touched Misha's temple with a single finger, then took a step back.

"All done," she said. "It's disintegrating rapidly. It'll be completely ruined in about five minutes, and then it will fail. No telling when she'll wake up, but I did remove some of those sedatives as well."

"Huh," Gus said aloud. He looked around for a chair to sit in, happy to wait.

The door opened, and three Elves walked in. The first two were Meadow Elves who looked very similar to Misha in appearance. The third was a Desert Elf, with dark-brown hair and light-brown eyes.

Before Gus realized what he was doing, he was halfway to drawing his weapon and killing the Desert Elf. It was through sheer force of will that he didn't, but he was losing control over his emotions.

Everything was bubbling up.

"Can I help you?" Vanessa asked, staring at the three Elves, unaware of Gus's plight.

"I'm Misha's mom, and this is her sister," said one of the Elven woman. She only looked to be in her thirties. "That's her cousin."

All three Elves were staring at Gus, though. Their eyes were wide, their faces rigid, and they looked for all the world like they were staring at a wild animal.

"It's him," hissed the sister of Misha in Elvish. "Isn't it? The Hunter! He's here for Misha."

"Hush, if it's the Hunter, he speaks Elvish," said the Desert Elf. "Doesn't he?"

"Both of you, be silent," said the mother to both of them in Elvish. None of them had looked away from Gus.

Trish and Vanessa were now looking at Gus as well.

"We're here to speak with Misha," Gus said. "We were hoping she could help us. The last time I spoke with her, she was… ah… indisposed. We believe she should be waking up shortly."

"Misha only… only screams," said her mother, a frown on her face.

"Yes, I saw it myself in person," Gus said. "We believe she'll wake up shortly, and in a normal disposition."

"He's the Hunter," whispered the Desert Elf in Elvish. "I know it. It's just like Uncle said."

"Hush, hush, he's looking at us," replied the sister.

Ok, I should probably address that now. Since we'll be sitting here for a few minutes together.

"Who's this Hunter?" Gus asked in English.

All three Elves stared at him in stunned silence again.

"The Hunter," said the mother. "He… he lurks in wait and hunts Elves who don't listen. He cuts their ears from their heads along with their scalps. He speaks Elvish, looks human, and can't be seen or heard.

"He's just a campfire story my brother told them to scare them. Ignore them, they're just silly girls."

"Your brother?" Vanessa asked.

"He was visiting us," said the daughter. "There's a war amongst the Elves and he was on furlough.

"And the Hunter is real! He's real and he's out there and he's waiting. Waiting to start collecting ears again."

"I see," Gus said, then let the subject drop.

Apparently, he'd made a name for himself amongst the Elves.

An hour later, Misha's eyes started to flutter and she made small moaning noises. The two separate groups both stopped their private conversations at the sounds coming from the Elven woman.

Then her eyes slid open, and she frowned. Looking around, she seemed lost. She blinked several times, and then her eyes slowly focused on her family. A small smile spread across her lips.

"Hello," she said in Elvish to them. "I seem to be myself today. Is this temporary or—"

Her mother was there in a flash, hugging her daughter tightly. She was sobbing, rocking Misha back and forth in her arms.

"Misha, I'm sorry to bother you," Gus said, stepping up to the side of the bed again. "I just really only want to ask you one question. Do you remember what happened to you?"

Misha looked at him, her eyes narrowing slightly.

"I remember you," Misha said in Elvish. "You broke through the haze."

"Glad you remember. Does that perhaps mean you remember what happened to you? Just before the haze, as you called it?" Gus asked.

"I was... I was driving home," Misha said, looking confused. Her mother hadn't let go of her, either, and was still latched on to her. "I can't remember anything after that. At least until you showed up and asked me to tell you my story."

"Nothing? Nothing at all?" Gus asked.

Misha shook her head. She looked tired and confused, but Gus had the feeling she was being honest.

"Great, thank you for your time," Gus said, and then he quietly left the room.

Trish caught up to him on his left, Vanessa on his right.

"She wasn't lying," Vanessa said. "I may not know Elvish, but that was just sheer honesty from her."

"I think so, too," Trish said meekly, tapping the fingers of her left hand into the palm of her right.

"Yeah, me too," Gus said, shaking his head. "I'd really hoped she could confirm it for us. Right now we've only got the theory with no evidence to back it up at all."

"We could—" Trish started, then stopped.

"Go on," Vanessa said across Gus to the Sorceress as she tapped the elevator call button.

"Uhm, what if we... what if we had someone give you their mask, see if it happens, and I just... break the enchantment," Trish said.

That's only violating like every rule out there, that's all. No big.

Mark won't care at all. He'd pay us to do it.

"My cousin. Let's go ask her pack. They'd do it to help their pack-mate, right?" Vanessa asked. "We just propose it like that to them."

Gus didn't like it. It would be numerous violations, put people at risk, and make them all liable for something they shouldn't be.

Except he didn't have any better ideas or even thoughts. It was all a guess at this point without any evidence or proof.

"Guess we're going to go see your family again," Gus said softly, and he stepped into the elevator. Both women got in, and they got behind him this time.

***

"Oh, I'm not so sure I should go in with you. I try to stay away from areas like this," Trish said, peering out the passenger window.

"What, because it's a barrio?" Vanessa asked, sounding annoyed.

"No, because it looks like a high-crime area," Trish said. "It's far more likely that something will happen around me in places like this. It has in the past."

"Well, you have two cops with you," Vanessa said, getting out of the car. "So come on. Just stay close to me or Gus."

"Ok," Trish said, getting out of the car but looking hesitant nonetheless.

Gus couldn't exactly blame her. Every time she had men around her, they seemed to gravitate toward her or try to get closer. He was constantly blocking people and they'd only been out and about for a few hours.

No sooner had they walked into the liquor store than a young man was walking straight for Trish.

Gritting his teeth, Gus looked at the man and lost control of his aura. There was a flash of promised violence after a long hunt, and the man being strung upside down and left to bleed out from a lamp post.

The man veered away wildly from the trio and hustled outside.

Fumbling with his control, Gus didn't know what to do with himself. He was tired of playing sheep dog and keeping men away from the one person who seemed able to help him solve this case.

"I'm sorry. This is why I don't go outside very much," Trish said. "I end up having to use magic when I shouldn't. It's been much worse without the minor enchantments I had."

She's right. She's the damn cause itself!

Feeling his frustration hit a boiling point, Gus flung his anger at the situation along with his aura at Trish, and he smothered her in it. Winding it about her, he practically detached it from himself and left her drowning in the center of it.

Except Vanessa and Trish didn't seem to notice it at all.

The man at the counter noticed, however. He was staring at Trish in terror rather than lust. Which was rather different.

Frowning, Gus felt instantly better. It was the first time he'd ever cut his aura away from himself, but it seemed to have taken his anger with it.

"Need to see your pack-master," Gus said, holding his medallion up to the man. "She in?"

"Y-y-yeah, she's downstairs," said the man.

"Great." Gus didn't bother to wait, just went to the back door. He started heading down to the basement where he'd met Elise before.

When he reached the bottom, he found Elise squatting down in front of the Were they'd seen previously. The bound, gagged, and tied Were was lying motionless on the ground, though its chest rose and fell steadily.

"Huh?" said the Were pack-master, frowning at the three of them. "What are you doing here?"

"Came to see if we could help your pack-mate, as well as if you could help us," Gus said.

"Has anyone in your pack gotten their mask updated in the last year?" Vanessa asked.

"I did," Elise said, looking at Vanessa. "Why?"

"Could you pull it out and show us? We think we have an idea of what happened to your pack-mate," Vanessa said, taking the lead on the conversation.

Elise nodded and walked over to a desk on one side of the room. Opening a drawer, she pulled out a pink purse, then opened it and drew out a driver's license.

Walking over to Vanessa, she held it out. "Here."

Trish stepped closer and leaned in over the license.

"It's reacting to your medallion, but… not in the same way. It seems to be responding to the presence of your mask, but not in the same way mine does," Trish said. "It's almost as if it wants to do the same thing, but… can't."

I have… no idea what that means. It's the same as hers, has a similar reaction, but not the exact same one.

Vanessa fished out her medallion and held it out near the license.

Before anyone could react, Elise tapped her license to the medallion.

And nothing happened.

Using a fingertip, Trish touched the license.

"It reacted the same as mine. It just… stopped, though. It looks like it wants to explode or mutate, but it can't," Trish said. "Something really is blocking it."

Makes no sense.

But it does confirm it's the mask, and it's for people who have had it updated recently.

"Alright. Could you please go fix that one over there, Trish?" Gus asked, indicating the unconscious Were.

"Of course, Gus," Trish said with a smile, walking over to the Were.

"You can fix him?" Elise asked, looking at Trish.

"Yes, and is there anyone else in your pack that had their mask updated in the last year?" Gus asked.

"Other than him, just me," Elise said, indicating the Were who was tied up.

"Right, ok. Thanks," Gus said, and then turned to Vanessa as Elise moved to stand next to Trish.

"So… we're more or less confirmed that it's masks, but I can't figure out why they're behaving in the way they are," Gus said.

Vanessa shook her head and shrugged her shoulders.

"No idea. Know anyone who had their mask updated recently?" Vanessa asked.

Shaking his head, Gus was about to say he didn't know anyone.

When suddenly his mom popped into his head.

His mom had gotten her license updated a few months ago. At the same time, she'd decided to get her mask reset as well.

"My mom," Gus said, frowning. "Time to go see my folks, I guess."

Chapter 30 - Apex

As he got out of the car, Gus adjusted his coat. Reaching into it, he fingered the safety to make sure it was on. It was one of the few places he always made sure it was on.

He'd tried calling his mom on the way over to give her a heads up, but she hadn't picked up.

She was a homemaker now, and his dad was the only one with a job. Which meant she was more than likely home but hadn't heard him call. Shaking the idle thoughts free from his mind, Gus turned to look at Vanessa and Trish.

They in turn stared back at him.

"Any questions?" Gus asked.

"No," Vanessa said.

Trish shook her head instead of responding. She looked like she was feeling self-conscious right now. Rubbing her hands together in front of her waist nervously.

Gus walked over to the front of his parent's house and pushed the doorbell.

Stepping into view of the camera he knew was there, Gus waited quietly. His mom would likely check the camera, then come get the door. She didn't answer the door unless she had to.

There'd been a few times Gus could remember from when he was a kid that men had become stalkers of his mom. Typically after she answered the door.

Didn't they just... vanish though?

I wonder. Maybe mom's a bit more vicious than I think.

The door opened and his mom appeared, a big smile on her face.

"Gus! Vanessa! What are you two doing here?" Jennifer asked, immediately hugging her son and then catching Vanessa up in one. "Oh, and who's this? Another girlfriend?"

Jennifer moved in on Trish before she could respond. The tiny Boogieman seemed to tower over the larger woman.

"Well, she's certainly beautiful, and... an Elf?" Jennifer asked, holding out her hand to Trish. "Call me Jen, or Jennifer."

Trish took Jennifer's hand in her own and shook it gently.

"I'm Patricia, but I go by Trish," murmured the Sorceress.

"Well, come in, come in. I wasn't expecting visitors. I'm sure I can put together a snack or a quick lunch, though," Jennifer said, putting a hand behind Trish's back and leading her in. She only stopped to catch Vanessa up in her herding, guiding them into her home.

Gus followed behind with a small grin and shut the door.

"First, she's not my girlfriend, Mom. She's just helping me with a case," Gus said.

"Oh? Pity. She's absolutely beautiful," Jennifer said, looking at Trish again. "I really thought she was. Especially since you marked her so powerfully with your aura and scent. Honestly, son, it's a bit much for someone you're just working with, isn't it?"

Trish only smiled at that, her eyes going to the ground.

"Marked her?" Gus asked.

"Mm, I suppose I never taught you about that. Then again, I never had a need to do that with your father," Jennifer said. Then she waved a hand at Trish. "You put your aura, scent, or mark all over her. It's like a black cloud surrounding her. It's very angry, very violent, and seems hell-bent on repulsing men and predators."

"You can see it?" Gus asked.

"Of course I can, son. I'd be a terrible hunter if I couldn't," Jennifer said, looking at him with a chuckle. "Next time just make it smaller. It doesn't have to be that large. It's practically a challenge due to its size."

"Alright. Got it. Thanks for the advice.

"Now, could you show me your mask? Make sure Vanessa or I don't touch it, though. We're trying to run something down and I know you had your mask updated recently," Gus said.

"Hm? Oh, sure. I'm still listed as a minor-magician though," Jennifer said, walking into the kitchen.

"Minor-magician?" Trish asked, looking at Gus.

"Can't really put down 'Boogieman' now can she?" Gus replied with a grin.

"Oh, I suppose not," Trish said, shaking her head. "I didn't even think about it. You and your family have to live in complete secrecy."

Gus shrugged. "Comes with the territory."

Jennifer came back in and held out her license to Trish.

"I assume this is why you're here, and why I'm not supposed to give it to them," Jennifer said as Trish took the license from her.

Trish only nodded and smiled.

Holding the license tightly in her hand, Trish walked over to Gus and slowly held it out towards him.

"Oh. It reacted just like mine did, but not. At least not in the same way," Trish said. Reaching to her back pocket, she pulled out her wallet. Opening it, she dug out her license. Holding one in each hand, she eased them toward Gus, then stopped.

"They're reacting differently, but the result will be the same. The runes will snap, and mutate, then the rage will happen," Trish said.

"Differently? Differently how, exactly?" Gus asked.

"The runes were written by different people," Trish said. "And they're... oh, that's what it is. They're failing. They're both failing but in different ways. The result will be the same, however."

"Failing," Vanessa said. "In other words, they're not supposed to break apart like they have been?"

"Yes," Trish said, handing Jennifer her license back. "Thank you, Jennifer."

"Of course, dear. Say... would you be interested in dating my Gus?" Jennifer asked. "I bet his Contractor would be happy to pick up a pure magic user into her group."

"What?" Trish asked.

"He has two girlfriends. Vanessa is one. Melody, a Contractor, is another. She'd probably try to recruit you based on your looks and ability," Jennifer explained.

"Mom, seriously?" Gus asked, and then he looked back to Vanessa. "Ok, so, they're not supposed to fail, but the end result that's happening is the goal. What does that mean exactly?"

"I don't know," Vanessa said. "If it's not meant to fail, but it's clearly not supposed to be there, that means it's... triggered? A timer?"

"I guess. Elise's had similar runes, but hers wasn't failing. Which means the goal is Elise's, and these two, and the other three we know of, are all errors," Gus said.

Vanessa nodded.

"It feels like a timer," Trish said, staring at her license carefully. "Like it's using some type of counting device to determine if it's ready or not. Mine is failing in that counting device. Jennifer's seems to be in the attachment."

Gus blinked, then laughed softly.

"It's because she's not human. In other words, people who lied for their mask are more likely to have a failed mask," Gus said.

"That makes sense," Vanessa said. "But we still don't know what to do with this, or if that's what actually happens."

"Can you stop it? Or make it go away?" Jennifer asked.

"What, the rage? Yeah," Gus said.

"I assume it's the lovely little Elf who does it," Jennifer said, nodding at Trish. "If so, then let's just break my mask and see what happens. Trish can fix it and you get your answer."

"Mom, I really don't like that idea," Gus said. "Not at all."

"No, I imagine not. But it's a good answer, and one you can implement right here and now," Jennifer said with a smile. "Just put me in handcuffs before you do it. I wouldn't want to hurt any of you kids if things went wrong."

Letting his chin drop to his chest, Gus thought on it. His mom was right. It was an easy way to confirm everything they suspected and get a few answers at the same time.

He just really didn't want to risk his mom—that was what it really came down to.

"Trish, how confident are you in being able to fix it?" Gus asked.

"One hundred percent. In fact, I could probably make it so it only lasts ten seconds or so. It's the same thing I put around my own head just in case my mask failed," Trish said. "It just prevents the runes from feeding on me, which is their target. The mask holder."

"Mm," Gus mumbled, looking back to his mom.

"Do it," Jennifer said with a grin and waved a hand at him. "It'll be fine. I really do have to insist on the handcuffs, though. Before I met your father, I was quite the wild-cat."

Looking at his diminutive mother, he couldn't see a "wild-cat" as she'd described. He knew she was pretty, and a hunter, but there was no anger or hostility in her.

"Gus?" Trish asked. "I'm ready… I already put the counter-measure on her brow."

"Alright, let's—"

"Handcuffs," Jennifer said, holding up her hands in front of her.

Vanessa pulled her set from behind her and quickly snapped them around Jennifer's wrists.

"Thank you, Vanessa. By the way, your hair looks lovely today," Jennifer said, smiling at her. "Would you and Melody mind going out with me sometime? It'd be nice to go shopping with a few people who know what I am and not have to worry about hiding myself."

"Uhm, sure, Jennifer. I wouldn't mind that," Vanessa said.

"Alright, here you go," Jennifer said, holding her license out to Vanessa.

Taking it, Vanessa held it in her hand.

"I'm just going to, uh… pretend I'm doing a check. Like a security run or something," Vanessa said. Peering at the license, she seemed to be checking it. Holding it at an angle, then flipping it over, she gave it a good once-over. "Looks fine to me."

Handing the license back to Jennifer, Vanessa looked to Trish.

"The runes broke the moment you touched it. They're slowly fading away from the mask right now. If I leave it alone, they'll fade in about thirty minutes all on their own," Trish said.

"Oh? Hm. Well, we could work on lunch and snacks while we wait," Jennifer said. Then she wiggled her fingers at the girls, the handcuffs jingling. "Though I'll need some help."

Twenty minutes later, everyone was standing around the breakfast table eating small baked things his mom had directed the others on how to make. Being so small, they had cooked up in no time.

"Mrs. Hell—"

"Jen or Jennifer," his mother said firmly, interrupting Trish. "Besides, I think you'll end up being one of Gus's girlfriends with how you keep looking at him. Start with Jen now, it'll be easier later."

"Jen," Trish said, looking down at the table, breaking eye contact. "How old are you, if I may ask?"

"Goodness, how old do you think I am?" Jennifer immediately asked back.

"You look like you could be my older sister," Vanessa muttered.

"Yes, you look like you're in your twenties," Trish added.

"Hmm. I'm closer to Melody's age, I think. I'm ninety-six," Jennifer said with a grin.

What?

"Don't tell your father. He thinks I'm younger than him," Jennifer said, winking at Gus. Then she frowned, tilting her head to one side. "I suddenly don't feel… well."

"The runes are about to fade," Trish said. "Maybe five minutes, maybe five seconds."

"Oh. I see," Jennifer said. Shaking her head, she looked confused, her eyes slowly clouding. "Goodness. I… I genuinely don't feel right."

One moment his mother appeared confused, and in the next, her head snapped toward him.

Her eyes were a solid black. There were no whites, no color, nothing. They were jet black. They were also angry and hungry looking. Like a drawn knife.

She faded away in the same instant, her body becoming almost insubstantial, fading into the surrounding. Her fingers shifted and changed, becoming long talons that looked like they'd gouge through anything and anyone.

A deep, dark, dangerous sense of imminent doom fell on him. The sense of being hunted pervaded the very air around him. That he was being hunted and would be brought down and eaten from.

Fear sprang out of him uncontrollably, and Gus wanted to do nothing but hit the ground and scurry away. As if death were waiting for him right there.

We've made a terrible mistake!

Then the aura faded and vanished in a blink, and Jennifer's eyes returned to normal.

Fading back into full visibility, his mom seemed unchanged, looking the same as she always did.

She looked confused, though. Her eyes were looking around to each of the three of them.

"You all reek of fear," Jennifer said. "And while I'm not adverse to a free meal, I'm concerned. I don't remember anything happening. I appear to be in the exact same spot and nothing has changed. Did I miss something?"

Looking to his left, Gus saw Vanessa and Trish as pale as bedsheets. Their faces were white, glistening with sweat, and they looked like they wanted to run.

Trish's fear tasted like blueberries.

Before he knew what he was doing, he'd fear-scented her, and then he gorged himself on Vanessa and Trish's fear.

"Now that's just bad manners," Jennifer said in a scolding tone. "I taught you better than that, Gustavus Hellström."

"You were terrifying," Trish said, her voice wooden. "You… you became this black-eyed monster and I wanted to run. I think I might need to go to the little girl's room."

Vanessa only nodded, not saying anything.

"Did I? Heavens, I'm so sorry," Jennifer said. Then she looked at Gus. "Good thing we had those handcuffs on."

She lifted her hands up and looked at them with a sigh.

"Though I fear I broke them," she said, holding them out to Gus. The middle chain was snapped, and the shackles themselves appeared bent and warped. "Sorry."

"No… no worries, Mom," Gus said. Those weren't ordinary cuffs. They were meant to hold Weres and other super-strength Paras.

Like Ogres.

"No worries, Mom," Gus said.

***

Sitting in the car, Gus wasn't sure what to say. He'd driven away from his parents' house, only to stop at the end of the block.

"Your mother was scarier than the Troll," Vanessa said. "I think you grossly understated how powerful your family is. I can see why those Elves in Misha's room were terrified of you."

That's not untrue, is it? I probably looked the same way to the Elves. And that's why everyone stayed away from me when I came back.

Except for Mark.

"Yeah, sorry. I don't really have a barometer on this one," Gus said. "I've never seen my mom like that. She's normally what you saw right there at first."

"I think what we saw wasn't really her," Trish said. "I think what we saw was her at a full head of steam, so to speak. She was angry. Beyond angry. Irrationally angry. Your mom might have been truly outside of herself when that happened."

"I'm sure she doesn't know what happened, but that was her. That was me, in a way. I'm not human. Never was, never have been," Gus said. "There's no doubt that she probably has been exactly what we saw before in her life. You heard her—she said she was a wild-cat."

Vanessa sighed, then reached over and took Gus's hand in her own.

"Well, knowing that, I'm glad your mom likes me," Vanessa said. "It'd be a lot harder going to holiday dinners with her knowing what she could do if she didn't like me."

Chuckling at that, Gus gave Vanessa's hand a squeeze.

"Thanks for that," he said. Then he turned to Trish in the backseat. "I didn't want to ask with my mother there since it was so weird, but did you find anything out?"

"Nothing beyond what we've already discussed. It's pretty much exactly what we thought," Trish said. "It failed the moment Vanessa touched the license, and the runes activated. It started a countdown, then attacked your mom.

"It triggered all of its conditions, then attempted to feed from her to refill itself so it could continue to work. When it couldn't and ran out of power, it simply went away."

"Ok," Vanessa said. "It's completely reversible, it's trackable, and we know about it."

"But we don't know how it's supposed to be used, or why some of them are failing," Gus said.

"I think some are failing just because they weren't done very well, or like I said previously, they made with an error," Trish said. "So cross that one off. It really just leaves the 'how' are they going to do what they're attempting to do."

"No idea," Gus said. "And when I hit a wall, I usually call Mark to walk him through where I'm at. Then he gives me an idea or a direction, and we move again."

"Mark?" Trish asked.

"He's our boss," Vanessa said. "He's also a vet. He served with Gus."

"Oh. Okay," Trish said. "Uhm, what should I do? I should probably go back to work."

"No, you're staying with us," Vanessa said, shaking her head firmly. "Right now, you're vital to our case, and you're the only one who can see the problem. We need you."

Trish grimaced at that, looking away and then out the window.

"I don't really want to be involved, though," she murmured.

His mom had mentioned that Trish was looking at him in an odd way. Even Vanessa had said it seemed like Trish had a crush on him.

They needed her, and right now, Gus was going to play what cards he could.

Letting go of Vanessa's hand, he reached back and took Trish's hand into his. It got her attention immediately, and her head turned toward him.

"Trish, I need you," Gus said, squeezing her hand. "Would you please help me?"

Trish gave him a broad smile and slowly nodded her head.

"Ok. I will," she said.

"Great, thanks. I'm going to call Mark now, ok?" Gus asked.

"Alright," Trish said, her fingers curling into his. Apparently she wasn't willing to let go yet.

Turning partway back into a normal sitting position, Gus got his phone out with one hand. Glancing to Vanessa, he caught her smirking at him. She didn't look jealous or angry. Though he couldn't miss the fact that she was frustrated. Or annoyed, maybe.

Tapping the button for Mark, Gus held the phone up to his ear.

It went straight to voicemail. Which made Gus very nervous.

Very, very nervous.

"Mark never turns his phone off, and he always picks up for me," Gus said, dialing seven-one-one next. "Always."

"PID non-emergency," said a woman over the line. "Agent Hellström, how can I help?"

"Can you put me through to Mark Ehrich?" Gus asked. "I can't get him on his cell."

"One moment please," said the woman, and the line was silenced. It came back only seconds later. "I'm afraid Captain Ehrich's hospital room isn't taking phone calls right now."

Hospital room?

"Which hospital?" Gus asked, his voice tight.

Chapter 31 - Wrong Tool

"And they really didn't know anything?" Vanessa asked as they trooped out of the elevator from the parking garage.

"They didn't know shit," Gus said. "They're just dispatch anyways. It was amazing they knew he was in a hospital, and which room."

Vanessa grumbled under her breath. Gus couldn't blame her for it either. His heart was hammering in his chest and his mind was racing.

For the life of him, he couldn't understand how Mark had ended up in a hospital. Let alone that his room wasn't receiving calls.

He wasn't about to call Kelly until he knew what was going on. It'd just panic her if he didn't have information and she didn't know either.

Gus blew past the nurses' station and went to the elevator doors that led up to other floors. Smashing the call button with two fingers, Gus waited angrily.

"I feel like I shouldn't be here," Trish said softly.

Glancing at her and then ignoring her, Gus looked back to the elevator. He didn't have the time, inclination, or patience to coddle her right now.

A moment later, however, he realized he needed to have the time, because he needed her.

"It'll be fine, Trish," Gus said. "Besides, no one's bothered you at all, have they?"

Trish shook her head and then frowned.

"You're right. No one's bothered me for a while now," Trish said, looking around. Men were walking wide around her, like she was sick or diseased. "I suppose I should thank you for marking me. That's what your mother said, right? You marked me?"

"Something like that," Gus said. "I honestly didn't know what I was doing. I was just mad that men kept coming up to you."

"Oh, alright. Well, thank you. Anyways. It's… nice," Trish said.

The elevator dinged and opened up. A group of people got out and then Gus, Vanessa and Trish got in. Gus thumbed the button for the third floor and then the close doors button.

The doors closed with a soft thump, and the elevator started moving.

"Do you think it's related?" Vanessa asked.

"I honestly have no idea," Gus said. He knew he probably sounded irritable and petty, but Mark was the only person he'd trusted after their time deployed. Everything right now was wrong. Bad and wrong. "It could be related. It could be that he had a heart attack. Maybe his pancreas exploded."

A cool hand slipped into his and squeezed it.

Looking at the partial reflection in the elevator, Gus saw Vanessa standing next to him, holding his hand.

"It'll be fine," Vanessa said. "He's already in the hospital. He's getting care."

Gus nodded, not really sure what to say.

"Thanks," he muttered.

Vanessa squeezed his hand again, then let it go when the elevator doors opened.

Stepping out immediately, Gus didn't bother with the nurses' station. He knew where he was going.

"Excuse me," said a nurse.

Gus just held up his PID medallion as he walked by, not stopping. Counting off room numbers as he went, Gus found Mark's.

Without knocking or waiting another second, Gus opened the door and walked right in.

Only to find Mark and Kelly.

Mark was laid up in a bed, surrounded by and drowning in machines. There was even a ventilator working to keep him breathing.

"Gus?" Kelly asked aloud as her eyes moved from her husband to Gus. She was in her mid-thirties, with brown hair and blue eyes. She was attractive, of course. Mark wouldn't have been Mark if he hadn't found and married a pretty lady.

"Hey, what happened?" Gus asked. "I went to call his cell and he didn't pick up, so I called dispatch."

"We're not sure," Kelly said. "He was at the PID building and there were gunshots, and something about a car. I didn't hear much and no one's really talking to me about it.

"But… but he's ok. He had a collapsed lung, and amazingly that was it. He was shot six times, but everything missed outside of his right lung."

Gus nodded. He wasn't a medic or a doctor, but he'd seen enough chest wounds to know that Mark was indeed ok. He was going to feel like garbage and have a chest tube for a short period, but he'd probably be able to go home in a week or two. Then he'd be off duty for a month or two.

In general, it was amazing how hard it could be to actually kill someone with a gun at times.

Sighing, Gus pressed a hand to his head, then laughed softly.

"Of course he just… waltzes away from something like this," Gus said. "Mark's Mark."

Kelly smiled sadly and looked back at her husband.

"They've got him loaded up on meds and he's just… sleeping," Kelly said. "He hasn't really been coherent since they brought him in."

"Probably for the best. Alright, I… I'm gonna go. I just needed to know if he was ok," Gus said, feeling incredibly awkward.

"I know, Gus," Kelly said. "I know he'd have rushed over to see if you were alright, just as you did. I understand. I'll let him know you came by."

There wasn't anything he could do here, and Mark was ok. Gus felt like nothing else mattered after that.

"I'll… I'll see you later, Kelly. I'll drop in again when I get the chance," Gus said.

"I know he'd like that, so please do." Kelly gave him a firm look. She knew he was prone to avoiding emotional things in his past.

"I will," Gus said, and he backed up out of the room.

Vanessa shut the door once he'd cleared it. Neither her nor Trish had joined him in the room.

"Sounds like someone tried to put a rune-car through the PID front door," Gus said, looking down and to his side. "Mark must have rushed down, caught the culprit trying to ram the building again or just trying to escape. Probably a shoot-out after that.

"And he's ok… before you ask. Looks like he'll be out of commission for two or three months… but ok. He's stable."

"Good. Now, let's see if we can't find that shooter," Vanessa said. "If we can find them, we can find another piece of the puzzle and maybe follow it back."

Nodding his head, Gus agreed. It was the best place to start right now.

"I'll check in with the nurses' station to see if anyone else was brought in. You call dispatch and ask there," Gus said, then rubbed a hand against the back of his neck. "Without the Fed, having our entire precinct scattered to the wind is making this incredibly difficult."

"Yeah, they definitely opened with a strong blow," Vanessa said, pulling her phone out and putting it to her ear.

Stuffing his hands in his pockets, Gus ambled off to the nurses' station.

"If… if we can get back to the scene where this all happened, and if magic was used, I might be able to trace it back," Trish said. "I have… I have a few other abilities I learned. I was taught how to track magic usage."

"Yeah, we have some tools that do the same thing," Gus said. "But I'm more than willing to give you a go of it. Usually the tools don't work so great because magic is more prevalent than you'd think."

Stepping up to the nurses' station, Gus threw a thumb back the way he'd come.

"Did anyone come in with Captain Ehrich? Or was there a perp checked into the hospital with him at the same time?" Gus asked a young woman at a computer.

"No, he was brought in by ambulance. Once they realized he was PID, they called it in before he got here," said the nurse, a frown on her face. "After that we haven't heard anything from anyone."

"Right, got it. Thanks," Gus said, stepping away from the station.

It was more or less what he'd expected given what Kelly had said.

With everyone's resources pissed away, there was little in the way of centralization for the PID right now.

"You might get that chance after all, Trish," Gus said. "Cause I have no friggin' clue on what to do next. Other than to call local police department and have them put guards on Mark's door. Just in case our shooter shows up and tries to finish what they started."

Sighing, Gus pulled out his phone and put it to his ear.

***

"I never park down here," Trish said as they pulled into the parking garage beneath their PID building.

"I don't either," Gus said. "But with the front of the building roped off, including the side entrance, we don't really have a choice. Even if it's easier to park outside."

"I don't park down here because it's a perfect place for something to happen," Trish said.

Oh. Huh.

Being a pretty girl sounds like it sucks.

"Wouldn't worry about it right now. The most dangerous thing in here is Gus, I'm betting," Vanessa said. "His mother is just a Boogieman. Gus is a telepathic Boogieman. I'm suddenly very grateful he plays by an internal set of rules and doesn't sit there reading my mind all day."

"I… I forgot he could do that," Trish said. Looking up into the rear-view mirror, Gus gave her a smile when he caught her watching him.

"Who says I'm not?" Gus asked, pulling into a space and throwing the car into park.

"Because of the simple fact that you've never reacted to any of my thoughts, no matter how dirty I make them. Or inviting," Vanessa said and got out of the car.

"That's… that's a good point. You don't react to anything, so… you clearly don't," Trish said, and then she got out as well.

Clicking his tongue, Gus suddenly regretted that he wasn't reading their thoughts after all. Except he couldn't. It'd be too much of an invasion of privacy.

He'd learned his lesson on reading people's minds years ago. Sometimes, you really didn't want to know what others thought about you.

People don't have perfect control over their thoughts. They change faster than the wind.

Getting out of the car, Gus flapped his coat and adjusted it.

"Guess we go check the scene and see what we find," he said. "If anything. Otherwise… I'm not really sure what else to do. We've exhausted everything I can think of."

Vanessa started walking up the exit ramp that would lead them back outside.

"I can't either," she said. "It's pretty frustrating to be damned, honest. I feel like we're little ants trying to fight off a cat. They're just so… prepared for everything, and their plan is already long since in motion. We're just barely groping at the edges of it."

"From what you've told me and what I've seen, I'd agree," Trish said, walking along next to Vanessa and Gus as they went back up to the main street behind the PID building. "You're not just playing catch-up, but you're trying to catch up when they've already lapped you once."

Gus didn't want to say anything, because it would only be negative. His partners were already far more negative than they needed to be, and him contributing to it wouldn't help at all.

"Whatever," he said. "We've already figured out how they did it and the problem with the masks. I already packed all that up and sent it to Mark's boss, as well as Captain Vard. Maybe he'll get more traction with it than we would. Beyond that, I don't even know who to contact."

"I never knew how much the Fed did," Trish said, rubbing her upper arms with her hands. She looked nervous. "It's rather frightening to know that it's all… gone."

"It's definitely disconcerting," Gus said.

"I updated Melody," Vanessa said, looking at her phone with raised eyebrows. "She apparently is getting on a plane right now. She thinks she'll be back here by tomorrow morning."

That's good news, at least.

Gus's mind froze on that thought.

He'd missed Melody. The warmth he felt the instant he knew she was coming back was a strange and funny thing to him.

Genuinely, he'd missed Melody Lark.

"I'm going to check in with Vard," Gus said, clearing his throat. "You walk Trish over to the scene to see if she scents anything.

Turning to one side as they approached the police barricade, Gus pulled out his phone. Trish and Vanessa ducked under the police tape after they were cleared, and went inside.

Looking at his phone, Gus frowned and unlocked it. Pulling up Melody's last message, he realized he hadn't responded to it.

Knowing Melody, she would always be the last message sent, and it was up to the other person to respond.

Tapping in his message slowly as he thought about what he wanted to send, Gus came to the end result after a minute.

I'm glad you're coming home.
I miss you, and I found myself thinking how great it would be to have you back.
For what it's worth, I do care for you. More than I'd like to admit.
Come back swiftly to me, Mel.

Closing his phone, Gus turned back to the crime scene.

Trish was bent low over a spot on the ground where there was an evidence marker. It looked like she'd found something, too. Her eyes were glowing now, the green of them taking over completely.

It's like they greened over or something.

Gus's phone vibrated in his pocket. As he pulled it out, he was expecting something from his mom, or Mark.

Except it was Melody.

Unlocking the screen, he tapped the message.

I'm going to buy a damn plane and leave right now. This moment. I'll learn to fly it myself on the way to get home to you as fast as I can. So I can see you.

I love you so much, Gus.

I know what a display of emotion is for you, and I know how much that little message of yours means.

When I get home, I'm going to smother you in love and affection. Then I'm going to bed you, even if Nessa isn't ready. I'm going to make your wildest fantasies come true. Perfect three-way plans be damned.

It's going to be messy, loud, and wet. And all over.

I'm going to break your bed.

BREAK YOUR BED.

Chuckling to himself, Gus took in a slow breath, then shrugged his shoulders. He'd dragged his feet long enough. Now he was just being stupid.

Ok, Mel. I agree.
Come home, and break my bed with me.
I love you.

There was a small prompt at the bottom that said, "Melody is typing," so Gus waited.

"The tracker failed. Trish got something, though, so we've got a trail. Let's go," Vanessa said, coming up behind Gus.

Tucking his phone into his pocket, Gus coughed once.

"Oh? Good job, Trish. Alright, let's go."

"Thanks. It was a trick I picked up from a friend. She… taught me a few things I never knew I could do," Trish said, her fingers interlocked together in front of her. "Didn't really ever think about using it like this. I just… throw out the trash."

Gus, Vanessa and Trish got to the ramp and started to walk down it.

"I take it we can drive and you can still follow it from the car?" Gus asked.

"Yes. I can do that," Trish said.

When they reached the bottom, Gus froze. Their car was at the back of the parking garage. They couldn't see it, though.

The entire garage was pitch black. Pitch black and seeming to be devoid of all light. A single light buzzed on, flickered several times and then stayed on. It hummed loudly, as if the bulb was about to burst.

Then it turned off again, with a click, only to flicker on and off.

"I… don't want to go in there," Trish said.

To Gus, this was a perfect set-up. It would elicit a primal fear and force someone forward anyways to get to their car. Everything seemed to be primed to create fear and discomfort in anyone.

As if a very intelligent hunter had put it together just for humans.

He could taste the warm chocolate of Vanessa and the blueberries of Trish. It had started subtly, but it was building quickly.

"Stay here, and be afraid. As much as you can," Gus said, and then he walked into the closest darkened corner. He had a strange feeling about this. A strange and truly unwelcome hunch.

Closing his eyes, Gus settled down in the shadows and steadied his breathing in a single second. There was no fear in him, because this was nothing he hadn't done to others.

He knew what this was. He'd mastered it with Elves. Warrior Elves who wanted nothing more than to crack his head open and pluck out his eyes.

This was nothing.

Gus brought his thoughts around to the here and now. To finding whoever it was hiding here in the darkness and taking them. Carving out a piece of them and eating it as a prize.

To hunt.

Opening his eyes, he couldn't see, but he didn't need to. He could taste Vanessa and Trish's fear. He could literally see how it was flooding into the garage, and where it was vanishing.

Where someone was feeding.

Gus didn't touch any of the fear, nor did he have any of his own.

"I know you're there," Gus said aloud toward the ceiling. He hoped it would help disguise his location.

The fear from Trish peaked, coming off her in a wave.

There was a new flavor in the air, though. Incredibly faint as it was, he could still taste it.

He'd fed from much less; he didn't need much.

It was sweet, and pure. As if it had been baked in an oven and made to perfection.

Like chocolate chip cookies.

"I can taste you," Gus said, getting up. He pulled off his coat and then stepped out of his shoes. It would minimize the noise he made and give him a chance to approach.

The sweet stink of cookies freshly baked grew.

There, two cars over from ours.

Gus approached directly, keeping several cars between him and his target. His plan was to approach, distract, and then relocate. Opening his mind and using his telepathy, he tried to collect anything he could.

What he got back was mildly surprising.

"Your fear is sweet," Gus whispered, two cars away from the other Boogieman. Because Gus was sure of it now. He was hunting one of his own kind. And a woman, if he didn't miss his guess. "I haven't eaten a Boogieman. Woman. I'll try your liver."

Pushing on his magic with a touch of his telepathy toward the other of his kind, Gus put out the idea of an abdomen bursting open with a wicked slash. Then of him perched over her, dying. Her stomach spread open. Her twitching and shivering on her back as Gus chewed raw liver with a smile, staring into her eyes as the light faded.

The fear from the woman spiked and become palpable.

"Shut up," she said. Her voice was confident and bold. "I'll hunt you and kill you. You don't know what you're talking about."

She sounded young to Gus. Whoever it was had probably found success against those who didn't know what she was. Against defenseless things like humans.

No one like Gus.

Slithering around a truck, Gus moved across the middle area and was now coming up behind the other Boogieman.

Now he was locked on to her. Her fear was delicious, and he could hear her mind. Her thoughts were whirling, spinning around one another. Fear, panic, and attempts to reassure herself.

Wedging his presence into her mind, Gus smashed it open. Looking for anything he could that'd tell him what he needed to know.

And he found nothing. The woman was a hitman, and little else. She was kept in a manor house and only let out to hunt. She received her orders by written letter and spoke to no one about anything.

She was a completely disconnected piece just here to kill him, Vanessa and Melody. Most surprisingly, Trish was on that list as well.

Which meant this had all came down after they'd brought Trish on board.

Her target after that was Mark.

She had no other orders, memories, or thoughts that would be worthwhile to him.

She was worthless.

Gus sprang out from behind her and wrapped one arm around her throat, his right hand slamming into her midsection.

Overwhelming fear that her stomach had been ripped open assailed Gus. The woman doubled over from the blow.

Her mind slowed down as Gus continued to apply pressure to her neck.

Then she passed out and slumped to the ground.

As soon as she did, the lights sprang on.

Looking up, Gus saw Vanessa and Trish standing at the ramp. They were staring at him.

"All done," Gus said. "It's a hitman. Hired by whoever is doing this."

Vanessa's fear was dying away rapidly. Trish's was as well, but much more slowly.

"She was watching Mark's room and tracked us back here. From what I gathered, she was dispatched a few days ago," Gus said. "Got new orders though once Trish got involved."

"Gus, could you take a moment and change back? If someone walks in here, we'll have to explain it," Vanessa said.

Change back? Oh. Yes.

I… must look like mother did.

Gus stood up, closed his eyes, and shook himself out. At the same time, he took in all the fear in the garage. Devoured it.

It filled him and gave him a mad rush of power and vitality.

And with a sigh, Gus pulled himself back. Back from himself. Opening his eyes, he turned to Vanessa with a smirk.

"Better?" he asked, not really needing to ask. Vanessa and Trish's fear had fallen to nothing almost instantly.

"Much," Trish said. "What… what should we do with her?"

"Dunno. Technically she didn't do anything wrong. Standing in the dark isn't a crime," Gus said. "If anything, the only person who committed a crime is me."

"Let's… ugh. Let's tie her up, throw her in the trunk, and take her with us. Go sit down in the car, Gus. We'll handle her," Vanessa said.

Not arguing about it, Gus went and got his coat and shoes, and he sat down in the car.
Add kidnapping to the list, I guess.
Reaching into his coat pocket, Gus pulled out his phone. There was a message from Melody.

I bought a plane! I'm coming, Gus. I'm coming right now. I'll be home as soon as I can.
You'll not regret this. We're going to be so happy. I told Nessa everything!
She said she'll help me break your bed.
My life is so perfect, so complete. I can't wait to Contract you two. I can't wait.
I LOVE YOU GUSTAVUS.

There was a second message several minutes after the first.

Who's Trish? Nessa sent me a photo.
She's beautiful! She's a Sorceress? We could use one!
I think you found our next girlfriend! Bring her home tonight. Maybe we can just drag her into a four-way and Contract before she can think of saying no.
I love you so much Gus! I'm going to make your world a paradise. Please don't be mad at me wanting to make my harem bigger. I promise to explain more later.
My women are your women though.
LOVE YOU. LOVE YOU. LOVE YOU.

The "love you" string continued till it looked like Melody had hit the character limit.
Great. Mom was right, I guess.
Sighing, Gus laid the back of his head against the head rest.

Chapter 32 - Converging Trails

Trish had her head partway out the window. Her nose was lifted and her eyes were closed. She looked like she was imitating a dog.

Shaking his head, Gus didn't know what to make of it. He'd never heard of a Para that could track a magical signature like this.

Then again, I track by fear. Is it that hard to believe?

Pulling up to a stop light, Vanessa sighed and looked over to Trish.

The busty Elf was practically standing out of the window now. She did this at every intersection they reached. Apparently it was helping her stay on the scent.

"Mel wants her," Vanessa said, looking at Gus.

"I know," Gus said, giving Vanessa a smirk. "She also said you'd be helping me break my bed."

Vanessa turned a faint red, then shrugged. "After the other night, does it even matter? I think I had both of my hands in your pants at the same time at some point."

"You did," Gus said, thinking back to the drunken make-out session. "Do you want Mel to add her?"

"I mean… I think she's gorgeous… but she might not be into women. I wouldn't be against trying," Vanessa said, then laughed softly, looking forward again. "Such a fucked-up life I have now. I'm going to tell Mel no more. I can't handle more than this."

"No more before or after that?" Gus said, hooking a thumb toward Trish.

Vanessa looked back, her eyes obviously going straight to Trish's rear end.

"After," said the detective, and she looked forward again.

Easing forward once the light turned green, Vanessa cut the conversation again. She didn't seem to enjoy talking very much if the car was moving.

Pulling out his phone, Gus looked at the last message Melody had sent him. He hadn't responded yet, and he wasn't sure what to say.

Chances were good that she was already in the air and probably wouldn't get any message he sent back to her.

Then again, she said she bought a plane. What'd she mean by that exactly… and would it have wi-fi? Most new planes have wi-fi, right?

Hm.

Gus started to type in his response to her, then stopped and started several times. He wasn't much of a texter, in all honesty.

"That's it, right there," Trish said, getting back into the car and moving up between the seats. She pointed up ahead at a building they were just starting to pass. "The brick building."

Pushing his phone into his pocket, Gus grabbed the laptop mounted to the dash and swung it over. He started to type in the address for the building just to see if he could get anything.

The building passed by them as Vanessa pulled the steering wheel to one side. She aggressively forced their way onto a side street and turned them onto a road that would lead them back toward the building.

Except she pulled into a parking space and leaned around Gus to look out his window.

"Looks like we can go in on foot from there," she said. "The question becomes: do we park here and walk over, or park out in front of the building?"

"This person shot the captain?" Trish asked.

"Yeah," Gus muttered.

"Then they wouldn't be averse to shooting us as we get out of a car," Trish said softly. "I would personally say parking here and walking would be better. But I'm not a policewoman."

"Yet," Vanessa said, staring hard at the alleyway.

"Yet?" Trish asked.

"I already put in a formal request to the captain to have you hired on. Our Contractor girlfriend, Melody, said she already did as well," Vanessa said, her brows drawing down as she thought on the plan of attack.

Seems a bit… odd. Mark already hired someone who didn't even go to the academy. Let alone do a patrol beat.

I don't think he'd be able to swing a second person like that.

Especially if they were coming in from the Facilities department.

"I really… really don't think I should… no. I'm just a cleaning lady and—"

We'll encourage it for now.

"Trish," Gus said, interrupting her. He hadn't found anything useful on the address other than that it was an apartment building. "I think you should seriously consider the offer. With your abilities, you could easily be a useful asset to us. Worst case, Mark could probably hire you part time for consultation needs. You'd still probably make more part time than you do cleaning full time."

"Oh. Oh, I see," Trish said. She sounded confused to Gus.

"I say alleyway; Trish is right. If they've already shot at a cop in broad daylight, there's no reason they wouldn't do it again," Gus said.

Vanessa shook her head slowly, then sighed. "You're right. You're both right. I guess I'm just afraid they'll have a car they can get to and we won't be able to catch up in time."

A fair worry.

"Alright, let's go," Vanessa said.

The three of them got out of the car, and Gus went around to the trunk.

"C'mere Trish," Gus said. He didn't really like this. Didn't like what he was thinking of at all. Except he'd already done enough to get himself fired, if not arrested. What was one more crime?

"Uhm, yes, Gus?" Trish asked, coming to stand at his side.

"Take your sweater off," Gus said.

"Gus, uhm, I really—"

"Take it off," Gus repeated, getting the trunk open.

Tied up, gagged, and bound tightly inside was the hitman. She squirmed around as soon as Gus opened the trunk.

"Forgot about you," Gus muttered, then shoved her to one side. Pulling open the spot where the spare would go, under a solid plastic hatch, he looked at all the gear he had stowed there.

It was unfortunate to sacrifice the spare, but carrying equipment was more necessary.

Good thing I forgot to load the rifles back in. Though that's also a bad thing. She wouldn't have fit if I did have the rifles, but now we can't use them.

I need a car specific for work, I think… with a mob-trunk.

Reaching in, he grabbed several sets of body armor. Vanessa appeared on his other side, apparently realizing what he was doing. After handing her one, Gus started pulling off his coat and holster.

Getting into the armor, Gus grabbed a tactical belt and slipped his sidearm into it.

"This feels a bit…" Vanessa said. Then she sighed.

Glancing over, he saw she'd gotten her armor on as well. She was also wearing a tactical belt with her sidearm in it.

"Overkill? Paranoid? I'm not so sure. Whoever it was, they were good enough to get several shots on Mark in the torso," Gus said. Checking on Trish, he saw she was wearing the vest, but it looked wrong on her.

"Doesn't fit very well," Trish said, pulling at the bottom.

"That's because your boobs are too big," Vanessa said. "Here, Gus, move over."

Getting out of the way, Gus wasn't sure what to do about Trish. If it didn't fit, it didn't fit.

Maybe get her to point it out and send her back to the car? That'd—

Vanessa reached into Trish's blouse and started shoving her breasts this way and that. Even going so far as to reach around Trish's back and unhook her bra.

"Ahhhh, I uhm, that…" Trish said as Vanessa literally handled her chest.

"There," Vanessa said finally. "That seems like it fits. Or at least, as best as I can get it. How's it feel?"

Trish looked down at herself.

"It's actually not bad. They're a bit squished, but nothing a good sports bra doesn't do," Trish said. She bounced up and down ever so slightly. Smiling, she seemed happy with whatever result she got.

Right. Ok… yeah.

Vanessa reached into the trunk, pulled out a tactical belt and fit it around Trish's waist. She completed it by putting a taser in the holster.

"Sorry, can't afford to give you a firearm," Vanessa said. "Even giving you a taser is going to get us fired, I'm sure."

"It will," Gus said. He put the plastic shell back in place over the spare, then shoved the hitman back into the middle of the trunk. "We ready?"

"Yeah," Vanessa said, pulling on one of Trish's straps. "We're ready."

Walking down the alleyway, Gus was on alert. He didn't think three people walking around in body armor was going to be very subtle. The alternative was infinitely worse, however.

Gus flinched when his phone suddenly started ringing. Reaching into his pocket, he checked the screen.

C&C Marketing?

Tapping the accept button, Gus pulled the phone up to his ear.

"This is Gus," he said.

"Hello, Agent," said a voice on the other end. He couldn't quite recognize it.

Falling behind Vanessa, Gus let the two women lead the way while he took the call.

"This is Leanne from C&C. I just wanted to say… thank you for the warning. You were correct," said the voice that was apparently owned by Leanne.

"Oh? Anything to share on that?" Gus asked.

"A car crashed into our building a short while ago. It was treated as a simple accident, but I had the car impounded when the driver fled," Leanne said. "It had runes all over it that did exactly what I think you were expecting them to do."

"Ah, yeah. Though I'm surprised you were targeted. Can you give me anything on that? Is this related back to Fitz?" Gus asked.

Vanessa and Trish walked up a flight of stairs that led them into the apartment building. Trish immediately pointed to the stairwell off to one side.

"I don't believe Michael is, but C&C is related I suppose," Leanne said. "The simplest answer I can give you is that C&C is interested deeply in the Para world. We want the two worlds to come together. But very slowly. So slowly that almost neither side notices."

"And Michael?" Gus pressed.

"Michael was working on something else for us, unrelated to the Para world. He was something of a… well, I suppose you could call him an armchair scientist," Leanne said. "His mind was a marvel, doubly so when you consider he was a full-blooded Troll."

"Got it," Gus said. "Alright. Thank you for your time, Leanne. I'll have someone come by and pick up that car later, if you don't mind. It'd be nice to have a finished car with working runes to study."

"Of course, not a problem. Thank you again for your assistance, Agent," Leanne said, then disconnected the line.

Slipping his phone back into his pocket, Gus looked around. They were still moving up the stairs.

"Was Leanne from C&C," Gus said aloud, mostly for Vanessa. "Someone drove a car into their building. It was covered in runes."

Vanessa let out a short, quick huff. "Suppose we have all the confirmation we'd ever need then. I take it they support a separation of the worlds?"

"Gradual blending," Gus said. "Might as well be the same thing as separation though."

"This is it," Trish said, breaking the two out of their conversation. She pointed to the door that led back into the apartment building. "It leads through that way."

Vanessa immediately stepped in front of Trish and walked over to the door, which had a push-bar opening mechanism. Pulling her weapon from the holster, she looked at Gus.

Gus moved up to the other side of the doorway and unholstered his own weapon. Vanessa gave the push-bar a shove and Gus went in quickly as the door swung inward.

He was in a hallway with apartment doors on either side.

There was no one here.

"Clear," Vanessa said from behind him.

"Clear here as well," Gus said. He really didn't like what they were doing right now. But with how deep they were, without Mark being able to assist, and the fact that a shooter had appeared when they'd radioed in for help, Gus wasn't going to hand this one off. Nor was he going to radio any of it in until he was done.

"Trish, come take a look," Vanessa said.

Walking in quietly with her shoulders hunched, Trish watched the ground. Her head turned to the left and followed something only she could see or sense.

Walking forward, Gus and Vanessa flanked her as she continued down the hall.

"This one," Trish said, indicating a door ahead of them.

"Alright," Gus said, taking a shaky breath. "Trish, you stay here. That taser of yours is a last resort. Your first resort is running away or hiding, ok?"

"I can fight," Trish said, holding her right hand up. A ball of fire appeared there and started to slowly rotate in her palm. "I just don't use the weapons you do."

He'd honestly forgotten that she was more than a tracker. It was hard to see her as anything other than a liability with how she carried herself.

"Second resort is spell-work; first resort is running or hiding," Gus said. He really didn't want her involved.

Looking at the door, he thought hard on how to do this.

"We're already in for a penny on this," Vanessa muttered. "Do we just... break in?"

"Kinda thinking that, yeah," Gus said. "Only takes me a few minutes per lock. Cheap apartment like this probably won't be longer than a minute or two each. Remember, our goal is to overwhelm and capture them. Quiet and alive, if possible. The last thing I want to do is explain why we broke into someone's place.

"It'll be easier if we can... well... just tie 'em up and dump them into the trunk next to the hitman."

Vanessa nodded at his words, her forearms flexing. Then she looked at him with a smirk.

"Cheap, huh?" Vanessa asked, her tone amused and soft.

"No offense, Ness, but you were living in a shit hole," Gus whispered, slipping his weapon into its holster. Getting down on one knee next to the handle, he reached into his pocket.

"Are you proposing?" Trish asked, looking extremely confused when Gus glanced her way. The Elven woman seemed to be looking everywhere but him. "This really isn't the time or place, is it?"

Looking up at Vanessa, Gus sighed and shook his head. Then he pulled out his lock pick wallet and tensioner, and he set to work.

"Oh. Oh! He's... yes, ok. Yes. Sorry," Trish said.

Gus ignored her, focusing on the pins as he pushed the pick into each one. With a click, he felt the cylinder come free.

Ever so gently, he pulled the tension wrench around, and the lock opened. Pulling the wrench out, he set it to the deadbolt and started again.

A minute later and he'd set all the pins. Holding the tension wrench, Gus put his pick back into the leather pouch it had come from and then switched the wrench to his left hand. Pulling his gun out with his right hand, he started to ease the wrench around, unbolting the deadbolt.

With a soft clunk, the lock fully retracted.

Wincing, Gus stuffed the tension wrench into the pouch and left it there on the ground. He grabbed the door handle and turned to Vanessa. She looked ready. Then she gestured to herself and held up one finger.

She wants point? I don't… Fine, whatever.

Shoving the door open, Vanessa rushed in with her gun drawn. They didn't shout PID, or that they were here. There was no warrant and they didn't know who it was, only that they'd been involved in a shooting with Mark.

Nothing about this would stand up in a court.

Unless it's criminal charges brought up against us, I suppose.

They moved through the kitchen and into a living room.

A woman was standing there, looking extremely surprised at having two people in her apartment.

"Ma'am—" Gus started, lifting his gun towards her. At the same time, he reached out with his telepathy to get her thoughts.

She drew faster than he expected and had fired twice before he got his gun up fully and pulled the trigger.

The booms of gunfire made his ears ring in the tiny apartment. And the solid punch to his guts told him he'd been hit.

Shifting to the right behind the kitchen counter, Gus continued to fire at the woman.

Vanessa was moving to the left behind a wall, firing her own weapon.

Blood splattered out behind the woman and painted the wall liberally in red.

Gasping, one of her hands came up to her chest. At the same time, contracts blossomed to life all over her face.

She had just as many as Melody did, which meant she was a Rainbow Contractor. They were incredibly rare, so Melody should have been the only one Gus would encounter in his entire life.

Her wounds closed up instantly, her gun still firing on Gus.

Dropping low, Gus hit the magazine release on his weapon and pulled a fresh load from his belt.

"Can't hide from me, Agent," said the woman. At the same time, a wave of icicles crashed through the cabinets in front of Gus and pelted him. Several struck his leg, and one bounced off his armor.

Shit. Shit, shit, shit!

Vanessa was already firing again, leaning out past the corner of the wall.

A block of ice came hurtling from inside the room and smashed through the wall behind Vanessa.

They were seriously outgunned fighting a Contractor that could just heal herself.

Trish stepped into the entry to the living room, her right hand held out. A cone of fire left her palm and spewed out towards where Gus had last seen the woman.

Unable to see what was going on, Gus could only guess at what was happening. The shriek of pain was unmistakable though.

Trish stood there with a blank face, flame pouring out of her hand like a hose held open.

What the actual fuck.

Gus was starting to feel seriously underpowered in the Para world. He could easily see how Boogiemen could be hunted down and crushed. It wasn't as if he had super regenerative abilities or inhuman endurance.

He was a hunter. A hunter with specific tools.

Apparently a Sorceress is the cavalry regiment of the Para world.

Trish finally let off the attack, the fire simply cutting off. Her eyes were completely greened over, her face a mask of nothing. She looked like a living doll with glowing eyes.

Gus heard whimpers and moans coming from the other side of the room.

Blinking a few times, Trish looked around and sat down on the ground right where she was. She seemed entirely focused on her shoes, brushing dirt off them.

Shit, she's in shock. Right here and now.

Standing up as quick as he could, and having to lean up against the counter in front of him, Gus leveled his weapon.

The Contractor was down on the ground in the corner. At least he thought it was her. She looked like a lump of cooked beef. There was little that would distinguish her as a living woman anymore.

Fucking hell.

Shuddering twice, the woman coughed, then fell still and silent.

Yanking his phone from his pocket, Gus started to call in the incident immediately. He needed to make sure locals didn't show up, and if anyone did, it was PID.

Need to think up a cover story as well. Shit. That got out of hand a bit quicker than I thought it would.

Vanessa was already moving forward to clear the rest of the apartment. With any luck, they'd find something that could help them figure out what was going on.

Gus felt like he was only a few pieces away from knowing if he was too late or right on time.

He wasn't trusting to luck, though. There was no doubt in his mind—he wasn't just too late, he wouldn't even be in time to clean up the mess.

Gus started to shiver uncontrollably, even as he heard the line ring out.

Closing his eyes, he fought through the shivers and quakes. It'd been a long time since he'd been shot at in close quarters.

The sniper fire really didn't register in his head in the same way.

Not in the same way staring down a barrel does.

And actually getting hit.

Opening an eye, Gus looked down to his midsection. There were several frayed spots on his vest that looked like they'd taken hits.

Why… why am I calling again? I need to check for wounds. And check Vanessa for them and… what…?

"Agent Hellström? Hello?" asked a voice on his phone.

Confused, Gus cleared his throat. Then he remembered where he was all over again.

Get it together, Gus! Get it together.

Clearing his mind, Gus got back on task. Looking down at his hands, he realized he had his radio in one hand and his phone in the other.

Fuck.

Sighing, Gus realized he was having a disconnect from his thoughts. He needed downtime to process everything.

Chapter 33 - The Quiet Thought

By the time the PID agents showed up to take care of the scene, Gus had worked out their story with both Trish and Vanessa.

Unfortunately, Trish seemed to be only marginally more responsive than she'd been originally. To Gus she seemed to have all the hallmarks of a Combat Stress Reaction, and she had literally CSRed right then and there.

Then again, he'd had his own minor break with reality. It'd been a while since he'd been in a close quarters firefight where he actually felt like he was on the weaker side.

Gus ran a hand along his stomach. The Contractor had hit him four times center mass. His chest and stomach felt like he'd been in a slugging match with a dumpster.

Even Vanessa had been hit once by the Contractor.

The whole thing brought up a slew of memories he didn't want to deal with right now.

There was one thing he couldn't doubt, though. Without Trish stepping in, Gus wasn't sure he and Vanessa would have made it out.

"I can't even begin to express how glad I am to be home," Vanessa said, the garage door opening in front of them.

After being debriefed by an interim captain while Mark was out, they'd been given paid time off for a week. Time off that wasn't going to be revoked. And if they came to the office…

They'd be fired.

"Oh," Trish said from the backseat. "You have a lovely home."

The Elven cleaning lady had come with them. She didn't feel safe going back to her own apartment. Not since the hitman in the trunk had been instructed to kill her as well.

"Thanks," Gus said. Then he glanced over to Vanessa as she pulled them into the garage. "We've been thinking about buying a new house together. Getting a good fresh start."

Vanessa smirked at that, and then sighed.

"We'll probably start looking in six months," she said. "We're waiting on me. I have some student debt that'll make it harder for me to pitch in my share."

"I never went to school," Trish said. She'd been recovering herself on the way out of the city. She seemed almost back to normal now.

Whatever normal for her is. She can be a little strange.

Then again, after Melody, can anything be strange in comparison?

Vanessa killed the engine and everyone got out, the garage door closing behind them.

Gus walked over to the trunk and popped it open.

Laying inside was the Boogieman he'd caught.

She was young. Probably in her late teens. Her eyes were brown, hard, red rimmed, and they looked scared. Her light-brown hair had tumbled around her head. Clearly the drive hadn't been easy on her.

Gus had the impression she'd been sheltered her whole life and hadn't expected to run into someone like him.

"So what do we do with her?" Gus asked.

"You said she didn't know anything," Vanessa said.

"Nothing useful to us, at least. She's just a weapon with little in the way of anything. I'm not even sure she has a personality, or hobbies, or anything like that," Gus said. "I think she literally lived just to kill people."

"But nothing we can prove," Vanessa said.

"Nope. Unfortunately, we've got nothing. She was just standing in the dark. She had no weapons on her and had made no aggressive move toward us," Gus said. "Realistically, she could have killed me, claimed self-defense after the fact, and gotten cleared with the way I went after her."

Vanessa blew out a short breath.

All the while the Boogieman was staring up at them. Her eyes moved back and forth as they discussed her.

"We could leave it to Mel," Vanessa said.

"We both know what she'll do," Gus immediately replied.

"I mean, what alternatives do we have? If we let her go, it's a crime on us, and she can just… come back again later," Vanessa said.

"I mean, that's really it. Let Mel take care of it or let her go," Gus said.

"She's kind of pretty," Vanessa said, turning her head sideways to look at the hitman.

"What? How is that even relative?" Gus asked. Then he had a scary thought and grabbed the trunk lid. "We'll talk about her later."

Slamming it shut, Gus promised himself he would dispose of her. If he let Mel do it, he might end up with her trying to force another girlfriend on him.

I'll just… knock her out, cut her head off, remove the limbs, make sure to remove fingertips and her lower jaw. Spread it out through the city, the freeway, and a park or two.

Won't even be an issue.

Trish was just standing there next to him. Watching him.

"What do I do?" Trish asked. She looked confused and lost.

"You? You are going to sit down, take your shoes off, and relax," Gus said. Grabbing the woman by the shoulders, he began leading her out of the garage and into his house. "Beyond that, we're going to raid Melody's closet to see if anything in there fits you. I know for a fact she has an overwhelming amount of clothes, and she probably wouldn't even notice if we borrowed some for you."

"Oh. That sounds… good," Trish said. "But… I meant, what do I do about my life? I have to go to work tomorrow. They're going to be waiting for me. To kill me."

Gus frowned at that, and he thought on how to solve it.

It was true. Trish needed to go back to her job tomorrow, and it would be rather likely that she'd remain a target. There was no reason to not go after her.

The simple reality was Gus and Vanessa were targets as well. There was no telling when or if the organization they were going up against would send another hitman. Or just wait to hear back from the one they'd already sent.

Gus pushed Trish down into the couch, then went back to the entryway to hang up his coat and holster.

"Honestly, Trish, I don't know how to answer that," Gus said. "The only answer that comes to me immediately is go on medical leave, call out sick, or vacation. You're welcome to stay here until this blows over."

"The house is rather large," Vanessa said. "There's four bedrooms, but only two have master bathrooms. I tend to use Gus's because… well… trying to take a shower in Melody's is a risk."

Looking up at the ceiling, Gus was momentarily surprised. He'd forgotten about the fourth bedroom because he'd turned it into a storage closet.

It wouldn't be hard to get everything out, though. He wasn't sure if he had an extra bed for it in his basement. He might.

"I couldn't. That'd just be imposing, wouldn't it?" Trish asked.

"Stay here, Trish," Gus said. "We'll clean out the bedroom tomorrow and make it yours. Tonight you can sleep in Melody's bed, mine, or on the couch. And if you choose my bed, I'll sleep in Melody's or on the couch."

Gus nodded, feeling better about the direction. It kept Trish safe.

To be honest, he felt responsible for her. He was the one who'd dragged her into this and put her life in danger.

Looking at the Elven cleaning lady, he saw the hair pin he'd bought her holding her hair back.

Smiling to himself, Gus couldn't deny he was also acutely aware of the fact that he wasn't exactly upset at the idea that Melody wanted to bring her into the relationship. He'd had a soft spot for her for a while.

Vanessa had flopped down onto the couch next to Trish. Her slacks were long gone, as was her coat and blouse. She'd somehow changed into a t-shirt and sweatpants.

Trish was still in her street clothes and looked fairly comfortable already.

Holding up the TV remote, Vanessa powered it on.

"Gus, can you beer me? Please?" Vanessa asked, looking over the top of the couch and giving him a sweet smile.

"Yeah, yeah," Gus said, shaking his head with a grin.

"Can… can you… beer me as well? Please, Gus?" Trish asked, turning her head slightly to look back at him.

"Looks like we're going to have to buy beer more often," Gus said. He'd never really been a drinker, so when Vanessa had started buying it in cases, he'd been surprised.

Going to the fridge, Gus kicked off his shoes and dumped them near the entryway to the garage. He grabbed two beers and a bottle opener, then walked them back to the two women.

Stopping behind the couch, Gus stared at the TV.

On it was a news broadcast talking about a football game.

"…tomorrow! It looks like it's going to be an exciting match for everyone," said the announcer.

Gus handed a bottle to Trish, then popped the top off it. He repeated the gesture for Vanessa.

"…sold out. We're looking at about a hundred and four thousand fans," said the newscaster.

"And that doesn't even include those watching the big game at home! Last year's viewership was about a hundred million. This year looks to be bigger than that, and possibly even breaking records," said a second news anchor. "Definitely something to tune in and watch."

"Security is going to be a damn nightmare for this one," Vanessa said, slouching low over the side of the couch. Apparently she'd ditched her bra as well, or so Gus discovered by the bare shoulder sticking out of her shirt. "Their fans are almost as combative as the players."

"That's because a lot of the fans are Weres. They tend to—" Gus froze in mid-sentence, staring at the screen.

Shit.

"What if… what if a whole bunch of people went to the game and their masks broke after the game started?" Gus said. "What if… a whole bunch of Weres went wild in crowds packed with Norms? What if the Feds weren't able to cut the feed to live television and everything was being broadcast to the world at the same time? On top of that, people live streaming from their phones."

Gus couldn't look away from the screen. They were running comparative numbers on previous years.

"A hundred million people, watching a hundred thousand people have a bunch of Paras go insane on everyone nearby in a stadium with nowhere to go." Gus ran a hand over his face. "And then random madness breakouts wherever someone else is getting their mask checked."

In a normal situation, he had no doubt the Fed was watching for things like this. Watching, waiting, and had a hand ready to pull the plug at any given time.

Except the Fed was gone.

"Oh my god," Vanessa said softly.

"That'd be… very bad," Trish murmured. "And it would do exactly what you said. It'd force… the Para world into the light. There'd be no turning around from there. No going backward."

Gus closed his eyes and scrubbed his hands back and forth over his face.

It all made sense to him. This whole thing was being conducted in a terroristic type of fashion so far. There was no reason to not suspect them of attacking civilians.

"Even the attack on C&C would fit," Vanessa said. "If C&C was taken down, there'd be one less spokesperson throwing money around trying to make it go away."

"Security checks are usually just pat-downs and a license check against a ticket, right?" Trish asked. "No one would be bringing in a weapon. They'd be the weapon. There was a timer on the runes in the end. Your mother's mask was faulty. It's likely the timer could have been an hour or two after being checked, or down to thirty minutes. There's no telling. It could be right in the middle of the game."

Gus went back to the kitchen counter and immediately called Mark's hospital room.

"Hello?" asked a voice on the other end when it picked up.

"Hey, this is Gus. Mark awake?"

"Oh! Hi Uncle Gus," Mark's daughter Megan said. "No, he's still asleep. They said they're trying to keep him under for a bit longer since he's on a ventilator."

"Got it. If he wakes up and can talk, tell him I called?" Gus asked.

"Sure thing, Uncle Gus. Will you come by later?" Megan asked.

"Maybe. If I can clear my case load, I will. Alright, see ya later Megan," Gus said and hung up the phone. Dialing the interim captain in Mark's place, Gus felt sick.

He had a bad feeling about this one.

Shaking his head, he waited as the line rang.

***

Growling in frustration, Gus smashed the hang-up button on his phone. Then he hung his head, sinking lower in his chair.

"No luck?" Trish asked, hovering over him. She'd been behind him in the kitchen while he was on the line.

"I can't get a hold of anyone in the Fed. No one. Doesn't matter who I talk to, how many times I read off my badge number or explain what's happening, no one seems to be able to help. Or they transfer me into a voicemail," Gus said with a dark laugh.

"Do you think your temporary captain might have had any luck?" Trish asked, laying a hand on his shoulder.

"Probably not. He's my rank and probably doesn't have any connections that I don't," Gus said. "In fact, I might have more than him. He's just the senior detective."

Shaking his head, Gus felt like he'd just been running into a wall for the last hour and a half. He'd even contacted Captain Vard, hoping maybe he'd have a contact or resource Gus didn't.

Every email he sent to the Fed about the situation seemed to vanish into the ether with no response.

Vanessa came back in the room, shaking her head and looking annoyed.

"I keep getting the run around," she said. "No one can tell me a damn thing. Nothing about who's doing security, who's in charge of the Para side of it, who I can contact, or even any direction on what to do.

"It's like we're operating completely in the dark and no one can get anything moving in the right direction."

"It's because we are," Gus said, putting his phone on the counter next to him. Sitting upright on the barstool, he sighed. "They did everything they could to knock the Fed out. To put them in a position where there was little they could do to stop them.

"And let's be honest, the PID isn't equipped in any way to step in and take their place. Nor is it able to reach into the government or the public in the same way."

Trish had continued to gently stroke Gus's back as he spoke.

"Could we go there?" she asked.

"Go where?" Vanessa asked.

"Go to where the game is being held. Could we go there, tell the security team what's happening, and get them to stop it? Or at least not do license checks? It's the license check that will break all the masks," Trish said. Smiling, she looked back and forth between the two detectives. "We could even involve the local PID departments, couldn't we?"

"I mean," Gus said, thinking the whole thing out. No matter who he called, hounded, or badgered, he hadn't been able to get a single person on the line who could help him. If he was there in person, with a badge and the local PID department, then there wasn't much he couldn't do.

"I'll look at flights, see if we can't get anything out of here tonight. Game starts early after all," Vanessa said, heading back out of the room quickly. She tended to have her laptop out at all times, and she used it far more frequently than Gus or Melody did.

Trish smiled and nodded, then patted Gus on the back.

"Good job, Gus," she said. "You're a good detective."

Looking at the cleaning Elf turned consultant detective Sorceress, Gus wasn't sure how to respond to that.

That and the fact that she'd put on one of Melody's blouses and it was very clear it didn't fit her. Particularly around the chest.

"I'll just stay here and take care of things and—"

"No," Gus said, shaking his head. "Come with us. I'd like you there. I know that was your first time in a real fight, but you did really well. I know it wasn't easy… and that you probably haven't really… processed… what happened, but would you come with me?"

Gus had no doubt she would eventually come to the realization that she'd killed someone. For some people, it was the beginning of a road that led to a slew of problems. Especially for someone untrained and un-indoctrinated.

Trish's mouth tightened, her smile becoming rigid. Then she sighed and closed her eyes, and her head dipped.

"You keep pushing me, Gus. You keep pulling me along and using me," Trish murmured. "I'm not… stupid. I know you're preying on me. Preying on my… apparently obvious feelings."

The guilt Gus felt immediately after her words hit him was intense.

"You're right. I am. And I'm not going to apologize for it, because I need you. I feel guilty for doing this to you, but it doesn't change the fact that I need you," he said. "Though… if we're being completely honest with one another, this might be your last chance to get out.

"If you're here by the time Melody gets back… it's distinctly possible you might not escape this. She seems determined to get you into a relationship with us."

"Us?" Trish asked, lifting her head and looking at him. "You mean… you, Vanessa and Melody."

"Mmhmm," Gus said. Then he pulled out his cell phone, unlocked it, flipped it to his conversation with Melody, and handed it to her. She could see firsthand what Melody was saying.

"Oh," Trish murmured, her eyes widening. "I see. She seems… very… interesting."

"She's a Contractor, so… that's just how it goes," Gus said, taking the phone back when she handed it to him. "So… come with me, Trish. I need you. But be forewarned that Melody is going to try and get you into our bed."

Trish shook her head with a small grin, her eyes darting up to his.

"I didn't think I'd end up in a grove, sharing a husband, but I suppose I will in the end after all. Just not in the way my sister expected," Trish said with a sigh. Her eyes were slowly greening over, glowing from within and becoming a solid color. "Since you're being honest, I'll be honest with you as well. I'm not just an Elf. I'm also a Dryad. An Elven Dryad Sorceress."

Gus opened his mouth, and then closed it. He'd heard tales of Dryads, but they were incredibly rare. Said to really only exist in the rural areas back in the old countries of Europe.

"Another term we Dryads are given is Nymphs," Trish said, reaching up to undo a button on her blouse. "And honestly… it's very difficult to control my nature at times around you. It isn't me who should be worried about getting in your bed; it's Melody and Vanessa. Because once I get in with you, I won't get out. It'll become my bed."

Trish was staring him down now. In a predatory way that made every alarm bell in Gus's head ring. He'd seen this look on her face before as well.

Back when this had all started in the garden. She'd looked at him in a very similar way.

It wasn't me stalking her at all, was it? She was stalking me.

A massive wave of magic washed over him, and he had an extreme sexual urge to throw Trish to the ground and take her then and there.

As sudden as the magic had hit him, it cut off almost as quickly.

"Sorry, Gus," Trish said, her eyes glowing brighter than ever. "I lost control for a moment. It won't happen again. At least for a while. We are what we are after all, and I can only fight my nature so much."

Not stalked—hunted.

Chapter 34 - Walls and Politics

Gus, Trish, and Vanessa napped.

They napped while waiting for the taxi. Napped in the taxi to the airport. Napped at the airport waiting for the plane. And napped on the plane itself.

Getting off the plane, the three of them trooped out into Larimer International Airport.

Looking around, Gus found a number of different signs. Finally, he saw one overhead that directed him to baggage claim.

"How much time do we have?" Trish asked.

"Something like four or five hours to kickoff—need to see if we changed time zones," Vanessa said. "Supposedly it's only about fifty minutes to downtown from here."

Moving with the flow of people toward the bag claim, Gus felt like his thoughts were foggy. He'd gone on little to no sleep often. The hardest part was waking up. Once his brain fully turned on, he'd be fine.

"I feel like that was a short flight," Vanessa grumbled. "Like I didn't sleep for two hours on it, even though I know I did."

"I'm not used to not sleeping," Trish mumbled. "I really want to go to bed."

"Can't," Vanessa said.

"I know. Doesn't mean I don't want to," Trish said.

Gus said nothing. He was entirely focused on what they needed to do. No one had responded to his calls, texts, or emails. It was like no one wanted to look into what he was claiming.

Walking down the escalator quickly, Gus hurried along to the next, and then to the train that took them from one terminal to another.

Arriving at the claim, he found that the baggage hadn't been unloaded yet.

Normally he'd never check anything, but when traveling with firearms and ammunition, you had to do what was required. Even if you were a PID agent.

"Apparently hirable ground transportation is right outside those doors," Vanessa said.

"That's nice," Trish said. "I was afraid we'd have to go wandering around looking for it."

"Apparently not," Vanessa said. "Sad that we missed Mel by an hour, though. Would have been nice to travel with her."

Gus grimaced, then nodded. It would indeed be nice to have Melody on board. She was skilled, intelligent, and well suited for this type of thing.

"She texted me a bit ago. She'll land here an hour from now, give or take," Vanessa said. "She probably could have beat us here except that she couldn't get her flight plan approved quickly enough."

"Is she a pilot?" Trish asked.

"No, she apparently hired one with the plane. I'm starting to wonder how much money she actually has," Vanessa said. She sounded suspicious to Gus.

Gus wasn't actually surprised. The Para world had plenty of opportunities to make a lot of money. Especially for talented people like Melody.

Even Gus had a considerable salary paid to him by the PID, simply because as a detective he had a near-perfect solve rate. Most of that was due to his telepathy rather than any type of detective skills, though.

On top of that, he'd received a hefty bonus from the Fed for his deployment, and his medical discharge had given him a nearly full salary retirement.

"Ness, how much do you owe on your student debt again?" Gus asked.

Vanessa sighed loudly.

"I think it's around eighty thousand right now," she said. "The interest killed me for the first several years. I couldn't make the payments very well and no one was hiring. Everyone wanted experience, my degree was worthless. Those that were hiring were offering unpaid internships with only a hint that it might become a job.

"Which is illegal, by the way."

That's not so bad. I could pay that off for her, or even just a massive portion of it, and not be at a loss. Maybe it's time to actually start spending some of that blood money.

Gus had a large and growing pile of money in the bank that he didn't touch. In his mind, it was blood money. Money given to him for the deaths of everyone he'd known and cared for when he was deployed.

Paying some of that towards Vanessa's debt seemed like a good use of it. He'd already sent huge checks to the families of everyone who had fallen while they were out there.

The pile still grew.

"There we are," Gus said as the machine buzzed to life and began spitting out luggage. "After this, we go to the closest PID precinct."

"Right," Vanessa said. "I'll pull that up."

"Ooooh. I'm getting nervous now," Trish said. "This is rather terrifying."

***

Vanessa pulled the rental car into a parking space in front of the PID building.

Peering up at it, Gus wasn't sure what to make of it. It looked significantly older than his own building. In fact, now that he was really judging it, it didn't just look old, but run-down.

"I suddenly feel like our chief takes much better care of us than I thought," Vanessa said, looking up at the building as well.

Getting out of the car, Gus sighed and gave his coat a pull. They'd driven straight here from the airport.

Trish was dressed in business-casual clothes much more similar to Vanessa and Melody now. They'd raided both Vanessa's and Melody's wardrobes to get her outfitted.

Slacks, a black coat, and a white blouse. It definitely made her look far more professional, though it did make it harder to not look at her.

Walking around to the front of the building, they got through security quickly with their PID badges. Trish's being a consultant visitor badge.

It was amazing how quickly they'd ended up in front of the chief of the precinct's office door.

Except that was where they now waited. Where they'd been waiting.

Looking up at the clock on the wall, Gus grimaced. They only had three hours till the game started. Most people would be heading into the stadium thirty minutes to an hour beforehand. They'd already been waiting here for thirty minutes.

Time was running out.

Getting up out of his seat, Gus contemplated what he wanted to do. Looking to the closed office door, his thoughts started to run around the idea of just opening it and marching in.

He couldn't deny that chiefs were usually busy. Their calendars booked out weeks in advance. The idea of just marching up to one and getting a meeting was fairly fanciful.

But Gus didn't have a choice. There just wasn't any time.

Knocking on the door twice, Gus waited. Vanessa and Trish were both staring at him as if he'd grown a second head and was babbling the end of the world at them. Shrugging his shoulders at them, he didn't really want to respond.

"What?" came a voice from inside.

Gus opened the door and stepped inside, not answering the chief.

Sitting in front of a desk was a man in his fifties with brown hair, blue eyes, and fair skin. He looked bored and annoyed at the same time.

"What the hell do you think—"

"Stop. Listen to me, Chief," Gus said, interrupting the man. "This is about the Fed bombings."

That got his attention. The older man looked angry, but he was at least willing to listen now.

Moving up to the desk, Gus stood there.

"The bombings are part of a centralized effort to force the Para world and the Normal world together," Gus said. "The—"

"Oh, it's you. I read your email," said the man, leaning back in his chair. "You're that PID agent from Saint Tony or whatever."

"Saint Anthony," Gus said, suddenly feeling extremely angry. If the man already read the email and dismissed it, this might be a waste of time Gus couldn't afford.

"Yes. So the three of you are from there, you believe there's going to be a bombing of the game today, and you want us to cancel it," said the chief, looking completely uninterested now.

"No, that's not it at all. Did you read the email?" Gus asked. Glancing over his shoulder, he saw Vanessa and Trish had joined him.

The man waved a dismissive hand at him and turned back to his computer.

"Read it, forwarded it to the Fed, and moved on. Not our jurisdiction and it doesn't matter anyways. Even if it was, there's no way they'd get through security with a bomb. It's going to be so tight it isn't even a concern," said the Chief.

"That's actually the problem! You didn't even read the email! Every mask that's been worked on for at least the last year is going to fail and make people crazy," Gus said. "They're going to go into blood rages the likes of which people have never seen. And it's going to be on live television."

"Uh huh," said the chief, typing away at his keyboard. "When are the aliens coming for you? What you're describing isn't possible. Masks are extremely complicated works of rune-magic. It's just not possible."

"It's not impossible; it's very doable. It's how they bombed the Fed buildings. I know that report got sent up! Did you not even read it?" Gus asked, getting angrier by the second.

"The Fed hasn't said a damn thing about what caused the bombings, so now I'm starting to wonder if maybe you're not with the PID at all," the chief said, looking at Gus squarely now. "I lost a lot of friends. So don't you go telling me lies about what caused it. Was probably damn Weres. It's always Weres. Should exterminate them all."

Holy shit. Ok. This… this isn't going to go anywhere at all, is it?

Keeping his tongue firmly at the roof of his mouth, Gus smiled, nodded his head at the chief, and turned around.

"Hey, where are you going? I didn't tell you you could leave," said the chief.

"You're not my superior, sir. I'm sorry for wasting your time," Gus said.

Because it wasted mine as well.

"Hold it right there. I can't just let you go running your mouth with your crazy ideas," the chief said. "You can stop right there, or I can have you arrested and then let you go tomorrow."

Gus stopped in his tracks, realizing just how badly this was all starting to turn out.

"I've got the mayor, two senators, and seven representatives all breathing down my neck to make sure this year's bowl goes off without a hitch," the chief said. The sound of his chair squeaking heralded that he'd stood up.

"That doesn't even include the Para communities. Do you have any idea the amount of money this stuff brings in for today? The amount of coverage and awareness?" the chief continued. "No. I can't have you running around making more out of this nonsense than there is. You're staying here till the game's over."

Frowning, Gus looked to Vanessa and Trish. They both seemed apprehensive. Nervous. Angry.

The chief hadn't actually wanted to hear anything Gus had had to say. He simply didn't want anything to get in the way of the big game and what it'd do for his state. It didn't matter how much evidence Gus gave this man—he'd never be convinced.

That much was certain.

And now he was going to try and keep Gus here. All to try and keep him from causing problems.

Without turning around, Gus pulled on his telepathic gift and slipped it into the Chief's mind.

It was a nasty political thing. One made of betrayal, money, and deals made behind closed doors.

A vast majority of it was all for the betterment of the people, the Para community, and his department, but there was always a good bit of it that was pure selfishness.

The chief seemed to be a blend of good and evil, much like everyone else in the world.

Gathering himself for something he hadn't done since he'd come back to the states, Gus cut the Chief's mind free from its body.

It'd reattach itself in a day or two.

With a crash followed by a thud, it sounded like the chief had fallen to the ground.

Looking through the man's mind and burrowing into his memories, Gus searched for anything and everything relating to himself.

Then he burned it all from the chief's mind, as if it had never existed. Even his knowledge of the email Gus had sent him.

There were still things Gus couldn't get rid of, like the email itself or anyone who had heard about it from the chief directly, but he could at least scour the man's mind of anything.

Marching out of the office, Gus pulled his power back from the other man's mind. He didn't dare leave anything in there, just in case they called on a psyker to come take a look at him.

"Help!" Gus called out to the desks. "The chief got up, seized, and fell over!"

Everyone got up from their desks and began rushing over to the office. In no time at all, medics were on the scene.

Gus, Vanessa, and Trish all repeated the same story to everyone who asked.

They'd come to talk about the Fed bombings, the chief had gotten upset, said he'd lost people, stood up, then fell over.

Then they left the PID building and were on the road. Heading for the event itself.

"How much time do we have now?" Gus asked.

"Two hours," Vanessa said angrily. "He didn't even want to hear it. He didn't want anything to do with it. He just wanted us to leave, till he thought we might make trouble for him."

"Yeah. Definitely politics oriented," Gus said.

"Why'd he fall over?" Trish asked. "Did you do something to him, Gus?"

"Yeah. I cut his consciousness free from his brain. In a few days he'll wake up just fine," Gus said. "I did take a moment to burn any memory of us from his mind, though. With any luck, he'll just take it as some kind of fit and move on."

"Ah. That's smart," Trish murmured. Then she reached up from the back seat and patted his shoulder gently. "Thank you, Gus. I appreciate you doing such things."

"Uh huh," Gus said, not really sure how to respond to that. Trish had gotten rather touchy feely with him since she had admitted she wasn't just an Elf.

"I suppose we just… go to see the organizer now and see what we can work out with them," Vanessa said. "We just have to make them listen and then change security or cancel the event."

"Yes," Trish said. "If we can just get them to not check licenses, it'll be fine. The runes don't self-destruct unless touched by someone with a medallion.

"Though… do you really think PID will be there to run security? I thought they normally hired people for things like that."

"It'll be PID, or a PID resource," Gus said. "It looks like it's a normal hire from the outside, but they're there to make sure certain types don't make it into events. There are some species out there of Para that just… aren't able to function on a human societal level. Which means they can't participate."

"There are?" Vanessa asked.

"Yes. Boogiemen are feared for the fact that we blend in with human society so well. That we eat humans—feed on their fear, sometimes a soul—only makes it that much worse," Gus said. "But I'd say a Lich, a true and real Lich, is probably much worse. They don't blend in very well. They don't get along with any other species. Their only goal in life is to feast on the living and make them part of their undead ranks."

"Oh, I never… really thought about it," Vanessa said.

"It's not so different from human society," Gus said. Vanessa turned them onto the freeway heading downtown. "There are those who fit in quite well, even though they could be serial killers. And then there are those who can't and are obviously deranged. They go on killing sprees and shoot people for no reason."

Gus's phone started to ring. Pulling it out, he looked at the front of it.

It was Melody.

Accepting the call, he put it to his ear.

"Hey Mel," Gus said.

"Gus! I love you!" Melody practically shouted. It was so loud Gus had to pull the phone away from his ear for a moment.

"Yeah, hey Mel. I uh… you too," Gus said, his face screwing up in a frown.

"No! Say it. Say it right. I deserve it," Melody said.

Rolling his eyes, feeling embarrassed and a little annoyed, Gus put a hand to his brow.

"I… love you too, Mel," Gus said finally.

Melody squealed into the phone, and then it sounded like feet stamping.

She's spinning in place, isn't she?

"We just landed. I'm going to have my pilot park it in a hangar till tomorrow. Sounds like maybe we'll be making some last-minute plans to flee the country," Melody said.

"I hope not," Gus said. "We're on our way to the event itself to see if we can talk to the organizer."

"Alright. I'll get a car and then head that way as quickly as I can," Melody said. "By the time I get clearance to disembark, the whole thing may have already started. Maybe I'll be the getaway car."

"Again, I hope not. But… I'm glad you're here, Mel. I did miss you," Gus said, feeling less embarrassed for saying that.

"Awww, thanks Gus. I missed you, too. I had to go, though. I needed to square all my contracts away and get them renewed for five years. Especially once I get you two contracted to me and you take colors," Melody said. "You're going to be Indigo. Vanessa is going to be Red."

"Oh? What does Indigo stand for? I never asked you directly. I know what I think it does, but… I actually don't know," Gus said.

"Mmm, you wanna know my secrets, huh?" Melody purred in the phone.

Chuckling, Gus sighed.

"Yes, I do Mel. If I'm going to be doing this, I do want to know all your secrets," Gus said.

"Okay! I'll tell you everything. Just make sure you make me spill them for you in a fun way. Ropes are okay, but you need to get nice ones. I have soft skin. As for Indigo… well, you could say it's sex, love, fidelity, and sharing of one's self."

"I see," Gus said. "That makes sense. And Red?"

"Violence, lust, power. I think having those two filled would be good for us. Or maybe Yellow. Yellow is emotions and empathy."

"Uh, I think you'll want to save Red for your third," Gus said, thinking on Trish's description of herself. "Use Yellow as the second."

"You're being vague. I take it both my old girlfriend and new girlfriend are in the car?" Melody asked.

"Yeah, why?" Gus asked.

"I wanna talk to Trish, my new girlfriend who doesn't know it yet. Can you pass the phone to her?" Melody asked.

"Yeah, no worries," Gus said.

"Thank you, Gus! I love you! I'm going to suc—"

Gus pulled the phone away from his ear and handed it to Trish.

"Good luck," he said with a smile.

Trish took the phone and pressed it to her ear, then turned a deep, dark red as she listened. After an entire minute, she cleared her throat.

"Uhm, Gus already gave me the phone," Trish said.

Snickering to himself, Gus looked back to the road ahead.

It was a moment of levity he needed.

Desperately.

Because if he messed up in the next hour, there was a good chance most of the country was going to implode.

Chapter 35 - Working in a Vacuum

Walking at almost a jog, Gus moved fast through the parking lot toward the stadium. He angled himself for the long line of people waiting to get into the stadium and headed for the front.

Moving past several people near the front, Gus walked straight up into the security aisle. It had six people standing in it, with one man out front.

"Whoa, hold up there, we're not letting anyone in just—"

Gus pulled out his medallion and held it up to the man who was talking, who also was the one out front. To anyone without a mask, the PID badge would look like a local policeman's badge.

Having a PID mask did have a few benefits.

"I'm Officer Gustavus Hellström. I need you to tell me where whoever is running the gates and security is," Gus said, staring into the other man's eyes.

"I-I what?"

"Tell me—where the person—who's running security—is," Gus said, breaking the request apart. "Now."

"Security office, home-team side," said the man, pointing backward behind him. "Mr. Grenth."

"Great. May I go by myself, or do you need someone to escort me? Because I need to go see Mr. Grenth immediately without delay," Gus said.

The man glanced at Gus's badge, then at the two women behind him.

"They're officers as well; you're welcome to look at their badges, but make it quick. This is deathly important," Gus said, doing his best to be patient.

The man stepped to one side of the security lane.

"Go ahead then," said the man.

"Thank you," Gus said, and then set off at a jog again. Their time was running perilously short.

Darting through the open double doors, Gus paused and looked for signs. He had no idea which side was the home team's.

Vanessa ran ahead down a tunnel, Trish coming to a stop next to him. She was panting softly.

"I hate running," she said. "I'm not built for it, and I don't have a sports bra on."

Glancing over at the Elven Dryad, Gus raised a brow. She was fanning herself, her cheeks red.

"What? I'm just a cleaning lady," she said. "It's not exactly a daily workout."

Uh huh. I can think of hundreds of women who would murder you for your body, given the opportunity.

Vanessa came back, pointed to the left and kept running.

"Home-team lockers are that way," she said, not stopping.

Gus gave Trish a grin and chased after Vanessa.

"Oooh, I hate this. My boobs and back are going to hurt so bad," Trish complained.

Vanessa held up a hand and pointed to a sign as she ran past it. It simply read "Security" and had an arrow.

Great! We're on the right path.

Jogging along through the open tunnels, it felt strange. There were employees here and there working at getting things ready, but otherwise it was fairly quiet.

Vanessa peeled off to one side, skidding partially, and then darted into a doorway. Gus prepared himself a bit better and slowed down, taking the same turn she had. He barely caught a glimpse of a sign that read "Security" as he ran through.

"...you Mr. Grenth!?" Vanessa asked, breathing a bit harder than normal. She was standing in front of a man sitting at a desk with a laptop open on it. There was a radio, cell phone, and a tablet on the table.

"Yes, yes I am. And who are you?" asked the man. He looked to be in his mid-fifties with graying hair and brown eyes, with a trim build and looking fit for a man his age.

There was also the telltale glow around him of a mask.

"I'm Vanessa Flores, PID," she said, pulling out her medallion and holding it out. "With me are Agent Gustavus Hellström and Patricia Ash, consultant. We've been working the Fed bombing case. Are you aware of it?"

"Yeah," Mr. Grenth said, looking from Vanessa to Gus, then to Trish, and finally back to Vanessa. "Why?"

"Because that wasn't their end goal. Their end goal was to make the Para world and the Norm world be aware of each other," Vanessa said. "And the first step was removing the Fed. The next step was making it so one world couldn't ignore the other."

Mr. Grenth shook his head.

"That's just stupid. Every time the Para world gets close to the Norms, we get massacred," he said.

"Well, that's what they're doing. And they're going to do it today. At this stadium. During the game," Vanessa said.

"I'd love to see them try. We have a good amount of PID security forces here today. Normally it'd be the Fed, but... well... as you know, they can't help," Mr. Grenth said.

"That's the problem. They aren't smuggling in weapons—they *are* the weapons," Gus said. "There's a... uh... a back-door rune-script, I guess you could call it, on anyone who's had their mask updated in the last year. At least the last year, maybe longer. If they turn their license over to anyone with a PID badge, it'll make them go crazy."

"It takes about an hour, give or take," Trish said. "They lose complete control over themselves."

Mr. Grenth looked suspicious, but also unnerved.

"And you know this? You know this is what they're doing?" Mr. Grenth asked.

Gus blinked, then looked to Vanessa.

They didn't actually know. There was no guarantee that this was actually what the enemy had planned this whole time.

This was all based on a guess Gus had made.

There was the distinct possibility they had it all wrong.

"No," Vanessa said, looking back at Mr. Grenth. "But we have no reason to not believe it to be true, and every reason to believe it."

Sighing, Mr. Grenth pressed a hand over his mouth.

What if we're wrong? What if this is all wrong? What if I've misjudged this entirely and there's nothing wrong here? Did I just... did I just ruin my career?

The self-doubt and crushing worry was pressing in on Gus. It was ruining him with every second that went by.

"Okay," Mr. Grenth said, letting his hand fall from his mouth. "You said it's all in the licenses. Okay, we can work with that.

"What if we only have the security personnel scan tickets and ask for names. They never touch licenses. Would that work?"

"Yes," Vanessa said immediately. "It would work, and it'd do exactly what we need."

"Alright. I can do that. It isn't much of a security change, and honestly... if the only thing I have to worry about is someone scamming someone else of a ticket, I'll call it a good day," Mr. Grenth said with a shake of his head.

Picking up his radio, he looked lost in thought as if considering how to relay the message.

Then he pressed the transmit button.

"This is Office," Mr. Grenth said. "Change in security. Do not ask for licenses. The machine reader isn't working, and any attempt to use it will make it harder for the technician to fix it. Do not use the license readers. Just ask for names, check them against the ticket, and do the normal security routine otherwise.

"Gates please check in and confirm."

Mr. Grenth let go of the radio and then looked at his laptop.

Over sixty people checked in after that, all reporting that they understood orders.

Nodding, Mr. Grenth smiled at them and set the radio down on the table.

"And there we go," he said, then blew out a breath. "Without much time to spare, too. We were going to start letting people in in about ten minutes. Takes a while to get that many people into a stadium and seated."

Leaning back in his chair, Mr. Grenth sighed and put his hands on his head.

"I'd hate to be in the stadium if something like you described actually happened. We have a very active Were population here. They tend to turn out in huge numbers for stuff like this. We once figured that half the audience at one point was Weres. Weres all cheering for the same team, despite being different species."

Huh. Universal enemy and all that, I guess.

Blowing out a breath, Trish laughed softly, clapping her hands together.

"I can't believe we did it!" she said excitedly.

Grimacing, Gus wanted to tell her to knock it off and not jinx it. You never celebrated a victory in a fight until your enemy was dead at your feet. Not unless you wanted lady luck to come butt-fuck you into the next life.

Mr. Grenth was staring at Trish, clearly not knowing what to say or do about her statement.

Vanessa's phone started to ring, and she pulled it from her coat pocket.

"It's Mel, I'll be right back," she said and then turned away, walking to a corner and answering the phone.

"So, you said it's the rune-script in the license itself?" Mr. Grenth asked.

"Hm? Oh, yes!" Trish said, smiling. "The whole thing is set up to begin to deteriorate once a mask is touched by someone holding a PID medallion. After that, the runes begin to fail. It seems to take somewhere between thirty minutes to two hours, but I'm not certain.

"Once it fails, the individual gets hit with the spell laid in the mask, and they go crazy."

"That's… rather intricate, isn't it?" Mr. Grenth said, suddenly looking concerned. "That sounds like a lot of planning went into it. A whole lot of planning. Especially if they subverted a few Enchanters at every DME, then bombed every Fed building they could.

Gus looked away from Vanessa and back to Mr. Grenth.

"Do be sure to keep that to yourself, Mr. Grenth," Gus said. "It's likely an organization is working in the background. They've been rather meticu—"

"All gates, this is Office," said a woman over the radio. "The technician has repaired the reader machines. It was a problem with the software, go figure."

Mr. Grenth snatched up his radio.

"Who is this? Who are you? Do not use the machines, I repeat, the reader mach—"

"Let's go ahead and get this show on the road, people. We're going to be behind if we're not careful, so let's use those license readers first and foremost. Do a quick compare, then get them moving," said the same voice.

"Who is this!?" Mr. Grenth practically shouted. "No one do anything. Don't do anything! Don't use the readers!"

"Great, let's do it to it, people. Chop-chop," said the woman.

"I repeat, don't use the readers," Mr. Grenth said into his radio. There was no response. "They cut me out somehow… how?"

Turning to Gus, Mr. Grenth looked dumbstruck.

Truth be told, Gus felt a bit shocked as well. Turning on his heel, he sprinted out of the office. Looking for the nearest exit, he started running down the tunnel.

And was practically ran over by a mob of humanity all rushing through the tunnel to get to their seats.

Struggling against the press of bodies, Gus was driven backward. Literally forced against his will to be backed up.

Cursing under his breath, Gus sprinted back to the security office. Vanessa and Trish were there, looking around.

"I can't even get out, for fucks sake," Gus said, throwing an arm back the way he'd come. "Like fucking swimming upstream. There's over sixty gates, and they're just machine-gunning people through."

"We can't just let them keep scanning people though, can we?" Trish said. "We have to do something for them."

"I'm... I don't know anymore," Gus said, shaking his head. They'd gotten all the confirmation they needed when that woman had gotten on the line and changed the orders.

They'd planned ahead and expected someone to try and stop them. They'd been ready to simply force the issue.

"What do we do?" Gus asked, losing his confidence entirely. The simple fact that people were having their masks breaking even now meant that the whole thing was already a failure.

"Where I come from is fairly brutal," Trish said. "If stopping the event isn't possible anymore, can we... can we prevent people from finding out about it? Could we kill all the attendees?"

Gus blinked at that, turning to Trish. It was a fairly extreme question. To slaughter over a hundred thousand men, women, and possibly children.

The Elven Dryad shrugged her shoulders.

"If your goal is to protect the world, would they not be expendable? Am I reading the situation wrong?" she asked.

Ok, need to really talk to her later about her background. Wherever the fuck she came from sounds like a hellscape country.

Gus pressed his hands to his head, still at a loss.

"Just looking at the crowd going by, I see a lot of masks. With broken runes around their heads," Trish said. "I can't even fix them, either. The runes are different from the ones I fixed for myself and your mother. I'd have to study one for a while, but... I don't think I could fix many of them before I'd run out of power."

"What if we shut down the ability for them to broadcast the game?" Vanessa asked. "Let's... let's assume we can't stop this. It's already happening. Happened."

"The broadcast room is on this side of the stadium, but on the top floor. I saw it on the security map when I was looking around. We could use the security elevator and get there quick," Vanessa said. "They had one just for them in the back that I saw."

"I mean, I don't have a better plan. That'll take care of exposure over TV," Gus said. Turning on his heel, he headed back to the security room.

"The question remains, what do we do about everyone in the stadium and their cell phones? Because we all know this is going to get recorded," Vanessa said.

Gus had an inkling of an idea, but it would probably get a lot of people killed. A lot of people killed, and he wasn't sure how to make it happen.

Sighing as he came to a decision, he pulled out his phone and called Melody.

It only rang once and was picked up. Looming over Trish, Gus followed her as she followed Vanessa to the elevator.

"Hey honey, I'm on my way to you guys right now. Ness told me the good news," Melody said.

"Situation's changed," Gus said. "We failed, and got confirmation at the same time. We're heading to the broadcast room to shut it down. That'll at least prevent everyone at home from watching it."

Melody didn't say anything. It was obvious she was driving, and completely at a loss for how to respond.

"Yeah, I know, same feeling here," Gus said, interpreting her silence. "But I need a favor, and I want to run something by you."

"Anything for you, honey," Melody immediately said.

"I'm thinking... I'm thinking this might be a good time to call in the Para National Guard," Gus said. "But I don't have the connections to make that happen, or even warn them. Know any way to get them heading this way?"

"Oh! That's easy. I'll just call in a threat to someone. I'll tell them there's a bomb and an elite terrorist Para unit right in the middle of the field," Melody said, as if it were nothing at all. "You knocking out the broadcast will make it beyond credible, too."

"Alright, thanks Mel. Don't do anything that would get you caught or in trouble, though," Gus said.

Melody laughed on the other end of the line as they rode the security elevator upward.

"I know. You're making a good woman out of me. I'll be good—bye dear!" Melody said, then hung up.

"A lot of people are going to die, aren't they?" Trish said, sounding disturbed.

"Yeah," Gus said. "Probably. I just… can't think of another way of doing this. With any luck, the guard can get in there and lock it all down before the insanity starts. Then you can tell their magicians and wizards and what-the-fuck-magical-ever how to fix it."

Vanessa pulled her pistol from her holster, then pulled the slide back to check the chamber.

Oh. Shit.

"If we're going up there thinking they're not waiting, that's stupid," Vanessa said.

Gus pulled his pistol out and thumbed the safety off, then pulled his slide back. There was nothing there.

Racking it, he sighed.

"Is fire ok to use?" Trish asked, holding up her hands. Small pinpricks of flame appeared in her palms and began to slowly build.

"Fire might be the best thing, actually," Gus muttered. "Melt people and equipment alike."

The elevator dinged and slid open. The three of them stepped out and looked around.

"It's right around the corner," Vanessa said, and she walked that way. "We just get in, shut down the cameras, and that's one of the problems done and gone."

Turning the corner, Vanessa stopped dead in her tracks. Then she lifted her weapon and began firing, diving back towards Gus and Trish.

Automatic fire was returned, a hail of bullets coming back to where she'd been.

"They're guarding the damn door," Vanessa said, pressing her back up to the wall.

"How far?" Trish asked.

"Thirty feet…?" Vanessa said, guessing.

Trish put a hand on Vanessa's shoulder and eased her back from the corner's edge. Pushing her further down. Trish walked up to the corner, took a quick peek, and then stuck only her arm around the edge.

Bright orange and white light lit up the corridor around them as Trish literally became a human flamethrower.

Screams and shouts came from down the hall, along with random gunfire. Seconds passed as Trish continued to dish out fire.

She squeaked suddenly, her face pinching up. She stopped after another ten seconds and pulled her arm back around the corner.

The tip of her ring finger was missing, blood pouring out of it.

"Lost control of the spell," she muttered.

Not wasting what Trish had gotten them, Gus let out a quick breath, raised his weapon, and went around the corner.

Six flaming lumps of flesh were on the ground, two of them writhing around. Walking past them, Gus gave each one of them a once-over. They were going to be dead shortly. Their faces were beyond incinerated and looked like wax skulls.

Moving to the door, Gus opened it and looked inside.

There was a mass of men and women with assault rifles all pointed at the door. No sooner had he gotten his head back around cover than the doorway was lit up with automatic fire.

Kicking the door shut, Gus shook his head and moved away from it quickly. There was nothing he could do here.

He'd only gotten a glance, but they'd looked like Weres. Weres, Trolls, and Ogres. His fear magic wasn't going to do shit to them with how amped up they were and how strong they felt. There had to be something he could build off of.

Falling back to Vanessa and Trish, he found Vanessa giving Trish's finger the once-over.

"Sorry, Trish, hate to disagree, but that's not going to grow back," Vanessa muttered.

"Sure, it will," Trish said with a severe frown. "It's just not going to feel the same for a year or two. Oooh, I hope the nail grows back quickly. It'd be awful if I couldn't paint it."

I don't even…

"There's an entire squad holed up in the broadcast booth with automatic weapons. Unless you can play flamethrower again, we're not getting in," Gus said.

"I might be able to," Trish said. "But… I don't think I'll be able to hold it for long. I kind of lost my focus when they shot my finger, and I ended the spell badly. It chewed up my power pool."

"And I really don't want her sticking her hand out there and doing this again. She's lucky it was just her finger and it didn't just go right up her arm," Vanessa said. "We're not equipped to fight them."

"Any spells you can use to get them without exposing yourself?" Gus asked Trish. "Weres, Trolls, and Ogres."

"I need to see them for something good," she said with a frown. "My cone spells work without sight, but only like a water hose, and I'm really not sure I have the power for it."

Honestly, Gus couldn't fault Vanessa for her reticence at having Trish use the same spell.

She was right.

Having Trish stick her arm around the corner wouldn't be a bright idea with that many people slinging automatic weapons.

"I'd kill for a damn 'nade right about now," Gus muttered.

"Ok, so… we can't really get into the broadcast booth," Vanessa said. "Not without Trish risking herself, and she might not be able to do it anyways."

Gus pressed a hand to his temple and thought.

"What about… what about the actual server room? There has to be a server room where everything is going to be sent out to the Internet or server or whatever they're doing, right?" Gus asked.

Vanessa nodded.

"I imagine so," she said. "Think maybe they're not guarding that in the same way?"

"Can't be any worse than that," Gus said, jerking his head to the corridor. "Can it?"

"Not really," Trish said, grimacing as Vanessa inspected her wound.

"We'll need to get it covered in gauze and sterilized when we can. Not much we can do otherwise," Vanessa said.

"Right. Ok, we're on a clock here. We need to knock out their ability to send this out into the world. Where would a server room be?" Gus asked.

"Grenth would know. Let's double back, get a medical kit, and go from there," Vanessa said.

Gus nodded his head. He didn't have a better idea.

Chapter 36 - Results

Walking back into the security room, they found Mr. Grenth messing with his radio and laptop with equal frustration.

"I can't get anyone to respond," he said, looking up to them. "They're not responding to their cell phones, the radio, or emails."

"It gets worse. The broadcast room is full of people with automatic weapons who want very much to keep this on the air," Gus said. "So it looks like we're going to have to approach this from another angle. It's probably not your area of expertise, but… the broadcast goes out through the Internet, right?"

"Yeah," Mr. Grenth said. "We handed that whole thing off to the Telecom team, though. We pay our provider for a hosted solution and they handle all the IT for it as well."

"Ok… so… it goes to a server room? IT room? Somewhere that has something I can go break so it can't transmit?" Gus asked.

"Oh! Oh, yeah, got it. That's actually just a floor up from here. It's a server room. They put it there because it would be cheaper for the cooling required," Mr. Grenth said.

Seems like a bit much for just a stadium, doesn't it? Or are they putting out that much bandwidth with their broadcasts? Suppose it's possible.

"I'll keep trying here to raise the gates," Mr. Grenth said, picking up his radio again.

Turning to Trish, Gus gave her a pat on the shoulder.

"You stay here. If we need you, we'll come back. For now, recharge your batteries and see if you can get your finger to stop bleeding," Gus said.

Trish sighed and nodded.

"That's fine. I can concentrate easier on my Dryad magic if I'm not moving. Should be able to get it to stop bleeding fairly quickly," Trish said, and then she sat down heavily. "I can suddenly see why my sister never wanted to go anywhere with her husband. We're just not made for this. Everything hurts and I just want to lie down and go to bed."

Smirking, Gus dropped his hand on top of her head and messed up her hair deliberately.

If only her worries were my worries.

I'm expecting the damn country to tear itself apart today and she's fussing over being tired.

Moving for the security elevator, Gus waited for Vanessa to join him before he tapped the two button.

Trish was fixing her hair with one hand while staring at him with lightly glowing green eyes.

Hungry eyes.

Then the elevator doors shut.

"She looks at you in a really weird way," Vanessa muttered. "And her morals and mentality are so… different. She makes Melody look well-adjusted at times."

"Yeah… she's clearly not from here. Though I wonder where she is from," Gus said.

The elevator dinged and the doors opened.

Gus pulled his pistol from its holster. Bracing himself, he eased his head out for a quick glance one way and didn't see anything. Then he looked the other way and saw nothing as well.

"It's to the left," Vanessa said from inside the elevator car. "At least according to that map in the security room. I checked it again."

Looking back that way, Gus exited the elevator with his pistol raised and his finger in the trigger loop. He wasn't about to risk anything at this point. With that many people running around with assault rifles, he needed to be able to shoot before they could. Any delay would get him killed.

Walking slowly and softly down the hall, Gus listened for any sound at all that might clue him in to someone being here.

Except all he could hear was the crowd getting settled in for the game. The announcer was doing some type of giveaway, contest, or just getting the crowd ramped up. The ground felt like it was vibrating to a degree.

"I've always wanted to be around for a bowl, just not like this," Vanessa whispered.

Gus didn't respond. He'd only been watching football recently because Vanessa liked to hang out on the couch on game days. She'd drink, eat, and cuddle with him or Melody and just watch.

Neither he nor Melody had any interest in the game, but they'd ended up deciding on taking turns just to keep her company.

"There it is," Vanessa said.

Blinking, Gus focused his thoughts and looked at the sign on the wall. It read simply as "Datacenter," and that was it.

Chewing at his lip, Gus reached for the doorknob and slowly turned it. Noiselessly, it opened up and swung inward.

The hum and churn of computers, fans, and a blast of cold air all rushed out from the inside.

Taking a slow breath, Gus waited. The door was wide open now. He could peek in or rush in.

Pulling his phone out of his pocket, he unlocked it. He turned on the camera and eased the top of the device around the corner.

Looking into the screen, he saw only server racks and some computers. Slowly, he panned his phone around through the doorway.

Nothing.

As far as he could see, there was nothing there.

Which didn't mean there wasn't anything there, just that he couldn't see it.

After turning off the camera and locking his phone, Gus put it back in his pocket. Taking a moment, he focused on the task at hand. He'd gone too far outside of his job duties. Far outside of his responsibility. And he had already committed a number of crimes.

In all of this, he had no doubt he was doing the right thing.

Turning his head, he looked to Vanessa.

Her eyes were on the door, but they flicked to his gaze.

He held up three fingers for her, then pointed to himself and the door.

Vanessa stared at him for a second, then nodded her head.

Looking back to the door, Gus held up his left hand with three fingers up. He counted down to one, put both hands on his weapon, and moved into the server room.

Scanning the room, he quickly found there were plenty of places someone could hide. Like between the server racks.

The floor looked strange to him, and even the ceiling seemed to be open for wiring. Everything looked sensitive and expensive. He now regretted the idea of shutting this down, since there didn't seem to be anything obvious.

Grimacing, Gus looked around, trying to figure out how he could shut the whole thing down without destroying it.

Off to one side, he saw a backup power generator. It was a black tower-like thing sitting off to one side.

He'd only noticed it because there was a small LED screen on the front that read "Backup Ready" on it.

Ah. Where there's a backup, one can usually find the primary. Follow that line and pull the whole thing. Maybe? If it even is a backup generator.

What if it's just a stupid computer?

Keeping his gun up, Gus moved forward toward what he believed was the backup. His steps were slow, measured, and he made sure to check every in-between space as he went. The last thing Gus wanted to do was be surprised.

Finally, Gus reached the end of the aisle and inspected the supposed backup generator.

Surprised and delighted, Gus found that it really was what he'd suspected. A backup power source that would give the servers enough power to hobble along for a few minutes. Long enough for emergency power, or for someone to fix the problem.

Reaching down, Gus pushed the very obvious power button on the top of it.

The LED screen read "Shutting Down" and then several seconds later, the power winked out.

Nodding his head, Gus looked behind the tower and started following the cables. They ran up along the wall, across into the other aisle, and into a metal panel.

Shit. This might work.

Lifting his hand, Gus began to follow the cables again, making sure he was keeping to it.

Then something slammed into his back and knocked him to the floor. A second after that, he felt something blast into his stomach and send him crashing into a wall.

Immediately, Gus felt like his entire stomach had been set on fire and he'd pissed himself.

Looking down, Gus saw a several long slashes in his stomach. None of his guts were spilling out.

That's good.

But there was a lot of blood fountaining out.

That's bad.

Looking up, Gus tried to lift his pistol and only managed to make his arms shake.

A Were was bearing down on him.

Two rounds punched through the big monster, sending it to the ground right there. An explosion of blood and gore came out from the other side of it.

"Don't move! If you move at all, I'll fire again," Vanessa called. "Gus, you alright?"

"No," Gus said weakly. Looking down at his stomach, he watched as more and more blood washed out of him. "I think I'm bleeding to death."

"Nessa," said the Were, lifting its head up. "It's Wendy."

The fuck?

Gus managed to get his left hand up onto his stomach, and he pushed down atop the clawed flesh of his middle.

"Wendy? What the… don't move! Stop moving!" Vanessa commanded.

"This is for us, Nessa. If we make the Para world visible, make the Norms see us, we can stop hiding," Wendy said, wheezing. She was slowly getting to her feet.

"Stop moving! Stop moving, now!" Vanessa said.

"Nessa, we just have to let this happen. The whole world will see us, and we can live freely. You could meet my pack, we could move in together—we could do everything you wanted," Wendy said, standing up fully.

"I said don't move, Wendy," Vanessa said.

"I have to do this. I have to make sure this happens," Wendy said. "I'll take care of that agent, and we can go home. I can give you everything you wanted of me. We don't have to hide."

Take care of me, huh? Fuck you.

Gus tried to lift his right hand, still holding his pistol. Slowly, he brought it up.

"No. Don't move," Vanessa said, her voice wavering.

"If I do this, I can give you everything I couldn't before," Wendy said, pleading.

"That's a lie! You could have given me everything I wanted when I wanted it. You lied to me. You lied to me about everything. All you had to do was explain it to me. I would have been okay with it," Vanessa said as her voice broke. "And it was explained to me! I was included in the Para world. I was given everything I asked for, and nothing bad happened. I got everything!"

Vanessa took a deep, shuddering breath.

"You're just making excuses! You were making them then and you are now, just like always," she said.

"No. I'm not. And everything is gonna be fine," Wendy said. "I love you, and after this, I can show you that."

Wendy turned toward Gus.

He hadn't managed to get his pistol up completely.

Wendy closed in on Gus.

Or tried to. The retort of a pistol going off was loud.

It took Wendy low in her leg.

"Stop! Don't move!" Vanessa called.

"Nessa, don't do this," Wendy said, going down to one knee. "I have to take care of this agent, and then we can—"

"No! Stop! Last warning. I'll not shoot to wound again!" Vanessa said.

Wendy's head turned toward Gus.

He saw it in her eyes. The moment she decided to leap at him. Coiling herself up, the Were leapt.

And then her head exploded as Vanessa put a round in it.

Pulpy bits of brain and skull went everywhere. Collapsing to the ground where she had stood, the Were stopped moving.

Vanessa rushed around the corner, looking for Gus.

"Ok, let's… no, no," Vanessa said as her eyes fell on him.

Smiling weakly at her, Gus let his right hand fall to the ground. Then he moved it over his left and pushed down with it as well.

"Glad to be your pick," Gus said. "Open that panel and see if it's the power for the room. If it is, pull them all, smash it, whatever."

Vanessa looked at him for another second, then stepped over him and opened the panel.

"I think this is it," she said, and then started messing around with whatever she saw there.

All the lights went out, and all the servers shut down. Everything went dark. Then there was the sound of something being bashed. There were several sparks from the box, and then there was silence.

"Good job," Gus said, closing his eyes. "Take care of the backup tower, too."

He heard Vanessa walk away from him. There was some rustling, followed by a crash and several bangs.

"Alright. We're done here. Let's… uhm… let's get back to the security office, ok? We can use the medical kit there," Vanessa said, coming back to him.

"I can't move things very well," Gus said. "I think the Were fucked up my back."

To be honest, he couldn't feel his legs at all right now. He felt numb from his hips down.

"Ok, uhm. Ok. Ok," Vanessa said. She holstered her weapon and then grabbed Gus by the shoulders of his jacket. Taking hold tightly, she began dragging him out of the server room.

Down the hall and to the elevator, Vanessa dragged Gus along.

All the while, Gus just held his stomach, trying not to notice the large blood trail he was leaving behind on the ground.

Blood was welling up between his fingers now as she dragged him.

Propping him up against the interior of the elevator, Vanessa mashed the one button and then the doors closed button.

When it opened next, Vanessa didn't pull Gus out; she left him there.

Taking in slow breaths, Gus felt strange. His vision was alright, but his head felt light. Light and fuzzy. Things didn't feel right at all, and he had the distinct impression there were several things very wrong with him.

Trish came rushing into the elevator, her hands immediately going to his stomach. Before he could phrase a question, he felt a wellspring of energy flooding into him.

Then it cut off abruptly.

Trish groaned and leaned forward, her head pressing to the elevator wall next to his own head.

"I just don't have any energy left," she murmured into his ear. "I'm sorry, Gus."

"S'ok. Am I gonna die?" Gus asked, feeling strange.

"Silly man, of course not," Trish said. "I just can't… fix you right now. I have enough to keep you going, though. To answer your question… without me working on you, you would probably die."

"Goodie," Gus said, then closed his eyes. "Am I paralyzed, by the way?"

"I don't know. I know your back is broken," Trish said. "But I can fix that, too. It'll take some time."

Gus laughed softly to himself.

"What's so funny?" Trish asked.

"Melody is going to be pissed. She was expecting to get laid," Gus said.

Trish choked for a second, then laughed as well. She sat down next to him, and her hand came to rest on his thigh.

"Give me a day or two and I'll have you walking again. I'm much stronger with healing than most Dryads. Helps being a Sorceress," Trish said.

Vanessa came back, dropping down to a knee next to him.

"Sorry," she said, and then pulled him down to the ground, laying him flat. "Alright, move your hands… I've got the kit."

Gritting his teeth, Gus removed his hands from his stomach and stared up at the ceiling.

He didn't want to see their faces, see what they were doing, or even think about it. It would be easier for him if he didn't know how bad it was, which would be reflected in their expressions.

There was a sudden burning sensation in his guts. It also felt like something cool was being poured down the sides of his stomach.

"Alright, that's… that's the most I'm willing to do right now for the wound. The hospital can do more for you," Vanessa said. "There's nothing I can see in it, and that's all the saline solution I had in the kit."

Then it felt like Vanessa was pressing things to his midsection. Several minutes passed in silence.

"Hey, I've been watching things," called Mr. Grenth's voice from inside the security office. "We've been offline for about twenty minutes now. The Telecom techs found a corpse in the server room, and the broadcast room was empty."

Oh. They must have pulled out after everything went dark.

"Alright. That's good. Are they going to delay the game or something else?" Vanessa asked, still working on Gus.

"They're talking about it, yeah. The corpse has really shaken people up," Mr. Grenth said. "They put a call out to the local PID office, but the response they got back was strange. They're on hold now."

"That'd be the Para National Guard rolling out then," Gus muttered. "So… we're minutes away from the Mask Madness possibly starting to kick off, and maybe ten or twenty minutes away from tanks, armored cars, and soldiers rushing in with guns to secure the stadium."

"That all sounds bad," Trish said. She hadn't left Gus's side, and she was sitting there with her hand locked on his thigh. He felt a trickle of constant energy flowing into him from her.

"It is. They're going to come in guns up, and at the same time, there's probably going to be a lot of angry Paras running around. Like Weres. Or Trolls. Ogres. Fae. Elves. Anything," Gus said.

"Uhm. Can we hide? I feel like this is going to go very badly," Trish said.

"We should hide," Vanessa said, agreeing with Trish. "Mr. Grenth, come on over here. We're going to lock the elevator between floors. Best we can do, I'd say. You've got the maintenance key for it, right?"

"I do. Let's do that," Mr. Grenth said.

That's a really good idea.

"Sorry, Gus, this is probably going to hurt," Vanessa said. A soft hand pressed against his forehead.

"S'ok, do what you gotta," Gus said.

"Thanks. Alright, move a bit for me, Trish," Vanessa said.

"Just put his head in my lap. I need to touch him to keep working on him," Trish said.

Trish moved away, and then Gus was forced sideways and pushed up to the side of the elevator.

Vanessa had been wrong. It didn't hurt. It was agonizing.

When Trish's hand landed on him, he felt instant relief. As if someone had dropped him into a vat of numbing medication.

"There you are," Trish said, one hand on his brow and the other on his chest. "I've got you."

The doors to the elevator closed and started to rise.

Gus heard the jingle of keys, and then a click. An alarm sounded for several seconds and then shut off.

Vanessa sank down to the ground next to him in the elevator. It felt like she put her head on Trish's lap as well.

"And… that's that, I guess," Vanessa said.

"We failed," Gus said.

"No, we didn't," Trish said. "The goal was to protect the two worlds, so they wouldn't turn on one another."

"We didn't stop them from getting people hurt. Killed," Gus said.

"That was never our job," Trish said. "None of this was. We did more than anyone else and stopped the ultimate goal of the enemy."

"Normally I'd be the first to say we failed, but I think… I think I'm willing to go with Trish on this one," Vanessa said. She took Gus's hand in her own and squeezed it. "We succeeded where we could. Not bad for a bunch of rookies and a torn-up vet."

Gus nodded his head fractionally, but said nothing.

With a chime, his phone started ringing.

He felt Trish reach into his pocket and pull it out.

"Hi Melody," Trish said into the phone.

"Yes, we're safe. We're hiding. Gus was seriously injured; I'm taking care of him," Trish said. "No, she's fine. Looks tired, but fine."

Faintly, the sound of Melody's voice reached him, but he couldn't make out what she was saying. She talked for about a minute.

"Alright. Thank you," Trish said, then stuck the phone back in Gus's pocket. "She's outside. The Para National Guard is already here, apparently. They're about to move in and separate everyone as fast as they can. Maybe they'll get lucky. Apparently they've been made aware of the Mask Madness breaks as well. With any luck they can limit the amount of breakage since this was country wide."

A deep, rumbling howl echoed dully from far away. It was followed by a deep roar, and then what sounded like an explosion.

Here we go.

Epilogue

Gus opened his eyes, feeling confused for several moments.

Then he remembered where he was. He hadn't had bad dreams since he'd come back from Larimer, thankfully. Just pleasant ones.

Most of the problem with waking up in fact had nothing to do with his mind.

It was the beautiful woman behind him who had forced her way into his bed and refused to leave.

Glancing over his shoulder, he found Trish snuggled up right behind him, acting like the big spoon. She had a hand on him at all times during the day. And was curled up to him at night.

Since he couldn't feel much below his hips, he needed constant attention. He was grateful at least for the fact that he knew when he needed to use the restroom, even if he couldn't quite feel his privates or rear end.

He wasn't going to question how he could feel those signals, but he was happy for them. He thought of asking Trish, but whenever he questioned her about his injury, she just smiled at him.

Smiled at him and promised him up and down that he'd start feeling everything soon. It'd been her statement every day since it'd happened two weeks ago.

Closing his eyes, Gus didn't know what to do with himself. Without the ability to walk, there were just too many things closed off to him.

He was sure he could eventually figure it out. Get over it. But it would take time.

Vanessa and Melody had been put on administrative leave while Gus was out on medical.

With everything that had happened, no one seemed to be taking chances. Everyone was on leave who had been involved, and what few Fed agents remained were being used.

Psykers and magical healing had been applied to Gus in equal measure.

Thankfully, the psykers weren't as strong as he was and couldn't get through to the thoughts he didn't want them to see.

The healers had taken care of everything they could but said there was nothing they could do for his back.

Trish had been against them healing him at all, claiming it would make her job all the harder.

"Good morning," Trish said softly from behind him. She always seemed to know when he was awake.

"Mornin'," Gus muttered.

"Today's the day, you know," Trish said.

"You said that yesterday."

"Today it really is. I thought for sure it'd be yesterday, but you're not human. So things are a little different. You're taking more time than I expected, and I'm sorry for that," Trish said. "Today's the day, though."

"Uh huh," Gus said. He couldn't really complain. He knew she was actually working on him. He could feel the constant energy from her vanishing into his body. It wasn't idle talk when she said she was doing all she could for him.

She'd even quit her job. And she hadn't returned home.

Melody and Vanessa had gotten a truck, taken it over to her place, loaded everything and come back.

Gus now had three women living in his home.

One of whom was babying him to the point of making him annoyed, the second touching him all day every day, and the third consoling him while also clearly getting over having killed her ex-girlfriend.

Trish pressed in closer to him, her cheek resting against his shoulder.

"Besides, are you really complaining about lying in bed with me all day? I've been taking care of you, haven't I?" Trish asked.

Again, Gus couldn't argue. She really had been taking care of him. Anything he could do with his hands, he did. But there was a lot he couldn't do without the use of his legs.

There was a rapid knock on the door, and then it swung inward. Melody stepped into the room, hopped into the bed and then squirmed up in front of him. She wrapped her arms around him and Trish, hugging them with all her might.

"Good morning!" she said happily, then kissed Gus.

Breaking it several seconds later, she slipped her right arm under Gus's head, and apparently Trish's, and snuggled in closer. Her left hand vanished under the sheets.

"So, what's the doctor think?" Melody said.

"It'll be today," Trish said. "I swear it should have been yesterday, but him being a Boogieman is throwing my sense of things off."

"Ooooh, good. So… if he recovers today, do you think I could do a little in-and-out type of stuff with him in a week?" Melody asked, lifting her head and looking at Trish behind him as if he weren't there.

"Probably," Trish said, lifting her own head. "Once things start reconnecting, his senses will come back first. And fast. He'll probably have to spend a little time figuring out how to walk again."

"Thrusting his hips shouldn't be too bad, though, right?" Melody asked.

"No. I'll be sure to report back to you once I find out," Trish said.

Melody laughed at that, grinning at her. "Is that how it is?"

"Okay, anyways," Gus said, growing tired of this. "What have we got going on today? Anything?"

"Mm," Melody said, looking at Gus with a smile. "A few things, actually. Mark sent an official email over last night. He's being promoted and moved out of the PID office. So we'll need to congratulate him later."

Gus nodded. Mark had handled everything very well. It'd be surprising if he wasn't promoted.

Unlike Gus's, Mark's career was trending upward.

With all the protocol Gus had broken, the number of people whose toes he'd crushed, and the simple fact that no one liked the idea that he'd warned everyone he could and no one had listened, Gus was probably done as a detective. Let alone done in the PID. But that was yet to be seen. And none of that had anything to do with his broken back.

"The mayor sent over the official commendation paperwork for you, and the chief sent over your medal and citation," Melody said.

"Whatever. Just… put 'em in the box with the rest of my crap, I guess," Gus said.

The mayor, governor, and the chief had all congratulated him and awarded him. Even the director of the Fed had sent him a commendation and a medal.

"What box?" Melody asked.

"Never mind," Gus said, shaking his head. He didn't want to talk about that right now. Despite having a lack of bad dreams, he didn't want to call the memories up. It'd definitely bring the dreams back.

"Other than that, I think your mom might visit today," Melody said. "I was chatting with her last night."

Really don't like that… but then again… she is my girlfriend. Trying to keep her from talking to my mom seems counterintuitive.

Doesn't it?

"There you all are. I should have known."

Gus lifted his head to find Vanessa standing in the doorway.

"Morning, Ness," Gus said, and he laid his head back down.

"Oh, come join us," Melody said. "You can snuggle behind me, warm up my butt."

"Pass, Mel, I'm not really sure I'm in the mood for any of that," Vanessa said. "We just got fired. Me and Gus, that is. Email came in. The new captain did it."

Figures. Then again, I still have a Boogiewoman hitman tied up in the basement, so that's not entirely a bad thing.

Sighing, Gus shook his head.

"I was expecting it, I guess. Whatever," he said.

"It's ok. I'll just quit, too," Melody said. "Then we can all make a PI agency together and do our own jobs. It'll be fun!

"That or I can contact my niece. She has connections with the PMC world. She's even part of an outfit. They might be willing to hire us on as an auxiliary squad for some contracts."

"While I appreciate the offer, Mel, and it'll probably work out, I'm afraid I kind of need a job now. My student loans won't pay themselves," Vanessa said.

"Oh, shit," Gus said aloud. "I forgot about that. Uh, Ness, do me a favor and write down exactly how much you need. I'll just pay it off for you. Then you can pay me back if you really want to. But at least you won't have to pay interest."

No one said anything to that immediately. Mel was looking into Gus's face with a strange and small smile.

"I can't do that. That'd be no different than taking the money from Mel," Vanessa said.

"It is, I promise. This is money I don't touch. It's money from my time in the service," Gus said. "I don't want to use it, or even think about it. It brings up too much baggage for me. But I think using it to squash your debt would… make me really happy.

"So… you can tell me how much it is, or I can just write a check. Then tell your mom I did it."

"What? No, I—"

"Ness, do it," Gus said. "Do it, and take it, so we can all be on the same page already. Or if nothing else, do it because I'm asking you to. I've asked nothing of you so far. Have I?"

"No," Vanessa mumbled.

"So, there ya go. Do that," Gus said, and he closed his eyes with a sigh. His patience was low and running out with far too many things. "Just let me pay it away and we'll move on, and you'll be in the free and clear. No strings attached."

"Fine. Ok. I'll… ok. Ok," Vanessa said, then sighed. "That'll… that'll take a load off my mind, I guess, so… ok."

"Good. Now shut up and get in the bed, or go away. I think I want to go back to sleep," Gus said.

She didn't say anything, but Gus heard the sheets rustle, and the bed creaked softly. She'd apparently chosen to get in behind Trish.

Moving deeper into the blankets, Gus put his forehead on Melody's chest and got comfortable.

"What do we do next?" Trish asked.

"Well, Gus is going to take a nap," Vanessa said. "We could go finish moving furniture around once he falls asleep."

"No, I meant… us. As a whole. Whatever group planned out this attack is still out there," Trish said. "Right? I mean… do we just… pretend it never happened? Do we walk away? Move?"

Huh. That's… a good point. We didn't actually catch them, did we?

"It's a good question," Gus said. "I don't have an answer, though. I'm just… grumpy. Grumpy, depressed, and trying to cope. Right now I can't even think much further than going back to sleep. I'm sorry."

"No, it's understandable," Trish said. "I think we should move."

"I can buy us a house. Using some fun channels and things, I can even do it in a way that'll make it undisclosed. Then it's just a matter of making sure we're not followed home," Melody said.

Gus frowned, a strange feeling coming over him. It felt like his body was getting lighter by the second.

When he opened his eyes, he wasn't quite sure what was going on.

Out of nowhere, his toes started to tingle. They were… cold as well.

"Oh, I think I got it," Trish said.

"Got what?" Vanessa asked.

"His spinal cord. I think I just got it to connect back to itself and fuse smoothly," Trish said.

"Ohhh?" Melody asked, a playful smile on her face.

The tingling and cold feeling began traveling up from his feet into his calves. His thighs. Finally, his hips.

It was like they'd all fallen asleep and were waking up now.

Sensations and feelings were coming back. Faster and faster now as he lay there.

And like a switch had been hit, everything "turned on" and he could feel his whole body again.

He could especially feel the fact that Melody had apparently been fondling him this entire time under the blanket. Now she'd moved on to something else entirely, the movements of her arm going back and forth somehow disguised.

When he looked at Melody, he only got a smile in return from her. The Red symbol between her eyes glowed, and her Indigo contract lit up like the sun was inside her.

"I love you, Gus," said the Contractor, her eyes looking a bit wild. "Going to be so much fun. Soooo much fun. My one and only. My Indigo."

Thank you, dear reader!

I'm hopeful you enjoyed reading Swing Shift. Please consider leaving a review, commentary, or messages. Feedback is imperative to an author's growth.

Oh, and of course, positive reviews never hurt. So do be a friend and go add a review.

Feel free to drop me a line at: WilliamDArand@gmail.com

Join my mailing list for book updates: William D. Arand Newsletter

Keep up to date—Facebook: https://www.facebook.com/WilliamDArand
Patreon: https://www.patreon.com/WilliamDArand
Blog: http://williamdarand.blogspot.com/
My Personal Group: https://www.facebook.com/groups/WilliamDArand
Harem Lit Group: https://www.facebook.com/groups/haremlit/

If you enjoyed this book, try out the books of some of my close friends. I can heartily recommend them.

Blaise Corvin- A close and dear friend of mine. He's been there for me since I was nothing but a rookie with a single book to my name. He told me from the start that it was clear I had talent and had to keep writing. His background in European martial arts creates an accurate and detail driven action segments as well as his world building.
https://www.amazon.com/Blaise-Corvin/e/B01LYK8VG5

John Van Stry- John was an author I read, and re-read, and re-read again, before I was an author. In a world of books written for everything except harems, I found that not only did I truly enjoy his writing, but his concepts as well.
In discovering he was an indie author, I realized that there was nothing separating me from being just like him. I attribute him as an influence in my own work.
He now has two pen names, and both are great.
https://www.amazon.com/John-Van-Stry/e/B004U7JY8I
Jan Stryvant-
https://www.amazon.com/Jan-Stryvant/e/B06ZY7L62L

Daniel Schinhofen- Daniel was another one of those early adopters of my work who encouraged and pushed me along. He's almost as introverted as I am, so we get along famously. He recently released a new book, and by all accounts including mine, is a well written author with interesting storylines.

https://www.amazon.com/Daniel-Schinhofen/e/B01LXQWPZA